GOLD COAST

"Jess, if you don't go home right now I'm going to jump your bones."

She blinked. "How sweet."

"Sweet?"

"Sweetly put."

"Oh, hell," he swore. His arm went out, pulling her to him as his mouth came down on hers. The contact was stunning for them both.

He kissed her deeply again and then again as her hand moved up and she slipped her fingers into his hair. She moaned against his lips, pressing against him. Bending, he swept her up into his arms and carried her to the bedroom . . .

TRIUMPHANT ACCLAIM FOR MARY PERSHALL'S ROSE QUARTET . . .

Berkley Books by Mary Pershall

DAWN OF THE WHITE ROSE
A SHIELD OF ROSES
A TRIUMPH OF ROSES
ROSES OF GLORY
BEHOLD THE DREAM
FOREVER THE DREAM
GOLD COAST

GOLD COAST
Mary Pershall

BERKLEY BOOKS, NEW YORK

GOLD COAST

A Berkley Book / published by arrangement with
the author

PRINTING HISTORY
Berkley edition / August 1990

ISBN: 0-425-12213-1

A BERKLEY BOOK® TM 757,375
Berkley Books are published by The Berkley Publishing Group,
200 Madison Avenue, New York, New York 10016.
The name "BERKLEY" and the "B" logo
are trademarks belonging to Berkley Publishing Corporation.

PRINTED IN THE UNITED STATES OF AMERICA

10 9 8 7 6 5 4 3 2 1

DEDICATION

ELIZABETH EMERY VANDERPAN

To Bess.

We go back—oh, a thousand years, or so . . .
On occasion we have slipped down a rabbit hole.
In moments, we have even glimpsed Wonderland.

ACKNOWLEDGMENTS

Very special thanks to Susan Elizabeth Phillips, a friend.

> You opened the doors,
> Brushed out the cobwebs,
> Let in the fresh air
> And sunshine.
>
> It was a dirty job
> But you never flinched.
>
> Thanks, Susan.

My deepest gratitude to Mary Birmingham Emery, Associate Dean of Law, Santa Clara University School of Law. With a deft hand, you fit together the legal puzzles.

And most of all, to Gregory Pershall, for all that you did.

GOLD COAST

PROLOGUE

There was a horse on the highway.

The heavy rain reflected the car's headlights, throwing up an aura of light, and for a moment Jessica thought she had imagined the animal. Then it was there again, and frighteningly real. As instinct overcame surprise, Jessica shifted her foot from the accelerator and plunged down on the brake.

Front tires grabbed the wet pavement as rear tires broke free and the Jaguar XJ6 began to skid. Feeling strangely calm, Jessica reacted by turning into the spin. She depended on the response of the car, and for a moment it worked.

A night of heavy rain had created a sheet of water on the isolated rural highway. Just as the car began to correct its spin, the wheels hit the water and the Jaguar began to hydroplane. It spun in a series of widening circles toward an embankment.

The car hit the embankment broadside.

There seemed to have been a loss of time, though it could have been only moments, she wasn't sure. She only knew that the car was stopped, and it was pitch black. The throbbing in her head told her that she was alive.

Jess felt something dribble into her right eye. She reached up and felt her forehead. It was wet. Oh, my God, she thought, I'm bleeding.

She reached down to turn on the interior lights. Nothing happened. She tried the switch again, punching the button repeatedly. Panicking, she tried to start the engine. The key turned over, but the starter just whined. So the battery was okay, she reasoned, trying to remain calm, but the lights didn't work and the engine wouldn't turn over.

She felt for her purse, which had been lying on the seat beside her. It wasn't there. She opened the glove compartment and felt around, finding a small package of Kleenex. Ripping it open, she pressed the whole stack to her forehead. Then she leaned back in the seat and waited. The tissue didn't seem to be absorbing much blood; perhaps the cut wasn't too bad after all.

Jess drew a deep, steadying breath. Okay, she thought, she was alive and apparently not badly hurt. So far so good. Now what?

Stay calm. Use reason; you're on a country road, it's pitch dark, it's pouring rain, and the car won't start. What did the experts say? Never get out of the car. Stay in the car. Lock the doors.

She checked—they were locked.

Then she realized that the whole time she had been sitting there not one car had come by. She had never felt such isolation, such total blackness. And the only thing that separated her from the elements was a locked car door. Thoughts of every mass murderer she had ever read about seemed to tap-dance through her mind. My God, she thought, here she was, all alone in the sticks . . .

"Oh, for crying out loud!" she cried. She winced as the effort of speaking caused a new throbbing in her temples. "I *won't* give in to this," she said more softly. After all the things she had dealt with in her life, she would not lose her sanity on a rural country road in the middle of the night. A piece of cake. Nothing to it. She was alive and dry. Not exactly warm, but dry.

Remembering the car blanket on the backseat, she reached around and grabbed it. She felt the blanket resist; then it suddenly pulled free as something fell to the floor behind her with a thump. Her briefcase, she realized. And inside it was the reason she was in this predicament.

Jess wrapped herself in the blanket, then readjusted the back of the seat to a more comfortable angle. Once she was relatively warm, things didn't look quite so bleak. She would just wait, she told herself—in the car, with the doors locked, as the experts advised. Eventually someone would be along and would go for help. A piece of cake.

Dammit, she thought, swallowing back a lump. Who was she fooling? She was tired and hungry, stiff and sore, and she wanted to cry. She thought again of the briefcase, and the letter and silver-framed picture inside it, of how they had brought her here. "Roxy," she said aloud, even as she fought a yawn, "here's another fine mess you've gotten me into."

PART I

Roxy

CHAPTER 1

September 1972

Jessica Bellamy was the only thirteen-year-old to be arrested by the Swiss police for protesting the United States conspiracy trial of Angela Davis. In fact, she was the only American who participated in the demonstrations.

Madame Emilie arrived in time to keep the scandal out of the newspapers. Madame was not the headmistress of Saint Michel's, one of the most exclusive private schools for young ladies in Europe, for nothing. The parents of Saint Michel's students expected, and received, total privacy. Notoriety was not tolerated.

"Are you going to write to my father?" Jess asked.

They were sitting side by side in the back of the Bentley as Madame's chauffeur drove them back to school.

"No, Jessica," Madame answered, her eyes fixed on the windy mountain road. "I will allow you to do that."

Jess groaned. "I only went into Gstaad to shop," she tried. "I really didn't mean to get involved in the demonstration." But she kept her voice level. Jess had never whined in her life.

"Then you should have refrained from participating," the tiny woman said. Madame's size was deceptive. "Moreover, you know the rules about leaving school by yourself." Then she glanced briefly at Jess before returning her attention to the road. "On the other hand, I imagine I should be grateful that you did not take one of the other girls with you."

"Yes, Madame."

Long moments of weighted silence passed until Madame once again spoke. "You do realize, of course, aside from the embarrassment it would have caused for the school, how unhappy your father would have been if I had not arrived in time to discourage the attentions of the press."

"Yes, Madame." Oh, yes, Jess understood how her father would have reacted. Under no circumstances would one of *the* Bellamys be permitted to associate with rabble, particularly when the press was involved.

John Morgan Bellamy was owner and chairman of the board of Bellamy Guarantee Trust of New York, the largest commercial bank in the United States. His name turned heads in world banking and commerce. His bank owned subsidiaries so varied that each new acquisition threw various government agencies into a frenzy of anticipation as they contemplated antitrust possibilities. Oh, yes. Jess understood. She had been bred to understand.

Jess stared from the car window at the swiftly passing landscape, trying not to think of how her father would react to her latest escapade. On the other hand, did she really care? Jeez Louise, she thought. She hadn't planned it, but she wasn't sorry she had joined the demonstration.

However, in spite of her bravado, Jess knew this problem couldn't have come at a worse time. She had returned to school early in order to escape her father's anger. There was just one more thing. . . .

"Madame?"

"Yes, Jessica."

"Who is Angela Davis?"

A few days later Jess lay on her stomach on her bed, penning the dreaded letter home as a song by Simon and Garfunkel played on her tape deck. The sky outside her window had become leaden, and leaves blew up in sudden gusts, tapping against the glass. From the hallway beyond her closed door there were muffled sounds of laughter, punctuated occasionally by exuberant voices. The school term would begin tomorrow. Everyone was back and settling in for the year, but Jess was oblivious to the excitement.

She rolled over on her back and stared at the ceiling, tapping her teeth with the end of her pen. This was not an easy letter to write.

How could she approach her father about this? He was

already on the warpath. In the last few weeks of summer Jess had outdone even herself. John Morgan Bellamy's anger toward his youngest child and only daughter had been cushioned by the fact that Jess had been shipped back to school and out of his sight.

Her last escapade in New York *had* hit the papers. Fortunately, because of her age, her identity had not been released. One newspaper headline had read: "Minor Manages to Maneuver into Musical." The reporter had written, "Tuesday night, as the new play, *Jesus Christ, Superstar*, moved into its final weeks of rehearsal, an unidentified minor appeared without warning in the chorus. . . ."

Her older brother, Johnny, had been the maneuvering force, but she would go to her grave before she would rat on him. Besides, she had just wanted to be in a Broadway play, even if it was just in a rehearsal. And it had been worth it.

Jessica never planned on trouble. She didn't look for it, not deliberately. She just loved life and wanted to feel it.

She was a slender child, with large, serious green eyes that belied the mischief that dwelled inside. Wheat-colored hair, which promised to darken, now pulled back into a ponytail, tended to relax into waves and soft curls about her face, adding to the angelic look that tended to put adults and peers off their guard. Few people, aside from her brother, really knew Jess. Few knew the child who dwelt in her private secret place, deep inside.

It had come as a surprise to Jessica that there were other kids who suspected that they were adopted. Jess loved her mother, and her father, too, at least most of the time. But there was a part missing. It was an empty place that she didn't understand; she just knew it was there. When she was seven she had made her mother show her her birth certificate. She had often wondered, in moments since, if it could have been forged. Her father could do anything.

Jess paused in her writing and slipped off the bed. Crossing to the bookshelves over her desk, she removed copies of three books: *David Copperfield, Nicholas Nickleby*, and *The Pickwick Papers*. During an inspection the previous term, Madame had been most impressed by Jessica's selection of Charles Dickens, commending her taste in literature and her willingness to tackle the longest of the novelist's works. Jessica had agreed, particularly about the length of the works.

After stacking the books on the desk, Jess pulled out a drawstring bag that had been hidden behind them. She perched on the desk and opened the bag, pausing for a moment to peruse the contents with a thoughtful frown. Finally she chose a Milky Way from the treasured stash of junk food that included candy bars, Snowballs smothered in unnaturally bright pink coconut, and teeth-sticking Jujubes that she had smuggled from home. Switzerland, for all its fine chocolate, had nothing to compare to a good ol' American Ding Dong.

There were benefits to not having a roommate, Jess thought. She would not have to share her stash or worry about someone ratting on its existence.

Jess had not had a roommate since her first term at Saint Michel's, the year before. Jess was what Madame Emilie called "high-spirited." Simply, Jess loved practical jokes. Not serious ones that might cause serious embarrassment or harm, but merely the usual Vaseline on toilet seats and honey on doorknobs. They were harmless jokes that caused a good deal of laughter and put life into otherwise routine days. No one minded except a few girls, like Mary Lou Harris.

Uptight, prickly Mary Lou was Jess's last roommate. Mary Lou had almost gotten Jess expelled, but Jess's father had proved to be more powerful than Mary Lou's father. The episode had left a sickening, soggy knot in the pit of Jess's stomach. It had also left her without a roommate.

Jess preferred to be alone anyway, she told herself. It meant no whining, no shrieks of outrage, no ratting. When laughter came from the hallway, she ignored it. Instead, while munching on the chewy bar, Jess scanned the room and began to plan how she would decorate it for the coming year. Madame did have rules, of course, but they were nothing compared to Mary Lou's.

Posters on the wall, Jess thought, then grinned. Yes! *Jesus Christ, Superstar*. And *Hair*. She would paint the walls red and get black bedspreads. Yes, with red and black pillows. Or should she do it in black and silver? The tackier the better.

As she perused the room, Jess's eyes came to rest on the clock by her bed. Her face scrunched up into a frown as she realized that she only had an hour to make the afternoon post.

Madame would check, and if Jess didn't send the letter out today, the issue would become "official." Heaving a dramatic sigh, she went into the bathroom, wadded up the candy wrapper, and flushed it down the toilet. Returning to the bedroom, she paused to turn the Simon and Garfunkel tape over and increase the volume; then she returned to the bed.

It was a few moments later, as drums and guitar were pounding and Paul and Art were singing "Cecilia," that the door opened and Jessica Benedetta Bellamy's life changed forever.

Standing in the doorway were two of the biggest men Jess had ever seen. They were giants with swarthy complexions, heavy mustaches, and large dark eyes. Dwarfed between them was a breathtakingly beautiful girl. Though she was dressed in a simple double-breasted navy coat, she was as exotic as her companions. She had shining black hair, golden skin, and solemn almond-shaped eyes, which she quickly lowered beneath thick black lashes.

The girl's companions, however, were not shy. They glared with apparent disapproval at the teenager sprawled on the bed. Then their dark eyes swept over the room, and they grimaced at the sound blaring from the tape deck. One of the men glanced back at the number on the door frame, as if hoping to confirm that they had the wrong room.

Jessica sat bolt upright and stared back. Her Milky Way–filled stomach clenched as she realized that they might have found the *right* room. She slid off the bed and asked the dreaded question: "May I help you?"

Paul and Art continued to belt out "Cecilia."

The men heard and understood the suggestive lyrics. Their eyes widened and shifted in unison to the offending tape player. Jess spun around and lunged forward, snapping the machine off. Then, in her best thirteen-year-old imitation of Madame, she turned back. She'd be darned if she would accept unsolicited opinions on her choice of music, particularly from two Neanderthals who had come into her room uninvited. Primly she repeated the question. "May I help you?"

One of the men looked as if the best he could do was salivate. However, the mustached upper lip of the other man twitched slightly—a hint of a smile? The voice did not match the body. It was smooth, cultured, with a hint of a British education.

"You are Miss Jessica Bellamy?"

Jess was reluctant to answer. "Yes," she said finally. Puzzled, she shifted her gaze to the girl, whose eyes were still shyly averted. Jess cocked her head to one side and tried to see the girl's face. "And who are you?"

The man ignored Jess's question and smiled at his young charge. "Your Highness, may I present to you Miss Jessica Bellamy, your roommate."

Jess's eyes widened. "Your Highness?"

"Indeed. The princess Raokhshna Sulayman Husayn."

"It would seem that this is to be Her Highness's room for the school year," the other man said, but he was clearly not pleased. He regarded the room with distaste and its occupant with disapproval.

Jeez Louise, Jess thought, you'd think he had just found himself in a rat's nest. And then the word sank in. "*Roommate?*" she parroted. Both men nodded gravely. Ye gods, Jess thought.

From somewhere, Jess was sure she heard Madame chuckle.

Then, as Jess began to feel smothered, Her Highness lifted her dusky gaze. Her protective companions' attention was fixed on the American teenager, and so they were unaware of what Jess saw. Though the girl quickly lowered her eyes again, Jess had caught the flash of a mischievous gleam.

Moments later the men left to fetch the princess's trunks. "Raokhshna Sulayman Husayn, huh?" Jess repeated, closing the door behind them. "Good thing I have an ear for languages. But we can't possibly call you that. The others will probably call you Roxanne or something. But I . . ." She paused, studying the other girl. "Roxy, I think. Yes—Roxy. And you can call me Jess." She plopped down and pointed to the other bed. "You can have that one—the first one in always gets her choice of beds. Sorry. The bodyguards will have to go, you know. They're not allowed at school. Madame's really firm about that."

"My father will be displeased," Raokhshna said, sitting down on the edge of the bed by the door. Her voice was already husky, a rich promise of what it would someday become.

"You can get along without them, can't you?" Jess asked

with a concerned frown. "I mean, you won't be afraid or anything? There's nothing to be afraid of here."

"I am not afraid."

"Good." Jess sat back, tucking her legs under her as she gripped a pillow and hugged it to her. "Where're you from? Saudi Arabia?"

"No." Raokhshna smiled. "Iran. Teheran."

Jess's eyes widened and she gave out a whoop. "A genuine Persian princess!" Then a thought struck her for the first time, right in her stomach. Her eyes narrowed and she regarded Roxy with suspicion. "You're a Muslim."

"Yes, of course. Is that a problem?"

Again Jess thought she heard Madame laugh.

"Well, of course not," Jess said, heaving a deep sigh of resignation. She almost groaned. It was going to be a very long year. "I mean, I respect your faith, of course, but you'll have to tell me what I need to know. I mean I wouldn't want to do the wrong thing, or anything."

Raokhshna smiled. "I will respect your beliefs as well. In fact, I would like to know everything about the West."

"Is that why your father sent you here?"

"This school wasn't his first choice," Roxy said with a soft smile. "My mother wanted it for me. Actually, Farah Diba is my mother's cousin. She talked my father into it."

"The empress?" Jess was impressed.

"Yes. A new liberation is coming to Iran, Jess. New rights for women, an end to repression. I want to be part of that."

Whistles sounded in Jess's head. Was it possible that Madame had misjudged this girl? My, oh, my. This called for a test.

"You may regret having me for a roommate, Raokhshna. I mean, you could probably ask Madame to change you now, before the term starts."

Roxy frowned, puzzled. "Why would I want to do that?"

"I have a reputation," Jess sighed. "People think I like practical jokes."

"And do you?"

Jess shrugged. "It's a sickness."

To Jess's amazement, Roxy laughed. It was a lilting sound that compelled her to smile.

A good sign, Jess thought, but not proof. "I'm thinking of

putting Limburger cheese under the senior girls' table in the dining hall."

Roxy thought about it, then shook her head. "No, don't do that."

"Are you going to tell?"

"No, but I think you're wrong. They'll find it. What you do is smear it on the light bulbs and heating grates in their rooms. They'll never find it, but the hotter it gets the worse it smells."

Jess stared, struck dumb with admiration.

She got up off the bed and, flipping on the music as she passed, went to the bookcase. Taking down the Dickens volumes she pulled out the stash. Then she turned back as Simon and Garfunkel joined them, the refrain of "Bridge over Troubled Water" filling the room. Jess swung the bag in front of her as she regarded Roxy with a challenging smile. "The culture of the West. Lesson number one: Ding Dongs."

Nine months later, when Jess asked Roxy if she, too, felt that she was adopted, she received a blank stare.

That was one of the things she liked about Roxy. Raokhshna might not have the vaguest idea what Jess was talking about, but they had long since agreed to disagree.

"You mean you never get the feeling that you don't belong to your family?" Jess asked. "I mean *never*?"

"No. I know who my parents are, Jess," Roxy answered calmly. Jess's questions never seemed to unsettle her.

"Ah! But that's just it, isn't it? *How* do you know? How can you be *really certain*? I mean, were there *witnesses* when you were born? Like someone writing down records, making sure there was no mistake?" Jess sat back on her heels and regarded her best friend complacently. She had her.

"Yes, as a matter of fact, there were."

"What?"

"There were witnesses. There had to be."

Jess stared at her, deadpan. "You're kidding."

Roxy looked puzzled. "No, it's a matter of custom."

"Never mind!" Jess cried, throwing up her hands in defeat. She jumped up and, with her ponytail swishing, strode toward the door. "Let's go ride camels."

And they did.

The girls spent the month of July rambling through the

mosquelike caverns of Roxy's father's palace. The official residence of the Husayn family was truly magnificent, with walls of white marble, vast halls covered by arching domes and projecting cornices that gave the effect of weightless elegance. There were minarets at the many jutting corners of the palace, delicious deep shadowy recesses where two girls could spy on the comings and goings, rich, colorful carpets and hangings and wonderful Byzantine mosaics.

On occasion they visited the shah.

Farah Diba became Jess's heroine. Beautiful, intelligent, and powerful, the empress was the epitome of everything Jess admired. What a fabulous thing, Jess fantasized as she hung on the empress's every word, to be in a position to lead women out of bondage.

Jess's impression of the shah was that of a smooth Continental and exceedingly polite gentleman. At their first meeting, however, he did a classic double take. With a slight acknowledging nod, he had begun to move on. Then his head turned back, like the snap of a stretched rubber band.

"Bellamy?" the shah repeated, bending down to stare into her eyes. "Your father is John Bellamy—of the Bellamy Guarantee Trust of New York."

Though he did not phrase it as a question, Jess nodded. "Yes, sir," she said demurely. She had seen this reaction all her life. Odd, she didn't think that the shah of Iran needed a loan.

"You will give your father my regards."

"Yes, sir, of course."

Roxy adored Merryhaven, the forty-three-acre Connecticut estate that had been in the Bellamy family since before the Revolutionary War. Away from the restraints of her family, Roxy flushed with the taste of freedom and blossomed.

Days were filled with sailing, horseback riding, tennis, swimming, movies, and spying on Johnny. In particular, Roxy adored John Morgan Bellamy the Third. She was smitten with Jess's brother.

John III was not totally immune to the infectious, dark-eyed princess. Though now insufferably mature with only a year to go before Yale, he seemed to puff up like a pouter pigeon when Roxy was nearby.

• • •

In that one year Jess's life became a splendid adventure. And all because Raokhshna Sulayman Husayn had become her most devoted ally, confidante, sidekick—and roommate.

On Jess's first visit to Teheran, it only took her a day to realize where Roxy had gained her considerable expertise in matters of tomfoolery. With four brothers and five sisters, not to mention innumerable nieces, nephews, and cousins, she had to be on guard every waking moment—and often while sleeping as well.

The Limburger Cheese Caper, as it became known, established the pair as the daring duo of Saint Michel's. School became a soccer field, the opposing goals being Jess and Roxy versus Authority. With each success the game became more complex, and their classmates depended on their acknowledged captains for leadership.

All in all, life was dazzling. Wonderful. Awesome. But that was before it all came crashing down.

CHAPTER 2

May 1, 1974

Jessica's world had suddenly become filled with black, shrouded shadows. Desperate to make an escape, she tried to edge around the room to the French doors and the terrace. She was stopped by a hand on her shoulder.

"In here, Jess." Johnny's voice was barely a whisper.

Jess was drawn by the softness in her brother's voice, but when she realized where he wanted her to go, she pulled back.

"I can't—" She choked out the words.

"Yes, you can. Come on." He took her arm and guided her into the small room, closing the door behind them.

Jess stared at the room. Her throat felt swollen closed with an acid lump of pain. The morning sun streamed through tall windows, bringing life to the English country flowers repeated on the upholstery and pillows of the white wicker furniture. Crystal vases, filled with flowers as they had been each morning of Jessica's life, sparkled in the sunlight. It had been Jessica's favorite room. Now she couldn't bear to be in it.

"See? It's quiet in here and no one will bother you. Sit down and I'll go get a couple of plates of food." He saw her look of panic and smiled gently, even though his bright blue eyes were dull with his own pain. "It's okay, twirp. It's gonna be okay."

It wasn't okay! Jess screamed silently. The denial reverberated in her brain as Johnny left the room. Her mother was dead! It wasn't ever going to be all right again.

She stood there, immobilized. This was her mother's sitting room, her favorite room, and Jess hadn't come in here since her mother had died. Johnny was right; it was better than out there, with all those people.

She could hear the din of their voices through the closed door. Mouths that moved, all saying the same thing as they thrust their faces into Jess's. "Poor dear," they said. "You poor, poor dear."

Swallowing forcefully against the lump, she managed to move to the small sofa under the window overlooking the garden. Her mother's private rose garden. She sat with her back to the roses, on the very edge of the seat with her hands clenched tightly in her lap.

She tried to make herself small. If she could disappear, the pain would stop.

The door opened and Johnny returned bearing a tray. As she was staring at the floor, Jess missed the concerned frown, the tightening of his jaw, the compressing of his lips as he saw his sister's suffering. He shut the door with a foot and brought the tray over to the glass table in front of her.

"I didn't know what you wanted, so I got a little of everything." He sat down next to her and handed her a glass of milk. "Drink something, Jess. Eat something."

She clenched the glass between her hands and stared at it for a long moment. Then she looked up with tear-filled eyes. "How long are those people going to stay?"

"I don't know," he shrugged. "A couple of hours, I guess."

"I don't even know all of them."

"No, me either."

She started to speak, then paused, swallowing heavily. "I—I couldn't look at her, Johnny. I know Daddy expected me to, but I couldn't."

"It's all right, Jess. Mom wouldn't have wanted you to if it hurt too much. Besides, remembering her is what's important."

He let her think about that for a moment, then encouraged her to eat a little. She managed a few bites of chicken.

"I wish I could have seen her before she died," Jess said in a small voice. She picked idly at the chicken leg.

"I know. There was no warning, Jess. She didn't tell anyone about the pain, not even Dad, until it was too late," he said, referring to the renal cancer that had killed Margaret Bellamy.

Jess had been playing soccer when Madame Emilie sent for

her. Miss Françoise, Jessica's house resident, had already packed a bag for her when Jess returned to her room. Madame sat on the edge of Jessica's bed and waited while Jess showered and changed into traveling clothes. Madame herself took Jess to the airport.

"Jessica. John. Your father wants to see you both."

They looked up to find their grandmother in the doorway. Her flawless complexion was sallow and there were new lines that had not been there before. Her ramrod-straight posture was stooped a little. Her glorious silver-gray hair was the only thing that seemed the same, but somehow that surprised Jess. She didn't expect anything to be the same again.

Benedetta Bradenberg kept grief for the loss of her only daughter tightly in check with a Germanic rigidity that had served her throughout her life. She motioned for the two young people to join her. "Your father wishes to see you."

Upon entering the library, Jessica wanted to rush across the room and throw herself into her father's arms. But of course she didn't. Instead, she took comfort from Johnny's touch on her arm.

"Steady, twirp," he murmured. "Don't let the old man see you shaken."

John Morgan Bellamy was standing in front of the massive marble fireplace that dominated the cherry-paneled room. Tall, well built, and extremely fit, with dark hair that had begun to gray only slightly at the temples, Jessica's father commanded a room even in silence. But then, as Jessica had been taught, and taught well, true power was quiet. It whispered.

A fire burned low, giving an illusion of warmth to the room. The reflection was repeated in the heavy beveled glass of the bookcases and glowed off of small bronze sculptures that John Bellamy had spent a lifetime collecting. They were pieces depicting ancient wars.

Jessica lifted her gaze from her father to the large portrait of her mother that hung over the mantel behind him. She felt her heart skip painfully before it regained a normal beat.

Auburn hair framed a lovely oval face in the portrait. Margaret had the same flawless complexion as her mother, the countess Bradenberg, a gift from her German heritage. Large blue eyes seemed to fix upon Jess, speaking to her with a silent message.

What do you want me to know, Mother? Jess asked silently. The only answer received was the same feeling of sadness Jess had always felt when staring at the painting. Once she had tried to tell her mother about what she saw, but Margaret Bellamy had only laughed softly and changed the subject.

Jess shook off the feeling as she forced her gaze over the beautiful white satin gown her mother was wearing. Her lovely shoulders were exposed above full puffed sleeves. Her beautiful hands were folded on a soft green lap robe that covered her knees. The toe of a white satin slipper peeked out from below the hem of the robe. And then Jess's gaze rose, as always, to the face and the soft, sad smile.

Johnny squeezed her arm and propelled her forward. There were two men and two women standing with her father before the hearth, but it was her father's expression that gained Jess's attention. There was no doubt about that look, or what was expected of her. Emotions were not to be displayed, no matter the circumstances. There were duties to perform, condolences to be received, and it was to be done well, with graciousness.

Somehow Jess got through the next half-hour. It proved to be somewhat easier than with those she had met earlier. At least those who were brought into the inner sanctum did not gush or offer false condolences.

Jess had finally managed to tuck herself into a shadow. She was sitting on the lower step of the book ladder, her chin braced on the heel of her hand as she propped her elbow on a bent knee. The ladder had been rolled into a corner behind a large bronze bust of Alexander the Great. At the moment the conqueror of the world was guarding her from the unpleasantness of having to be gracious to the seemingly never-ending stream of her father's closest business associates.

Poor Johnny. He was still there at the elder Bellamy's side. But then, Johnny was the heir apparent; his responsibilities were greater. Jess was not expected to conquer the world. She glanced up at the bust and grimaced. She was, however, expected to marry someone who would.

Suddenly she missed Roxy so much it hurt.

Roxy had had the ability to make Margaret Bellamy laugh, and Jess loved her friend for that. Jess hadn't even had time to talk to Roxy before she had flown home; she wondered if Madame had told her.

Jess looked up just then to see Matheson, the Bellamys' butler, carrying in the most beautiful arrangement of flowers Jess had ever seen. The arrangement was enormous and totally nonfunereal. It consisted of a fabulous array of colorful spring flowers.

Jess was struck by the wonder of it. She felt a soft stirring of happiness, the first she had felt since her mother's death, and she wondered about the identity of the sender. Who could have been so perceptive of one of the greatest joys of Margaret Bellamy's life: spring flowers.

Matheson placed the flowers before the doors to the terrace and handed the card to John Bellamy.

Jess watched her father's expression as he read the card. And she saw the rage that gathered. When he spoke to Matheson, his voice was low, but Jess heard the anger in it. As the butler removed the bouquet from the room, Jess watched her father crumple up the note and thrust it into the fire.

Johnny was staring at his father with bafflement. He tried to speak, but John Bellamy cut him off with an angry gesture.

Jess waited with Alexander until everyone else had left the room; then she got up and walked to the fireplace. Impossibly, the note was there. It was crumpled and singed, but it had rolled away from the fire and survived.

Jess smoothed it out on her knee, then turned it to the fire's light. Disappointingly, most of the message was too badly singed to be read. She could just make out the last line and the signature: "My love is with you at this time of loss. Amanda."

My, oh, my, Jess thought, as a line from one of her favorite childhood stories wandered through her mind: "Curiouser and curiouser." For the first time since she had been called in from the soccer field three thousand miles away, Jess felt a spark of defiance. It felt warm and good. It flickered, then went out almost before it had begun, but it burned, if just for an instant.

Roxy arrived on the twenty-third of June, two days after the end of the term. The summer began quietly.

For the first time Roxy had come to stay at Merryhaven for the entire summer. Both girls knew that John Bellamy had called Roxy's father and invited her to visit in an attempt to assuage Jess's grief. It also freed him of worrying about his daughter's solitude at Merryhaven while he stayed in New

York during the week. Johnny was home, but he spent most of his time with his college-bound friends, dealing with his grief in his own way.

The numbing comfort of shock over her mother's death wore off bit by bit, striking Jess with flashes of hot, searing pain that left her breathless. Roxy was there in those moments, silently supportive. No false sympathy, no platitudes, but always the comfort of her quiet presence; a touch to the shoulder as her dark eyes pooled with understanding.

The girls went through the motions of a normal summer of sailing, swimming, movies, shopping, and spying on Johnny and his friends. But even the pursuit of Yale-bound men did not bring the usual satisfaction.

There was some distraction in August when Roxy entered the high holy days of Ramadan. Johnny and Jess conferred, then decided that they would observe some rituals of Ramadan in support of their friend's beliefs. Thus, with the cooperation of Mrs. MacMurphy, the Bellamys' cook—and to the consternation of John Bellamy, Sr.—the trio fasted each day from sunrise until sundown.

The first few days of the fast caused serious doubts in Johnny and Jess, and renewed admiration for Roxy. Not a drop of food or drink passed their lips for thirteen to fourteen hours each day. Then, on the fourth day, a peace descended over them, bringing a sense of commitment neither had known before. For Roxy it was a holy pledge. For Jess and Johnny it became a way of remembrance, a pledge of honor for their mother.

Mrs. Mac, busy in her kitchen, watched and waited each day until the sun disappeared over the rolling Connecticut hills, whereupon she would present them with a nightly feast in the formal dining room, complete with candles, crystal, and the 175-year-old Bradenberg silver.

As the weeks passed Jess's pain began to ease, but it took a sudden shock to return her to life. It was a humid Friday afternoon in mid-August when Jess thought about the letters. That particular day both girls were bored, hot, and restless. Besides, Jess had cramps, a condition they treated with the utmost respect.

Jess had gotten her period first, ten months earlier at school, and it had established her as the leader in such matters. Roxy had felt slightly miffed and definitely at a disadvantage as her periods came and went without much to comment upon. She took Midol anyway, on principle.

The girls had sought out the coolest room in the house, John Bellamy's study, which was located in a corner of the east wing. The large room was light and airy, with white wainscoting, bleached oak furniture, and accents of pewter and gray-blue. Dominating the room were several tall, arched, deep casement windows shaded by large maple trees. The girls were sprawled on parallel sofas throwing lazy questions back and forth in a halfhearted attempt to discover something to do.

Then suddenly Jess remembered another time, shortly after her mother's death that involved this room and Johnny.

"I have a grandmother," she said suddenly.

Roxy turned her head. "I know. I've met her a couple of times."

"No, I don't mean Grandma Bradenberg. I mean another one. A mysterious one."

The word caught. "Mysterious? How?"

"My father won't talk about her. I mean *ever*."

Roxy sat up. "Why not?"

Jess shrugged, playing the moment. "I don't know why, but he never will. For a long time I thought she was dead or something. But Johnny told me that Dad keeps her letters."

"How does Johnny know?"

"He saw them. He walked in here one day, about a week after the funeral, and caught Dad reading them. Dad was pretty angry, I can tell you that."

Roxy noticed that this was the first time Jess had referred to the funeral without getting solemn or weepy. "Because of something in the letters?"

"No. Because Johnny caught him reading them. As Dad put them away, Johnny saw the postmark on one of the envelopes. It was only a week old."

Roxy frowned pensively. Facing Jess, she pulled her legs up under her. "This is your father's mother, right?"

"Yeah."

"And you never met her?"

"Met her? I told you, we've never even *talked* about her. I asked Mom about her once, and she told me her name was Morgan, like my dad's middle name. But Mom said that if I wanted to know more I'd have to ask Dad. He would never even talk to Mom about his mother."

Roxy looked confused. This concept was beyond her reasoning. In her culture the paternal mother-in-law was the matriarch, with everything that implied. She ruled the women of the family. She said as much to Jess, then asked, "Do you know where they are?"

Jess frowned for a moment. "Oh, you mean the letters?" She gestured over her head toward her father's desk, a massive oak partner's desk in front of the French doors. "They're locked in a drawer."

"Don't you want to read them? Aren't you curious?"

Jess thought about it for a moment. "Yeah, kinda."

"Kinda? Jeez, Jess, are you kidding?"

They looked at each other for a moment. Then they both broke into grins. Jess slipped from the sofa, took down a volume of Voltaire from one of the bookshelves, and extracted a key hidden within. Another discovery of childhood.

As Roxy slipped off her perch to lock the door, Jess unlocked the desk drawer. She took out a rosewood box, which she carried back to the sofa. The girls sat side by side, staring at the box, which Jess had placed on the coffee table in front of them.

"Well?" Roxy said impatiently.

Jess opened the lid. Inside the box was an assortment of envelopes stacked unevenly, as if they had been tossed into the box. She took one out, glancing at Roxy, who was watching expectantly. As she pulled the folded letter from its envelope their heads came together over the page.

A moment later Jess gasped.

"What?" Roxy asked. The letter seemed rather disappointing, actually. It was merely a mother's polite inquiry into her son's life.

"The name! Look at the signature!"

Roxy frowned, puzzled. "Amanda?"

"Yes, don't you remember my telling you about the flowers—the spring flowers that someone sent to the funeral? How angry my dad was? The note was signed"—she paused dramatically—"*Amanda*. Remember, I told you about the note."

Roxy looked doubtful. "Your father saved these, yet he burned her card and wouldn't accept her flowers?"

That caused a moment's doubt, and Jess frowned. Then her eyes cleared and she half smiled. "Yes . . . because no one knows about these letters. Maybe it's us, Rox—Johnny and me. Dad doesn't want to talk to *us* about her?"

"But why?"

Jess shrugged. "Why do parents do anything they do?"

Before Roxy could respond, Jess had taken another letter from the box. "Well, I want to find out more about someone who knew my mother well enough to know that she loved spring flowers!"

Roxy could feel Jess's excitement. Slowly she smiled. Welcome back, Jess, she thought.

There was little in the letters that gave a clue to Amanda Morgan's nature, or her relationship to her estranged son. Nevertheless, reading them seemed to give Jess the bandage she had needed to soothe the wound that her mother's loss had caused. The wound was a long way from healing, but at least it no longer openly bled.

John Bellamy did not question the sudden change in his daughter; he simply accepted the improvement as something that had come in its proper time.

When Johnny cornered Roxy to thank her for the change in his sister, Roxy felt she had to explain what had happened.

"No, Johnny, it wasn't me," she said. "It was the letters."

"What letters?" he asked. They were sitting in his mother's rose garden, and the air was heavy with the fragrance of the cultured blooms.

"Your grandmother's letters. Amanda."

Johnny looked stunned. "She read them?"

In the next moments John Morgan Bellamy III fell in love with Raokhshna Sulayman Husayn, though he would never acknowledge it. Though his grandmother was a German countess, this Persian princess was beyond the reach of even the Bellamy wealth and power. Roxy was not yet betrothed, but Johnny knew it was only a matter of time before her family chose for her.

"Yes, Johnny, she read them," Roxy said, her voice husky

with understanding that was far beyond an American fifteen-year-old. "And it brought her mother back to her."

He frowned. "Did Amanda Morgan know Mother that well?"

"I think—she knew her as well as anyone in this house," Roxy said, thinking of the spring flowers and remembering Margaret Bellamy. "But that is not what I meant. Family . . . a sense of it tells us who we are. My mother tells me of those who have gone before, as her mother recounted to her, as I will for my children. It is not right that Jess does not know of her grandmother. What will she tell her children?"

"I don't know much about Amanda either." Johnny shrugged.

"It isn't the same thing. It is a woman's spirit that cares for the traditions of the family. A man's soul roots itself in his politics. He becomes too grounded in this world to sense another dimension."

Johnny stared at Roxy for a moment, marveling at the wisdom of a girl just approaching sixteen. He wondered if it had something to do with culture—but it was the same culture that undoubtedly would promise her, body and soul, to some high-muck-a-muck two decades older than she was. "How can I help Jess?"

"What she needs from you is love, and she knows she has that. Go about your business, Johnny."

He knew how deep his sister's pain still went. "Roxy, she needs more. If I don't help her, who will?"

"I will," Roxy answered. "And beyond that, she will find the answers for herself."

CHAPTER 3

September 1977

There were other events of importance that year: The King of Rock and Roll died, there was a serious crisis at America's gas pumps, and Leonid Brezhnev became President of the Soviet Union. But for Jess, nothing was more important in 1977 than Curtis Caldwell, Ph.D. from M.I.T.

He taught Jess's only Monday afternoon class as a freshman at Middlebury College in Vermont, and the only class she truly dreaded. She had always been good in math, but loathed it. Nonetheless, her SATs had placed her in Calculus II and John Bellamy had insisted that she take the course. Five minutes after class began, Jessica began to think there might still be some hope for her father's brain cells—at least, she was glad she had listened to him this one time.

Curtis Caldwell, it was perfectly clear at first riveting glance, had been born in the wrong century. A brown tweed jacket, a white shirt open at the collar, and dark brown slacks established him in the present, as did the penny loafers he wore. The resemblance ended there. Everything else about Curtis Caldwell reminded Jess of an early nineteenth-century poet.

His voice was a rich, deep baritone that seemed to vibrate through her. The man spoke higher mathematics, but when it reached Jess in the fourth row she heard sonnets.

His rich brown hair fell into natural waves that curled about his ears and tended to slip repeatedly onto his forehead. He would push the stray lock back, rather absentmindedly, with long fingers that would have been better placed about a quill than a thick piece of chalk.

Percy Shelley, Jess thought.

His eyes were blue. "Blue, darkly, deeply, beautifully blue, in all its rich variety of shades, she thought, quoting Southey, a contemporary of Shelley's. His brows were full and nicely arched, accentuating a fine Grecian nose and a strong squared chin that sported a romantic cleft to match a deep dimple in his left cheek when he smiled.

Lord Byron, Jess sighed.

After class she approached his desk. He finished putting papers into his briefcase, then looked up.

"Yes, miss?"

"Bellamy. Jessica Bellamy."

"Miss Bellamy," he acknowledged. "Is there something I can do for you?"

"Professor Caldwell, I just wanted to tell you how much I enjoyed your class today."

An eyebrow hitched up slightly, but those blue, blue eyes were unreadable. "I see. Do you have a particular . . . passion for mathematics, Miss Bellamy?"

He was just tall enough that Jess could stare directly at his mouth. His perfect mouth . . .

"Miss Bellamy?"

"Oh—no, sir. I mean, I have always enjoyed mathematics, but . . . you bring such—logic to it."

Then that mouth slipped into a smile and the dimple appeared. "Truly, I'm gratified," he said.

Jess's toes curled, but he was gone.

The moment Jess returned to her room she threw down her books and began a letter to Roxy. It was at moments like this that Jess missed her best friend the most.

Upon graduation from Saint Michel's the previous spring, they had hugged, cried, and sworn that they would be best friends forever. Two weeks later they had met for a glorious two-month sojourn in Europe. Then Jess had returned to the States to attend Middlebury and Roxy was off to Oxford.

Jess realized that the past six weeks constituted the longest period she had been separated from Roxy since they had first met, five years before, and Jess missed her terribly.

Roxy's return letter came back at a record speed of two weeks. Jess had begun to make other friends, as Roxy had three thousand miles away, but that did not lessen the importance of the constant stream of letters between Vermont and London. Jess and Roxy remained, for each other, the one person to whom each could reveal her innermost feelings, fears, hopes, and passions.

As the months passed, Jess noted that the tone in Roxy's letters became more intent regarding women's rights. While Jessica and her classmates debated ideologies, Roxy was endeavoring to learn practicalities—how she could bring increased freedom to the women of her country in ways that would truly work. Once, when Jess suggested that she come to America to study women's rights, with her usual droll humor Roxy had replied that she needed the British to explain American rights to her.

The reception given for those who made the president's honors list was held on a beautiful spring day in late May. The air was unusually warm for that time of year. The flowers had bloomed and bees buzzed about the gardens in frantic activity. Jess walked with two other students along the long gravel path leading up to the terrace of the university president's home.

"How long do you think this will take?" Dennis Klein asked as he ran his fingers through his unruly red hair.

"Nervous, Dennis?" Sarah asked. She winked at Jess, who was walking on Dennis's other side. "You're the next Einstein, you know. You're going to have to learn to endure these little fetes."

"No, I won't," the young man grumbled. "This is the last one I'm coming to and—"

"Sarah's right. You have to learn how to play this game," Jess interrupted. She smiled at the young man's bemused expression. "Grants, Dennis. Federal grants, state grants, private grants. The stuff of which research is made. It does little good to be the next Einstein if no one will fund your work. If you want funding, you have to sell yourself as well as your ideas—at to-dos like this."

Dennis's freckled complexion flushed. He looked totally miserable.

"It doesn't have to be painful," Sarah urged, touching his arm.

Jess noted the touch and smothered a smile. Sarah Talbot-Burke was madly in love with Dennis Klein. Unfortunately, Dennis barely knew the tiny attractive blonde existed, which went a long way in demonstrating Dennis's total absorption in physics.

The thought was sobering—Jess knew how Sarah felt. Though she had dated throughout the year, Jess had steadily carried the burning torch of unrequited love for the Ph.D. from M.I.T. On the few occasions when she had spoken privately with him, the professor had seemed to look right through her.

No, Jess thought, her situation wasn't the same as Sarah's and Dennis's. Dennis might not be aware of Sarah, but then, he wasn't aware of any girl. His mind was firmly and completely bent toward quantum physics. No, it wasn't the same thing at all.

If Jess had managed to see Dennis Klein as anything but a good friend, she would have seen how wrong she was. Dennis had been in love with Jess since the first moment he saw her walk into the math lab, three days after the beginning of the school year.

She was the most beautiful girl he had ever seen. She was tall, which he liked, slender, and substantially curved in the right places. Her beautiful face—she had what his mother called "good bones," which meant she would age well—was dominated by large, expressive green eyes. Her deep, rich auburn hair was cut in that severe new style that all the girls were trying, but few of them looked like Jess.

She had smiled at him that morning and his throat had clenched. It had proved to be the most bittersweet year of his life.

"Come on, Dennis," Jess said, slipping her arm through his as they approached the president's terrace. He noticed, for the hundredth time, that her voice had the mellow resonance of the D string on a cello. "I'll show you how to balance a teacup and a plate of canapés."

"You can do that, too?" he asked, clearing his throat. He was vaguely aware that Sarah had taken his other arm.

Jessica laughed. "I've had a little practice. Yes, indeed, a little."

Jess stayed with Dennis and Sarah through the reception line and long enough after to establish Dennis with faculty members and students with whom he was comfortable. Then she slipped away to mingle.

She was talking with the president's wife when a conversation behind her gained her attention.

". . . It is time that our government ceased supporting that despot . . ."

Jess tried to focus on what Mrs. Simms was saying, but the voice continued, dogmatically, to present some of the most closed-minded statements she had heard in a long time. While Mrs. Simms was distracted, Jess turned a little and stole a glance at the speaker. It was one of the professors from the political science department, and there was no ending his diatribe.

"The shah is an unconscionable tyrant," he continued, addressing his small group of listeners. "SAVAK is merely an expression of the man's true character. He has never done one damn thing for the country that can be considered redeeming."

That did it. Jess could no longer remain quiet. When the professor paused to take a breath, she stepped into the group. "Excuse me, Professor Flynt," she ventured politely. "But I don't think that SAVAK's existence tells the whole story of the Pahlavi shah."

The man looked down from his greater height at Jess, his brown eyes narrowing as he appraised the source of the interruption. "Indeed."

"Indeed not," Jess smiled, ignoring the warning implicit in the single spoken word. "I do not defend the mistakes Mohammad Shah has made, such as his repression of democratic opposition to his central government or the fact that many, including those in his own family, still enrich themselves at the expense of the people. However, this is no time for our government to withdraw its support."

"But you support the actions of the shah's secret police, ignoring the brutality, the injustices SAVAK commits daily upon the people? Miss . . ."

"Bellamy," Jess said, unaware of the group that was gathering about them. "And no, of course I do not ignore the actions of SAVAK. However, I do not think we can judge the actions in Iran by our standards. The shah is endeavoring to

bring a medieval country into the twentieth century. It takes
great wealth to accomplish this. Iran's wealth is its oil—which,
unlike that of Saudi Arabia and other Gulf States, is quite
limited. In fact, there are some estimates that Iran's oil reserves
may last only a few more decades . . ."

"So you are saying that the shah commits atrocities—and
must be forgiven them—because he is rushed for time," the
professor said with disbelief.

"I am saying that he has made astounding strides for his
people." She paused, then purposely selected particular accomplishments of the shah. "He has broken up great estates
held by a wealthy few and redistributed land to the people. He
has dramatically improved the standard of living for the
masses—"

"And padded his own pockets in the process," Flynt
interrupted sharply.

Jess stared into the man's angry eyes and noted the stubborn
set to his jaw. Professor or not, Jess thought, she was looking
at a fool. She tried to repress her own anger. "The real trouble
in Iran is that the jackals are gathering," she said with control.
"Specifically, disgruntled vested interests who have crawled
under a bed together to dispose of the shah. In fact, I believe
that you support one of those factions, Professor Flynt." While
she had never taken a class from him, Jess knew from fellow
students where the professor's political leanings were.

Jess was unaware that almost everyone was listening now,
including the president of the college. However, Professor
Flynt, from his vantage, was well aware of the fact.

"Are you accusing me of something, Miss Bellamy?"

"Of course not. I am merely referring to your well-known
political leanings, which could make you sympathetic to the
Tudeh party and its Islamic Marxists."

"The Iranian government accuses the Tudeh party of being
Marxist."

"As would any reasonable person who is aware, as I'm sure
you must be, that its leader is Iraj Eskandare, who is, at this
moment, residing in Moscow. You do not find it strange,
Professor Flynt, that Eskandare has embraced the Muslim
conservative fundamentalists? What goal could those two
factions possibly have in common but the overthrow of the
present government?"

"The Tudeh party and the conservatives in league with each other?" The professor actually guffawed. "Next you'll be telling me that the mullahs are preparing for revolution. What an absurd notion."

"It is not a notion, Professor," she said, now openly angry. "Nor is the fact that the shah has listened to our government and is planning to dissolve SAVAK."

"Miss Bellamy, where do you get your information?" he asked contemptuously.

"I have my own source, Professor, quite a reliable one."

"It certainly sounds as if you do, Miss Bellamy," a congenial voice interjected. It was President Simms. He was smiling his diplomatic smile. "Moreover, I think this would make an excellent topic for our next round table! I shall look forward to attending the debate." He laid a friendly hand on Flynt's shoulder. "For the moment, however, there is someone who has been wanting to meet you, Jerry." Still smiling, President Simms took Flynt's arm and, with a departing nod to Jess, led him away.

It was then that Jess noticed she had become a center of attention. She groaned inwardly, horrified that she had single-handedly ruined the president's reception. The guests drifted away, re-forming into congenial groups. Jess wanted to slither into a hole somewhere.

"Well done."

Jess stiffened, identifying the smell of his pipe tobacco even before she recognized the voice. She spun around. "Pro-Professor Caldwell," she stammered. She wanted to die.

"Very impressive, Miss Bellamy. Flynt should be called on his politics more often."

"But this wasn't the time, or the place," she said, flushing with embarrassment. Oh, God, she silently groaned. He had heard the whole thing.

Incredibly, Caldwell smiled and the dimple deepened. "Probably not. But then, it's been my observation that Flynt uses social gatherings like this one to pontificate. He knows that no one will start a row—he depends on it."

"Until now," she said miserably.

"Until now," he said with a chuckle. "Tell me, who is this mysterious source of yours? Or was that a bluff?"

The fragrance of his pipe tobacco was rich and heady. She

noticed that as the smoke wafted up it gave him a Clark Gable squint. "No, it wasn't a bluff," she said. "My best friend from school is Iranian. She keeps me apprised."

"I see—"

"Nevertheless, I'm terribly embarrassed," Jess added, glancing in the direction of President Simms. "I'm afraid I must make my apologies."

Caldwell followed her gaze and smiled. "I commend your parents on raising such a polite young woman. However, I wouldn't worry about Gerald Simms; he would be the last to want an apology in this instance." His smile widened at her puzzled expression. "Simms and I were undergraduates at Berkeley together. In his day, our president was quite the radical; he believes in defending one's principles. Besides, he loathes Flynt."

"Really?" She glanced again toward the subject of their discussion.

"Truly. Besides, there is no time for regret: 'Come, fill the cup, and in the fire of spring your winter garment of repentance fling.'"

She turned back to him, her eyes widened with pleasure. And she finished the quatrain for him, "'The bird of time has but a little way to fly—and lo! the bird is on the wing.'"

He looked impressed. "You know *The Rubaiyat?*"

"Do I know Omar Khayyam?" She laughed. "My best friend is Persian, remember?" The argument, with its accompanying adrenaline, now coupled with Curtis Caldwell's attention—at long, long last—was making her reckless. She actually, and quite boldly, flirted with him. "Isn't Khayyam rather . . . fanciful for a professor of mathematics?"

"Ah, well, I fear that my soul is that of a romantic."

Jess knew that.

"In any case," he added, viewing her with interest. Apparently this time her efforts had not been lost on him. "I have had about enough of this affair, but not of the company. I know a small coffee house on a rather unobtrusive side street a few blocks off campus. Would you like to join me for a sandwich and a cappuccino? You can tell me more about your Persian friend and what she knows about what is happening in Iran."

"A coffee house? Really? Like in the fifties?"

He winced, then laughed. "I'm afraid so. Complete with jazz."

"Oh, that would be fantastic!" Then her smile became wry. "Or should I say groovy?"

"Oh, please," he groaned. "Don't say anything of the sort." Then he sighed. "I guess I was born in the wrong time."

Jess knew that, too. And it was wonderful.

"I would love to go for coffee," she said. "I really would."

"Have you slept with him yet?"

Jess looked up at Roxy and rolled her eyes.

At Roxy's request they had met in Ibiza. They had spent the day on the beach, sunning beneath the warm Mediterranean sun, and after some deliberation had chosen an outdoor café for dinner.

The sky was a black canopy, reaching from horizon to horizon and studded with winking points of stars. The slowly rising moon laid a shimmering silvery path across the inlet to the beach. The terrace of the café was deserted except for two couples who were far too engrossed in each other to pay attention to two single females. They were also unaware of the hidden figures in the shadows nearby.

"Well, are you going to answer me?" Roxy demanded with a teasing smile.

"Not yet." Jess shrugged, moving a shrimp around with her fork. Then she looked up and smiled. "He quotes Omar Khayyam."

Roxy drew back, feigning shock. *"The Rubaiyat?"*

"Of course."

"From the infidel's mouth to Allah's ear," Roxy said dryly. "Dare I hope that he reads it well?"

"Roxy, he quotes it in Farsi."

"No kidding?"

"Well, kinda. He makes enough mistakes so that I know that he doesn't thoroughly understand the language. But at least he tries."

"The man's a paragon."

Jess picked up a large prawn and bit into it slowly, her eyes flaring at Roxy. Then she licked her lips suggestively before they curved into a wicked smile. "He kisses like a devil."

"Ah, now we are getting somewhere. So, are you going to

bed with him? Don't put me off, Jessica Bellamy. You've never planned a conquest in your life without painstakingly laying your groundwork—pardon the pun." She paused, glancing at the shadow-forms. "As it is more than likely that I shall remain a"—she shuddered—"virgin until my wedding night, I have no choice but to live vicariously through you. I want to hear every sordid, delicious detail, including the moment you lose your own 'treasured defenses.'"

"I promise."

That wasn't good enough. "By our oath on the blood of our thumbs, which we exchanged at the age of thirteen, in spite of Mary Lou Harris's shrieks, to be broken only by the pain of death? By that promise?"

"You know that you probably committed yourself to hell for exchanging blood with an infidel, don't you?" Jess said. "I've always meant to bring that up."

"Don't change the subject." Roxy leaned forward, her black almond-shaped eyes gleaming in the candlelight.

"I promise." Jess laughed.

Roxy leaned back, studying Jess across the table. Apparently she had actually caused Jess to blush, though Roxy couldn't be certain in the meager light afforded by the flickering candle between them. So this *was* serious, she thought. She would have to tread very carefully.

"Sometimes I wish we were thirteen again, Jess," she said. Her voice sounded wistful. "The only thing we had to worry about then was zits."

"And Madame Emilie."

"Yes, and Madame."

Jess glanced at the forms in the shadows, one by the low wall separating the terrace from the beach, and the other by the door to the café. Then she looked back at Roxy and grinned. "You know, if you want to get rid of Frick and Frack, I could distract them while you make your escape. I could set the table on fire or something."

Roxy laughed, following Jess's gaze to her ever-present bodyguards, who tried to be as unobtrusive as possible, and failed, as usual. It was tempting. "No, I don't want to escape, Jess," she said after a moment. "They do have their purpose, now more than ever."

Jess sobered, peering at her friend with concern. "Is it as bad in Iran as I've been reading?"

"It's worse. But that's not what I want to talk to you about. It's not why I asked you to meet me here."

Jess leaned forward, resting her arms on the table. "So? We always spend our summers together, Roxy. What's up?"

Roxy suddenly grew interested in her iced tea, absently pushing an ice cube around with her finger. This definitely was not going to be easy, she thought. She drew a quiet, steadying breath. "Jess, over the years you and I have crossed some pretty formidable barriers. We love and respect each other. I know you understand about the life I must eventually choose for myself; and you understand that I do so willingly. I know you accept it, in spite of any reluctance you may feel because of your"—she paused with a smile—"distorted Western views."

"Yes, I know." Jess smirked. "You're going to ignore everything you've learned about women's rights and disappear beneath a veil into some man's harem."

"Very funny. But I'll ignore it because I want to say something very important, Jess. And it has to do with you, not me."

"Me?" Jess looked puzzled.

"A harem can be a state of mind, Jess. That is, if you regard a harem as a restricted, confined way of life."

"Roxy, what are you talking about?"

Roxy sighed softly, wondering how to reach her oldest, dearest friend, one she loved more deeply than any of her sisters. She didn't want to alarm Jess, but things were far worse in Iran than the world was aware of—especially since the riots of the past month—and she and Jess might not be able to see each other for some time. She hadn't told Jess that she wouldn't be returning to Oxford. Her father had ordered her home. This month in Ibiza was a gift from him, a stopover on the journey because he knew how important it was to her.

"Jess, you have always been the most serendipitous person I know. You taught me how to expect joyous discoveries in my life. It's the most wonderful thing I've ever learned. . . ." She paused, grappling with what to say next.

"What, Roxy?" Jess reached out and touched Roxy's hand. "Is it this thing with Curt? You can talk to me about it, I won't mind. I know you only want the best for me." Then she punctuated her words with a grin. "And, as always, if I don't agree I'll simply tell you to go to hell."

"There's that." Roxy laughed. But the humor was only on the surface. Life was closing in. . . . Incongruously, from somewhere a woman's laughter drifted on the night air, filling the silence. "Jess, do you remember the emptiness you felt when your mother died?"

Jess looked stunned. She hadn't expected this. "Of course."

"I mean more than the loss of your mother," Roxy said. "I mean the loss of yourself, who you were, what you were. You lost a sense of where you were going."

"I remember," Jess said softly. "What about it?"

Roxy closed her eyes for a moment, searching for wisdom. So little time. "Jess, sometimes we tend to fill ourselves up with noise so that we don't hear the whispers inside. But we can't survive unless we can hear those whispers. They are the connection to our spirit.

"Johnny is content with the life he has mapped out for himself," she continued. "His destiny is to be the heir to your father's life. But you need more."

Jess frowned. "Roxy, what are you talking about? I have no intention of living the life my mother lived. I couldn't abide the loneliness."

Though she couldn't say it, Roxy was more concerned that Jess would live the life her father did, that someday Jess would decide that Dad was right, that caring was painful. Instead, she merely said, "Someday, Jess, you'll have to stop, to stand in place. Don't struggle against it. You need to find out about your grandmother. If you don't look back, you'll never know where you came from. Until then, you'll never trust who you are."

Jess was listening intently. Her elbows were propped on the edge of the table and she had braced her chin on the heels of her hands. When Roxy finished speaking she smiled at her friend.

Just then a waiter flambéed a crepe at a nearby table, gaining Jess's attention. "Oh, look at that!" She sat and looked back at Roxy with a wicked flaring of her eyes. "Come on, Rox, let's have a gooey, rich, sinfully fattening dessert. Just this once."

Roxy smiled sadly. She had tried. "Okay, Jess. Why not?"

Jess motioned to the waiter and ordered crepes with orange-almond butter, flambéed. As they watched in anticipation, the waiter brought the cart and began his preparations.

It was then, as the waiter added the sauce to the pan, that "Frick" had to step aside from the doorway to allow a family of tourists to enter the terrace. "Frack" was, at that moment, as fate would have it, bent over tying his shoe. Simultaneously, Jess's and Roxy's eyes shifted to the butane and igniter on the waiter's cart.

They began to laugh.

CHAPTER 4

Dear Roxy,

The fortress on the mount has been breached. So much for "treasured defenses." The battle was remarkable, the actual taking of the wall was—ah, dare I say, anticlimactic? Perhaps the troops need more drill.

He met me at the door with his pipe lit. He knows that his tobacco drives me crazy. (Could it be the southern blood in my background via Grandpa Bradenberg? Never mind.)

Can you believe it? The man *actually* has etchings! Fortunately, he did not ask me to come up to his place to view them. If he had, I think I would have lost it right then and there. My nerve, I mean.

Okay, okay, the details.

At 8:05, precisely, I entered his apartment. (I know because I checked my watch, knowing that you would want to know.) He looked fabulous. But then, so did I.

We viewed the etchings, drank a credible wine. Listened to some Miles Davis and Ahmad Jamal. (Don't say anything about that. I've learned to like Jazz. Kinda.)

Besides, I thought that asking if he had any Beatles around might break the mood.

He kissed me. It was a very long kiss. It took a long time.

He unbuttoned my blouse and . . . (Okay, I have to add a note here: I had worn a blouse with easy-to-open buttons and a front-snap bra. Yes, I wore a bra. I wanted

40

him to unsnap it. I thought about not wearing panties but chickened out.)

Anyway, he got it all off, piece by piece, and . . . Well, Roxy, it is really wonderful. Having someone you love make love to you, touch you like that, is like being ten years old and eating an ice cream sundae with your pockets filled with candy. It tastes fabulous, filling every sense including satisfaction, yet there's the impossible anticipation of more to come. Like you're finally going to get enough.

He took me to bed then, Roxy, and the "treasured defense" was breached. He was gentle and it didn't hurt. However—and I know that this is what you are waiting for—the earth did not move. It shifted pleasantly, but there were no shooting stars or time spent in the cosmos.

I'm sure this will improve with time. . . .

P.S. I'm sooo glad that your dad let you go back to school! It would be *crazy* to stay in Iran right now if you didn't have to. Besides, what would you do without your degree—get married to some fat old mullah and have his babies?

October 1, 1979
Oxford

Dear Jess,

Thank you for your letter. I appreciate the time you took from your busy schedule to correspond with me. Jeez, Jess, what a boring letter. Ho-hum.

P.S. It's a good thing you didn't mention the Beatles. He might have been quite insulted. " 'Hey, girlie, there ain't no bugs in this place. . . .' "

October 23, 1979
Vermont

Dear Roxy,

Very funny. And while we're on the subject: You can call him backward, you can call him boring, you can call him an inept lover. But whatever you do, my friend, don't call him *old!* I'm warning you, Roxy, you had better take heed or I'll call Jimmy Carter and cut off your foreign aid. On second thought, I'll call Dad.

Now I shall torture you. No mercy from this infidel; just like water, drop by drop, while you are dying of thirst. I shall tell you of the last two times I have made love with Curtis Caldwell. In detail, as you have requested. And I'm sending copies to your father. . . .

> November 7, 1979
> Oxford

Dear Jess,

How could you *ever* become involved with a math person? Ugh! I absolutely *detest* calculus! Gack! If I get through this course without losing my mind, it will not only be by the will of Allah, but a bloomin' miracle! Tell Caldwell he's a geek. . . .

P.S. Are you going to Merryhaven for Thanksgiving? That is one American holiday that I miss celebrating with you. Boy, can Mrs. Mac cook a bird.

Give my love to that gorgeous brother of yours.

> WILBURTON INN
> Manchester, Vermont

> November 26, 1979

Dear Roxy,

As you may have guessed from the hotel stationery, I did not go home for Thanksgiving this year. Instead, I am here with Curtis, for skiing and one of the most romantic weekends of my life.

This is a great hotel. It's a Georgian mansion that was once somebody's estate, really well done. Besides, the ambience is absolutely perfect for Curtis. I finally feel that he is at home.

Look, I know you don't approve of Curtis. I can understand that—aside from the fact that he's a math person. I'm somewhat surprised at myself, since I never thought I could be interested in a man of thirty-six, but there's just something about him.

He treats me differently than anyone I've known. Not

just like I have a brain (which *boys* our age couldn't care less about) but he—well, he swept me off my feet. I know, I know. It's corny. But how many men our age would bring flowers, recite sonnets, open doors, and remember what your favorite food is? I know, as liberated women we're not supposed to care about those things anymore, but no one let me vote on that. . . .

P.S. I talked to Johnny last week and he sends his love. I wish I could make it to Teheran over Christmas break—thanks for inviting me—but alas, after this holiday defection the family will expect me home for yuletide. Why don't you come to Merryhaven?

January 3, 1980
Teheran

Dear Jess,

Oh, Jess, now I can tell you why I couldn't come to Merryhaven for Christmas. Forgive me for not telling you before, but I was forbidden to breathe a *word* until it was definite. (Funny, Father specifically said I wasn't to tell *you*. Do you think he thinks you have a big mouth?) Anyway—the Big News! You won't believe it, Jess. The first news is that I am betrothed. Yes, the B-word! "It" has happened! Ooops—make that a small "it."

The second news is that I do not plan to take the Cleopatra exit. Simply—and listen to me carefully—he is the most gorgeous man I have ever seen. And (are you listening?) he is the most divine prince I have ever met. And I've met a few.

Yes, boys and girls, he's a Saudi prince. A really high-muck-a-muck. My father outdid even himself. My sisters are weeping. My mother is visiting every friend she ever had. Oh, yeah, one other thing: My prince could buy your father.

So. How's your old man? And I don't mean your father.

CHAPTER 5

February 1980

Jess studied her reflection in the mirror with a critical eye. The black wool Valentino dress clung to her body in suggestive curves, subtly perfect.

"Good God."

Jess looked up to see Sarah's reflection in the mirror. Her roommate's eyes widened with admiration as she shut the door behind her. "Is that for Caldwell?"

Jess ignored the criticism in Sarah's voice. "It's for me. I picked it up in New York over Christmas break. Do you like it?"

Sarah dropped her books on the desk and collapsed into the armchair next to it. "It's fabulous."

Jess studied her friend's reflection in the mirror. "Are you and Dennis going out tonight?" Sarah and Dennis Klein had been dating since the beginning of the school year, and Jess was delighted. The year before she had become aware that Dennis felt something for her. She was greatly relieved when he seemed to transfer his feelings to Sarah.

"Yes. We're going to the game." She glanced up at Jess. "Are you going to see Caldwell tonight?"

"No," Jess said, studying her own reflection, deliberately avoiding Sarah's eyes. "He has a meeting."

She didn't miss the other girl's soft snort of disbelief. "It's too bad you can't go to the game, Jess. You should, you know."

Jess knew that the reference was to the fact that she could not go out in public with Curtis Caldwell. "It doesn't matter." But she knew that Sarah would not let it be. Tonight she couldn't handle the criticism. "In any case, have a good time." She took a coat from the closet and headed toward the door. "I'll see you later."

The night was crisp and cold. The air smelled of the promise of snow. Jess walked across campus, her hands deep in the pockets of her coat, not certain where she was going. Her breath turned to mist, and her cheeks and the tip of her nose had already turned pink from the chill air, but at the moment she didn't care if she got frostbite.

She wondered just when it was that she had begun to lose her self-respect.

She knew Curtis was using her. She knew he lied to her—regularly, as a matter of fact. She allowed him to use her and she didn't even call him on the lies. She wasn't his first coed, and she certainly wouldn't be his last.

The s.o.b. Ph.D. from M.I.T.

Well, if there was any residual Judeo-Christian guilt left in her, she should feel better. She had done penance. The troops had not improved in their performance. Simply, the man was a lousy lover.

Just then she stepped into an icy puddle. Letting go of a particularly nasty expletive, she jumped back, shaking her wet foot. It was then she felt the full force of the cold, and she realized that she hadn't even taken the time to put on boots. She was wearing a pair of glove-leather-thin flats, one of which was now completely ruined.

She stood there, trying to decide what to do. She couldn't go back to her room until Sarah left. Everyone she knew was going to the game. With dates.

Jess couldn't remember the last time she had felt like crying, but the urge hit her broadside now. Then, as she stood there, alone on a strangely silent campus, with tears streaming down her face, it began to snow.

Oh, fine, she thought. Great.

In the light of the street lamp the large flakes of snow floated silently downward. She became aware of the absolute silence. It was one of those moments that one didn't quite understand or want to analyze, when something shifted inside and deep feelings were discovered.

Voices that had been silent whispered softly. But she heard them: Fool, he snaps his fingers and you jump. You can minimize it all you want, but you gave him something precious and he didn't value it. Simple Simon, Simple Simon, can Jess come out to play? Booby. Lunkhead. Rube.

But, Jessica, the voice whispered then, it doesn't have to be this way. . . .

Slowly Jess smiled. Then suddenly something burst and she laughed and cried out loud at the same time. "By god, Scarlett!" she shouted. "As God is my witness, I'll never let a man hurt me again!" Her voice resounded through the quad and echoed.

For some reason she thought that was very, very funny.

"Okay, okay," she murmured finally, when she had regained some composure. She slipped back into the wet shoe. "It's time to go see the old man."

Jess was not surprised when a young, beautiful woman with stunning red hair, wearing a blue silk robe, opened the door of Curtis's apartment. Jess did not wait to be announced. She stepped past the redhead and into the living room. Turning around she glanced briefly at the woman, giving her a quick amused smile, then let her gaze take in the setting. It was painfully familiar. Miles Davis. Two glasses of wine.

"Where is he?" she asked. "In the bathroom?" She leaned over and picked up the open bottle of wine from the table. "Son of a bitch," she said. This wine was more than just credible. She should know; she had given it to him.

"Who are you?" the redhead asked.

"The other woman," Jess said. "But don't let it concern you. We're just two of a herd."

"Pardon me?"

"He likes to work a herd."

"Jessica! What are you doing here?"

Jess spun about to find Curtis standing in the doorway to the hall. She enjoyed the stunned look on his face. "Close your mouth, Curtis. And your bathrobe. I know this isn't my night, but I thought I'd break the rules just this once."

"Curtis, who is she?" The redhead's voice had risen to a shriek.

"Crissy, go into the bedroom," Caldwell said, with amazing calmness. "I'll handle this."

Jess watched her go and waited until the door closed. Then she looked back at her former lover. "She's obedient, I'll give her that."

"Jessica, what do you want?"

I'm sorry, Shelley, Jess thought as she regarded the man standing before her. I'm sorry, Byron. Forgive me for associating you with this slime. On the other hand, she realized, Shelley absconded with virginal Mary while he was still married to someone else. And Byron—oh, where did one begin with Byron? He cut a wide swath through many a bed. But at least those poets had talent.

"I don't want anything, Curtis. Really." She took the bottle and walked past him into the kitchen. Crossing to the sink she poured the rest of the wine down the drain.

"Jess, that's a good wine!" he blurted, staring at the departing liquid with horror.

"No kidding, Professor," she said, giving him a droll glance. Then she went back into the living room. "As I said, I don't want anything—except to see this, that is. I always knew when you were lying to me. Now I needed to admit that I knew. I always knew you were cheating on me. I needed to confirm it." As she reentered the living room, she noticed that she had left a muddy track across Curtis's precious snow-white carpet. Yikes! A bonus. Life had its moments.

"Oh, it will take some time to get over the painful realization that I made an absolute, total ass out of myself with you," she said. "And I do regret having given my precious defense to someone so inept. However . . ." She paused, realizing that he was staring at the muddy carpet.

"Your what?" he said absently. "What did you give me?"

"Nothing, Curtis," she said. "Nothing of any importance."

She crossed to the door and opened it. Then she paused, turning back. "Oh, just one more thing." Then she spoke, in fluent Farsi: " 'Make the most of what we yet may spend, before we too into the dust descend; dust into dust, and under dust, to lie, sans wine, sans song, sans singer, and—sans end!' "

He looked at her blankly. "What?"

She laughed, deep and throaty. "I thought so. You memorized it, didn't you? Oh, Curtis, even the Farsi was a farce."

• • •

The walk back across campus was wonderful. The snow was beautiful, the air clean and crisp. There was a definite bounce in her step. Oh, she had meant it when she said it would take some time to get over feeling like a fool. Jess had not been born and bred to act the fool; it didn't come easily. And she did regret having given her virginity to someone like Curtis Caldwell. However . . .

As for the first problem, one did not die of foolishness. One did recover. As for the second, it was hardly a problem. She knew that the chances of losing her virginity to the perfect man—perfect in character as well as skill—were almost nil. That only happened in romance novels.

Tonight, however, felt good. It was delicious to have one's self-respect back. And then, remembering Curtis's dumbstruck expression, she began to laugh. God, Roxy was going to love it!

She got back to her room and was surprised to find the door unlocked. Her surprise deepened to find Sarah and Dennis inside. "Hey, you guys, I thought you were going to the game," she said, closing the door behind her. She took off her coat and opened the closet door to hang it up. "I'm glad you haven't left yet, though. Wait until I tell you what I did tonight." When she turned back, she realized that Sarah was dialing the phone.

Puzzled, Jess glanced at Dennis with a frown. "What's up? Why haven't you guys left?" Then it struck her. Oh, no, how insensitive. "I'm sorry, you guys. You want to be alone?"

"No, Jess," Dennis said softly.

Jess realized then that Dennis was even more somber than usual. And paler. She glanced at Sarah, who was speaking into the phone. Then Sarah looked up at her, handing her the receiver.

"Jess," she said gently. "It's your father. He wants to speak to you."

"My father?" Jess stared at her. She looked down at the phone and took it without thinking. "Dad?" she said.

"Yes, Jess, it's me. I've been trying to reach you." His voice was strained.

Jess's stomach clenched. Oh, dear God . . . "Johnny—is something wrong? Is it Johnny?"

"No, Jess," he said firmly. "Your brother is fine. He is here with me now. In fact, he is taking the next flight out there. He'll be there with you in a few hours, Jess."

"He's coming here? Why?"

"Jess, Sarah and her friend are still there, aren't they?"

Jess glanced at Sarah and Dennis, who were staring at her oddly. "Yes, they're here. Dad, what is it? What's happened?"

"I've been dealing with this for the last forty-eight hours. I didn't want to call you until we were absolutely certain. Do you hear me, Jess?"

"Yes, I hear you. What is it?" She laughed brittlely. "What's the problem, Dad, are we broke?"

"Jess, you will read something about this in the morning papers. But they won't tell the whole story, not yet. Since the Ayatollah Khomeini's return to Iran from exile, the entire country has gone completely mad. The mullahs have taken over totally. They are determined to return Iran to Islamic fundamentalism, not in the future but now. Immediately. The shah has left Iran. Imam Khomeini has assumed absolute power."

Jess felt herself grow cold. She began to shiver. She couldn't swallow. "What—what has he done?"

"Jess dear, I would do anything not to have to tell you this. Ferras Husayn's family was arrested."

She couldn't breathe. "Everyone in the family?"

"Everyone, Jess, including Roxy and her sisters and her brothers."

"Oh, God. Dad, you have to *do* something! You have to get her out of there!"

"I've been in touch with everyone, Jess. That's what I've been doing for the last forty-eight hours. We—almost made it."

She could not bear it. "What do you mean, you almost made it?"

"Jess. My darling Jess." She heard him sigh heavily, and his voice was thick. "They— The entire family was shot this morning."

They were sitting cross-legged on the floor in Jess and Sarah's room.

Sarah, Dennis, and Johnny sat facing Jess, a brazier smoking with sandalwood incense burning next to them. All four of them were drinking wine. An extra glass sat on the rug between Jess and her brother. It was half full.

"I thought Muslims didn't drink wine," Dennis murmured.

"They don't," Johnny said softly, never taking his eyes off his sister. They silently communicated the pain they were feeling. "But we decided that we would not mourn Roxy's passing with the customs of the current . . . of those in power. We prefer, and we think Roxy would agree, to observe it as an ancient Persian would have."

They drank their wine, and set their glasses down. Then Johnny picked up the extra glass. His eyes glistened with unshed tears, but his voice was steady: " 'The moving finger writes; and, having writ, moves on: nor all your piety nor wit, shall lure it back to cancel half a line, nor all your tears wash out a word of it.' "

Tears were streaming down Jess's face as Johnny slowly poured the wine on the brazier. The steam gusted up, filling the room with the heavy aroma of sandalwood. Then he handed Jess the glass. She took it from him and managed her part: " 'And when like her, O Roxy, you shall pass among the guests star-scattered on the grass, and in your joyous errand reach the spot . . . turn down an empty glass.' "

As tears streamed down her face, Jess turned the glass over and set it on the carpet. Her voice softened, breaking, but she managed a whisper: "Good-bye, my dearest friend. May you have love and an eternity of joy. And may the prophets be with you on your journey."

PART II

Amanda

CHAPTER 6

November 1989
San Francisco

Jessica stared at the letter as icy fingers of disbelief tingled up her back and over her cheeks. She grew warm as she fixed on the name and address inscribed on the envelope in the broad angles and loops of what appeared to be her own hand, even to the distinctive way she looped her y's. Sent by a woman she had never met.

Swallowing hard against a suddenly dry throat, Jess turned the envelope over and slipped her thumb under the sealed flap, ripping it open as she mentally scolded herself for reacting so strongly to a simple letter.

The door to the office opened, and a slender young man entered Jessica's private world of dark, comforting wood, objets d'art suggesting the deep, rich colors of the old masters, the warmth of leather chairs emphasized by the burnished gleam of brass and copper.

Tom Bradin was the only human trusted to enter, uninvited, Jess's inner sanctum nestled among the executive suites of the law partners of the San Francisco firm. The privilege hadn't come easily.

Jessica had been his boss for two years, since the day he had left Boalt Hall at Berkeley to set the legal world on fire. When he was hired by Reynolds, Armisted, and Royce, his expectations had soared. Headed by Aaron Reynolds, an ex–Supreme Court justice, the firm, though small, was one of the most prestigious in the country. Then Braden found that he had been assigned to a partner who was not only brand-new but was also—Gloria Steinem forgive him—a woman.

Then he got to know her. Swiftly, and with a good deal of chagrin, he came to understand why she had been made a partner at age twenty-eight. She was superb with corporate work, but her specialty was criminal law. It was nothing short of breathtaking to watch her before a jury. With her husky voice that could make a man's spine turn to jelly, she'd go for the jugular, and the witness wouldn't know what hit him. By the end of the first month she had won Tom's total loyalty.

"I brought the papers on the Cardenas case," he said, laying the papers on her desk.

She glanced up from the letter she was reading, and for a moment she looked confused. Then his words registered. "Fine," she said, tossing the letter to one side as she pulled the papers toward her. He noticed that her hands were trembling.

Tom propped a hip on one corner of the large mahogany desk, his hazel eyes shifting with curiosity to the letter and back to Jessica as she skimmed the brief.

"Bad news?" he asked. Jessica looked up, and he nodded toward the letter. "You look as if you've seen a ghost, Jess. You're as white as a sheet."

His youthful face was somber as he attempted not to show the concern he felt. He had never seen her like this before. Jessica Bellamy was the most composed, self-assured woman he had ever met.

"No, it's not bad news," she answered, studying the report. "Just strange."

"A new case?"

"No. It's personal." She glanced up at him with irritation, which he answered with an unperturbed smile that she suspected must turn the ladies of his acquaintance to cream of wheat. Moreover, she knew it was sincere.

Besides being talented and bright, Tom was one of the most sincerely caring men she had ever met. She had liked him the first moment he walked into her office—even though his initial reaction to her had been akin to horror.

He had denied this reaction, of course. Once, much later, when well into his cups at an office Christmas party, he admitted that from the first moment he ached to take her to bed—but he had *not* wanted to work for her. But, he assured her, he had been duly punished. He insisted that he had begun to see visions of Phyllis Schlafly as the ghost of feminism future. Jess never mentioned the conversation to the sober version of the man.

Since that time respect had grown between them, and they had become friends. However, this one time Jess did not want to talk about what was bothering her. She continued to glare at him, hoping he would take the hint and skulk away. The smile remained planted, as did he. Capitulating with a heavy, resigned sigh, she slumped back in her chair.

She picked up the letter, fanning it. "It's from Amanda Morgan."

"Your grandmother?" His eyes widened with surprise.

"Yes," she answered tightly. "My esteemed paternal grandmother. She wants me to visit her."

"No kidding," he said. Hot damn, he thought. He remembered how shocked he had been when he had learned, quite in passing one day, that Amanda Morgan was Jess's grandmother. Anyone who read a major newspaper in California knew who Amanda Morgan was. With understandable curiosity, he asked Jess what she was like, only to have his surprise turn to incredulity as Jess merely shrugged indifferently, stating that she hadn't the vaguest idea—she had never met her.

"Well, are you going to visit her?" he asked.

"I don't know."

Christ, what was going on here? he wondered. It was obvious that the letter had shaken her badly. From her expression he could see that it wasn't likely she'd confide in him, so the only reasonable approach was head on. "You're right. You probably shouldn't bother." He shrugged. "After all, it's a whole thirty-five-minute flight to Monterey. And why rush it? You've only been here in San Francisco for six years."

Her eyes glittered as the lovely mouth drew into a smirk. "Tom, buzz off."

"She's never asked to see you before, has she?"

"Perhaps that's the point." She picked up the papers and handed them to him. "These look fine. Send them out by messenger."

"You bet." He stood up and crossed to the door, then paused. "I'll make your flight reservations."

"Go away, Tom."

"I'm gone, I'm gone."

"Rick?"

Jess rose up on an elbow to look down at him in the moonlight that crossed from the window to the bed.

He was already asleep. She reached out a finger, lightly tracing his heavy black eyebrows. He was even better looking when he was asleep, she marveled, not for the first time. There was no doubt about it—besides being her stockbroker, Rick Logan was classically handsome, a fabulous escort, and great in bed.

She leaned back and stared at the shadows on the ceiling for a moment, then closed her eyes, sighing softly as she tried to relax. After a moment her eyes flew open. It was no use—she was wide awake and restless. Even Rick's considerable expertise as a lover had not helped.

Slipping from the bed, she pulled on her robe and left the room, closing the door quietly behind her. Glancing around the large living room of her apartment, she felt suddenly gloomy. In the bright moonlight everything looked gray, like her mood.

The effect that had been created with such care was missing: the earth color accented with rose; the clean, uncluttered lines structured for contrast to the office, to give separation from days, to ease a battered spirit. Tonight the room just seemed lonely.

Without turning on a light she crossed to the bar and poured herself a brandy, thinking a drink might help her sleep. Sipping from the snifter, she leaned against the bar, watching the twinkling lights of the city through the wide windows. She could hear the faint sounds of traffic far below. Where were people going this time of night? she wondered idly. The noise never seemed to stop.

Restless, she strolled across the room, trailing a finger over an inlaid library table behind the deep-cushioned sofa, hesitating as she passed her briefcase. Then her hand stopped at a small silver-framed picture.

She picked it up, turning it to the moonlight. Funny, she mused, how you can live with something for years, yet at some undefined moment stop being aware of it. At some point it merely became part of the furniture.

She smiled at the two bright smiling girls in the picture. Like two peas in a pod, Madame Emilie had said, more than once. Strange, Jess thought, we were as different as night and day. She was gazing at a snapshot taken on a sunny spring morning in Gstaad as she and Roxy stood arm in arm before a large banner declaring some momentous school event. The letters were partly hidden—Jess could not remember what the banner said. The fact that she had forgotten suddenly filled her with regret.

I guess we were alike, Jess reflected. Both in tight mini-skirts, cashmere sweaters, and heavy charm bracelets, both looking terribly pleased with ourselves.

The "event," whatever it had been, evidently was one of those occasions when "free dress" was allowed—occasions that were tolerated but despised by the faculty, which meant that everyone observed them. Except Mary Lou Harris, Jess thought suddenly, grinning. Mary Lou wore her uniform every day for the seven years she was at Saint Michel's, thinking that it would earn her extra points with Madame. Too bad for Mary Lou.

Jess set the brandy on the table and gently traced a finger over the cold form of the other girl beneath the glass. She smiled softly. How could she have gone so long without remembering the warm, cozy comfort of those days with Roxy? They were so much a part of what she was.

The answer came with the pain. Those final memories of Roxy rushed over her, leaving her breathless. "Damn," she gasped. "No!" It had taken years to become numb and now she had reopened the wound. She didn't want to bleed like that again, ever.

Setting the picture down, she reached for the brandy, determined to end her journey to grief before it began. Then, as her gaze came to rest on her briefcase, she hesitated. Opening the lid slowly, she reached in and lifted out a small blue envelope. She stared at it for a long moment, then sighed raggedly. Jessica Bellamy, who are you kidding? she wondered.

There was no mystery as to why she had been on the verge of tears all evening—or why she had noticed Roxy's picture after passing by it for years. And why now, the realization had made her sad. It was all because of spring flowers at a funeral.

Jess picked up the picture again. "Roxy," she whispered, her eyes suddenly filling with tears, "I got a letter from Amanda today."

She carried the letter to a deep chair by the window and turned on a lamp. She nestled into the cushions, tucking her legs up under her, and hesitated for a moment before she pulled the letter from the envelope. Again she was struck by the uncanny similarity between Amanda's handwriting and her own. She pushed the thought aside and began to read:

> My dearest Jessica,
> I do hope everything is well with you—but then, I am certain that your life moves splendidly. However, as busy and as fulfilled as you must be, I am going to ask a favor of you which will seem, considering our situation, unusual and possibly even unreasonable.
> Unhappily, I find myself facing a distasteful and awkward legal situation that could have serious ramifications. I need you, Jessica, or I would not ask. It is really quite urgent. Please come.
>   With love,
>   Amanda

It was totally impossible and irresistibly intriguing. Jessica's gaze shifted from the letter to the small picture on the table. She silently laughed. Intriguing? Roxy, she thought, it was nothing short of totally compelling. Finally, at long, long last, to find out about her father's past.

"Jess?"

Startled out of her thoughts, she jumped at the sound of Rick's voice. She turned her head to find him standing by the bedroom door, buttoning his shirt. "Are you leaving already?" she asked, her voice shaken.

"Yes. I have an early appointment in the morning. What are you doing out here?" he added, glancing up at her as he buttoned a cuff.

"I couldn't sleep."

He crossed toward her and perched on the arm of a chair.

"Business problems?" The question seemed rhetorical as he gave his attention to his tie.

Do you really care? she wondered silently. Even as she had the thought, it surprised her. Now where did *that* bitchiness come from? she mused. They had gone to the theater—the play was wonderful, an A.C.T. production of Molière's *School for Wives*. Jess had enjoyed herself thoroughly.

When Rick brought her home and kissed her good night, she suddenly didn't want to be alone. Not that having a man in her bed was the answer to anything. It never was—beyond a pleasant experience. Not that she had so many men. Aside from Rick there was one brief relationship with a fellow student in law school. And of course, there was Curtis . . .

No, she thought, angry with herself. She wouldn't think about *that!* One reflective relapse was enough for one night. In any case, men were certainly nothing to be wound up over.

Rick stood up and retrieved his jacket from the back of the chair where he had thrown it earlier. "Oh, I almost forgot," he said. "About Saturday—I'm sorry, but I've got a client flying in. He insists that his portfolio won't wait till Monday. I'm afraid we'll miss dinner, but we should still make the performance."

Puzzled, she frowned at him. "What are you talking about?"

He paused as he pulled on his jacket, his expression turning to one of irritated disbelief. "The Getty fund-raiser. The opera, remember? Duty calls. How could you forget?"

"Oh . . ." Damn, she had forgotten. "Rick, I'm not sure I can go. I may have to go out of town this weekend."

He cocked a questioning brow at her.

"Family problems," she said.

He stared at her, now openly worried. "God, Jess, what is it? Did someone die?"

She blinked. "No! For heaven's sake, would I be sitting here if someone had? Nothing that dire. It's . . ." Oh, Lord, she couldn't explain this to him. She didn't even want to. "Someone in the family needs me, that's all."

The stare continued; then his brow furrowed in disbelief. Suddenly he laughed. "Jess, for crying out loud, you haven't even been home for Christmas in four years! You're telling me now that the self-reliant, reticent Bellamys are having 'family problems'? What is it? Someone new in your life? It's okay, we agreed—"

"Dammit!" she cried, jumping up from the chair. She suddenly felt raw, exposed, and she turned away from him as she struggled to control her emotions. She felt shocked at her own behavior. "I told you the truth! It has nothing to do with someone new in my life! I—" But it did. It was someone new—so very new. "I told you, it's a family matter." She forced out the words, then braced herself against the silence that followed.

"Okay, I'm sorry." His voice was gentle as he came up behind her, drawing her back against him as he kissed her ear. "Call me when you get back."

"I will," she said softly, swallowing. "I'm sorry I lost my temper."

"Don't worry about it." He kissed her again and then, crossing the room, grabbed up his overcoat from the sofa. "I've got to go." Pausing at the door he looked back at her and smiled. "Call me if you need me, Jess. I mean it."

She nodded and returned the smile, then stared at the door for a long moment after it had closed behind him. Slowly, she returned to the chair, sinking into it with a sigh. How quickly life could change, she mused, just like that. He wouldn't call again—not after tonight. In spite of his reassurance, he hadn't believed a word she had said. Exit Rick Logan. Maybe tomorrow she would care. At the moment she was numb.

She picked up the letter from the table where she had dropped it. She stared at it for a long moment, then tapped it thoughtfully against her chin. She had always believed that the past was better left in its place. She had learned that at her father's knee, and learned it well. Now she was letting someone from the past totally upend her life!

She hadn't even thought about how she would approach Justice Reynolds. He probably wouldn't let her have the time off. But she hadn't had a vacation in almost two years, she argued with herself, she hadn't wanted one. She had cases pending. It would be difficult to reassign them. But then, she was a partner now. With the position came privileges.

Face it, Jess, she thought, you're frightened. You're facing a door with a lady behind it—who may well turn out to be a slavering tiger, ready to chew up and spit out your neat, patterned, comfortable life!

Then, suddenly, Jess found herself laughing softly. Roxy, she thought, if I believed in ghosts I would believe that you had orchestrated this. Then like a dam breaking, memories came rushing:

They had been hiding side by side in a closet in the music room, huddled together with a bag of marshmallows Roxy had somehow managed to procure during their flight. It had been a particularly daring adventure, and Madame was in hot pursuit—though they hoped that, given time, she would forgive.

Chewing on a marshmallow, Jess had observed, in a rare moment of doubt, that perhaps just this once they had overreached themselves. If they were caught they were doomed. To which Roxy had responded, her mouth full: "Shoot, Jess, what if we are? It was worth it, wasn't it? Life is nothing if you don't feel it."

CHAPTER 7

Jess knew that either she was doing exactly the right thing or she was about to make one of the biggest mistakes of her life. So her chances were fifty-fifty, she thought. She'd had worse odds in her life.

It began to rain, and she turned on the windshield wipers. Then she flipped on the turn signal, pulled into the left lane, and passed a slower-moving car. The Jaguar's engine responded happily, and Jess settled deeper into the soft leather seat, gaining comfort from the car's power and maneuverability in the face of the developing storm.

Jess smiled as she recalled the reaction of those within the inner offices of Reynolds, Armisted, and Royce. Tom Bradin had been a champ. Outwardly he had accepted her news with panache, though occasionally she had caught a look of extreme satisfaction on his face. That was okay; she'd let him take credit for the whole expedition if he wanted to.

Once she had made her decision, she called in favors from the partners. Their eager acceptance of her work load came as a surprise. In spite of the burdens it placed on them, they actually seemed happy to help. Their reaction puzzled her until she spoke to Joseph Armisted.

When she apologized to the senior partner for leaving on such short notice, he had peered at her over the tops of his half-glasses. It was an effect that made the co-founding partner of the firm resemble a middle-aged Ben Franklin. Then, with a slight smile he had said, "Don't think anything of it, Jessica. It's about time that you asked a favor. We are all greatly relieved."

The comment had stunned her—and it had confirmed the

62

wisdom of her decision. She had become, over the years, horrifyingly predictable and, she was beginning to suspect, somewhat boring.

She managed to wind up the most pressing business around nine-thirty that evening. Suddenly she felt intensely restless. It was a feeling she often experienced before a particularly difficult trial. Normally she would have gone home, changed into her sloppy old robe, and curled up in front of the TV to watch an old movie, preferably with Cary Grant. Tonight, however, her mind turned to a different solution.

"Tom?"

"Yes, Jess?" He glanced at her warily. That was the voice she used when she wanted him to do something. He just wanted to go home to bed.

"How far away is Monterey? In hours."

"For normal people about three hours. The way you drive, about two. Why?"

She ignored the question, frowning at his comment. "I do not exceed the speed limit."

He sputtered.

"I do not!" she insisted. Then her voice softened. "Well, maybe a little. But never past sixty or sixty-five."

He should have let it go, but he was so tired that a certain perverseness took over. "Right. You don't ever go over sixty. I'll give you that. However, Jess, that's your only speed. Zero to sixty. Regardless of the street you're on. You do sixty on the freeway and you do it on the Embarcadero."

"I do not."

"You do it in front of the Civic Center. Every time I have to go to court with you, I want to go to mass first."

"You're not Catholic."

"That makes my point."

She chuckled. Even when he was insulting her, Tom Bradin could make her laugh. On many a late night while preparing for a case, they had been reduced to silly, sanity-saving banter. Then she noticed how weary he looked. "God, Tom, you look awful. Have I done this to you?"

"Yes."

"Well, you can go home and go to bed. Moreover, you can take the next couple of weeks off."

He brightened considerably. "Seriously?"

"Absolutely. As for me . . ." She turned off her computer, got up from the chair, and rolled it under the desk. "I sent Amanda a wire that I was coming tomorrow. But I'm not going to wait until morning. I'm going to Monterey now."

Tom's eyes widened. "Jess, it's the middle of the night!"

"No, it's not," she scoffed. She began turning off lights. "I'm too restless to sleep anyway. If I pack quickly and get out of here, I should be there by one or two o'clock."

He knew better than to argue with her when her mind was made up. "Well, it's midweek and off-season. You can probably find a hotel room. Or you could sleep in your car. Take a blanket."

She ignored the quip as she snapped her briefcase shut and grabbed her purse. "Yep, I'm going to do it. Lock up, will you, Tom?" She left a tired, but happy assistant and went home to pack.

With some delays she was on the road by eleven-fifteen. By the time she neared Palo Alto it had begun to rain. She pulled off the 280 freeway and bought a cup of coffee at an all-night convenience store. As she continued on, she still felt very right about her decision. She sipped the hot coffee, wondering if what she was feeling could actually be excitement. It had been so long since she had felt it. She also wondered how her father would react if he knew what she was doing. She suspected that he would be furious.

While she had been raised in the relatively sheltered cocoon of her mother's heritage, Jess had the impression that John Morgan Bellamy joined the human race as a feeling, breathing, vital adult, full-formed and ready for life at the age of seventeen. Many times, when she was very small, Jess had asked her father about those early years of his life. He had always managed to evade her questions.

Finishing her coffee, Jess realized that the exit to Highway 101 was just ahead. She glanced in her rearview mirror and changed lanes, taking the exit just as the storm opened up in a deluge. Headlights reflected off of the sheets of rain, restricting visibility, but fortunately there was little traffic. Nevertheless, Jess found herself gripping the wheel. She hated to drive in the rain. To calm herself she slipped a Bach tape into the stereo. As the sounds of flute and harpsichord filled the car, she could feel the tension ease in her shoulders. As she relaxed, thoughts of her father seeped back.

Though it had not occurred to her before, she realized that John Bellamy's attitude toward his mother reminded her of what she had learned about racism in a sociology class taught by a professor named Blackstone. Prejudice was not exclusive to screaming bigots, Dr. Blackstone had said. Real bigotry was subtle. It was taught without fiery crosses, violence, or raised voices. It was taught by parents who insisted they were not racists; who instructed their child in the evils of bigotry; who claimed to care for those of color. Possibly the parents even believed it. Then, when the child was walking down the street holding the parents' hands, a black person passed by. In that moment the child felt a tightening, just a brief suggestion of tension in the hands holding his. The message was transmitted. The message was driven deep.

And so she had been taught about her grandmother, Jess realized. When a child's questions turned a parent's warmth to reserve, when laughter faded and eyes turned cold, questions were no longer asked and attitudes were born. What remained was an unspoken understanding that Amanda Morgan had caused her son so much pain that he had stopped loving her. Unable to contemplate such horror, Jess had allowed her questions to sink into dark recesses, never asking him about his past—or about her grandmother—after the age of ten.

But now, Jess realized, she was about to meet a ghost. Amanda Morgan Bellamy Alger. Over the sounds of Bach, Jess tried the name out loud. She knew that her grandmother did not use either of her married names, preferring to be called Amanda Morgan. She wondered why.

Why have you contacted me now, Amanda, after all these years? Jess wondered. The letter said that she had a legal problem, but that couldn't be the reason. Amanda Morgan had more than adequate legal council at her beck and call. The family company had begun with Amanda's grandfather back in 1846, but it was under her own hand that it had developed into a large international business with heavy political influence. And that information, gained while working as an attorney in California the past six years, was the total extent of Jess's knowledge.

Jess drove on through the heavy rain. The tension had

returned to her shoulders, and she realized she was clenching the wheel again. She changed the tape to an old Three Dog Night, turned up the volume, and sang along, belting out "Joy to the World" and "As Sure As I'm Sittin' Here." Thus she passed the next forty-five minutes. She was so absorbed in the music that she almost missed the Highway 156 turnoff to the Monterey Peninsula.

Jess became aware in the next fifteen minutes that it was very dark. Not just nighttime dark, but pitch-black dark. And the reason for it came to her: there were no lights. No traffic lights, no streetlights, not even lights from overpasses. The highway cut across the foothills, and Jess was out in the rural countryside. It was totally dark and it was still raining buckets.

Then, suddenly, without warning, there was a horse on the highway. Jess slammed her foot down on the brake. . . .

Her first thought was that she had been dreaming. She didn't remember falling asleep, but she woke up suddenly, her body protesting from every stiff, aching joint. In a rush, it all came back: the crash, the fact that she had survived, the fact that she was all alone out in the middle of nowhere. . . .

Suddenly there was a bright light shining in her face. She threw up her hand to fend it off, and disjointed thoughts shouted in her brain. Sweet Jesus, it was a mass murderer! Then, squinting against the light, she realized the intruder was wearing a khaki rain slicker and a hat. And the hat had a gold badge on it. The assailant was a cop.

Jess tried to punch the window button but it was dead. She tried again, swearing at it. The cop knocked on the window and pointed to the ignition. She tried the key; fortunately the battery wasn't dead and the window still worked.

"Are you all right?" he asked as the window slid open.

Jess stuck her head out the window. She leaned way out, looking left and right. "Officer, do you have a gun?"

The highway patrol officer stepped back, instantly alert. "Yes, ma'am." He pushed the slicker aside and reached for the unsnapped holster as his eyes darted about to spot the trouble.

"Good." Her voice was filled with authority as she got out of the car. "There's a goddam horse out here somewhere and I'm going to shoot it."

• • •

The Jaguar wasn't a total loss but it couldn't be fixed in less than a week. That was if they got the parts in time.

At midafternoon Jess found herself sitting on the hood, trying to look casual and somewhat dignified. A group of teenage boys, who had gathered around a shiny new pickup truck about twenty feet away, seemed to find her somewhat of a curiosity.

Castroville was not a bustling metropolis on a Thursday afternoon. It was a beige town with one wide street bordered by masonry buildings built in the thirties and forties. The only tow truck in town was occupied and could not haul her car to the British Motors dealer in Monterey until that afternoon. The way it looked, however, the Jaguar would get to Monterey before she did.

She shifted uncomfortably, trying to recover circulation in her tailbone. She should have bought a BMW, she thought. But she knew she was denying the love-hate relationship she had for her car. What other car owner bragged that she had crossed the country at an average of seventy-five miles an hour and the engine had only caught fire twice?

Her short relationship with the California Highway Patrol the previous night had been a blessing. The officer was friendly, helpful, and exceedingly polite. Once he realized she wasn't serious about dispatching the horse, he drove her into Castroville, arranged for a tow truck to bring the car after her, and dropped her at the only motel in town.

Jess had collapsed into a dry, clean bed at 4:15 and slept the sleep of the dead until 11:30 in the morning. She had found a café and eaten breakfast. Still exhausted, she'd spent an hour sitting at the counter, drinking coffee and listening to a cluster of farmers settle the problems of the world over their lunch. Then, at 12:30 she had walked to the garage where the car had been left the previous night. She spent the next half-hour being ogled by a lecherous mechanic.

She had dressed in a blue Ellen Tracy silk shirtdress. She had always loved Linda Allard's designs for their exquisite tailoring. Gracefully, tastefully, they fit the body. Now she rued her taste, wishing she had worn a large, baggy sweat shirt.

When the mechanic was through goggling at her breasts and she was able to gain his attention, she was able to determine

that he had absolutely no idea what to do with the car. He did,
however, provide her with a phone book. She called the British
Motors dealer in Monterey and almost wept when she was
connected to the head of the service department, an exceedingly polite gentleman named Percy who spoke with a clipped
British accent. Not to worry, he assured her, British Leland
would come to the rescue.

However, it would take at least a week.

Then Jess made a difficult decision. She called Amanda.

Jess spoke with her grandmother's butler, Henley. Another
British accent. According to Henley, Mrs. Morgan was,
regrettably, not able to come to the phone. However, he was
certain that she would want to dispatch a car immediately.
Henley, who proved to be totally officious, took down the
details, confirmed that Jessica was safe, and asked her to wait
at the garage where a car would pick her up.

That was at 1:00. At 1:37 the teenage boys clustered about
the pickup truck had something new to stare at. One of them
poked another boy in the ribs with his elbow, gesturing with his
head toward a point beyond where Jess was sitting. Jess turned
as a Mercedes limousine pulled into the garage lot. The door
opened and as the boys gaped, a middle-aged driver in an
immaculate dark blue suit approached Jess.

"Miss Bellamy? Mrs. Morgan sent me." As she slipped off
the hood of the car he was already retrieving her luggage,
which had been stacked by the rear door of the Jag.

As they pulled out onto Highway 1 and drove south toward
Monterey, Jess found her stomach tightening into a knot of
anticipation. Taking a deep breath, she tried to concentrate on
the breathtaking scenery. On her right was the cobalt blue of
Monterey Bay and the Pacific Ocean beyond. To the left were
sand dunes, which gradually changed to a landscape dense with
pine, fir, juniper, and cypress trees.

It was a unique forest, with trees that seemed at once
domestic yet wild, as if they allowed humans to live among
them in a strange kind of coexistence. Particularly intriguing
were the Monterey cypresses, of which pictures could not do
justice. They were fascinating, unlike any tree she had ever
seen, twisted and gnarled, as if shaped by a spectral wind.

They turned off the highway and slowed down at the
gate-house entrance to Del Monte Forest. A uniformed guard

leaned out, checked the identification plate on the grill, and nodded them through. The forest became more dense as they drove along well-paved narrow streets that twisted and turned along hills and dips, passing an odd mingling of modest homes and large, secluded estates.

The car stopped at a large black iron gate. The driver pressed a remote-control switch, and the gates swung open slowly. Then the limousine moved forward down a long, winding drive, pulling up before a large, rambling two-story English Country–style house of stone and heavy timbers, with tall windows of thick diamond-shaped beveled-glass panes.

Jess gathered up her purse and briefcase. As she stepped out of the car the front door opened and a distinguished-looking man of medium height in a gray coat, with hair to match, hurried down the steps. With his clipped English accent he introduced himself as Henley, then informed Jess that Mrs. Morgan was on the fifteenth green.

As they entered the large entry hall of the house, Henley asked if Jess wished to refresh herself. Jess declined the offer and said that she would prefer to meet Mrs. Morgan immediately. With a smile, she suggested that Henley lead the way; she would be right behind him.

From his pained expression, Jess knew that she had shocked Amanda's butler, but it couldn't be helped. The thought of waiting alone now, perhaps for hours, to see Amanda was more than she could bear. Following him through the house, she dropped her purse and briefcase on an eighteenth-century Queen Anne writing desk as they passed. She ignored Henley's wince as she encouraged him, brightly, to carry on. Not that she blamed Henley for her impulsiveness—or for her grandmother's absence. But then, it wasn't his Queen Anne, and Amanda apparently had three holes to go.

As they crossed the rolling lawns reaching down to the lush golf course that abutted the grounds, with the deep blue Pacific crashing against the rugged coastline just beyond, Jess began to regret her decision. The weather was much warmer here than it had been in San Francisco. Her blue silk dress was in serious jeopardy of being ruined as she felt a trickle of sweat roll down her back. In addition, she could feel her two-inch heels sinking into the soft earth. She plodded along behind Henley, ineffectively glaring at his back. Finally, when she had almost decided

to return to the house, they rounded a grassy knoll and she
spied a small group of golfers dead ahead. One, in particular,
took her attention. She recognized her from her pictures in the
newspapers: a short, trim woman, bent in a stance as she
readied for her drive down the fairway. Silver-haired and
fragile-looking, she was garbed in bright yellow and green
plaid knickers and an eye-opening yellow sweater. As she
raised the wood, Jess fought a compulsion to shout out her
name.

The club swept down and the ball shot off the tee. The heads
of Amanda's friends moved in unison, as if on a connecting
string, following its progress. But Jess's full attention was
fixed on the object of her journey. She was surprised at how
young and vital Amanda looked. Her body was trim and
surprisingly supple for her age—probably as a result of
excessive golf, Jess observed wryly. And her skin was beautiful, soft and almost unlined. Phenomenal, Jess thought.

As they approached, Amanda finally saw them. Her expression, which had been one of studied concentration as she
watched the ball, turned into a brilliant smile. "Jessica! Good
Lord, child, I'd know you anywhere!" She passed her club to
her caddy and strode toward Jess, grasping her in a surprisingly
strong hug.

Amanda introduced Jess to her golf companions, then
abandoned her game and her friends. They returned to the
house on a golf cart, which Amanda drove like Mr. Toad. Then
Amanda took a shaken Jess into a high, vaulted library.

Three walls of the large room were occupied by book lofts.
In the fourth wall was a massive stone fireplace. Below the
lofts, two of the oak-paneled walls were dominated by paintings. With a slight, surprised arch to her brow, Jess recognized
a rare Vermeer, a Rembrandt, and two Rubens sketches.
Amanda, apparently, had a fondness for the baroque. The wall
facing the fireplace was composed entirely of thick beveled-
glass windows, bayed in three graceful scallops to hold
deep, cushioned window seats. Glancing around at the furnish-
ings, Jess began to understand her father's preference for
English decor mixed liberally with Early American antiques—
a sharp contrast to her mother's taste, which had run to French.
Odd that he should carry tastes of a woman he could not even
bear to talk about, she thought. With this realization, her
curiosity returned.

Sinking into a deep leather chair, Jess glanced with dismay at her ruined shoes and then dismissed them from her mind as Amanda ordered tea. "Or would you prefer coffee, Jessica?" she asked, as Henley waited with studied patience in the doorway. Jess assured her that coffee would be fine. She found herself growing irritated as Amanda ordered sandwiches and cakes as well. She was in no mood for high tea. Settling back in the chair, she gripped the overstuffed arms as she peered through narrowed eyes at Amanda, who had perched on the heavily padded arm of the sofa across from her. She realized, as she viewed the other woman warily, that the back of her neck was a knot of tension.

"I want to thank you for sending the car for me," she said stiffly. "However, I was somewhat surprised, considering the urgency in your letter, that you were not here to greet me."

Jess wasn't certain what reaction she expected her words to bring, but certainly not the embarrassment they apparently caused. Amanda actually looked chagrined. The moment stretched uncomfortably as Henley entered and set the tea tray down between them on a low, heavy oak table.

"I'll pour, Henley; you may go," Amanda said, glancing at the butler, who nodded and left the room quietly. Jessica watched as Amanda picked up a silver coffee pot and poured the steaming dark beverage into a delicate Limoges cup. She frowned slightly, noticing that Amanda's hand was shaking. It was the same hand that a short time before had wielded a heavy wood with steady power that had driven a golf ball down the long fairway. Jess was suddenly stunned by the truth: Amanda was nervous! Was that why she had not been here to greet her? A last-minute flight to the greens? The realization that her grandmother was as uneasy about this first meeting as she was touched her gently. This was the Amanda of the flowers, she reminded herself, and inside a spot suddenly softened.

"Tell you what, I'll forgive your oversight in not being here to greet me," Jess offered with a smile, "if you will forgive my impatience in dragging you away from your game. Deal?"

Amanda's eyes grew warm. "Agreed." She smiled. "This is not easy for either of us, is it?"

"No, it isn't. How could it be? I was stunned when I got your letter."

"But you came anyway. I'm glad, Jessica. More than you

can know." When she handed Jess a cup and saucer, her hand was steady. "How much has your father told you about me?"

Jess took the cup and leaned back in her chair as she regarded Amanda steadily. "Absolutely nothing. He never talks about you."

Amanda sipped her coffee, apparently weighing Jess's answer. "Well, perhaps that is best. You will have to form your own opinion of me. It's not a bad beginning."

"My own opinion? Not entirely." Jess carefully set her cup on the table. "I've read about you, so I'm not completely ignorant about Amanda Morgan. But I've also lived with the knowledge that you are estranged from your son. I love my father, I respect him, his feelings are important to me. I would be less than truthful if I said that his attitude won't affect my opinion of you."

For the second time Amanda surprised her by not taking offense. "You are bluntly honest, Jessica. I'm glad. The only way we will be able to find a common ground to deal with this is by being honest."

"'This'?" Somehow Jess knew the word encompassed far more than just their present discussion.

"Our relationship, of course—and what I'm going to ask of you."

Here it comes, Jess thought.

Amanda set her cup on the table and rose from her perch, taking a few steps to the fireplace, where she paused and turned, her expression one of resolve. "Years ago, to my deep regret, your father and I had a falling-out. Neither of us is to blame—outside events controlled our lives in those years. I will not discuss that with you; it has nothing to do with why I asked you here."

She fixed her penetrating blue eyes on Jess. "You said that you've read about me. I assume that means you know about the Morgan Land and Development Company. It is a diversified corporation, Jessica, reaching one way or another into practically every country in the free world. I've spent a lifetime building on what my grandfather founded and his son passed on to me. But nothing, no part of it, is more important to me than the land where it all began, the core, the beginning, which became Altra Grow. Altra Grow is not just an agribusiness, Jessica; it is the land. I cannot expect you to understand how I truly feel about this, not yet. But you must come to understand it soon if you are to successfully defend my company against the criminal charges."

Jess wasn't surprised by her last words; she had expected them. "Amanda," she said gently but firmly, "there is absolutely no way I can represent you as counsel. It is totally impossible."

"Impossible? Quite the contrary." Amanda smiled. "You are the only one who can."

Jess swallowed heavily as her mind raced. No, no! she thought. She had come here out of curiosity, not commitment! She spoke slowly. "It is impossible. You have legions of attorneys. Besides, I know nothing of your business. I don't have the background required to represent your best interests. Additionally—"

"Jessica." Amanda's soft, firm voice ended the plea. "Yes, I have legions of lawyers. And I am quite aware that you are unacquainted with the intricacies of the company. But none of that matters. I hire and fire whom I please, legal counsel included. You are the only one who can represent me in this matter. Don't look at me with such dismay, my dear. I assure you that I am in control of all of my faculties. Jessica, I am seventy-nine years old. I have one child—who will have nothing to do with me. I have two grandchildren. Your brother is firmly established in John's business and will someday take over for him. Who, Jessica, who in this world is to inherit what I have accumulated?"

Oh, my God.

Amanda laughed softly at Jess's thunderstruck expression. "Come now, Jessica, I know you are successful in your profession, and in no way do I demean what you have accomplished. Also, I am quite aware that you are financially secure through multiple family trusts—I should be; I established most of them. Beyond all of that, can it be that you have never considered this possibility?"

She hadn't. She honestly never had, not once. All her life she had been encouraged not to think about Amanda. She had not been real until today. But Jess couldn't say that to her; she wasn't that unkind. Stunned, she said the first impulsive thing that came to mind. "I don't want it."

"Why?" Amanda's voice was compellingly soft, though

there was a flicker of amusement in her clear blue eyes. And there was a glimpse of something else that made Jess uncomfortable. "Why, Jessica? Because you never considered it? I'm not surprised. You were raised by your father. Everything I represent is anathema to him. If you never considered this possibility, it is because you were taught not to think of me at all. We both know that, so let's be honest about it."

It was unsettling to have her thoughts read with such accuracy. "You're right; we should be open." Jess drew a leveling breath. "Tell me why— Tell me what happened between you and my father."

"No. That is the one thing I will not discuss. That is between your father and me and no one else. As I said in the beginning, you will have to judge me yourself, from your own viewpoint and experience. Be assured, Jessica, I am not giving the company to you because of some misguided sentiment. I have followed your progress carefully, and I named you in my will because I believe you are worthy of my trust. Otherwise, I would choose a total stranger if I had to, but one of talent. Do not doubt it."

Their eyes locked and Jess caught a glimpse of that look again, this time recognizing it as strength and determination. She understood then how this woman had accomplished so much: Amanda Morgan was accustomed to having her way. She had failed only once. Whatever had happened between them, Jess began to get an inkling of why her father had left home. Had he been fed up with manipulation? Tired of having Amanda rule his life? Or was he so much like her, beyond the strong physical resemblance Jess could see, that to live his own life he had to separate himself from her? And now Jess had the strong uncomfortable feeling that she was to assume the role he had abdicated. Restless, she stood up and moved away from Amanda, aware that those penetrating eyes were following her, waiting, anticipating. Composing herself, she turned back, with equal determination.

"Amanda, I don't want to hurt you. But I cannot accept your offer. I suggest that you find that talented stranger. I am content with my career; it is important to me. I have no intention of—"

"Don't make a rash decision. You owe her that much."

The deep male voice came from behind her. Startled, she spun around to find herself eye to eye with a tall man in his mid-thirties who had quietly entered the room. How long had he been standing there? she wondered, stunned by his sudden appearance. Before she could collect her wits to respond, Amanda took control.

"Michael!" She crossed the room, stepping between them. Her voice and manner made it clear that she was pleased by his sudden appearance. "Jessica, this is Michael Rawlings. You are prompt, Michael, as always. Michael is the general manager of Altra Grow, Jessica, and I asked him here to meet you. You will be working with him on the case."

Jess opened her mouth to protest, but Amanda was already halfway out the door. "There are other matters requiring my attention, my dears. I'll leave you two to become acquainted. When you wish to be shown to your room, Jessica, pull the bell cord by the desk to summon Henley. I'll see you at dinner." With that, she was gone.

In the awkward silence that followed, Michael Rawlings crossed to the far wall and pressed an unseen mechanism between the Rubens sketches. A panel slid back to reveal a wet bar. Obviously, Jess realized, this man felt at home here.

"Drink?"

"No." I'm losing control, Jess thought, if I ever had it. The situation was out of hand, and her immediate impulse was to grab her bags and head back to San Francisco. She contemplated leaving a note for Amanda as her eyes traveled over Michael Rawlings. He was an inch or two over six feet, with brown hair heavily streaked by the sun. His face and arms, exposed by the rolled-up sleeves of a plaid cotton shirt, were deeply tanned. From the broad shoulders and lean form to the Levi's he wore and the boots flecked with mud—flakes of which had dropped onto the Chinese silk rug—her first impression was that his appearance and manners were more appropriate to a field hand than to the manager of anything. The opinion was confirmed as he turned around. Brown eyes fixed on her with barely concealed irritation. Then they swept over her rudely, and, to Jessica's amazement, he smirked.

"Your shoes are muddy," she said, finding some satisfaction in pointing out his lack of social graces in his employer's home.

His eyes snapped down to her feet. "So are yours."

She felt her cheeks grow hot. "I—I was out on the golf course—" Oh, God, she thought, now I'm stammering.

"You don't have to explain to me." He leaned back against the bar and sipped his drink.

What an insufferable man, she thought. And he was very angry with her. Well, that brooding look might work on other women in the singles bars, but not her. It was too bad—the man would actually be good-looking if he wasn't such an insufferable hick. She crossed her arms and gave him one of her quelling looks of contempt and dismissal. A dark brow arched with surprise. Ah, she thought, we are getting somewhere. Then he laughed, a deep, easy sound.

"Is that look supposed to make me tremble?" he said. "Is it natural or something you learned at Harvard Law? The look that will reduce an opponent to a quivering mass."

Jess just barely managed to smother a gasp. A point in his court, she admitted, drawing a calming breath, but the match would be hers. She smiled in return. "Why, Mr. Rawlings? Are we opponents?"

"Apparently we are, Ms. Bellamy. If you meant what you said to Amanda just now."

"My conversations with my grandmother are none of your business."

"Oh, but they are. I won't allow you to hurt her."

The comment almost undid her. She dropped her arms and stepped forward, struggling to keep her voice level. Who did this person think he was? "How dare you—"

"I dare." He pushed away from the bar to cross the room and drop into a chair. "Sit down. We have a lot to talk about. Oh, come on—don't just stand there glaring at me. Sit. Unless, of course, you want to leave and go back to that flourishing law practice of yours. Frankly, I hope you do."

He emphasized his words by leaning back in the chair, crossing his legs ankle to knee, and resting his drink on the arm of the chair. He was watching her reaction, and she realized that he actually did want her to scurry out of here with her tail between her legs. Well, not damned likely.

She sat down on the arm of the sofa where Amanda had perched earlier. "Please," she said in a honeyed voice, "go on. I can't wait to hear this. Why does my presence cause you such discomfort?"

"Ms. Bellamy, your presence here does not affect me in the least. I don't give a damn where you are."

The insufferable s.o.b. "You just said quite clearly that you hoped I would leave. Do you have something to hide? Would it bother you if I should, say, go over Altra Grow's books while I'm here?"

The ball was in his court—and she had slammed it right into his stomach. She had the satisfaction of seeing anger flare in his eyes. "Feel free. With Amanda's permission, of course."

"Of course."

His expression grew hard. "All right. If you want to know why I'd like to see you out of here, you've got it. You didn't even invite her to your graduation from college or law school, or to your precious debut—that was quite an affair, as I recall. Don't look so surprised. Amanda showed me the clippings from the New York papers. Did you know that she keeps a scrapbook on you? All of your accomplishments—all of the things you excluded her from."

Jess was speechless—and humiliated that this man should know so much about her life. "I told you before—"

"That this is none of my business? You asked. And don't attempt to blame your behavior on your father. You've been living in San Francisco six years. Not once in those six years did you attempt to make contact with her. Why are you here now?"

"Apparently Amanda has confided in you—that was her choice. But I see no reason why I should be subjected to your rudeness."

"Amanda is my friend. I don't want her hurt any more than she already has been. When she told me that she had sent for you"—he paused and sighed—"I hoped at first that you would come and that I was wrong about you. But from what I heard when I entered this room I know I wasn't. If you stay, you'll only hurt her more. For God's sake, if you care for her the least bit go now, before that happens."

She stared at him for a long moment as her thoughts tossed conflictingly. She wanted to put him in his place, but his honest concern for Amanda was hard to combat. And, as much as she hated to admit it, everything he said was true. Regretfully true. But he didn't know anything about her. He had no right to be so angry with her. Finally she glanced at his drink and then forced her eyes up to meet his. "May I have one of those now?"

Her response surprised him and he shrugged. Placing his glass on the table beside him, he rose and crossed to the bar, giving her a moment to collect her wits. Until this moment she hadn't given any thought to how this visit would affect Amanda.

He returned and handed her the drink, then settled back into his chair. Avoiding his eyes, she took a long swallow of the liquor, drawing a breath against the burning that hit her throat. Scotch. She hated scotch. But it did serve to clear her thoughts.

"Michael— May I call you Michael?" she asked, attempting a conciliatory tone. He offered a slight smile and nodded. "I am here because Amanda asked me to come. I have absolutely no intention of discussing my family or my personal life with you, regardless of how much you think you know about us. However, I appreciate the fact that you seem to care about my grandmother; therefore, I will assure you of this much: If she is in trouble, I will do everything I can to help her in the short time that I plan to be here. I cannot represent her in the case, but I will look into it and advise her. Whatever I find, I will turn over to her attorney. Can you be content with that?"

"Would it matter?"

"No."

He studied her for a long moment, then seemed to come to a decision as he set his half-finished drink on the table. "Okay. Personal considerations aside—for both of us. Agreed?"

"Agreed." She took a deep breath, wondering if she was making a mistake. "Now tell me about the case."

He paused a moment, as if weighing his thoughts. "Late in September, one of our workers was accidentally killed. The district attorney has brought charges of criminal negligence against Altra Grow. And there are other considerations, aside from the case itself. If the D.A. proves negligence, there could be ramifications that would hurt us badly. The unions are already difficult to work with, and contracts are coming up; they'll use this case against us. Beyond that, there are suppliers and, at the other end, wholesalers and retailers for our crops, many of which we sell directly. All we have to offer is our reputation, in an extremely competitive, difficult market. Public sentiment matters, and we're a Goliath. There are a lot of Davids out there that are more than anxious to crush a giant."

Jess added an observation of her own: "Not to mention the law suits that are almost certain to follow a guilty verdict."

"Absolutely. And there's more. The last five years have been difficult ones for farming companies. A few years ago Amanda went public with the parent company. Now she has stockholders and a board of directors who have been pressing her to dump Altra Grow. They look upon farming as the albatross of the Morgan Land and Development Company. So far Amanda has been able to keep them at bay by pouring her own money into the farming operations, but the scandal caused by a criminal verdict would be the excuse they've been looking for. You should realize that the dumping of Altra Grow would finish Amanda as well. She couldn't survive the loss of Altra Grow. It's the most important thing in her life."

Jess regarded him silently for a moment, weighing what he had said. It occurred to her that if Altra Grow fell, Amanda would not be the only one to lose; Michael Rawlings would be out of a job. But she believed that his concern for Amanda was real—and her instincts had not failed her yet. So be it. "I'll need all of the documents on the case: the court files, the personnel files of the worker who was killed—by the way, how did he die?"

"A grape harvester."

"I beg your pardon?"

"He was crushed by a grape harvester."

"Jesus," she murmured. Then, after a moment, "I'll need to acquaint myself with the weap—the machine. And I'll need to speak with those involved—whoever was in charge, witnesses, family, and so forth."

"Whatever you need."

"Company records."

"Whatever."

She took a long drink of the scotch, then regarded him steadily. "What if I find that Altra Grow was culpable?"

"You won't find that."

"But if I do?"

"You won't."

"We'll see, Mr. Rawlings." Before she took another drink she gave him a pleasant but poignant smile. "I'll give it my best shot. But I warn you—you may come to regret the day you asked me to get involved."

CHAPTER 8

When had she become so jaded? The thought darted like a pesky gnat through Jessica's mind as she sat slumped in the box seat, her hands shoved deep in the pockets of her corduroy slacks. The morning fog had lifted from Del Monte Forest's polo field, and the day promised to be warm. The heavy fisherman's sweater that had felt so good only a quarter of an hour before had begun to feel heavy. The hollow thwack of mallet on ball cracked in the still morning air as hooves pounded down the grass toward the goal. Jess heard polite voices commenting on the play amid voices given to other conversation.

She had come downstairs that morning prepared to talk business, only to have Amanda usher her into a waiting car. She had discovered a few moments later that Amanda didn't want to miss that day's polo match. Before Jess could mount a serious protest, they arrived at the field just as the second chukker began.

"Splendid cross reverse!" Amanda remarked, gaining Jessica's attention.

I am jaded, Jess confirmed glumly, aware of the pâté and champagne being served from baskets to men who had nothing better to do on a Friday morning than watch a polo match. Their wives would disappear following the last chukker for hairdresser appointments, aerobic classes, or an hour with a tennis pro. Perhaps they'd even play some tennis.

Not that she could afford to be too critical; this life was still far too much a part of her. She had learned the value and satisfaction of hard work and the pleasure it brought, but she could never embrace poverty. She enjoyed a good pâté or beluga as much as anyone else, but she had come to despise the lack of direction.

Jess stole a glance at Amanda and felt a strange twinge of disappointment. For some inexplicable reason she had thought Amanda would be different. Her expectations had been founded in the knowledge that Amanda involved herself in her company, that her contributions were viable. But then, Jess really did not want to judge her on such a brief acquaintance. Amanda had earned her pleasures and was now reaping the well-earned benefits of hard work.

"Why, Sam, how delightful to see you!"

The tone of Amanda's voice gained Jessica's attention. Many people had stopped by their box to chat with her grandmother and to be introduced to Jess. She had greeted them politely, and over the course of the morning they had melded into a blur. But now Jessica's instincts sharpened on the casually offered greeting and the heavy irony in her grandmother's voice. Her gaze shifted to the two men who stepped into the box, taking the two empty chairs at the linen-covered table with a familiarity that claimed a relationship with Amanda.

"Jess, I'd like you to meet Sam Borgini and Elliott Westbrook. They are members of the company's board of directors. Sam, Elliott, I'd like you to meet my granddaughter, Jessica Bellamy."

"How do you do, Miss Bellamy," Samuel Borgini said genially. "Amanda, you didn't tell me your granddaughter was coming to visit." The voice was warm, but Jess caught a touch of surprise that went beyond the comment.

"I don't tell you everything, Sam." Amanda smiled, returning her attention to the action on the field. "And how is Helen?"

"She's fine. She'll be sorry that she didn't come today and missed you."

Jess studied the two men during the exchange, wondering about the amusement in her grandmother's voice. In a heavy sweater that was unflattering to his girth—probably thirty pounds overweight on his five-foot-seven-inch frame—Samuel Borgini looked as out of place as anyone she had ever seen. His face was round and tending to jowl, his broad forehead was intersected with frown wrinkles, and his large nose was mapped with broken capillaries that suggested he enjoyed his drinks. His brown hair was thinning across his head, thickening over the ears. His large, intelligent brown eyes flicked to Jess with interest.

Elliott Westbrook was Laurel to Borgini's Hardy—taller and rail-thin. He was impeccably dressed by Ralph Lauren in forest green and gray, not a graying sandy hair out of place. As his partner conversed with Amanda, his hazel eyes kept stealing guiltily to the action on the field. Watching him, Jess sensed that his inattention had less to do with interest in the match than a reluctance to be sitting in Amanda's box seat. If Jess was any judge, the man was nervous.

"I understand they've been having an unseasonal storm on the East Coast," Borgini said, turning his attention to Jess. "You should feel fortunate that you are here in California, enjoying our climate."

"I don't live in the East." Jess returned Sam Borgini's steady gaze. "I make my home in San Francisco."

"Is that a fact? Amanda, you never told me you had a granddaughter living on the West Coast."

"I never had any reason to, Sam," Amanda replied without taking her eyes from the field. "Oh, did you see that cut shot? Jessica is an attorney, Sam. She's a partner with Aaron Reynolds."

Borgini's eyes widened slightly as he regarded Jess with interest. "A partner? You must be a very good attorney, Jessica. Either that or Aaron Reynolds isn't as far into his dotage as I thought. The old man still has an eye for beauty."

A veil lowered over Jessica's eyes but her smile remained intact. Amanda, however, now leveled her gaze on the board member. "I advise you never to meet her across a courtroom, Sam."

"She's that good, heh?" Borgini grinned.

"She's my granddaughter."

Amanda said it softly, but Borgini's eyes flickered. Elliott Westbrook was now listening, a slight smile playing at his thin lips.

"Well, if you're that good, perhaps you can talk some sense into your grandmother," Borgini said. He chose a deviled egg from a plate on the table and took a bite, his tongue flicking out to wipe his lips. "Amanda, that distasteful matter in the valley has to be resolved. I'm glad I ran into you today; I was going to call you later."

"It's being taken care of, Sam," she said, her attention again on the field.

"The board has decided not to fight it," Borgini continued. "The Occupational Safety and Health Administration is investigating. That hydraulic hose was faulty, Amanda; OSHA will prove negligence, and the damn labor union will have us by the balls. We're not going to let this go into court. We're going to plead guilty and negotiate with the D.A. for a fine."

"When was this decided?"

"Last night."

"Without the chairman?" Amanda turned to her granddaughter. "Jessica, I need a legal opinion. Is it appropriate to hold a board meeting without notifying the chairman?"

Jess picked up a finger sandwich of ham salad. "No, unless, of course, the chairman is incapacitated. Were you incapacitated last night?"

"No . . ." Amanda said thoughtfully. "I was having dinner with you."

"Well, then, apparently the board met without duly giving notice. If they discussed company business, they were in violation of federal regulations."

Amanda turned to Borgini, her eyes widening. "Sam, you didn't do that, did you?"

"Amanda, don't play games with me," he said, now glowering. "You know damn well that we've been discussing this matter. It came up last night at the Alcotts' party and—"

"And a quorum of the board was present?" Jess interrupted.

"Coincidentally, yes," Westbrook said.

"Then, gentlemen, you should have known better," Jess said coolly. "Whatever was discussed has no legal bearing."

Borgini stared at her, his facade of friendliness dissolving as his eyes glinted with anger. "A formal board meeting will be called, Amanda. This nuisance will not be allowed to jeopardize the company."

Nuisance? Jessica fixed her eyes on Borgini. "I believe a man was killed, Mr. Borgini."

"Damn Mexicans are always getting hurt," Borgini said, dismissing the comment. "The union's demands would have finished Alta Grow eventually anyway. You know that,

Amanda. We can't allow the farming division to pull the rest of the company down. I have a buyer for Altra Grow, and I think we should consider selling it."

"You are annoying me, Sam," Amanda said wearily. "I came here to watch a polo match. This is world class, and you're missing it. Besides, I don't want to bore Jessica with our problems. Behave yourself and go away."

After the two unhappy men left, Jess picked at her sandwich, thinking about what had just happened. Sam Borgini, aside from his offensive bigotry, was not to be underestimated. Crude and coarse, she suspected that the man was also shrewd and knew exactly what he was doing. Westbrook was a shadow—not that Jess hadn't seen it countless times before. The public envisioned board members of large corporations as brilliant, capable men of industry and finance. Too often they tripped into their positions by accident. Thank God most men earned their positions, but if the general public realized how many found themselves there by sheer luck or accident of birth it would shake the foundations of their belief in capitalism. Wealth was no guarantee of intelligence or ability. She had watched too many men bumble, stumble, and piss away their advantages.

She suspected that Westbrook had found himself on the company's board by invitation of his good friend, Borgini. Westbrook had inherited wealth, most likely. And he was manageable in his acquired position. What she couldn't understand was how Amanda had gotten herself into this position. She knew her grandmother was no fool, so how had she allowed those two to assume so much control of her company? Her gaze shifted to Amanda, who appeared to be totally absorbed in the action pounding down the field toward a goal. One thing was certain, and the realization caused a spark of interest: Amanda had not brought her here this morning to watch a polo match.

They returned to the house to find that a packet had arrived for Jess from Michael Rawlings containing the personnel records of the dead worker. There was also a file from Altra Grow's attorney, Julian Alcott. He was out of town, but his office had sent over the requested material. Jess excused herself from Amanda, who met the request cheerfully, as apparently she had a one o'clock tee-off time.

Settling down in the library with a pot of coffee, Jess began to pore over the contents of the thick envelope. The Occupational Safety and Health Administration's initial investigation team had reported the basic facts, that Rafael Martinez had been crushed by a falling grape harvester. The accident had occurred on a terraced slope, which contributed to the death. Levelers and a faulty hydraulic hose were mentioned. The pathology report confirmed that Martinez died from internal injuries caused by the accident.

The district attorney claimed that the death had been caused by careless maintenance of the equipment, thus he had filed a joint action of criminal negligence against Altra Grow and its head mechanic, Peter Maloy. Jess appreciated the seriousness of the charges. If the D.A. proved that Maloy had knowingly practiced shoddy maintenance, the shop foreman could face a fine, a jail sentence, or both. And, if the company's officers were shown to have foreknowledge of unsafe practices within Altra Grow, they could join Pete Maloy in a guilty verdict.

The district attorney's prospective witness list included the foreman, Dan Herrera, the Federal Safety Board investigator from OSHA, and Juan Ramirez, the victim's co-worker, along with various expert witnesses.

Rafael Martinez, twenty-three years old, unmarried, had worked for Altra Grow for almost seven years, beginning the summer of his seventeenth birthday. The personnel file listed his parents as Aguilar and Manuela. There were two brothers and a sister, each of whom worked for Altra Grow. Beyond the employment record, there was no other personal background.

Jess flipped back to the witness list. She scanned it quickly, and frowned. There were no members of the family on the list, not even the siblings who also worked for the company. She thought about it for a moment, then reached for the phone, dialed and waited. A warm feminine voice answered: "Good afternoon, Altra Grow, may I help you?"

"Michael Rawlings, please. Jessica Bellamy."

After a moment he came on the line. "Jessica, what can I do for you?"

"I've read the papers you sent over. I appreciate your promptness."

"My pleasure."

"From what I've read you don't have a snowball's chance in hell."

"Is that a legal term?"

"I have a favor to ask."

"Ask."

"If you aren't busy tomorrow I want to see where it happened. And I need to see the grape harvester."

There was a pause. "I have a meeting early in the morning, but I should be free by nine o'clock. Could you meet me here at nine-thirty? Amanda can give you directions."

"I'll be there."

"Then it's a date." There was another pause. "Did you bring jeans?"

The question startled her. "As a matter of fact I did."

"Good. Wear them. And some shoes that will withstand a little mud."

"I'll see you at nine-thirty," she said, then hung up. She opened the folder again to see if she had missed anything.

The next morning Michael hung up the phone with a grim smile. It had taken a month to close the deal, but at last it was done, at his price: $520 a ton for the Pinot Noir and $1,300 a ton for the Chardonnay. Normally he would have been jubilant; instead he wondered if it would be his last harvest of grapes. And, there was the added, sobering fact that he had just finished a grape harvest that Rafael had begun. He was staring thoughtfully at the phone when his secretary knocked and came into the office. She placed letters on his desk for his signature and gave him more messages that had come through while he was on the phone. She sat down across from him while he scanned the letters and signed them, pushing them back to her. "How is Billy?" he asked, scrawling his signature across the third letter.

"He's fine. I think his flu is schoolitis."

He glanced up with a smile. "I remember that bug; don't be too hard on him."

"I know," she said, returning the smile. "He's bored."

He finished the letters and picked up the memos. Glancing at the first one, he frowned and handed it to her. "Call him back and tell him no, we won't accept that bid." While she made a note, he flipped through the rest of the messages, setting them aside for himself, reaching the last one. "And tell this one I'll call him next week."

When she had left the office, he leaned back in his chair, tapping his pen on the desk thoughtfully. Carolyn was one of those secretaries who could balance intricate schedules, soothe ruffled feathers, deftly handle customers, organize his life, and probably run the company if he should suddenly drop dead. And she was a single parent of two lively, healthy boys.

Michael knew that Carolyn's life was hard, and often lonely, but then nothing was perfect, and no one knew that better than Michael. Life was trade-offs, but if you were lucky the good outweighed the balance and in the end you profited.

Michael had grown up in a small house on a corner of Morgan property in the valley, the home Zack Rawlings had built for his family when he came from Oklahoma during the depression. Michael's grandmother had died in that house, worn out from the effects of the dust bowl and depression years, and from it his father and mother had left one night for an evening in Salinas. They had never come home, killed in an auto accident two months after Michael's eighth birthday.

One night, two weeks after being dropped from the high school track team, Michael had finished his homework then made a supper of baked potatoes, broiled pork chops, and salad. His grandfather had come into the small kitchen just as he was taking the potatoes from the oven. Lanky, with long, wiry limbs encased in Sears overalls, Zack went to the sink and washed his hands as his grandson put the food on the table behind him. They had sat down and Zack stared at the food for a moment, then glanced up at Michael, his brown eyes narrowing over a straight, long nose, narrow lips pursed as he studied his meal. "I wouldn't mind some gravy."

"It's not good for you, Grandpa." Michael handed him the salad bowl.

"I've been eating gravy on my chops all my life, and on good mashed potatoes, not these things still in their jackets. Why can't you make mashed potatoes?" Zack frowned, taking the bowl. He stared at the mixture of greens, cucumbers, radishes, and sliced carrots. "Vegetables ought to be cooked."

"Wrong. The fresher the better. Raw vegetables have more vitamins." It was a discussion they'd had several times since

Michael had begun to be responsible for their meals six months after his parents had died.

"Where do you learn such stuff?"

"I read. Eat your salad, Grandpa. After all, you grow it, so you might just as well eat it."

"I'd rather have gravy."

"Then make it yourself."

Zack slathered his potato with butter and they began to eat. "Did you do your homework?"

"Yes, Grandpa."

"Did you learn anything?"

"I hope so."

"Tell me something I don't know."

"Hannibal invaded the Roman Empire after crossing the Alps with elephants."

"Why in the hell did he do that?"

"Why did he invade the Roman Empire or why did he use elephants?"

"Elephants."

"I don't know. My teacher didn't say."

"Ask 'im. Damn foolish, if you ask me. Seems like they'd have slowed him down. Who's Hannibal?"

They discussed history for a while, as they did each evening. Michael knew that his grandfather hungered for learning, and they were working their way through high school together. Michael had learned that there were two kinds of smart, one book-learned and one common sense. Zack Rawlings might be short on formal education, but in the latter no one could hold a candle to him. They learned from each other.

Zack had learned to eat potato skins, though he thought they'd taste better with gravy. As he popped the last bite into his mouth he leaned back in his chair and glanced around the tiny kitchen. His eyes lingered on the shelf above the sink and the cheap porcelain figures that his wife had collected: a bulldog and a dachshund, a fawn with its mother, an assortment of rabbits and cats, and a young girl in a bright blue dress that had faded over the years. He remembered the pleasure it had given her to look at her collection. Then his gaze shifted to his grandson. "You know why he did it?"

"Who? What?" Michael paused with his fork halfway to his mouth.

"Hannibal. Think about it. Do you think he'd have tried it if he'd known how high those Alps were? And do you think he'd have taken elephants if he'd really thought about it? Not on your life. He did it because no one was there to tell him different. No one to tell him it couldn't be done. He just had an idea and he did it. And he scared the shit out of the whole Roman Empire."

Michael set his fork down and leaned back, sensing a message was forthcoming. "Yes, Grandpa, he sure did."

"It makes a man think," Zack said, his eyes narrowing. "It sure does. It makes a man think that he could do anything if he just set his mind to it."

"That's a fact, Grandpa."

"It sure is." Zack pushed his plate back, leaning his arms on the table. "Now, if someone had stopped him, say mid-Alps, and told him he was crazy, gave him all the reasons why he couldn't do it—the mountains being too high and the fact he was crazy to use elephants—he might have given up. At least he would have if he listened. I wouldn't be surprised if someone did tell him that. One of his generals. That general could've knocked the props right out from under him, if he had listened and given up."

So that was it. Michael stared at his plate, realizing that his grandfather knew he'd been cut that day from the track team. "Maybe no one tried to stop him," he said quietly.

"Sure they did. The man did a weird thing, something no one else had ever done before. There's always somebody, Mickey, who will try to stop us. Other people don't want us to succeed because they aren't real happy with themselves and they want us to fail, too. That's why they don't support our dreams."

"But what if they *can* stop us? I mean, what if they have the power to stop us?"

"No one's got that power, Michael," Zack said, fixing his gaze on his grandson. "Not unless we give it to them. Don't let anyone tell you who you are."

"But what if they have the power to control what happens to you?"

"Then you find another way. The bank took our farm in Oklahoma, Mickey, and I could have just laid down and died. A lot of people did. But I found out that sometimes someone puts a roadblock in front of you and it turns out he did you a favor. Somewhere I heard that when one door closes, another opens. But you've got to look for it. You're only beaten if you don't try. Then they've won."

In the fall Michael went out for football. He realized that he had avoided it before because it was *the* ultimate sport at Saint Patrick's School and he would be competing with the best athletes. But, fed by his grandfather's words, he had developed a burning obsession to prove the track coach wrong. By his junior year Michael had become a star.

"The best arm I've seen in fifteen years," the head coach said, "and, Christ, can that kid run."

By his senior year Michael's star status had also brought him to the attention of Noreen Keegan. Noreen was a cheerleader for Holy Martyrs, a member of the student council, and the most beautiful girl God ever made. Slender with blond hair and sky-blue eyes, she was a goddess whose image kept him awake at night for two months. He knew she was spoiled and manipulative beneath her expensively dressed exterior, but it didn't matter much to his seventeen-year-old way of thinking. Besides, he was nuts about her and he knew the feeling was mutual.

They remained a "heavy item" for the next year. Then, as they approached graduation, Noreen began to talk of plans that did not include him. She had been accepted at USC, and he was to enter Davis in the fall. They discussed being together during holidays and summer break and how they could keep the relationship going with phone calls and letters.

The letters and phone calls were frequent at first, then began to drift off as they settled into their new lives four hundred miles apart. While Michael returned each summer to work for Altra Grow, Noreen spent her freshman summer with her parents in Europe, the sophomore summer with friends back east. It wasn't until the summer after he had graduated and was preparing to enter graduate school that they met again. A meeting that led them into disaster.

"The good and the bad," Michael murmured. "It's all trade-offs."

Then the intercom buzzed and he shook off his thoughts along with the unpleasant memories that accompanied them. "Yes, what is it, Carolyn?"

"Your nine-thirty appointment is here," she said.

Nine-thirty? He glanced at his calendar—there was no nine-thirty. Then he remembered. Amanda's granddaughter, the high-powered eastern-bred Ms. Bellamy. He pressed the intercom button. "I'll be out in a moment." Great, he thought irritably, just what he needed right now.

Jess had announced herself to the receptionist and waited in the well-appointed lobby, a large sunny room with a dark green carpet, beige leather chairs, and a profusion of plants. The walls held brass-framed posters of the company's labels and breathtaking photographs of the valley. She had barely made herself comfortable when she looked up to see Michael striding down a long hallway toward the reception area. Once again he was dressed in Levi's and a blue plaid shirt. He had suggested that she wear a similar outfit, but his appearance didn't fit with the surroundings. His expression was distracted, but it set well with her that he had not made her wait. She stood, slipped the strap of her bag over her shoulder, and went to meet him. He looked up at that moment and saw her, his expression slipping into an easy grin.

"You're prompt," he said. His eyes dropped over her jeans and sweater with apparent approval.

"I'm anxious to see the accident site," she responded. "I don't want to waste anyone's time."

"I appreciate that. My truck is parked in back. Let's go this way." He touched her arm, turning to lead her back the way he had come. The hallway was almost entirely of glass, affording her a view of the offices they passed, which were filled with busy, well-dressed employees. Of the men she spied, Michael was the only one not wearing a suit.

They left the building through a rear door to an employee parking lot, and Michael led her to a green pickup truck parked near the door. He opened the passenger door for her, and the gesture disturbed her oddly. As she slid into the seat she looked out the windshield and her eyes widened. On the wall of the building in front of the parking space, in neat, small black letters, was stenciled "Rawlings," and below it, in smaller letters, "president, general manager."

Michael got in beside her and slammed the door. He set his

key in the ignition and turned on the engine, slipping his arm over the seat behind her as he backed out.

"I didn't know you were president of the company," she said, studying his profile.

"Just Altra Grow," he said, turning to accelerate through the lot. "Paul Iverson is CEO of the Morgan Land and Development Company. Amanda is chairman of the board, of course, and holds controlling stock in the parent company."

She stole another glance at him as he turned onto West Market Street. "All right, let's begin with that."

"What do you want to know?" he asked, glancing in his rearview mirror as he changed lanes.

"Altra Grow holds a great deal of land," she observed. "There are the nineteen hundred acres here plus acreage for winter crops in Arizona and New Mexico; apple, cherry, and pear orchards in Washington; and citrus groves in the Imperial Valley. All together over twelve thousand acres."

"You've done your homework."

"I had a few days to look into it before I left San Francisco; it's a matter of public record. If you're the president of the company, how many general managers are there?"

"Just me."

Her gaze shifted to him. "Just you?" she asked incredulously.

"I have good managers and foremen at all of the locations. I believe in hiring good people and leaving them alone. I only have to make three or four trips a year to check on the orchards and groves—visually, that is. The row crops require much more attention because we realize two to three harvests a year, except for grapes and asparagus, which are annual. Asparagus is our risk crop, so we grow it right here where I can keep my eye on it."

"Risk crop?"

"Yes, that and the cherries in Washington. A lot can happen to cherries, and you only get one, maybe two good years out of six or seven. But when you do they yield big money. Like berries."

Of course, like berries, she thought. They left the city behind, and Jessica's gaze moved over the beautiful valley nestled between two mountain ranges. It was an endless stretch of varying shades of green under a deep, clear blue sky.

Michael pulled off the road suddenly, onto a hard-packed shoulder edging acres of neat rows of puffy green and white plants. They got out of the truck, and Jess stepped forward toward the first row, curious to identify the plant with something she had seen in the grocery store around the corner from her apartment. She heard Michael's warning voice as he came around the truck. "Be careful, they've just irrigated—"

She had heard the expression "stepping on a cloud," and it had always seemed a fanciful, appealing notion. Suddenly she felt oddly short. She had dropped a full six inches, and she looked down to find that her feet and ankles had disappeared into thick, black mud. She tugged, attempting to pull up a foot. It gave way with hesitation, then a sudden sucking sound. The foot felt like lead; it had at least five pounds of thick black mud sticking to it. Slowly she stepped back, only to find that her foot disappeared again. If she ran fast, could she make it to safety? Would speed make a difference? Old black-and-white movies flitted through her mind; she was disappearing into a muck of quicksand, her mouth open in a silent scream as she disappeared from sight.

Suddenly an arm went about her waist, lifted her from the mud, and set her on glorious, firm earth. Her thoughts were tossed between embarrassment, an awareness of the strength of that arm, the brief contact with a male body, and the feel of solid ground beneath her feet. "Good thing you're wearing boots," he said.

She turned as he stepped into the row, missing the quagmires that seemed so obvious to her now, darker, damp areas bordering harder, dry earth. A good thing, she mentally repeated, glancing down at her feet, her heart sinking as she viewed the sticky mud that was clinging to her Ferragamo boots. Sighing, she attempted to stomp off the mud, watching the sad demise of four hundred dollars' worth of Italian leather.

Gingerly, she minced across the apron and joined him, watching as he withdrew a knife from his back pocket and cut off a plant, then removed the outer leaves quickly. "It's lettuce!" she exclaimed, staring at the familiar vegetable in his hand.

He glanced up at her with a flash of amusement. "What did you think it was?"

"I had no idea," she said, glancing at the field.

"Specifically, it's iceberg lettuce," he said, dropping it into her hand. "We should be harvesting in about two weeks."

They returned to the truck and were soon on the highway, heading south. The tiny head of lettuce was sitting on the seat between them. Jess was horrified when Michael attempted to throw it away, appalled by the waste.

"Jessica, there are two hundred acres of the stuff," he said when she retrieved the little head, his eyes glinting with humor.

"It doesn't seem right." She shrugged. "I'll give it to Amanda's cook."

"She should be pleased."

Jess knew when she was being humored, but she didn't care. It didn't seem right to throw away such a perfect little head of lettuce. A four hundred dollar head of lettuce.

They made two more stops. The first, which caught Jessica's imagination, was an asparagus field, a hundred acres of brown dirt spiked with six- to twelve-inch spears, like some strange astral desert. Glancing at her, Michael reached under the seat and extracted a paper bag and an object about eighteen inches long with a small spade at the end. He got out of the truck, but she remained where she was, looking for patches of mud. She watched as he moved from stalk to stalk, slipping the spade deep into the ground, pulling up the stalks with his other hand, dropping them into the sack.

Fifteen minutes later he returned to the truck and set the bag by her feet before returning the spade to its place under the seat. "Take that back to Mrs. McNeely," he said, referring to Amanda's cook. "It's late in the season, and asparagus is selling in the East right now for four-fifty a pound."

The next stop was a broccoli field, and its smell preceded it. Michael, however, drew in a deep breath, declaring that he could judge the quality of broccoli by how bad the odor was. Jessica glanced at him, wondering if he was kidding, but as they moved through the rows and he explained its characteristics, his enthusiasm almost made her believe him.

It was eleven o'clock when they passed Soledad and turned off the highway. They drove toward the mountains, and Michael turned into a vineyard. Jess was transfixed. Sprinklers were chugging in a jerky rhythm. The late-morning sun made rainbows in the spray over the dark green vines that ran in row upon row to the foothills. Beyond was a background of mountains covered with soft green velvet.

"Oh, it's beautiful," she said, letting out a breath.

His voice was grim over the sound of the idling engine, shattering the beauty of the moment. "This is where Rafael was killed."

CHAPTER 9

As they drove on, Jess glanced impatiently at Michael. "I'd like to have stopped there. I need to see where it happened."

"We'll go back later." He had pulled onto the road before she could protest. "I thought you should see the equipment first. It will give you a better picture of what happened."

She couldn't argue with that, and she fell silent, watching the small farm houses and fields they passed. They were on a back road that was slightly elevated above the valley, and as they drove she marveled at how richly productive the valley seemed to be. Mile after mile of land, as far as she could see, was covered with trim rows of vegetables and acres of alfalfa and oats. It seemed impossible that so many acres could be so neat, like some gigantic garden tended by hundreds of persnickety caretakers. She commented on it to Michael.

"We don't like weeds," he said with a shrug. "Besides the fact that they take too much water, it's become a source of pride. I think our farms look better than anyone else's, and our production isn't bad. This valley provides a fifth of the world's produce."

They pulled into a large compound that looked to Jess like something from outer space. Large, strange machines were parked in neat rows. Some looked like giant inverted U's spiked with thousands of metal fingers pointed inward between their legs. There were V-shaped stainless-steel tanks and others shaped like half-circles with the tops cut off. And there were rows of tractors of every size, including some about the size of small houses. "What are those for?" she asked, craning her neck for a better look.

"Those are D-eights and D-nines," he said dryly. "We use them when we need something big."

She glanced around at his droll comment with a retort on her lips. It died when she saw his expression. She followed his gaze as he brought the truck to a stop. Before them, parked away from the other machinery at the side of a large shed, was one of the inverted U–shaped machines. "Is this it?" she asked.

"This is it." He got out of the truck and waited for her to join him, and they walked toward the grape harvester. It was about twelve feet high, and up close it looked dangerous. She knew she was being ridiculous—it was just a piece of equipment—but the thought that this strange thing could kill someone made her feel eerie. Her eyes settled on the twisted metal of the side facing her. It looked like an abused toy, the mere size of which had turned it into an instrument of death.

"How does it work?" She hoped her voice sounded normal, analytical.

"The machine straddles the vines. These fingers vibrate." He pointed to the hundreds of metal extensions several feet long that were suspended in two vertical rows between the machine's legs. "They grab the vine and shake it. The grapes fall into these conveyor belts and are carried up along that arm, which swings out over a gondola that is driven alongside."

"A gondola?"

He pointed to the half-shell tanks parked a few hundred feet away. "They're pulled by tractors. When the gondolas are full, the musk is either taken in bulk to the winery or crushed in the field—in one of those machines." He pointed to several cylindrical stainless-steel tanks with platforms on either side. "Those are portable presses. We were field-crushing that night—" He fell silent as they both thought the same thing—that grapes were not the only thing that was crushed that night. "All right," he said brusquely, "I'll take you back to the vineyard now and you can see where it happened."

"Then harvesting the grapes is a two-man operation?" she asked as they walked back to the truck.

"Yes, one man drives the harvester, and the other pulls the gondola. The only time a worker might be alone on a harvester is when he's roading."

"Roading?"

"Driving between locations, between varieties or vineyards."

As they drove back to the vineyard, Jess thought about the tons of metal crushing young Rafael Martinez. "It does look rather unstable," she said suddenly. "The harvester," she explained when he frowned.

"It's not. Those machines are well designed and quite stable."

He drove back to the vineyard set at the base of the foothills. Unlike the acres that ran down into the valley, it was terraced on deep ridges cut in the side of the mountain. She got out of the truck and walked a few yards into the rows. Studying the topography, she frowned as she tried to deal with the questions that were crossing her mind. Finally she turned back to him. "Michael, I don't see how that machine could be safely operated here. No wonder it toppled. That is what happened, isn't it?"

"Yes."

"Well, I'm surprised it didn't happen sooner, given the slope of these rows."

"You don't understand," he said, coming to stand beside her. "There's a leveler on each harvesting machine. It works automatically when the harvester is taken on uneven ground. In fact, it works so well that when they are roading and they come to a poorly banked corner, they have to override the leveler manually to keep the machine from listing. Juan Ramirez was working with Martinez that night, following Rafael with his gondola, and he swears that the leveler and the override were both working perfectly on the roads."

"The OSHA report said there was a faulty hydraulic hose."

"Yes." Michael sighed. "The hose is part of the manual override. Pete Maloy, our shop foreman, checked that harvester himself just that day—including the hoses. It's in his log."

"There's a log?"

"Yes, of course. All our maintenance people keep daily logs of their work. We keep careful records of each piece of equipment."

"Michael, that's good news. That log could definitely help your case." Then she noticed his frown. "What is it?"

Michael shrugged. "The DA seems to feel there's a problem

with the log. When OSHA came to collect it later in the morning, we couldn't find it."

"What happened to it?"

"The log had just been misplaced, that's all. Look, you have to understand that harvest had just begun. The maintenance crews had been working overtime to get the equipment ready. The shop was a mess."

"Who found it?"

"Pete. He found it the next morning and immediately turned it over to OSHA."

"Maloy found it," Jess repeated. She didn't say anything for a moment, then she shook her head with dismay. "How long has Maloy worked for you?"

Michael's gaze shifted to her and his eyes narrowed. "He's worked for Altra Grow for thirteen years." He flared. "There's never been a serious accident involving his equipment. I *won't* believe that Pete is responsible for Rafael's death."

"I'm not your enemy, Michael. If I'm going to help, I have to ask these questions." And she would ask him more about Pete Maloy and his misplaced log. "Tell me what happened. Where were you?"

"I was home in bed."

"In bed? Were you sick?"

"It was two o'clock in the morning."

"You harvest at night?"

"Grapes we do. It has to do with the moisture and temperature of the grapes. Anyway, Ramirez came running into that compound about two-fifteen." He pointed to a clearing below them with a few small buildings. "He had run about two miles; it took him twelve to fifteen minutes." He paused, growing grim. "Apparently the leveler suddenly gave way, and the harvester rolled over, taking Rafael with it. According to Ramirez there wasn't even time for Rafael to jump clear."

"Wait a minute," she said, frowning as she stared at the rows in front of her. She thought about the machine she had seen back at the equipment yard. "The arm that reaches out to dump the grapes into the gondola extends to the left, doesn't it?"

"Yes."

"The gondola is pulled alongside. That would place the

gondola downhill from the harvester. Why didn't the harvester fall on it?"

"It would have if they had been going south, but they had turned at the end of a row and were heading north. The gondola was uphill. When the harvester collapsed, there was nothing but vineyard wire to break its fall. It rolled down three rows before it stopped—with Rafael beneath it."

"Who was in charge?"

He frowned at her cool response, then forced himself to ignore it. "Dan Herrera is foreman of this ranch, and he was here that night. When Juan came for help, Dan immediately pulled the tractors off of the other teams working in the vineyard and radioed to the shop for help. Pete Maloy was here within fifteen minutes with equipment. When they reached Rafael, their first thought was to use a cutting torch to free him from the wreckage, but because of the spilled diesel fuel, they were afraid of a fire. They chained the tractors to the harvester and tried to pull it up, but it was impossible. The tractors had to back down the rows, which took time. They cut some of the vineyard wire to allow them to find a better angle, but that plan didn't work. They would have needed a crane to pull the harvester upright, and the nearest crane is in Salinas. Meanwhile Dan had radioed the fire department in Soledad to bring the jaws of life. That's what finally freed him, but by then it was too late. He died before he reached the hospital."

They were both silent for a long moment, each imagining the confusion, the voices and terror of that night. They returned to the truck but sat there for a while, unwilling to leave just yet. "Tell me about Rafael," Jess said at last. She turned and looked at Michael. "Did you know him?"

"Yes, since he was fourteen, old enough to get a work permit. His father would bring him out in the summers, and Dan would find odd jobs for him to do. After he graduated from high school, he came to work full-time. When he was twenty he began taking classes at Hartnell College. He was driving a tractor by then, and Dan had him spraying herbicides and fertilizers in the morning—they work early, before the wind comes up—so he could go to class in the afternoon. The last time I saw Rafael, he was excited because he had just earned his associate's degree and was planning to attend San Jose State next fall. He wanted to be an accountant, a job where he wouldn't have to get his hands dirty anymore, he said."

"There's more, isn't there?" she asked after a moment of silence. When he gave her a puzzled look, she smiled. "I have an ear for what isn't being said, Michael."

He shrugged. "You'll probably hear things about him. Rafael wasn't a troublemaker, but he had deep convictions and passions. I warned him more than once to ease off. He had a head-on approach to life that got him into a lot of trouble."

"Such as?"

He reached down and turned on the ignition. "What does it matter now?" he said gruffly. "He's dead."

As they bumped along the rutted dirt road, she studied his profile. "Of all the hundreds of people who work for the company, how is it that you knew this boy so well?"

"I was raised in this valley, and I spend a lot of time in these fields. You get to know people if you want to."

"And he stood out; he made you care."

Brown eyes shifted to her, and she saw the anger and pain before they turned back to the road. "Yes, I cared about him. But that doesn't matter now, does it?"

"There are some who view what happened as a nuisance that would be best forgotten."

"Who?" he growled.

"Samuel Borgini, for one."

"You met him?" Michael asked, now looking at her.

"Yesterday. I met Elliott Westbrook, too. Apparently they have a buyer for Altra Grow."

"I'll bet they do," he said, scowling. "But then, I warned you about that."

Considering what she was learning, she wondered if Amanda wouldn't be wise to accept the offer. But she kept the opinion to herself.

"Are you hungry?"

He asked the question with the same angry tone, and it took a moment to register. "Yes, I am. Are you offering me lunch?"

"Yes. Besides, there's someone I want you to meet."

Fifteen minutes later they pulled into the driveway of a small, compact, one-story house that was similar to countless others she had seen that morning. The yard was painfully neat, with new plantings of spring flowers and manicured shrubs.

Jess wondered what Michael was up to, but she didn't have much time to think about it as he took her around the side of the house and knocked at the back door. He smiled at her baffled look and glanced down at her feet. "Around here you come to the back door at lunch time."

At that moment the door was opened by a small middle-aged woman in jeans and an oversize shirt. Her short hair was auburn, feathered in soft curls around her face. Seeing Michael, she broke out in a broad grin; her large hazel eyes which dominated a thin, angular face sparkled with pleasure. "Come in, Michael!" As she stepped back to admit them, her eyes shifted to Jess with friendly curiosity.

"Cathy, this is Jessica Bellamy. Jess, I'd like you to meet Cathy Maloy."

Jess tensed. She threw a swift glare at Michael. Why hadn't he warned her that he was bringing her to the Maloys? She swiftly hid her dismay and smiled at the other woman graciously. "I'm happy to meet you, Mrs. Maloy."

"Friends of Michael call me Cathy," the woman said. "I assume you're here to see Pete, Michael. He's in the kitchen with Norman Taylor." She turned and led them into a spacious kitchen dominated by a huge table where two men sat eating their lunch. On the table was a large platter of sandwiches, a basket of chips, and a bowl of fruit. Cathy Maloy gestured them toward two vacant chairs as she introduced Jessica to her husband and the other man.

Pete Maloy smiled during the introductions, casting an appreciative look at Michael, which Jess didn't miss. He was leaning on the table, his shirtsleeves rolled back to reveal large forearms covered with thick black hair and huge hands that were wrapped around his coffee cup. His wavy dark hair was peppered with gray. His face was long and narrow, his features contained within a third of the space, over a jutting chin. His dark eyes were as friendly as his wife's, though at the moment they were curious.

"Jessica is Amanda's granddaughter," Michael said, settling next to her. Cathy Maloy had placed plates in front of them, and he was reaching for a sandwich.

"You don't say?" Pete acknowledged. "Showing her around, heh? What do you think of Altra Grow, Jessica?"

Jess was embarrassed at having arrived at mealtime—though

apparently the others thought nothing of it—and she was more than a little irritated that Michael hadn't warned her whose home he was taking her to.

"What I saw today was quite impressive," she said. "But I'm not here just for a visit, Mr. Maloy. I'm an attorney, and my grandmother has asked me to look into the Martinez incident."

Jess watched the foreman's reaction, which was one of sad regret. "Rafael Martinez. God, that was terrible."

"The whole thing is absurd," the other man said. Norman Taylor, a man in his mid-thirties with sandy hair and a sunburned complexion, glowered. "It was tragic, but that's all it was, a tragic accident. Now the county is trying to make a federal case out of it. Farm equipment is dangerous; anyone with a warm brain knows that. The fact that there are so few accidents proves how careful everyone is and how many precautions are taken. My company—I'm the manager of Campbell and Sons—has a good record, but it's not as good as Altra Grow's. This is the first accident they've had in four years, and the first death ever. But the state and the Feds are all over them like ticks on a dog."

"Do you think they should ignore it?" Jess asked.

"Of course not. But criminal negligence? If they compared farming accidents with those in any other industry, we'd come out smelling like a rose. It's the damn union—they've got the sympathy of every bleeding-heart liberal in the country, and a story like this makes for good press. In fact, if Rafael hadn't been Mexican this wouldn't be an issue."

Well, Jess thought, there was a new point of view. She fought to keep her expression neutral, realizing that this would be an emotional issue for the manager of another agribusiness company. "I don't think this case will be decided on the basis of the ethnic background of the deceased, Mr. Taylor."

"Where do you practice law, Ms. Bellamy?" Norm Taylor asked.

"In San Francisco."

"Ah, I see. Then you should understand. You have a lot of minorities up there. If a case involves race or sexual prefer-ence, it makes a difference, doesn't it? I mean, you're not going to tell me that emotional issues don't affect a court case."

"Of course they do, but regardless of what is reported in the press, inside a courtroom you would be amazed to what degree those sentiments are set aside."

"Do you really believe that?" Taylor pressed.

"I know it," Jessica responded calmly. "Have you ever served on a jury, Mr. Taylor?"

"Yes," he said, becoming guarded.

"What was the case about?"

"Drunk driving."

"Do you drink?" she asked, smiling to soften the question. He hesitated, glancing at the others. "Yes—of course."

"What was the outcome of the case?"

"We convicted him."

"Ahh," she said softly. "Commendable. But didn't you feel any sympathy for the defendant—after all, you both drink."

"I don't drink and drive," he said firmly.

"Never?"

He glanced again at the others, knowing he couldn't lie. "I have, but—"

"But you were never caught. Yet, knowing that, you judged the case on its merits. Apparently we have both experienced that strangely wonderful thing that often happens to an individual when he or she is impaneled on a jury. There is a real attempt to place prejudices aside. That is what makes the system work."

"She's got you there," Pete Maloy laughed. The sound was deep and wonderful, and drew Jess's attention.

"On the other hand," Michael drawled, smiling at Jess, "I've heard it said that the case is decided during jury selection. Doesn't the attorneys' ability to select jurors have a lot to do with it?"

"Both sides attempt to choose jurors who will be sympathetic to their case," Jess answered. "But that's not the point. The issue is how much public sentiment would affect the outcome of a trial. I am saying that we can sit here and discuss the merits of this case for hours, but it will not affect what will happen in that courtroom. If it does, the attorney is at fault for not filing for a change of venue."

"Okay, I'll accept that," Michael said, "*if* the attorneys in that courtroom are equally talented in choosing jurors. But what if they're not?" His voice softened on the last words as he challenged Jess silently.

"Well, Michael, we're not going to decide anything here, so leave the poor woman alone," Pete said affably against the sudden tension of the room. "Jessica, you haven't eaten anything. Try one of Cathy's chicken salad sandwiches; they're fantastic."

The sandwiches were good, and the rest of the lunch was pleasant enough in spite of the awkward beginning. The men shifted easily into the topic of work, and Jess listened, noting that Cathy chose to ignore the men as she busied herself with making coffee and cleaning up. She offered to help clean up but Cathy declined the offer and as the hour wore on, Jess began to feel superfluous. The conversation had been interesting at first, but after a quarter-hour of discussing bunch rot, she found herself struggling to stifle a yawn. It was then that she felt a tap at her shoulder.

"Jessica, I have some things to do outside. Would you like to join me?" Cathy Maloy asked.

The distraction was irresistible, and Jess rose eagerly from the table. She followed the other woman outside, feeling somewhat piqued that neither Michael nor the others had even looked up when she left the table. Cathy pulled off her shoes in the laundry room and slipped into boots. As they left the house, she glanced down at Jessica's feet. "Good lord, those are Ferragamo boots, aren't they? You've ruined them!" Cathy sighed. "Try some saddle soap; you may be able to save them."

Jess followed the older woman to the back of the house. Cathy went into a large shed and emerged with a bucket filled with some nondescript substance resembling oatmeal. They circled the building and went to a large pen filled with pigs. Jess's eyes widened as they came to the fence and Cathy dumped the bucket in a trough on the other side. The pigs gamboled over, sticking their snouts into the mush.

"My God, they're so big!" Jess exclaimed. Then she broke into laughter as a scurry of tiny pink piglets emerged from the shadows of the shed, rushing with squeals of protest to join their mothers.

"These are breeding sows." Cathy smiled. "They can reach four hundred pounds."

Jess smiled, transfixed by the piglets. She had never seen anything so adorable. Then she sobered, realizing what the outcome of their short lives was to be. "They're so cute," she said wistfully.

"I know how you feel," Cathy said, leaning her arms on the wall of the pen. "When I first came here, I was the same way. The first week, a mouse ran smack through the middle of my living room. I managed to trap it under a bowl—then called Pete to come home. I had to go into the other room while he dispatched it, and the poor thing's death haunted me for days."

"You weren't born here?" Jess asked.

"Nope. I was born in San Jose. I met Pete after college, through mutual friends."

"What did you study?"

"Graphic arts. I worked for a design company in Silicon Valley for two years."

They fell into silence, watching the snorting antics of the pigs as Jess dealt with her surprise. But why should she have assumed that someone who lived in a farm community had not been raised here?

"You're here to check on Pete, aren't you?" Cathy said quietly. "You're trying to decide if that faulty hydraulic line was his fault."

"No," Jess said gently. "I didn't know we were coming here. It was Michael's decision."

"Same thing. He wouldn't have brought you unless there was some question about Pete. It doesn't matter, though," she said firmly. "I know my husband. If his log says he checked that line, then he checked it."

Jessica didn't answer; she couldn't give platitudes to this woman. But Cathy Maloy's next words surprised her. "You were wrong about what you said in there. You'll find that it's different here, and you can take that from someone who knows. This is a small community. Public sentiment will make a difference in this court case." As Jess began to protest, Cathy shook her head, her eyes remaining fixed on the action in the pen. "When I came here, Pete brought me out to see the house. The people who lived here then invited us in, showed us the house, and gave us lunch. I was amazed at their hospitality." She turned and glanced at Jess. "Can you imagine anyone in San Francisco doing that? Anyway, after a while, the woman told me something that has stuck with me until this day. 'Don't expect to be accepted,' she said. 'You're an outsider.' She said that she had been here for twenty years and people were just beginning to accept her. She was right.

"I told myself it didn't matter," Cathy continued, reaching over to scratch one of the sows behind the ear. The pig grunted with pleasure, raising its head for the attention. "And it didn't, for a long time. I had my family—two girls and a boy—and I was busy with them, school activities, and 4-H. And I had no complaints. The people here were warm and friendly. Accepting. And that woman was wrong. They will accept outsiders—to a point. They'll allow you to work in their clubs, work your ass off for projects, charities, and school. Just don't expect them to invite you to their family gatherings. It didn't bother me. Who wanted to be invited to someone else's family gathering, after all? But I didn't understand then, Jess. I do now. You feel it when the kids are gone. The two oldest are married and moved away. The youngest is at school at Berkeley. And after a while you get burned out and can't involve yourself with the charities anymore. People don't forgive you for that." She reached into her pocket, extracted a lump of sugar, and tossed it to a pig. It seemed to inhale the treat with a snort, then moved back across the pen where it lay down. It was immediately swarmed by piglets who rushed with frantic squeals to find a place for lunch.

"You know what's been the hardest?" she asked. "In thirteen years I've never had a real conversation with another woman I've met here. Perhaps, in the bosoms of their families they discuss world events and politics. I'm not privy to that, and so I can't say. It took me a long time to realize that if big issues were discussed at all, they were talked about with those who counted, not with outsiders. And now I'll get to the point," she said, turning to regard Jessica evenly. "Life in this valley is lonely and painfully unstimulating, Jessica. There's no way in hell that I would have stayed here all these years if it hadn't been for Pete. This job is important to him, not because he couldn't find another one somewhere else—he's been offered other jobs because he is good at what he does. He stays here because he cares about the company. He's loyal to it—and to Michael and Amanda Morgan. And no matter what, I'll stay here with him."

The back door slammed just then, and the two women turned as the men came down the back steps and headed for their trucks. With a backward glance at the pigs, Jess kept pace with Cathy Maloy, thinking about what she had said.

"There's one other thing." Cathy's voice was quiet as they approached the men. "I don't know how many people you've met here yet, but I should warn you: Don't believe everything you hear."

"What do you mean?"

"Just that. Don't accept everything at face value. These people protect their own. And keep in mind that you're not just an outsider, you're a Morgan. That's two strikes against you."

Jess glanced at the other woman with a puzzled frown, but she couldn't pursue the strange comment. They had reached the men, and apparently Cathy Maloy had said all she was going to say on the subject. "Don't make yourself such a stranger, Michael," she said, then turned back to Jess. "It was nice meeting you, Jessica. I hope your visit here will be everything you hope it will be." Her eyes fixed on Jess for a moment, as if judging an opponent; then she turned and went back into the house.

CHAPTER 10

"Why didn't you tell me you were taking me to Pete Maloy's?" Jess asked irritably as they drove back to Salinas.

"I was angry," Michael answered. "I thought that perhaps after you met Pete you'd understand that he isn't the sort to doctor a log."

"Then you wasted your time, because meeting him didn't prove a thing. Yes, I like him—I like Cathy, too—but that's irrelevant. There's a death involved. Desperation pushes even honest men to do things of which they thought themselves incapable." She took a deep breath, and let it out slowly. "All right. It wouldn't hurt to look at the log."

"I'll give it to you when we get back to the office," he said stiffly, fixing his eyes on the road ahead.

She understood his frustration, but it didn't make any difference. If she had become jaded it was from experience. She had seen normal men and women commit far more heinous acts than doctoring a log when they felt cornered. "Look, if it's any consolation, I want to believe him. However"—she paused, glancing at his angry profile—"there is the fact of that hose."

"That hose was not a fact; it was a judgment call. Pete noted in his log that it had begun to show wear, but the damage was only superficial. He's an expert; he would have known if that hose needed to be replaced."

"OSHA said it broke because it was worn out."

"It also could have broken from the stress of the accident. If you press the OSHA agents, they'll admit that."

He just wasn't going to understand. How could she make her point? she wondered. "Michael, I'm not afraid to fly but I have a healthy respect for the fact that something could go wrong with an airplane. Hundreds and hundreds of flights take off from airports all over the country each day, and yet there are few accidents."

"What's your point?"

"Only that planes are machines, checked by fallible human beings, and yet those planes take off, fly, and land with rare mishaps. However, accidents *do* occur, Michael."

"This isn't being treated as an accident, Jess, but as criminal negligence."

"I know. And just as the FAA would not pass off an occasional plane crash with a shrug of their shoulders, this accident must be dealt with seriously. If there was a hose that should have been changed and the hose was carelessly overlooked, and the neglect caused a death, it could be criminal negligence. The fact that you're a close friend of the Maloys doesn't matter, any more than if you were close friends with the mechanic who overlooked a loose bolt in an airplane engine."

"Peter didn't overlook that hose. It was noted in his log."

Quite possibly after the fact, she added silently.

When she didn't say anything, he felt a surge of anger. "So you're going to hang Pete Maloy for this."

She whirled around to face him. Now she was angry. "Just a minute, Michael Rawlings; don't make me the heavy. I'm not the prosecutor. I said I'd look into this case and give Amanda my honest opinion. I also recall telling you that you might come to regret my involvement. If you have any doubts, express them to Amanda. One word from her and I'm on my way home—and good riddance."

The cab of the truck was weighted in heavy silence as he thought about what she had said. "I'm sorry. I know the case looks bad and that's what's making me crazy. But there's more to this and I'm hoping you'll find it."

"Could that actually be a vote of confidence?"

"It's an expression of hope."

Or wishful thinking, she mused. She still had a great many things to check, but at the moment everything was pointing to negligence.

Changing the subject, she related some of what Cathy Maloy had said to her, leaving out the more personal aspects. "Then she said something I don't understand," Jess concluded. "She said that I had two strikes against me here—one, being an outsider and, two, being a Morgan. What did she mean by that?"

Michael had listened without comment. He glanced at her, then fixed his eyes back on the road. "I don't think that's something we should discuss."

"Why not?"

"It's something you should discuss with Amanda. If you have questions about your family, ask her."

His dismissal left Jess nonplussed. It was as if she had suddenly run into a wall.

A few hours later Jess joined her grandmother for dinner. They were eating in the sun porch, which Amanda preferred to the cavernous dining room. The moon shone through the windows, spreading its light in a gray-green cast over the fairway that abutted the grounds. Beyond, the sawtooth sky-line of pine forest was broken by the outline of craggy rocks and the reflection of the moonlight on the ocean.

"How was your day with Michael?" Amanda asked.

Jess had returned late that afternoon and had spent the two hours before dinner going over the personnel records of those involved, and reading Pete Maloy's log. The hose in question was noted in the log, but, as it was the last entry made, there was no way to tell when it had been entered. In answer to Amanda's question, she gave her a brief account of her day. "Amanda, there is nothing to suggest that the accident wasn't exactly as is reported in the OSHA file. Their work was quite thorough."

"Well, just keep looking, dear," Amanda answered, unruf-fled.

Jess bit her lower lip in frustration. Amanda was attacking her dinner of French onion soup and Caesar salad with gusto, barely pausing at Jessica's observations. How could she make her grandmother face reality? After meeting Sam Borgini and Elliott Westbrook, followed by what she had learned today, Jess knew that Amanda had not overstated her problems. But no amount of wishful thinking would change what was to be the almost certain outcome of the pending trial.

Putting the case aside for a moment, Jess studied her

grandmother across the table. Amanda Morgan, the business-woman, was undeniably fascinating. But it was Amanda of the flowers Jess had come to discover.

Jess knew she couldn't just blurt out the questions that were bothering her. Amanda had made it clear that she wouldn't discuss her relationship with her son. Jess would have to take a subtle, roundabout approach to that subject. "I was impressed by what I saw today," Jess said suddenly. "I can understand why you are so proud of Altra Grow." She paused, taking a bite of romaine, blue cheese, and an anchovy. The strong flavors bit pleasantly into her tongue. "It's amazing, Amanda, that you've done all of this by yourself."

"I'm delighted that you appreciate what you saw, but I hardly did it by myself. Michael's been a very important part of the last few years. Before that I did manage things, but then I had Nicky to help me."

"Nicky? You mean Nicholas Alger, your second husband." She watched Amanda covertly but it was unnecessary. Amanda's expression became openly wistful at the mention of his name.

"Yes. He was the love of my life, Jessica. I miss him terribly." She regarded Jess with eyes that sparkled with sudden mischief, and her face seemed to slough off twenty years. "Is that what you wanted to know?"

Not for the first time, Jess realized that her grandmother was nobody's fool. "Yes," she said. "I'd like to know something about your life. I'd like to know about my family—the part my father would never talk about." She paused, pushing her salad around on her plate with her fork. "It's my family, too, after all."

"Well, then, I'll tell you what I can," Amanda said, leaning in her chair as she drew her wineglass toward her. "But to keep the story brief, let's skip the early history of the pirates in our family and pick up when the Morgans moved from ships into boardrooms, to become pirates of industry, as it were."

"Pirates?"

"Oh, yes. Did you think your father developed that business of his totally on his own? Not that he hasn't done a fine job with it."

Jess hesitated, pushing her plate aside. She tried to recall the few bits and pieces her father had told her. "Morgans have been in banking and shipping since the late seventeen hundreds."

"Well, in the seventeen hundreds their shipping was accomplished as privateers, and their banks consisted of locked chests." Amanda laughed softly. "But by the mid–eighteen hundreds, they had become respectable," she added, pausing as Henley removed their dinner plates. "Coffee, Henley. Would you like something else, Jessica?"

"Coffee would be fine," Jess said.

Amanda nodded at the butler and then returned to her story. She told Jess of Jeremy Morgan who came to California in 1844 and eventually fell in love with a niece of a great California don.

"They were my great-great . . . great grandparents," Jess observed.

"Yes. Just leave it, Henley," she said to the butler as he put a coffee tray on the table. "I don't think we'll be needing anything else tonight." Just then there was a rustle from the aviary off the sun porch. The aviary had surprised Jessica at their first breakfast. No dogs or cats here; Amanda was addicted to tropical birds. A temperature-controlled, glass-walled aviary abutting the breakfast room was filled with cockatiels, parakeets, and parrots of every size and shape. It was dominated by a large, rather ill-tempered parrot for whom Amanda had a special fondness. "Henley," Amanda asked suspiciously, listening to the rustling in the darkened aviary, "did you feed Conrad this afternoon?"

"Yes, madam," he said, straight-faced. "He had a particularly nice ear of corn."

As the butler disappeared, Amanda, apparently satisfied, returned to her story. "Jeremy and Ariana established the first ranch near Soledad in the valley. By the 1870s, they owned over sixty thousand acres. Must of that was sold off, of course, or leased out. Now we have only twelve thousand acres, though I've left most of it to pasture land, a commitment to Jeremy and Ariana's memory I suppose. Consider it an old woman's quirk."

"Why was so much sold off?"

"In those days land wasn't irrigated; it was used to graze cattle. You might say that the company had to shrink and then grow again to operate with today's standards of production.

But counting the acres in Washington, Arizona, and other parts of California, we have almost what we had originally. But now it's diverse farming, orchards, and dry farming such as wheat."

Jess waited as Amanda added some cream to her coffee. "Tell me more about the family."

Amanda took a sip of coffee, then launched into a recounting of the generations that had passed since Jeremy Morgan. She told of men and women who built upon what Jeremy had begun—the ranchers, lawyers, and ministers in the family as well as those who had come across the country in a covered wagon.

"And now there is only one other member of my generation left," Amanda concluded. "My cousin, who married a correspondent for the BBC."

"Doesn't she have any interest in the company?" Jess asked.

"No, not an active interest. She owns stock in the Morgan Company, of course, including those divisions of the company that your father controls. You may not have known this, Jessica, but the Bellamy holdings are part of the Morgan Company."

"I didn't know that."

"I'm not surprised. Along with the Bellamy Guarantee Trust, I gave your father twenty percent of the Morgan Company's stock on his twenty-first birthday. Though he hasn't shown any interest in his shares."

The images of people ran through Jessica's mind. People who, until the last few months, had never existed for her. Now they took on form and shape in a sudden birth. Men and women who had lived, loved, laughed, felt pain and despair, and whose blood ran through her veins. The German ancestry that she had inherited through her maternal grandmother, the countess Benedetta Bradenberg, now joined hand in hand with German stock from Minnesota, immigrants who had traveled across the country in a covered wagon. She wondered what Etta would have thought of that. Etta died when Jess was seventeen, but her laughter still rang through Jessica's memory. It filled a room in unconscious bursts, bringing smiles from anyone who heard it. It was young laughter, filled with wit. Some said that Jess had Benedetta's laugh, though she could never hear it in her own voice. Now there were Saldivars, Randals, Brauns, and Morgans to add. And then she remembered something else she had heard that afternoon, and her enthusiasm waned.

"Cathy Maloy said something strange to me today," she said abruptly, bringing a curious look from her grandmother. "She said it was a warning. She told me I had two strikes against me: one, that I was an outsider and, two, that I was a Morgan. I asked Michael about it, but he said I'd have to ask you what she meant. So I'm asking: What do the people in the valley have against Morgans?"

Amanda regarded her for a protracted moment before she seemed to come to a decision. "What time is it?"

Baffled, Jess glanced at her watch. "Eight o'clock."

"Good, it's early yet," Amanda said, rising from her chair. "Get your coat and I'll call for the car. There's something I want to show you."

A few moments later the car was pulled around to the front. Amanda ignored Jessica's puzzled looks as they left the forest and drove toward Monterey. They drove through the oddly angled streets that seemed to have merged with no plan, intersecting wildly. Then the car pulled up before a small, out-of-the-way bar on a quiet, almost forgotten side street. The name of the establishment, Pasquale's, declared itself in chipping, faded red letters on a hinged sign swinging over the doorway.

Amanda ushered Jess into another world, a time-forgotten long, narrow room. Ceiling fans turned lazily, and time-worn chairs and tables had generations of names and once-important comments carved into their thick wooden surfaces. The floor was covered with red tiles, and a long bar extended along one side of the room with rows of bottles and glasses behind it. Potted palms, rubber plants, and ferns attempted to disguise the shabby condition of the room. The few customers barely noticed their presence as Amanda led Jess to the back of the room, taking the farthest table, which was set off from the others in a small alcove.

"Pasquale's descendants sold this bar over twenty years ago," Amanda said as they sat down. "Some hippies bought it in the early seventies, and fortunately they thought the decor was suitable. Since then it's become a historical landmark, and the present owners have treated it as such." Amanda slipped

out of her coat, dropping it on the empty chair next to her.
"There are plans to restore the building next year."

A waiter came to the table, and Amanda ordered them both
a brandy. When he had left, she smiled at Jessica's expression.
"Your great-great-great grandfather would have had a brandy
about this time of the evening. We'll join him in a nightcap."

Whatever feelings of manipulation Jess might have felt
dissolved in a rush of curiosity. "Jeremy Morgan came here?"
She glanced around the room. "How old is this place?"

"It was built in 1842." Amanda followed her questioning
gaze with a small, pleased smile. "It looks pretty much as it did
then—you would be amazed at how many records were kept.
Pasquale's account books were quite detailed, even to the
furniture and glasses he ordered. In fact, Monterey was the
original capital of California, Jessica, and the historical society
has done a bang-up job of maintaining and restoring the town.
You must take time to see it all while you are here."

Jess felt a stirring of frustration and she suddenly lost interest
in the room. "Amanda, I'm not here as a tourist—as you well
know."

Amanda's gaze shifted to her. "I do wonder, Jessica, why
you are so impatient."

"I have two weeks," Jess said, emphasizing her words.
"You asked me here to help you; I'm trying to do that. I don't
have time for this."

"All right, Jessica." Amanda sighed as their drinks were set
before them. "I brought you here to answer your questions; I
am trying to do that. The attitudes of those in the valley began
here, in this room. Jeremy Morgan used this table—its
predecessor, that is—as his office. From this table he bought,
leased, or sold land. He made loans to people and called them
due. He planned the future of the company here and visited
with friends."

She paused, emphasizing her words as she took a sip of her
brandy, letting Jess digest what she had said. "But to answer
your question. Jeremy was sitting here the first time someone
tried to shoot him—a squatter who felt that Jeremy had dealt
with him unfairly. He stood by the front door"—she glanced
toward the entrance, as if seeing the moment—"and he fired.
Fortunately for both of us he was a poor shot."

"Had Jeremy dealt unfairly with him?" Jess asked, glancing on impulse toward the doorway.

"No, but resentment over land ownership began during those years."

"Resentment of the Morgans began in the eighteen hundreds?"

"It began then, but there was much more, of course. Each generation experienced much the same story. The have-nots resented anyone who had, regardless of how they'd acquired what they held."

"What did your generation experience?" Jess asked bluntly.

Amanda smiled, not taking offense at the question. "I made my contribution to the resentment in the thirties."

"The depression?"

"Yes. And I'm certain that it came, as it most likely did with each generation, because I was unprepared. I had thought I was a person who cared for others, but naïveté is no excuse. Prior to the—advent of the situation, I was totally caught up in the very important issue of myself."

"Why?"

"Why?" Amanda repeated the word as she laughed softly. "Because I was eighteen years old. And, as any affluent, self-directed eighteen-year-old in 1928, I was in Paris."

"You were in Paris in 1928?" Jess asked. My God, how fantastic, she thought, momentarily forgetting her other questions. Pre-depression, pre-war Paris. She and Roxy used to fantasize about what they thought of as the Great Age. "What was it like in the twenties?"

"It was wonderful." Amanda smiled. "The depression was coming, but mercifully we didn't know that. It was a time of innocence, of discovery. I was eighteen years old, in the company of three of my very best friends, Kristen Elliott, Melinda Wilson, and Michelle Donat. Our chaperon was Michelle's aunt Maria, who was considered suitable by our parents because she had been raised in Paris"—Amanda's eyes took on a mischievous glint—"though she was getting on in years and was deliciously inattentive."

"The perfect chaperon." Jess grinned.

"Indeed. It was a heady time for us, to find ourselves in Paris without any vestiges of the Victorian priggishness that our ancestors had brought with them to America. Paris in the

1920s—the scandalous artists, the radical poets, the fanatical political idealists, the spring flowers, fountains, and music. I'm afraid we became quite unmanageable, not that Aunt Maria was ever a match for us."

"What did you do?" Jess asked, her eyes wide with expectation. Images of cabarets, mysterious men, and clandestine love affairs passed through her mind. Amanda did not disappoint her.

"What does a young woman do in Paris in spring?" she smiled. "I fell in love, of course."

"What was he like?"

"Ah, well." Amanda smiled at her granddaughter's eager expression. "He was the most handsome, romantic man I ever met, before or since. I would come back to the Ritz each night—the others would cover for me with Aunt Maria, and I would slip in after she was asleep—and we would sit on the bed. I'd tell my friends of my dark-haired, fiery-eyed lover, a Marxist-Leninist poet I had met in a cabaret. In the evenings he would read his passionate poetry to me, we'd drink wine, and later we would make fantastic love to each other. Or so I would tell my friends."

Jess frowned on the last words. "I don't understand."

"It's simple. Years later I looked back, able to view that time with a maturity that recognizes the devastating mistakes of youth that seem so vitally important, so logical at the time. But that was later. Lies seemed innocent then as I sat with my friends each night and related my love affair, like Scheherazade, feeding on their envy. It was preferable to admitting that I had traveled six thousand miles only to fall in love with someone from home. In truth, he wasn't dark but had sandy hair that fell across his forehead in an unruly and totally charming fashion. His eyes were blue—very blue, clear, and bright like cornflowers. And he wasn't a communist, he had just graduated from Yale and was taking his grand tour of the Continent with some of his classmates."

"You fell in love with an American? What happened to him?"

"Eventually I married him. He was Nicky Alger." Amanda smiled at Jessica's baffled expression. Jess was confused; these pieces didn't fit. "But he was your second husband," she frowned.

"Yes. 'Oh, what a tangled web we weave.' Which is just what happened as I wove my wild stories. Unfortunately, I didn't know that Nicky was doing the same thing with his friends, for much the same reason. The outcome was unpleasant and unfortunate. Unbeknownst to me, Nicky had to spend an obligatory weekend in the country with friends of his parents. He hadn't told me he would be gone. One night, in his absence, I spent an evening in a cabaret with my friends. There, quite by accident, we met up with Nicky's classmates. During the course of the evening they entertained us, quite innocently, with the reasons for Nicky's absence. I believed them when they told us that Nicky had gone off for the weekend with a lover—just one of many he had enjoyed during his sojourn in Paris."

"You believed that?"

"I was very young and very immature. And they were very convincing."

"Did you confront him with it when he returned?"

"No. I took the first ship back to the States without seeing him again. My heart was broken."

"That's horrible!"

"Yes, it was. Nothing destroys with such pain as the loss, through disillusionment, of that first deep love that answers childhood dreams. At the time, of course, I thought I would never recover. Home was security, and I fled back to it, although I could never view life again in the same way. Needing distraction, I plunged into the company's business. My father and I were very close. He knew that something had happened in Paris, but he respected my privacy. He also believed in me, in a world from which women were normally excluded. Oblivious to the criticism of others, he encouraged me and I found solace in work—helping him to build the company.

"The Morgan Company's main business then was in sardines and mackerel." She smiled at Jess's surprise. "We revolutionized the fishing industry here. My father, David, gambled and won—becoming a partner in one of the largest fish tonnage ports in the world."

Jess listened with amazement, then glanced around the room. She didn't want Amanda to see what was reflected in her eyes. Amanda's story had touched her own memories. With the remembrances, the room changed subtly, its romantic sheen shifting to a time-worn bar, shabby and neglected.

"Tell me about him," Amanda said quietly.

Jess looked back at her grandmother and frowned. "Who?"

"The man you're thinking about right now, though you're trying not to. It takes a man to create that particular expression of dismay and regret, Jessica. Of course," Amanda went on gently, "we don't know each other very well yet. I imagine that you see me as a meddling old lady who couldn't possibly understand how you feel."

Irresistibly, Jessica met her grandmother's gaze. Amanda's clear, sharp blue eyes softened with understanding and Jess felt something shift inside her, a tug that made a small, vulnerable opening. She fingered her brandy glass, giving it her attention as she tried to close the gap, to shut off the sudden impulse that was pushing it to widen. "Curtis Caldwell," she said quietly, shrugging her shoulders in a gesture that seemed to belittle his importance. She glanced up at Amanda with a regretful look. "But I wasn't as strong as you were. When I learned that he was using me—and it wasn't a misunderstanding—I hung around for more. I was eighteen and he was thirty-six. I took a class from him and fell in love with him the first day. God, Amanda, he even had etchings—can you believe it?" she laughed self-deprecatingly. "That should have been my first clue. But I wanted to believe it all."

Jess leaned forward, wrapping both hands around the large snifter and staring into it. "I walked into it with both eyes closed. Perhaps that's why I hung on so hard; I couldn't admit that I had been such a fool. And I didn't give it up until I had no self-respect left. Not a pretty story, is it? Certainly not one of the proudest times of my life."

But it answered a lot of questions, Amanda thought. Jess had been bitterly hurt by an affair, and yet what Amanda heard now was not anger toward the man who had caused it but self-loathing. She wondered what had happened to make her granddaughter so deadly serious. For a few moments, as she told of her months in Paris, she had seen the control fall from Jess's eyes, to be replaced by a smile of innocent pleasure—only to see the veil drop again.

"Apparently you've extracted full payment from yourself for

the costly error," Amanda said, editing any sympathy from her voice.

Jess frowned, puzzled. "I don't know what you mean."

"You made a mistake. But that was many years ago, Jessica. You still seem to be very angry with yourself."

"I'm not really," Jess said with a sigh. "It's just tonight, I guess, listening to you. It brought the memories back."

Now Amanda suspected that Jess wasn't being honest with herself, but she let it pass. She knew better than to push against the tenuous bond that was developing between them. Instead, she deliberately led away from the subject. "I suppose there've been others over the past years," she smiled. "More pleasant associations."

"A few friends," Jess shrugged. "Only one affair that was somewhat serious. That ended recently and mutually." She thought about Rick Logan for a moment, then dismissed him. "Actually, I've been too involved with my career for the past seven years to think about relationships. Or perhaps I just haven't been lucky enough to meet the right man—as you apparently did with my grandfather." Jess smiled. "It was only a few years later when you met him, wasn't it? I mean, it had to be. My father was born in 1933."

"Yes, I married Jack Bellamy in 1931, three years after I returned from Paris. Jack was handsome, polished, and capable of sweeping a woman off her feet." Amanda glanced around with a sudden frown. "This old bar has grown rather drafty. If you've seen enough, I think it's time that we went home."

"I agree," Jess said, then hesitated. The words came out tentatively. "I'm glad you brought me here, Amanda."

"So am I," Amanda said, punctuating the words with a quick smile. "Apparently this old wreck of a place hasn't lost its appeal for the Morgans. Somehow I think Jeremy would be glad."

CHAPTER 11

Something had awakened Jess. She was warm and comfortable, lying on her stomach beneath a heavy down comforter as her arms clutched the pillows that cradled her head. The clock on the night stand announced it was 8:10 in the morning. The memories of a pleasant dream lingered, though she could not give it form, and she nestled deeper into the bedding, hoping to fall back to sleep. Then she heard the noise again, an odd scratching, and knew that it had awakened her.

Rolling over, she rose up on her elbows and confronted a large parrot perched on the foot of her bed. Any remnants of sleep disappeared as she sat up abruptly and pulled the bedding around her in startled defense. The bird shifted its weight, turning its head to regard her with a large, staring eye. It spread a huge wing and ruffled its feathers in an innocent gesture, as if in response to Jessica's hostile reaction.

Conrad, Jess thought as her heart resumed a normal pace. The bird had Amanda's look about it—in control and totally certain of its position. But how had it gotten into her bedroom? Jess glanced at the door. It was slightly open. She had gotten up in the middle of the night with an attack of indigestion. Stumbling through the house in the dark, she had made her way to the kitchen for a glass of milk. Apparently she hadn't closed the door behind her when she returned.

"Go away," she told the bird.

Unaffected, it continued to stare at her.

She eased out of the bed, never taking her eyes off the bird, though its eye followed her as she edged toward the closet. As Jess pulled on a robe, her eyes fixed on the huge bird's long talons and curved beak, wondering if parrots attacked. Just then there was a soft knock at the door. "Come in!" Jess said.

The door swung open to reveal a slightly flustered butler. "Miss Bellamy, your door was open," he said, with mild disapproval in his voice. "You have a phone call—" He halted mid-sentence and his brows shot up. "Conrad! There you are; I've been looking for you."

Jess marveled at his unruffled tone as he walked to the end of the bed and slipped a hand under the bird's breast. Conrad stepped obediently onto the offered hand. "I apologize, Miss Bellamy. He should not be here."

Jess expelled her breath at the understatement, clutching her robe around her. "A phone call?"

"Yes, it is Mr. Rawlings," Henley answered, shifting the bird to his shoulder. "Though it is early, I told him I would see if you were up."

Jess regained her composure now that the bird was in his control, though the sight of the large parrot perched on the shoulder of the staid English butler struck her funny and she had to struggle to maintain a straight face. "Thank you, Henley. I'll take the call."

He nodded, then left the room with the bird riding on his shoulder. As he closed the door behind him she heard a squawking voice declare, "Close the door, dammit, the birds will get out!"

When she picked up the phone she was laughing.

"What's so funny?" a deep voice asked.

"Nothing," she said, biting her lip. "It's early for a call, isn't it, Michael?"

"Is it? I've been at work for an hour. Sorry if I woke you up."

"You didn't. What can I do for you?"

"I'm calling to see if you'd like to have lunch with me."

The statement surprised her. "Lunch?"

"Yes. I have some business in Monterey later this morning and I thought we could have lunch."

She thought about it for a moment, wondering about his motives. If he needed to see her he could have asked her to come to his office. "I guess so."

There was a pause at the other end of the line. "Don't put yourself out."

"I'm not. Is there anything you want to discuss?"

"What else? I'll meet you at the Del Monte Lodge in Pebble Beach at twelve-thirty. In the Taproom. Is that okay with you?"

"I'll be there."

"See you then," he said, then hung up.

She replaced the receiver slowly, feeling disturbed. It was odd how the mind seemed to lie dormant, then suddenly toss up memories when they were least expected, like a catapult at a wall of defenses. First Amanda last night, and now Michael Rawlings, triggering memories she had thought buried. There had been similar phone calls from Curt, and like Kipling's army she had ridden pell-mell into disaster. Or perhaps she was giving herself too much nobility. She had responded to Curt's demands for far less elevated reasons than God and king, a fact that had left her with total self-disgust. But that had come later, much later.

She trembled suddenly, alarmed that she had allowed herself to dredge up old, best-forgotten memories. Pushing aside her thoughts, she went into the bathroom and turned on the shower. Slipping out of her robe and nightgown, she stepped under the water, letting it run over her face and body. It seemed impossible that two weeks ago, before Amanda's letter, her life had been well planned, controlled and normal. And now she was embroiled in a fantasy world of people who refused to accept reality—and she awakened to parrots on her bed.

As the hot water eased her turmoil, she thought about the things Amanda had told her. In one evening another world had been revealed, though its residents still seemed to have little to do with her. Names and lives that were distant, brought to life in stories that might have been read to her as a child. The Little Golden Book of her ancestors.

Turning off the water, she stepped from the shower, toweled herself off, and slipped back into her robe. She was kidding herself, she thought; this wasn't fantasy. In the past three days Amanda had become real; her history added a new dimension to Jessica's life, tipping that life into balance. And the characters were disarmingly real. Amanda had loved and lost in her youth. Jess could certainly identify with that.

As she dressed in slacks and a sweater, she thought about her own situation and her time with Curt. She understood Amanda's drive to lose herself in work, but that work had also brought success. Pain and disappointment could be a great stimulus. Jess wasn't a deeply religious person. She believed in God, but she felt sure that destiny was brought about by will and determination. She had often argued with Roxy about that. . . .

There she was, thinking of Roxy again. Roxy had insisted that destiny was in God's hands. And together they had faced life with an open, innocent eagerness, until Jess learned how much life could hurt. She had been left with that legacy from Roxy and her mother, and then from Curt, each step of growth teaching her caution.

And now, like Alice in Wonderland, Jess found herself slipping through a hole into craziness. Conrad was on his way back to his cage, and that was a definite first step. Amanda and Michael Rawlings would simply have to accept reality as well.

The Taproom was busy even on a Tuesday afternoon. Jess was shown to a table by the window, barely noticing her surroundings as she fixed her mind on the pending meeting. She was early, a result of her determination to get the lunch over with. While driving to the lodge she had confirmed her decision that there was nothing more she could do for Amanda.

She ordered a club soda and waited, glancing around the room for the first time. Above the wainscoting, the walls were covered with photographs of golfers and celebrities who had visited the lodge for the Crosby Clambake, or the AT&T Celebrity Pro-Am, as it was now called. Her gaze passed over pictures of Bing Crosby, Bob Hope, James Garner, Clint Eastwood, and Jack Lemmon, all in attitudes of mischief that seemed to have little to do with golf. And there were countless others she assumed to be professional golfers, though the only one she recognized was Jack Nicklaus. Another who looked familiar had signed his photograph in heavy, broad strokes: "Fuzzy." Perhaps she should get out more, she thought.

"I'm sorry I'm late." Michael slipped into the chair across from her. "Last-minute problems." His grin was disarmingly boyish, and she wondered if the effect was deliberate.

"What did you want to talk with me about?"

"Always right down to business, aren't you?" A dark brown brow arched independently of its mate, and she felt something warm catch in her chest.

"You called me, remember?" she said, forcing her thoughts away from the growing awareness that she found Michael attractive. It was a complication she didn't want or need in her life.

"Yes, I did." The waiter appeared, and he ordered coffee. "I wanted to know how you felt about what you learned yesterday. Did it help?"

She understood his anxiousness, and it made what she had to tell him all the more difficult. "Michael, I wish I could tell you what you want to hear. I appreciate your commitment to Amanda and to the company. I know we got off to a rather bad start, and I apologize for the things I said to you when we first met."

His brows gathered together above his eyes. "I don't mean to be rude—I appreciate the gesture—but is this apology meant to soften the blow?"

"I'm sorry, Michael." She found that she really meant it and she drew in a shallow breath against the regret she felt. "I don't think there's anything more I can do. Everything I've seen, read, and heard merely confirms OSHA's report. My best advice is for you to plead guilty and negotiate. If you do, the DA will probably settle for a large fine."

"So that's it, just like that?"

"I'm sorry."

"Don't apologize to me," he said, shifting in his chair. He glanced out the window, staring at the putting green below. Finally, looking back at her, he said, "Do you give up on all of your clients so easily?"

"I understand your disappointment," she said, ignoring the insult.

"No, I don't think you do," he countered, regarding her steadily. "And I wonder how much your decision was affected by the fact that you never wanted the case in the first place. What a relief it must be to have your prejudgment confirmed."

"That's not fair."

"Isn't it? You told Amanda you'd be here for two weeks. Can't you give it that?"

She glared at him, regretting the peace offering she had made a few moments before. "What do you want me to do? Create evidence that isn't there? Or ignore the evidence that is? Whether or not you choose to believe it, I had hoped the outcome would be different. But two weeks or two months won't change the facts. Nor will wishful thinking."

He was silent for a long moment, leaving her words hanging awkwardly between them as he regarded her with an inscrutable expression across the table. Made uncomfortable by his silence, she found her gaze shifting from him to the window and the golfers below on the putting green.

"I concede to your wisdom and to your experience," he said quietly. "But credit Amanda and me, at least, for not being fools. We know it looks hopeless. We wouldn't have asked for your help if it had been easy."

"It's not just difficult, Michael, it's impossible."

"Perhaps. But I know the people involved; I have to believe that there is more to what happened than what you see on the surface, as damning as it looks. Look, put it this way. Assuming for the moment that it was negligence, Amanda will need you more than ever. The fact that you're here means a lot to her, more than you realize. Stay, give it the two weeks, be here for her. If she loses Altra Grow it's going to be very hard on her."

Jess sensed what the plea cost him, just as she wasn't immune to what Amanda was going to face in the coming weeks. Could she actually walk out on Amanda now? A few days ago her answer would have been a brief, unequivocal yes, but now she wasn't as certain. "All right," she sighed, regretting that she couldn't give him any hope. "I planned to stay awhile in any case. But, Michael, I honestly don't believe there's anything I can do." It was an open-and-shut case, she added silently.

In the small office off her bedroom, Amanda finished another letter and laid it aside. The room was furnished in shades of green and yellow, meant to give the feeling of the outdoors. Normally the room soothed her, but this morning it seemed entirely too cheerful.

She leaned back in her chair and swiveled around to view the panorama beyond the large window behind her, looking past the trim, immaculate fairway and through the open spaces of the forest to the ocean beyond. She fixed her gaze on the horizon, as distant as the memories she had tried so hard to forget, and had been forced to recall the previous night. It had begun innocently. After all, she never had to be encouraged to think about Nicky. God, how she missed him. It seemed to grow harder to accept his loss as the years passed, and thinking about him, talking about him, always helped to bring him nearer. But she hadn't been prepared to think about Jack. What could she have told Jessica about Jack Bellamy? Perhaps that when Jack Bellamy entered her life she was susceptible to his carefully cultivated charms.

She had met Jack at a small dinner party given by friends. He was a houseguest, and it didn't take Amanda long to realize that she had been invited specifically to meet him. Throughout dinner she could feel people's eyes shifting to them, watching their reaction to each other. Part of her was amused; her friends had been trying to match her with a constant stream of suitable prospects for two years. And this time she was interested. She was attracted to his dark good looks. He was startlingly reminiscent of Rudolph Valentino.

His eyes smoldered—she had read that once in a book and now she knew what it meant—when he looked at her. His humor outmatched hers, a fact that quite possibly impressed her more than anything else. And, she came to realize that she had no reason to suspect he was a fortune hunter. He was well set financially, with a modest but adequate trust from his parents.

As they spent more time together, Amanda grew aware that Jack had no ambitions beyond pleasure, but in that endeavor he was a master. He was not unwise with his money—he didn't gamble and he was sober—but he had no ambition to increase his financial position beyond what was needed to maintain his life-style. Jack's area of expertise was play—parties, dancing, golf, polo, tennis, and entertaining. When he asked Amanda to marry him, by a comical serenade beneath her window that had her slumped in hysterical laughter against the windowsill, she said yes.

She had been married to Jack less than a year when she realized that she had made a terrible mistake. Perhaps, in honesty, she had always known that Jack had answered her need for some sort of respectable stability. And he would not be a threat to the company or to her involvement in it, as long as it didn't interfere with his pleasures. Eventually he came to resent her wealth and, more important, the fact that his position in society paled beside hers. He knew he was sought after as a pleasant, amusing entertainment, but Amanda had power and authority. His resentment grew, subtly at first, then openly. But in spite of their differences they developed an understanding: he left her to her business, and she left him to his pursuits, including other women.

Oddly, it was during those years, with all of their pain, that her life became most meaningful. But then, moments of great unhappiness often led to search of self and purpose, and through her discoveries Amanda kept her sanity. Perhaps because of the restlessness Jack had caused in her, she needed something to commit herself to beyond mere profits. Whatever the reason, she was totally receptive the day that she met Zack Rawlings.

Her car had become stuck in the mud up to the rims of its spoked tires. One of her foremen was with her that day, but he seemed as helpless as she to extricate them from their problem.

Zack seemed to emerge as a natural part of the landscape. Over the years, she had come to realize that this was close to the truth. Zack Rawlings was as natural as the tumbleweed that fed its nutrients into the ground, then broke loose and careened wildly over the land, pushed by the wind. Like a jackrabbit, he was lean and wiry, with large, dark eyes, trusting yet alert, friendly while darting about to warn him of unexpected threats. His pickup, which had long since forgotten the luxury of paint, lurched out of nowhere to bear down on them suddenly. And it stopped, heaving its sides in a shudder.

Zack stepped out, leaving the door open as he strode over to them. He shoved his hands down into the pockets of his Sears overalls and stared at the mired vehicle. " 'Pears that you've gotten yourself stuck."

"It appears that we have," Amanda said. In spite of her need for help, she wondered what this stranger was doing on her land. "And may I ask who you are?"

"The man who's going to pull you out of that mud," he responded dryly.

Those moments were the beginning of a thirty-year friendship. Zack pulled them out; then they sat on the hood of his truck, sharing the sack lunch he produced from the cabin of his truck. And they talked. Amanda remembered biting her lip against Zack's declaration that he wasn't a squatter. He was camping down by the dry river, and he had set out a small garden on a piece of land that wasn't being used, but only until he could find a job. She remembered that flourishing garden— snap beans, tomatoes, squash, and a few unrecognizable vegetables. He had chosen a piece of ground no one else would use, and it flourished like a small Garden of Eden. She hired him that day.

It was from Zack that Amanda learned to love and value the land. Together they built Altra Grow, adding to what Jeremy Morgan had begun over eighty years before.

It was from Zack that Amanda learned about the balance of nature. He accepted the necessity of large farming operations, knowing that his methods would not feed the world. But his methods were caring, and they helped to make Altra Grow successful. "You need to know when to put on the brakes, Amanda," he would say. "Pull back, use natural methods when you can make them practical." And she found that some of his methods worked, such as his way of dealing with predators. While other farmers were busy eliminating "pests" from their land, Altra Grow cultivated its wildlife. Hawks, badgers, weasels, and bobcats were given protection on Morgan land. And even nonpredators such as quail and jackrabbits were left unmolested as they drew the predators, and a natural balance was established. Altra Grow had never found a need for pesticides or pest control that plagued other growers. As Zack had promised, the critters did it. And Altra Grow saved a lot of money.

In all of those years together, Zack would never accept her help beyond what he earned, with one exception. She'd never forget that day, or what it had cost him. He came to her, his hat in hand, and asked for a loan. He wanted to send his grandson to Saint Patrick's. It took a moment for her to deal with the sudden humility of this man she respected so much. And then she found a solution for them both. "Why, Zack, this is fate," she had said, feigning wonder. "For some time I've been thinking of setting up a scholarship at Saint Patrick's. And here you are, as usual, prodding my conscience. You always seem to know when I'm procrastinating. I am absolutely delighted that Michael will be the first recipient." She had continued the practice ever since.

Zack died in 1975. His pickup truck ran off the road into a

eucalyptus tree when his heart suddenly failed. Amanda made good on a promise she had made to him. She made sure that Michael finished college. And in spite of the fact that she asked nothing in return, Michael repaid her tenfold. He had his grandfather's touch with the land, coupled with a knowledge of modern farming. And Amanda loved him.

Too bad she couldn't love Jack. Except for those moments when she was involved with building Altra Grow, Jack Bellamy was always there, like a nagging sore in her life, a self-inflicted wound that festered and refused to heal. She would look at him across the breakfast table, hating him, wondering what she had once seen in him. In such moments she would force herself to look at him analytically, wanting to remember the redeeming qualities she once saw in him. And she wondered how many other women found those lips inviting. But her view of him had become distant; it was like looking at something she had once craved and while she could still appreciate its beauty, she didn't want it anymore. Unfortunately, she had bought it.

Jack, sensing her rejection, was too much of a coward to confront her privately but took special delight in embarrassing her before her friends and business acquaintances. He savored such moments, making hurtful remarks about her before an audience. Unfortunately he was bright and cunning. He knew better than to mention her business acumen, but he played on her vulnerability as a woman, her lack of physical desire for him, her need for friendship. His remarks hurt because they rang with truth, spearing her heart, leaving her speechless and wounded. Later, of course, he would regard her with innocence when she objected to his barbs.

It became a standoff, painful to both, but they were unwilling to confront each other, knowing the agony that confrontation would bring. Then, in 1932, Amanda went to New York to deal with Morgan Land and Development Company shipping interests. Minor problems, actually, but the prospect of a trip east proved irresistible. It was an impulse that would change her life.

In New York, Amanda quickly concluded her business. She could have taken the next train home but simply couldn't bear the prospect. A few days to herself, with nothing to do but shop, became undeniably attractive. She had a stack of invitations suggesting what she might do with her evenings, but she wasn't particularly drawn to dinners and parties with people she hardly knew who had extended invitations out of loyalty to her father or because it might prove advantageous for business reasons. But there was one invitation that interested her—a fund-raising event for the present governor of New York, Franklin Delano Roosevelt, who was campaigning in the Democratic primaries. She had read about him, and in spite of his party affiliation she had found herself drawn to his policies, particularly his success as governor involving tax relief to farmers and lower utility costs to consumers. Besides, she didn't have anything else to do. She thought it might be nice to spend the evening with someone besides business associates, even if they only wanted money from her, and even if the candidate was a Democrat.

Not long after she entered the ballroom of the brand-new Waldorf-Astoria, she began to wonder about her decision to come. She was greeted upon her arrival by James Farley, Roosevelt's campaign manager, who graciously welcomed her and introduced her to a few other people before he departed to welcome other guests. Over the next half-hour, Amanda began to feel young, uninformed, and painfully aware that she was a political cretin. People showed some initial interest when they learned she was from the West—apparently Roosevelt needed California delegates—but when she was unable to answer questions about the political situation in her home state, their interest quickly waned.

Totally humiliated, Amanda decided to leave as unobtrusively as possible. In fact, she hoped that no one she had met would remember her name. She hurried toward the cloakroom, curbing an impulse to break into a run. She gave her claim tag to the hat-check girl and waited as the young woman disappeared into the racks of fur and cashmere.

"Miss Morgan, you can't be leaving so soon." Amanda turned to find James Farley standing at her side. "We haven't even served dinner yet!" Amanda attempted to stifle a feeling of panic, but he had seen it. "Is something wrong?" he asked.

"No, of course not. I mean—I'm not feeling well. I'm afraid I have a headache."

"I'm terribly sorry. Is this your coat?" he said as the girl returned to the window. He took the fox coat and dropped it about her shoulders. "Is your driver waiting for you?"

"No, I came in a cab."

"Then you must allow me to have my driver take you back to your hotel."

"That really isn't necessary, Mr. Farley."

"Nonsense, I insist. Your father would never forgive me if I let you go off like this. Wait in the lobby, and I'll have one of my assistants see you home. It will just be a moment."

Knowing she had no choice, Amanda waited. She was tempted to just walk out and have one of the doormen hail a cab, but she could imagine Farley's reaction if his assistant returned to inform him that Miss Morgan had simply disappeared. One thing was true about what she had said to him, however; she now had a headache.

"Miss?"

Amanda turned. Her eyes grew wide and she stared unbelievingly as her heart began to pound. She was looking up into familiar deep blue eyes that were equally astonished. "Nicky," she breathed.

"My God. Amanda . . ."

The door to Amanda's office opened, abruptly drawing her from her reverie. "Henley said you were up here," Michael said. He paused at the door, regarding her startled expression with concern. "Amanda, are you all right?"

"Of course," she said, refocusing her thoughts. "Where is Jessica?"

"She was driving the station wagon, and it wouldn't start again." He came into the room and perched on the arm of the sofa. "You really should get rid of that lemon, Amanda. I dropped her off at Julian Alcott's office. She said she'd take a cab home."

"Julian's? Oh, yes, I recall now. She had a meeting with him today." Amanda had called Altra Grow's attorney the day after Jessica's arrival, informing him of her decision to involve Jess and requesting that he make his files available to her. "Has she said anything to you about the case?"

"Yes. She said that there was nothing she could do. I convinced her to give it a little more time, and that's what I want to talk with you about." He paused, regarding her with concern. "Amanda, are you certain of what you're doing?"

"You mean my decision to involve Jessica in this?"

"Yes. She's going to stay, and she's going to keep digging. She may find out more than you bargained for."

"I realize that. It's a chance I have to take."

"Do you? Look, after all these years, you have a chance to develop a relationship with her. Why risk it?"

"Because if anyone can find a solution to this messy case, it's my granddaughter, and not just because she's a good attorney. There are others who could fit that profile—quite a few of them already work for me. It's because she'll learn to care, Michael, as no other lawyer will."

"And if she discovers more than she should? You have to face the possibility, Amanda."

"I know, and I have. In that event I will lose something far more important than the case. But I'm not accustomed to losing, Michael, and I have no intention of doing so now."

CHAPTER 12

Upon arriving at Julian Alcott's office Jess was ushered into his private suite. The attorney for Altra Grow met her at the door, extending his hand with a warm greeting. He was a tall, slender man, possibly in his early sixties, with silver hair and brows over bright, friendly blue eyes. "I'm delighted to meet you, Ms. Bellamy. Aside from the fact that you're Amanda's granddaughter, your reputation precedes you."

"Thank you for seeing me on such short notice, Mr. Alcott."

"Not at all. Shall we sit over here? I think we'll be more comfortable," he said, gesturing to deep armchairs by a window overlooking the bay. "I'm sorry I was out of town when you arrived. Did my assistants give you what you needed?"

"Yes, they were quite helpful, thank you. I hope Amanda explained to you that it was not my intention to take over this case. I agreed only to look into it and advise her, on a very personal level."

"Yes, she called me. However, I had the feeling that she hoped you'd become more deeply involved. I want to assure you that my professional ego would not be offended."

Jess smiled. "I appreciate that, but I'm sure you would agree that further investigation really isn't necessary."

Alcott's brows lifted slightly. "Then you've already come to a conclusion?"

"Yes, and I am in total agreement with your assessment of the case. I plan to advise Amanda of that fact this evening."

"I see," he sighed. "I admit that I had hoped you would find something I overlooked. It's a very unfortunate situation.

Aside from the tragedy of the boy's death, the loss of Altra Grow is going to be a blow to Amanda."

Jessica regarded Alcott with surprise. "The loss of Altra Grow? What do you mean?"

"Well, that will be the eventual outcome, I'm afraid."

Jess frowned. "Perhaps I did miss something. With Altra Grow's previous safety record, I believe the penalties would be negotiable, perhaps a heavy fine. What is the district attorney's position?"

"I haven't spoken with him yet."

"What? Not at all?" Jess was dumbfounded.

Alcott seemed unruffled by her reaction. "Not personally. I felt that such a meeting was premature."

Premature? Jess stared at him as a warning bell went off in her head. She kept her voice calm. "Just what is your advice to Amanda going to be?"

"That she sell Altra Grow. I believe that if the district attorney is approached on that level, we stand the best chance of negotiating the penalties."

Surely he wasn't serious? "First of all, Mr. Alcott, the district attorney is not likely to negotiate on that basis. Selling Altra Grow will not absolve the parent company of liability. However, it will suffer additional, heavy losses by a sale at this time. You'd be lucky to find a buyer who would pay fifty cents on the dollar. Lastly, you do not work for the Morgan Land and Development Company; you are Altra Grow's attorney. I cannot believe that such a decision is in its best interest—or Amanda's."

"I understand your dismay, Ms. Bellamy. And that your— personal involvement might color your view of the situation."

"My view of the situation is not colored, Mr. Alcott." My God, he was patronizing her.

"Possibly not, but you should know that I've been in Los Angeles the past few days and have met with the Morgan Company attorneys. They concur with my approach."

Jess found that difficult to believe, but she wasn't in a position to argue about it. She suspected that if the L.A. firm concurred with Alcott they had been fed some rather selective information. "Under the circumstances, Mr. Alcott, I will have to revise my decision. I cannot advise Amanda to agree to this."

"I understand that," he said solemnly. "However, I do feel that if you understood the history of the company, and of Altra Grow, you would be in a better position to understand my decision."

Jess gathered up her purse and briefcase and stood up. "Thank you for your time, Mr. Alcott," she said. "Perhaps I'll take your suggestion."

"Pardon me?"

"I think you're correct; I do need more information. I should look into the history of the company."

"Excellent." He smiled, walking her to the door. "If I can be of any help, please let me know."

Not likely, she thought, controlling her anger as she left the office. But there was one place to start.

She took a cab to the main library in Monterey and prepared to take up Julian Alcott's challenge, though she doubted that he had meant it as that.

Jess slipped out of her jacket, dropping it onto the empty chair next to her. Then she checked the notes she had made in her search through the microfilm catalogs of the area newspapers spanning the last fifty years. They were categorized in notations under headings of the Morgan name, Altra Grow, and more recently, the articles written on the Martinez case. The list was lengthy, though she shouldn't have been surprised. Monterey was a relatively small community, after all, the Morgans had been prominent in the area since the mid 1800's, and newspapers had been reporting their activities since 1873. Turning on the microfilm viewer, she opened the first box from the large stack the librarian had selected from the list Jess had given her.

The first tape was fairly recent, dealing with 1983 and 1984. She flipped through to locate the dates she had noted for those years, briefly skimming the social columns and the many pictures and articles of Amanda attending functions for local charities, donating land to the city of Monterey for a park, opening a day-care center—typical philanthropic activities for a woman in her position. The next two tapes, of more recent years, were much the same, along with articles about the Morgan company's public offering of stock, the new board members and their backgrounds. Among them, however, were articles about Amanda and pictures of her with the governor and members of the state legislature. There were reports of visits with U.S. Senate committees in Washington, D.C., and of visits to the White House. As she studied them, Jess was surprised by the amount of influence Altra Grow had held with the past three administrations, both Democratic and Republican.

As the tapes moved back through the years, Jess became fascinated with the growth of the company. Reflecting on what Amanda had told her the night before, she began to see a pattern in Amanda's experience and confidence paralleling Altra Grow's expansion and influence. Though the company hadn't been without its problems. She finished a long article about the formation of labor unions, dating from 1903 when the first agricultural union was formed at San Jose, the bracero program following World War II, and the formation of the United Farm Workers in the sixties. Jess leaned back in her chair, rubbing her neck against the stiffness that had begun to set in over the past hour.

"Would you care for some coffee?"

She looked up to find the librarian standing next to her, holding a Styrofoam cup. "That would be wonderful," Jess said with a grateful smile. "Is this typical service around here?" she asked, taking the cup.

"Occasionally," the older woman said, taking the chair next to her. "On a slow day. Are you finding what you need?"

"Probably more than I need." She glanced at the tall pile of microfilm still waiting for her. Or perhaps nothing, she added silently. She'd know if she saw it. She was looking for background, anything that might support or undermine Altra Grow's reputation and methods of doing business. And there was the added benefit of learning more about Amanda, information that she might never learn directly from her grandmother, not because of any attempt to hide anything but because it seemed unimportant.

"I see you're reviewing articles about the farm unions," the librarian said, glancing at the screen.

"Yes. Seems that Altra Grow, like most of the other companies, went head to head with Cesar Chavez over his union."

"Not really," the woman countered. "There is a lot of hostility between the union and the growers, of course, but

Altra Grow is one large company that has dealt pretty fairly with the workers."

Jess had dealt with many librarians over the years and the extent of their information no longer surprised her. Most librarians she had met were literally walking encyclopedias. Over the years—to the dismay of her opponents—she had found occasion to call them as expert witnesses. And their information was never disputed.

"I always wondered if Altra Grow's policy arose from a sense of fairness or if it was just good business—keeping its people happy so they wouldn't want or need the union," the woman continued. "Amanda Morgan's always done things her own way, but then the Morgans always have. Most of the other growers have been furious with her for years because of her policies, including the high wages she pays. Their anger really flared up, though, in the fifties. Look at the articles from 1950, around July or August. You might get an idea of what I mean. And then there was the trouble in the thirties, with the migration from the dust bowl— Oops, there's the phone." She stood up and pushed in the chair. "I hope I helped."

"You did, thank you." Jess smiled. "And thanks for the coffee."

"Don't mention it. Call me if you need anything else," she said, rushing away to answer the phone.

Jess unloaded the machine, reloaded it with the tape of 1950, and turned it to July. She stopped suddenly on July 17. The headline declared, "Four Dead in Bloody Riot." She read the lead of the story: "The unusual warm spell peaked today in a bloody confrontation between a gang of Mexican youths and local residents. Meeting in an angry confrontation . . . they exchanged words, and then mayhem broke out. Four Mexican youths were killed by gunfire. Despite exhaustive investigation by local police, the perpetrators have still not been identified."

"Mexican youths and local residents?" Apparently the Mexicans were not considered residents of the area. And after "exhaustive investigation" the killer of four youths had not been found? In a community of eight hundred residents? God, she would like to have been on that case.

Expelling a disgusted breath, she read on: "Amanda Bellamy, owner of Altra Grow, a subsidiary of the Morgan Land and Development Company, protested to the district attorney over what she claimed to be 'a totally biased review of the situation.' She referred to the police chief as 'an addle-brained incompetent who should be replaced immediately.' Mrs. Bellamy threatened to go to the state attorney general over the matter. She vowed to commit Morgan Company resources to get to the heart of the matter."

Good for you, Amanda, Jess thought.

"Sam Ballard, of Ballard Growers," the article went on, "told this reporter today, in response to Mrs. Bellamy's statement, that Amanda Bellamy was misguided in her emotional reaction to the situation, though he conceded that she probably meant well. It was understandable that a woman would have a soft spot that would keep her from clearly understanding the issues. 'The riot,' Mr. Ballard went on, 'was clearly incited by malcontents who could not understand American principles and who did not appreciate the work ethic. If they want jobs here, they better learn our language and our laws,' Ballard said."

The article ended there, with the reporter apparently agreeing with Mr. Ballard's comments. So much for Amanda and the loss of four young men's lives, Jess thought.

Disgusted, Jess flipped through the next few weeks. Suddenly a headline and picture caught her eye and she paused, turning back to it. She focused the machine. The date was October 24, 1950. There was a large studio photograph of a younger version of Amanda. She was as beautiful as Jess imagined she had been—a finely boned face, high cheekbones, and large, bright eyes. In the picture, Amanda's expression was devoid of her customary self-control. Her lovely face was infused with happiness as she stared up at the tall, incredibly handsome man at her side. He was broad-shouldered and trim with pale eyes and fair hair. Jess leaned forward, studying his features. Oddly, there was something familiar about him. The caption read: Amanda Morgan Bellamy weds Ambassador Nicholas Leighton Alger. The accompanying article was a typical news release of a wedding, apparently a private ceremony in the home of the bride, attended by close friends. It struck Jess that family was not mentioned. Hadn't her father attended the wedding?

The article went on to state that Amanda was the mother of John Morgan Bellamy and the widow of Jack Leland Bellamy.

It was a first marriage for Ambassador Alger. The background on the groom was brief but to the point: a graduate of Yale; assistant campaign manager for Franklin Delano Roosevelt in his 1932 and 1936 campaigns; a captain in the United States Navy, served in the Pacific during World War II, decorated with honors, assistant to the Secretary of the Navy, 1947–1948, ambassador to Brazil, 1949.

Jess wondered if perhaps John Bellamy's estrangement from his mother had something to do with Amanda's remarriage. Had he been loyal to his father, who had died only a year before? More pieces of the puzzle, yet each one seemed to make the puzzle larger.

Glancing at the clock, Jess removed the tape and sorted through the remaining stack. Finding the one marked 1930, she threaded the machine. It didn't take her long to find what the librarian had referred to—angry, disparaging articles about the immigrants who were "descending upon California in hordes," or "Okies, refuse of the dust bowl, who were blatantly squatting upon land throughout California." And mentions of Amanda and the Morgan Company began to pop up. Apparently she had allowed "Okie" squatters to stay on her land. She was hiring and even leasing small sections to them, angering the other farmers in the valley. As she began to page down the film, Jess stopped, turning back to a name that caught her eye. There, in a brief article, was the name Zack Rawlings. Apparently, to the displeasure of the farmers being interviewed, Mr. Rawlings had been hired as a foreman for Altra Grow's Soledad acres.

Well, that corner of the puzzle was beginning to take shape, Jess thought. Sitting back in her chair, she felt her mouth twitch with a smile. Then she chuckled softly. Apparently her grandmother was a bit of a maverick. "Roxy," she murmured, "I think Amanda could have refined the Limburger Cheese Caper." Jess was learning that the Morgans had been alienating the establishment since the mid–eighteen hundreds. Feeling full and satisfied, Jess turned off the machine and gathered up the tapes, returning them to the librarian.

"Did you find what you need?" the woman asked, taking the tapes from her.

"Yes, more than you know. Thank you for your help," Jess said warmly. She asked to use the phone and called a cab, then went out to wait by the front door. Fog had crept in from the ocean, and Jess pulled the collar up on her jacket, shoving her hands into her pockèts to keep them warm. Wishing she had worn a warmer coat, she stamped her feet, shivering against the dampness. To her relief, the cab appeared within ten minutes and she got into the backseat and gave the driver directions. As they drove out of Monterey onto the highway, Jess settled back, her thoughts turning to what she had read over the past few hours. And she thought of the contrasts between her mother and Amanda—and Roxy.

Margaret Bellamy had lived life according to her husband's rules, Jess thought. After her marriage, her art and paintings, which had been her passion, became a hobby. Margaret Bellamy was the perfect wife, mother, hostess, and philanthropist. Her entire life was given to the needs of others. She had an almost ethereal beauty that warned one not to touch. Only Jess and her brother dared to approach that beauty, knowing the warmth and love that lay beneath. And with it, they knew the sadness.

By contrast, Amanda pulsed with life. She had the strength and resolve Jess recognized in her father, but Amanda also had a lust for life, a determination to take on life's challenges. Jess hadn't experienced that zest for living since her years with Roxy. She had embraced those years, flourished within them, and then they had torn life from her. Dad was right, caring caused pain. Could she risk that pain again?

The cab pulled up to the gate to Del Monte Forest. As a guard leaned out from the gate house, the cabby glanced at Jess over his shoulder. "Whose name should I give?" he asked. Jess hesitated, then fumbled in her briefcase, looking for an address. "I want you to take me to Pacific Grove," she said, giving him the address.

"Lady, you wanted to come here," he said impatiently.

"I changed my mind." She leaned back against the hard seat. "Take me to the address I just gave you."

"Whatever you say." The cabby turned the car around.

As he headed toward Pacific Grove, Jess tried not to question the decision she had made. They drove along a winding road edging the forest, and she focused on the darkened landscape they passed. Coming out of the forest, the street edged along the coastline, with the ocean to their left.

Soon the cab came to a stop before a large house, nestled between its neighbors on a steep hill overlooking the Pacific Ocean. Paying the driver, adding a tip that she knew would make up for the inconvenience, Jess stood looking at the house as the cab drove away. At least someone was home, she thought, as evidenced by the lights that were on in the house. She walked up the steps, hesitating a moment before she knocked.

After a long moment, the door opened. "Jessica," Michael said, his eyes widening with surprise.

"May I come in?" He looked different, she noted, in his ever-present Levi's but with the addition of a sloppy fisherman's sweater and Topsiders, without socks. His hair was tousled. As he stepped back for her to enter she brushed past him, aware of his masculinity and the fact that he looked disturbingly handsome. She wondered if she was making a big mistake. "I need to talk with you."

"It must be important," he said, shutting the door. He took her arm, gesturing beyond the entry hall. "Let's go into the living room."

His voice rumbled in her ear and she was aware of the firm touch of his hand on her arm as she let him lead her into a large room. What she found surprised her. She didn't know what she had expected but certainly not a room created with such taste and care. There were chairs and a large sofa upholstered in soft brown leather, warm woods of cherry and oak, brass lamps, and American primitive paintings. Two windows gave an unobstructed view of the ocean.

"You had something you wanted to talk about?"

The question brought her out of her reverie and she turned to find him watching her. From his expression she knew that he knew what she had been thinking. "This room is beautiful," she said.

"Thank you, Miss Bellamy," he said, his mouth pulling into the lopsided grin that she was coming to recognize all too well.

"I should have called first," she said.

"Yes, you should have. It could have saved you some embarrassment."

"Excuse me?"

"I might have had a guest."

The thought hadn't occurred to her. Realizing it, she

flushed. The fact made her bristle. "Your cowgirls aren't my concern, Mr. Rawlings."

"Cowgirls?"

My God, she thought, had she actually said that? This man was making her crazy. "Whatever type of woman you prefer." Her eyes lit on an open book lying face down on the coffee table, and she realized that he had been reading when she rang the door bell. Impulsively, she picked it up. It was a spy thriller, a recent best-seller. "I see you enjoy popular fiction."

"For relaxation, you bet. Do you have a problem with that?"

"Of course not," she said, setting the book down. "It's none of my business how you entertain yourself in your leisure hours."

"Fine. Now that we've discussed my taste in literature and women, would you mind telling me why you are here?"

It took a moment for her to remember why she had come. "May I sit down?"

"Of course. Sit, by all means."

She chose the corner of the sofa. "I came by tonight to tell you that I want to meet with the Martinez family."

He frowned, confused. "Can you do that? Wouldn't Rafael's family be off limits, or something? I mean, you're representing Amanda."

"First of all, I am not representing Amanda or anyone else, remember? Second, no one in the family is on the DA's prospective witness list." Which was, Jess added silently, a curiosity in itself. One she planned to investigate.

"However, even if they were on that list," she continued, "and even if I was the company's attorney, the defense attorney has very few limits in regards to witnesses. The prosecution has less leeway—which is probably what you are thinking of. As a defense attorney, I can talk to anyone who will talk to me. They can refuse, of course, which is another matter. Which is why I want you to intercede with them for me."

"Why?" he asked quietly. His eyes had become hard. "Why do you want to talk with them?"

"I need to talk with them about their son, of course. They might give me insight . . ."

"Insight?" he interrupted, staring at her incredulously. "My God, they lost their son! What insight can they give you? A look at their pain?"

"You don't understand."

"You're damn right I don't! First you'll look into the case, then you won't. You say you came to Monterey to get to know Amanda, but you criticize everything she does. You tell me the case is hopeless; then you prance in here unannounced, make snide comments about my way of life, and demand to see a family that is grieving so you can get their insight! I don't know what your problem is, Miss Bellamy, but whatever it is, I'm fed up with it!"

She opened her mouth to protest, then clamped it shut. He was right. From his viewpoint she was guilty of everything he had accused her of. "I'm sorry," she said. He glowered at her. "I said I was sorry. You're right, I've behaved deplorably."

Her words diffused his anger and he looked confused. "Well, I wouldn't put it that strongly. But you do have a tendency to act like you have a burr up your butt."

"This hasn't been easy, Michael," she sighed. "I respect your loyalty to Amanda; I admire it. You expect me to feel affection, even love, for a woman you've known all of your life. But I was virtually unaware of her until a few weeks ago. Then, without warning, I received a letter from her asking me for help. And I'm expected to give that help without qualification, even though I might ask why she has never tried to make contact with me before this. Why was it my responsibility, Michael, and not hers? Why did she wait until now to contact me? Nevertheless, I came. Now I'm expected to take on a case that her attorneys have advised her to settle out of court. Moreover, I am supposed to discover some miraculous solution that will absolve her company from responsibility! Yet I'm considered self-centered. I should never have agreed to stay here under these circumstances. Do you want to know why I did, against my better judgment? Because I wanted to get to know Amanda, and I used the Martinez case as an excuse. Perhaps I thought that if I didn't agree to look into the case I wouldn't be asked to stay."

When she had finished, he stared at her for a long moment. His expression had softened as she spoke, and now he took a deep breath, letting it out slowly. "Jess, I'm sorry," he said quietly. "I owe you an apology. I have a very narrow viewpoint when it comes to Amanda. I'd do just about anything for her, but I was wrong to expect the same from you. Look, if it will help, I can explain it to her. You're right, there's no reason for you to stay."

"But you're wrong, there is." She smiled at his look of puzzlement. "That's why I came here tonight. I think I *can* do something."

"What?" he asked, baffled. Then his expression shifted to expectation.

"I'm not sure yet, so don't get your hopes up. I'm not promising anything."

"Okay, you've made that point," he said, his smile slipping into that unsettling boyish grin. "We'll take it a step at a time. Have you eaten?"

"No, but—"

"Come on," he said, turning abruptly. "I'll fix you something to eat and we can talk."

"It isn't necessary," she insisted, but he was already gone. She found him in the kitchen.

"How about a cheese omelet?" he asked as he rummaged through the refrigerator.

"Michael, really, it isn't necessary."

He paused with an egg carton in his hand, his eyes dropping over her as he peered over the top of the refrigerator door. "You're not anorexic or something, are you?"

"Do I look like it?" she asked, arching a brow.

"No, you look great." He grinned. "Sit over there and we'll talk." He gestured to a table set in a deep bay window.

She obeyed him, partly because she was at a temporary loss to do anything else and partly because she was hungry. Since he seemed intent on feeding her, she decided to make the best of it.

As he rattled pots and pans, she took note of her surroundings. The room was large and spacious, with the same dimensions as the living room. Like the living room, the kitchen was at the front of the house. The bay window where she sat gave a breathtaking view of the ocean. The room had the feel of French Country, with copper pots hanging from heavy beams, hand-painted blue and white delft tiles, and rich golden oak cupboards and paneling that was repeated in the wide planks of the floor. The room—once again, like the living room—was a pleasant surprise. She wondered if he had hired a decorator, not that it mattered. He appeared at ease in his surroundings and she knew they reflected his tastes. At the very least she suspected that not one item had been chosen without his approval. There was something solid about Michael Rawlings—

She realized, with some embarrassment, that he had spoken to her. "I'm sorry, what did you say?"

"Jack, cheddar, or Swiss—in your omelet?"

"Oh—jack." She watched as he worked, admiring his dexterity as he flipped the omelet, sprinkled it with cheese, and slid it folded onto a plate. "You seem to be at home in a kitchen."

"I am," he said, adding toast and sliced melon to the plate. "My parents died when I was eight, and I learned how to cook in self-defense." He set the plate down in front of her. "Eat," he ordered, then returned to the stove. "The only things my grandfather knew how to cook were beans and pancakes. We ate them for breakfast, lunch, and dinner for six months. It didn't take much intelligence to figure out that if I was going to survive I'd have to learn how to cook." He poured them each a cup of coffee then took the chair across from her.

"Oh, Michael, this is delicious," she said sincerely. "What's that flavor?"

"You don't expect me to divulge my secrets, do you?" He grinned. "Not about my cooking, at least."

"I never learned how to cook. I'm afraid I'm a dismal failure in the kitchen."

"Now, why doesn't that surprise me?"

She glanced up sharply, but there was no criticism in his expression. "I just never had any reason to learn." She shrugged. "I have a woman who cooks and cleans for me. But I can make salads," she added, seeing the glint of amusement that crept into his eyes.

"Fabulous. I hate making salads."

The comment unsettled her; there was a familiarity about it that suggested something beyond the present conversation. Something she was totally unprepared to deal with. "I'm sorry for barging in on you this evening. In the past week I seem to have lost my sense of propriety. I'm not normally this rude, or this defensive." At least she didn't think she was. "I made some discoveries and I wanted to talk with you about them."

He waited until she finished the last bite of the omelet before he responded. "So tell me."

"So far they're just feelings, Michael," she said, leaning back in the chair. "I spent the afternoon searching through old newspaper files. It gave me a broad view of Amanda and the Morgan Company. I can't articulate it now; they are feelings more than form." She sighed, glancing through the window at the silver moonlight reflected on the ocean. "What I heard from Julian Alcott today convinced me that he is not working in Amanda's best interest. The man is incompetent. Furthermore, what I discovered at the library gave me some clues and a strong urge to delve deeper into the case." She wrapped her hand around her coffee cup as she shifted her eyes to him. "Michael, you were right, instinct often keeps me on a case when it seems hopeless. Sometimes it proves to be nothing more than wishful thinking and the fact that I care about the client. Or sometimes I keep on it simply because pieces don't fit. And that's the situation here. Beyond that, I care about Amanda and I'll do my best for her. She doesn't deserve these legal problems but she may have to live with them. However, even if Altra Grow is found culpable, I think I can diffuse the penalty somewhat."

He frowned on her last words. "Diffuse it? How?"

"I hope to lessen the judgment. Altra Grow's record is its best defense. I think I can show that the accident occurred in spite of the company's normal practices, not because of them."

"Would that make a difference?"

"Even if you were found guilty, it could lessen the judgment."

"What changed your mind?"

"I told you, Alcott's an idiot. Amanda has spent a lifetime fighting for those who are less fortunate, even to bucking popular opinion. Under intense criticism, she fought for what she thought was right. I can offer a portrait of a woman, the owner of this company, who would never, ever be oblivious to the well-being and safety of someone who worked for her, not for profits or for the approval of others."

"How can I help?"

"You can arrange that meeting with the Martinez family. It begins with them."

Doubt entered his expression, the first she had seen since he sat down at the table. "I can arrange it, of course. But they're in pain, Jess. I don't want to hurt them any more than they have been."

"Do you think I do?" she asked. "Look, they've already been hurt in the worst way. But don't you think they want to know the truth even more than you do?"

He regarded her for a silent moment. "All right, I'll arrange the meeting. But I wish they didn't have to go through this."

"So do I. Try to trust me, Michael. I spend my life dealing with these situations. But arrange it soon. I have a feeling that there's no time to lose."

CHAPTER 13

Helen Borgini finished addressing the last envelope and set it on the stack of invitations she had been working on all morning. They should have been in the morning mail, but it had been difficult to concentrate on the task; she was still upset over the argument she'd had with Samuel the previous night. It seemed that they were arguing more and more lately. It was upsetting. She had promised herself years ago that she wouldn't argue with him anymore.

She placed the pen in its holder and leaned back in the chair. Her eyes moved over the room with satisfaction, noting that everything was in its place. The room, in their home in Del Monte Forest, had been created with studied care, as had everything in her environment. If only her life with Sam could be so well ordered.

She thought she had made peace with him, but in the past two years, since he had taken a position on the Morgan Company board, everything had begun falling apart. She was still confused as to how it had happened, and he never explained anything to her. She was expected to keep a lovely home and be the consummate hostess when he required it of her—not that those tasks were burdens, they were the only true pleasures in her life, now that the children were grown with lives of their own.

She had been happy in Maryland. It wasn't fair that he had uprooted her at this time in their lives. But of course she hadn't had a say in the matter. She had learned the reasons for their leaving through gossip and innuendos from well-meaning friends. Until then she had never heard of the Morgan Land and Development Company. Not until the Bellamy Guarantee Trust had foreclosed on Allied Tool and Die and Sam had somehow found a position on the Morgan Company's board. She would never understand how business worked. He had come home one night to inform her that he had sold the house and they would be moving to Monterey. She had one month to pack and move, one month to resolve her feelings and say good-bye to the home in which she had lived for twenty years and raised her children.

The Monterey coast was said to be one of the most beautiful in the world, and the Del Monte Forest was lovely, but it was dismally foggy so much of the time, particularly in the summer when the heavy ocean fogs would cling to the forest until noon, then drift in again a few hours later. The fog depressed her, reminding her of the misty gray areas of her life—like the early years when there had been other women in Sam's life. Poor Sam, he thought she didn't know about them. Little had he realized that she was relieved to be free of his insistent rutting. It had been fifteen years since he had sought her bed, but even now she tensed when she heard him pass by her door in the middle of the night. Sam's idea of foreplay was to take off his pants.

Revolting memories, it seemed, were never forgotten. Such as Sam's staying power. She bit her lip and tried to think of more pleasant things than the way he pumped away at her, grunting, until he collapsed. Once, long ago, she had been curious about satisfaction. She could have had affairs when her body was firm, before the age spots appeared, before she felt the need to hide her aging body. She remembered the young men who would have satisfied her curiosity, men who moved in and out of her life as they did business with her husband. But despite the overt, sometimes clumsy offers, she had never seriously considered it, not once. Life was trade-offs and she never would have risked her security to satisfy her curiosity. So why had she argued with Sam now? It had surprised her more than it had him.

Sam was up to something. She had known it for months, which probably meant he'd been at it for years, since she chose not to see much of what was happening around her. She had mentioned it. He had told her that it was none of her business, which it probably wasn't, but what he didn't know, and had never cared to know, was that when something was important to her, her mind was like a sponge. She pigeonholed what was needed and tossed away what she didn't want to hear or deal with. But this matter forced itself to consciousness and ate away at her until she found herself voicing her objection. Sam was plotting to destroy Amanda Morgan, not just idly, but with calculation and a vengeance.

Secure in her neat, patterned life, Helen had found herself uprooted and tossed into the terrifying strangeness of new surroundings three thousand miles away from home, friends, and children. Amanda Morgan had befriended her, taking her under her wing, establishing her in her new surroundings where she was given total acceptance by those she met. Her gratitude toward Amanda was boundless, and so she had found herself arguing with Sam, shocking them both. She hadn't meant to eavesdrop; she had come into the room off the library to finish the invitations. As she gathered them together, voices from the open door to the library had floated into the room, catching her attention.

"I don't think we have any reason to worry," Julian Alcott was saying. "As Altra Grow's attorney I've advised Amanda to sell. I've been in contact with the Morgan Company attorneys and they concur. The case is not winnable; she has to agree."

"That granddaughter of hers is nosing around," Elliott Westbrook had said, his voice worried. "She could be a problem."

"There's nothing she can do," Julian said. "Let her stick her nose in wherever she wants. In fact, I've encouraged her to do so."

"Let me refresh your drink, Julian." It was Sam's voice then. "I agree with Elliott. That little chit couldn't have come at a worse time. She's been hanging around with Rawlings, sticking her nose in where it doesn't belong. She was down at the ranches the other day, and she's been talking to people."

"It doesn't matter," Julian insisted. "What is she going to learn? Think about it, Sam. She's good, very good, and that's going to help us."

"I don't see how."

"Then I'll try to explain, if you'll listen. Jessica Bellamy is a very hot attorney. Oh, don't look at me like that, Sam. Try to put your prejudices aside for a moment. Women have made a few marks outside of the sheets, whether you approve or not.

She's regarded as one of the best criminal attorneys in the state, and this is a criminal action. More important, she's Amanda's granddaughter. She's going to ferret out the facts of the case, which are indisputable. Eventually she'll come to the same conclusion and advise Amanda accordingly. Amanda doesn't want to believe me, but she's going to have to believe her granddaughter."

"You had better be right," Sam said, his voice edged with anger and doubt. "I spent an hour on the phone with our backer yesterday. Altra Grow goes or everything crumbles. That means a few careers in this room will crumble along with it."

"Trust me," Julian said. "Everything is going as planned."

"It better," Sam said angrily. "This is a thirty million dollar deal to us, Julian. If it fails you'll be the first to go."

Helen had waited until she heard the cars drive away. Then she went to the library and found Sam sitting before the fire with a brandy. What had compelled her to do such a thing she would never know, but she told him what she had heard. She said she couldn't understand why he wanted to destroy someone she had come to consider a friend. He was furious.

Now Helen glanced around the sunny room, trying to dismiss her morose thoughts. There was nothing she could do, after all, and it probably wasn't any of her business. As Sam had pointed out, Amanda Morgan was not a child who needed her protection, and this was business—his business. And after all, Sam had always provided for her, giving her a lovely home and security. Then her eyes fell on the stack of invitations and she glanced at her watch with alarm. It was almost noon, and if she didn't hurry she would miss the afternoon mail. Besides, Sam was probably right. He always was in such matters.

Jessica had studied French and German, and now, not for the first time, she regretted her choices. As she listened to Michael converse with Aguilar and Manuela Martinez she regretted her lack of Spanish. It left her in silence with an uncomfortable awareness of her surroundings. The room was spotless, speaking of almost destitute pride. The furniture was poorly made; the upholstered pieces were shrouded with ill-fitting slipcovers. The wooden tables were worn and littered with inexpensive knickknacks. The walls were bare but for a handwoven striped rug, which hung from two hooks, and a large picture of the Madonna and Child flanked by votive candles on two small shelves.

She had been stunned when Michael drove up and stopped in front of the house. Set on a side street in Soledad, it was old, its siding badly in need of paint, the yard empty but for rosebushes on either side of the steps leading up to the front door.

"What did you expect?" Michael said, glancing at Jessica's horrified expression. "The Martinezes are not typical of Hispanics in the area. Many have better jobs and live well, but many are not this well off, living in labor camps. But that's something else for you to see. I think we'd better discuss this before we go in." He turned off the engine and settled back in the seat of the pickup. "Don't make the mistake of lumping all Hispanics together. There are those who are descended from the old Spanish land grant families. Their families have been here for two hundred years. Aguilar is one. In spite of hard times, he has a pride in his heritage as great as yours—though his ancestors were dons when yours were pirates.

"Then there are the Mexicans who have come here in the past one hundred years, emigrating to California much as mine did, but they came from Texas, New Mexico, and Arizona as they followed the crops. And there are recent immigrants from Mexico. Many of them were made legal residents by the recent amnesty program, but some are still illegal. There's antagonism between the groups, often even resentment and hatred. They have to deal with enough problems from Anglos; the divisions within their own people just make life more difficult."

"If Aguilar is from an old California family, why is he living like this?" she asked.

"You mean if he is 'old blood,' why is he so poor? Jessica, the Yanquis stole everything from the land grant families in the eighteen hundreds. You can't compare his family with yours. The Californios lost everything while your people built upon what they had begun. The Californios were trusting and couldn't compete with Yankee enterprise and greed. They have great pride; they once based a society on it and the Yanquis used that pride to defeat them. Anyway, Manuela was raised in Mexico. She still doesn't speak English well, but then, she is part of a culture that confines women to the home. And the kids are Chicanos. But you can best see for yourself. Let's go inside."

They were greeted by Aguilar Martinez. Manuela stayed in the background, looking almost painfully embarrassed. Anselmo, Mario, and Josefa were in their early twenties, and while they deferred to their father, Jess saw the resentful looks they cast in her direction. She caught Josefa's gaze only once, and the younger woman looked away quickly, but not before Jess had seen the flash of anger and distrust in those dark eyes.

"Miss Bellamy, you have come to my home to speak with me of my son," Aguilar Martinez said in accented English. "What do you need to know?"

"Thank you for seeing me," Jess said, glancing at Manuela with a soft smile of understanding. She deliberately kept her voice calm and unemotional. "I realize how difficult this must be for you. Please understand that my only motive is to find the truth of what happened. I know you are aware that this matter will soon be brought into court. You may be asked to testify, Mr. Martinez. The questions I need to ask of you now are those that would be asked in court. Your son worked for Altra Grow for many years before the accident. Did he ever express to you any fears, any doubts or reservations, about his job?"

"No, señorita, my son was proud to work for Altra Grow. It was very good to him. Señora Morgan even helped him to attend college. That was very important to my son."

"How did she help him?"

"She had a scholarship for those who attended college."

Jess glanced at Michael with surprise. He hadn't told her that. "I understand that Rafael had finished his studies at Hartnell Community College and planned to attend San Jose State University in the fall."

"Yes, he was going to become an accountant," Aguilar said with pride.

"Mr. Martinez, your son's untimely death was terribly tragic, and I offer you my deepest sympathy. I regret having to ask you these questions, but I must ask you about his frame of mind at the time of his death. Understand that Rafael is his own best witness. Do you recall his ever mentioning any reservations about the operation of the company? Policies, attitudes, lack of attention to maintenance of equipment? Anything that might help me to understand how this tragedy might have happened?"

Aguilar thought about the question for a moment, apparently giving careful consideration to his answer. "No, Señorita Bellamy, he never said so to me."

Rafael's older brother, Anselmo, turned to Jessica, his face contorted with sudden anger. "What do you want here? Why are you doing this? You are not here for us, but to prove that the company was not at fault! To the company Rafael is just another dead Mexican!"

"Anselmo!" his father shouted, his dark eyes glaring at his son. He switched to Spanish, obviously berating his son for his rudeness, then turned apologetically back to Jessica. "You must forgive my son. He thinks of himself as a Chicano, not understanding that in doing so he brings dishonor upon this family. Chicanos are nothing more than *cholos*—scoundrels who demand rights without having to earn them. They do not understand the meaning of pride."

The room fell silent. Jess noted Aguilar's stiff-necked pride and felt the rage from his sons and daughter. This family was deeply divided. Rising, she thanked Aguilar, glancing covertly at the younger members who were barely concealing their anger, and once again her eyes fell on Josefa, who had remained silent, her eyes downcast. Then, as Michael spoke to them and they made ready to leave, Josefa's eyes rose to catch Jess's for another brief moment. Those dark eyes were filled with sadness and despair, an anguish that went beyond politics and social injustice. Shaken, Jess left the Martinez house, unable to utter more than a few trite and superficial words of comfort to Rafael's grieving family.

Neither spoke until they drove out of Soledad. Jess thought about what she had seen and heard. As usual she had learned more from their attitudes and reactions than from what they had said. No wonder they were not on the DA's list. They shifted from passive to volatile, and each refuted the other.

They passed a row of large, imposing buildings set back from the highway and surrounded by barbed wire and guard towers. She hadn't noticed it before, but then she had been arguing with Michael. "That's Soledad prison, isn't it?"

"The Soledad Correctional Facility," he corrected grimly. "A kind name for a maximum-security prison."

"Yes, I know," Jess said. "Sirhan Sirhan, Charles Manson, and other notables are housed there."

"It also contributes to making this area a drug capital, and it gives aid and comfort to La Familia."

"La Familia?"

"The Mexican mafia, which is more powerful than I like to admit. One of our foremen was murdered by them a few years ago. They made him eat battery acid."

"My God. Why?" Jess asked, horrified.

"He worked for them until, apparently, he decided to start his own business. He ran prostitutes and drugs out of his house and decided to keep the profits for himself."

"What does the prison have to do with the Mexican mafia?"

"Everything. The flow of drugs into the prison supports La Familia."

"I can't believe that the prison officials allow drugs to come in."

"Allow it?" He glanced at her with a smirk. "Jess, they don't have much choice. Though it's never been proven, there're plenty of rumors to that effect, and some of the guards will admit to it privately. Besides, that's not so hard to understand. That's no country club; it's a maximum-security prison. The inmates are barely manageable because of under-funding and overcrowding. Gang factions are a reality, and there's not much the guards can do about it. Drugs keep the inmates happy. If you were a guard in a crowded, understaffed prison, wouldn't you look the other way if drugs helped to prevent riots? The best the local police can do is try to keep the drugs off the streets, but that effort is ineffective. A couple of years ago the authorities dug up hundreds of linear feet of heroin and cocaine that had been buried outside the walls. There are gangs in the valley communities that periodically raid other towns, warring with each other to win dominance in the drug trade."

"I knew that was happening in large cities, but I thought people in farm communities were simpler and more innocent."

"Hayseeds in bib overalls chewing on wheat stalks? We are part of the real world, Jess, in this case unfortunately."

She considered what he had said, then thought about the Martinez family. Then she opened her notebook, wrote a quick note, tore out the page, and handed it to him. "These are people I want to see. If you can't arrange it tell me and I'll find another way."

After measuring the traffic, Michael glanced at the list. "The growers associations and the union? I can do that." He turned his head to regard her keenly. "What do you hope to find?"

Jess remembered Josefa's look of anger and desperation and shrugged it off, along with Michael's question. "I'm just pursuing all avenues, Mr. Rawlings. As I promised I would."

"What were your conclusions about the Martinez family?"

"They are a tragic family with a lot of anger that goes beyond Rafael's death."

Silently folding the note with one hand and tucking it into his pocket, Michael made a sudden decision. He turned the truck, taking an off-ramp. "Where are you going?" Jess gasped.

"Sorry," he said, decelerating as they left the highway. "It just occurred to me that there's something you might want to see. Chalk it up to my instincts."

They drove out into the countryside past neatly planted farms to the foothills, where he pulled off the side of the road and turned off the ignition. "Come on, I want to show you something," he said, getting out of the truck.

She followed him to a knoll overlooking a dry riverbed. She glanced around, noting the dense brush along the riverbank, the stillness of the early evening, the warble of a dove. "It's lovely, Michael. What did you want to show me?"

"There," he said, pointing to several depressions in the bank. "Come on." He took her hand and led her down the embankment. As they grew closer, she could see that the depressions were actually entrances to small caves. There was litter strewn around—cans, bottles, evidence of campfires, and even disposable diapers. She noticed then that the cave floors were lined with cardboard from packing boxes. She glanced at Michael with horror. "My God, people lived here."

"Farm workers lived here," he corrected. "This was the housing promised to them by the labor contractors who bought them from coyotes—men who charge fat fees to bring illegals into the States. Workers lived here with their families, using bushes for bathrooms and campfires for kitchens. Not all labor contractors are unscrupulous, of course, but there are enough who are. And the worst of them are Mexicans, not Anglos."

"Doesn't the border patrol stop this?"

"As much as it can. Sometimes the coyotes actually help by turning in the families they brought here. Then they can charge them again, later on, to reenter the country."

"God, Michael, I've read about this but . . ." She couldn't finish the statement for trying to imagine what it would be like to live in these conditions.

"This contractor was caught," he said, following her horrified gaze, "but there are others. The worst part for these people is that as illegals they don't have any recourse. The amnesty program helped, but for those who were not included this will go on. They'll simply find new angles."

"But an employer must see proper identification now, proof of citizenship or employability," she argued.

"Yeah, sure," he scoffed. "So the honest people will become more honest, and perhaps a few others will join them out of fear of prosecution. It will make things more difficult, but not impossible, for the dishonest ones. Forged identification will cost the coyotes more, but they'll just charge more for their service. And what would you do if you were an employer? You can't question a Social Security card, unless maybe you see the same number twice."

"Has it happened to Altra Grow?"

"Of course, but not too often with labor contractors. There are good ones and we use them. But we'll always have the bad ones with us because there's so much money to be made. Illegals are just part of it. I've had foremen turn in fraudulent time cards for nonexistent workers. I've known foremen who demand sexual favors from the women for the privilege of a day's labor in the fields. They charge the men a portion of their paychecks. Labor contractors will house their people in substandard camps and make them pay rent, of course, or offer something like this as an alternative. And some deal with growers for kickbacks from workers' pay. They control the workers with fear. After all, whom can the illegals go to for help? The amnesty program will protect those who comply with its regulations, but it won't stop the next flood who come up here looking for wages they can't find in Mexico. They're going to keep coming in order to feed their families, even if they have to put up with this shit."

Jess felt sickened. "At least the Martinez family doesn't have to live with this," she said quietly.

"Don't they?" he asked, turning his eyes on her. "Every Hispanic lives with this, just as every black lives with the memory of slavery. Aguilar Martinez's family has been here since 1832, but on his wedding night a motel wouldn't give him a room because he was a Mexican. Mario married last year, and a motel proprietor in Carmel turned on his No Vacancy sign when Mario requested a room. Mario called me and I went over to the motel and took a room with no problem. The owner was cited, but the problem is with attitudes, Jess. Laws won't change that."

She looked up at him, sympathizing with his outrage. "Let's go back to Amanda's. I've seen enough."

Amanda greeted them upon their return and persuaded Michael to stay for dinner, then led them into the library for cocktails. "You two seem to have settled your deferences," she commented with a pleased smile as she settled onto a sofa with a dry martini.

Jessica's eyes shifted to Michael. He was watching for her reaction. "We're trying." She smiled. "After all, Amanda, you threw us together without preamble. If there was some initial distrust, you have to accept the responsibility for it."

"Me?" Amanda said with an innocent expression. "I merely introduced my granddaughter to my general manager."

Jess smirked, gaining her stride. "Save me your innocent looks, Amanda. You knew exactly what you were doing. And it almost backfired on you. I came very close to leaving that night. I don't like being manipulated."

"Oh, Jessica, we're all manipulated from the day we are born. By parents, friends, lovers, and business associates. We do whatever we have to do to encourage others to see our point of view."

"That's a very cynical statement," Jess said.

"No, it's not. Your father was a terrible student, Jess. He simply refused to study. I tried everything—taking away his privileges, punishing him—but nothing worked. Then, in his sophomore year in high school, I promised him a sports car if he earned an A-minus average by the end of his junior year. It worked, and I gave him the car. That was certainly manipulative on my part—it was out-and-out bribery—but it worked. And he benefited."

"You had to bribe him to get good grades?" Jess asked, fascinated.

"He flunked two courses in his sophomore year."

"Which two?" Jess asked.

"Science and math."

"No kidding?"

"It's a fact. His teachers said he would never amount to anything. But then, they didn't have my gift for manipulation, and they didn't believe in him the way that I did. Manipulation isn't a sin, Jess, unless it's used for hurtful reasons. I threw you and Michael together to get my way, but I never would have done it if I'd thought either of you would be hurt by it."

Michael handed Jess a gin and tonic. She looked up and their eyes met. She smiled, then turned back to her grandmother. "Have you ever lost, Amanda?" she asked quietly.

"Many times." If you only knew how often, Amanda thought. But I won't lose this time; I can't.

Jess regarded her grandmother for a moment. "I need some clarification, some history," she said, aware of Michael's interest as he leaned against the bar, just out of her line of vision. "To begin with, what was the Morgan Company's relationship with the Associated Farmers of California?"

Amanda looked nonplussed. "Good Lord, Jessica, what has that to do with anything? You're going back to the thirties!"

I'm going to go back at least that far before this is over, Jess thought. "I wouldn't ask without a reason," she said. "Were you part of that group?"

"Certainly not!" Amanda said indignantly. "My father was running the company then, and he wouldn't have anything to do with those vigilantes."

"The association was formed to resist strikes organized by the Communist party, wasn't it?"

"Yes," Amanda sighed. "For all of the hysteria over the 'red menace' in later years, there was no doubt then or now that those particular strikes were spearheaded by the Communist party. The communists were determined to unionize migratory farm labor."

"From what I read today," Jess said, "there was considerable support for the Associated Farmers, but the Morgan name was conspicuously absent from the reports. That was your father's doing, then. I assume that his position was an unpopular one."

"Yes, very unpopular," Amanda said, settling back into the sofa. "But in business matters, Morgans act; they do not merely react. It's a principle handed down to us by Jeremy Morgan, and it's always stood us in good stead."

Bull's-eye, Jess thought.

"The growers had been fighting to keep unions out of farm labor since before the turn of the century," Michael interjected, "and they had pretty effective methods to do so. By the thirties, almost every county sheriff was allied in some way with farming interests. In some counties, migratory workers were required to register with the sheriff before they could work. The Associated Farmers provided those sheriffs with lists of those workers they considered dangerous radicals or agitators."

"And you only had to be a member of a union to get on that list," Amanda added. "The association broke the back of any attempt to unionize. The worst character was a retired army colonel by the name of Henry Sanborn, the publisher of an anti-communist journal. The association hired Sanborn to coordinate the anti-strike forces. He formed a citizens' army, arming them with shotguns and pick handles. The state's leading law enforcement agencies, including the attorney general's office, gave their approval."

"So the Morgans didn't support the vigilantes," Jess said, leveling her gaze on her grandmother.

"No, we didn't . . ."

Henley came into the room just then. "There is a phone call, madam, from Mr. Iverson. It seems urgent that he speak to either you or Mr. Rawlings."

"I'll take it, Henley," Amanda said, rising to cross to the phone on the desk near the fireplace. She set her drink down and picked up the receiver. "Yes, Paul, what can I do for you?"

"Can I refresh that for you?" Michael asked Jess, glancing at her drink.

"No, I'm fine, thanks," she said. She was watching Amanda's expression, which had grown concerned. Jess wondered what the Morgan Company's CEO was saying.

"How bad is it?" Amanda said sharply. "I see. Thank you,

Paul, for catching it so quickly. . . . I'll be at the office at nine in the morning. Good night, Paul."

She hung up slowly, staring at the phone for a moment before she turned. Jess and Michael were watching her expectantly. "Apparently small blocks of Morgan Company stock have been bought up each day for almost three weeks. Paul caught it quite by accident while he was preparing stock reports for me."

"That doesn't sound ominous," Jess said.

"No, not in itself," Amanda said, "but apparently they were all purchased through the same broker, a company in Dallas."

Michael frowned. "Are you saying they all went to one buyer?"

"We don't know yet."

"How much stock is involved?" he asked grimly.

"Over a hundred and twenty thousand shares."

Michael let out a soft whistle. "Jesus," he murmured.

"What percent is that?" Jess asked. Amanda looked unshaken, but as she had picked up her sherry, Jess noticed that her hand trembled slightly.

"About sixteen percent. But don't worry," Amanda said, turning her gaze to her granddaughter. Her voice was calm, but her eyes were bright with anger. "I might have been talked into making this company public, but I'm not a fool. I made certain that the Morgans retained fifty-seven percent. They'd have to kill me before I'd give up control of the company."

But if the company's CEO was right, someone was trying to take that control, Jess thought.

"Dinner is served, madam."

The calm statement startled them from their thoughts. No one in the room was particularly hungry, but at the moment it was something to do. "Well, then, let's go in to dinner," Amanda said. "Mrs. McNeely has prepared Scampi Blue Grotto, Michael. You wouldn't want to disappoint her by letting your favorite dinner get cold."

Business was not discussed during dinner. Conversation was given to lighter, more pleasant matters, including appreciation of Mrs. McNeely's efforts. The scampi was delicious, but Jess hardly tasted it.

The past week had been a series of revelations, all of which contradicted Jess's preconceived ideas. She had expected to dislike Amanda, but she found herself growing extremely fond of her. And of Michael—she glanced at him and drew her eyes away with some reluctance. The man was no hick, but an educated, bright, dedicated, and—she admitted it—extremely attractive man. Beyond that, nothing had fit since she came to Monterey and it disturbed her. Admittedly, a few days before she insisted that there were no missing pieces, but no longer. Alcott was a piece out of place. Altra Grow's history did not fit with the profile the district attorney presented. And now, the sudden stock purchases.

"I've made a decision," she said suddenly.

Amanda and Michael looked up at her, regarding her with puzzlement. Their expectant expressions caused Jess to laugh softly. She realized then how much emphasis she had put into the statement. "Just a personal decision I've reached. I don't like puzzles that don't fit." That was an understatement, she thought. Since she had arrived her life seemed to be ruled by a jabberwocky, and she was as confused as Alice had been in Wonderland. And now she was about to step through that looking glass. "I'm going to take the case. If you want me, Amanda, I'm now your attorney of record."

CHAPTER 14

Amanda left early the next morning before Jess came down for breakfast. As Henley served her morning coffee, he informed her that Mrs. Morgan had suggested Jess use her office upstairs if she needed a quiet place to work.

"Thank you, Henley, I think I'll do that. I do have some phone calls to make." After a light breakfast she took a mug of coffee upstairs, stopping by her room to collect her briefcase and notes.

She was struck by the loveliness of the room. Amanda's home was exquisite, filled with fine art and antiques, but there was a personal beauty about her grandmother's private sanctuary with its white wainscoting and soft green linen wallpaper. There was a small white sofa with needlepoint throw pillows patterned in English garden flowers, and an armchair upholstered in fabric printed with large blossoms of mauve and yellow on a white background. A wide panoramic window admitted a profusion of light, and in front of the window stood a delicately carved Queen Anne desk.

Jessica sat at the desk and set her coffee mug on a coaster. She pressed her hands on the desk, smoothing them over the rich, polished wood. She felt her grandmother here more than in any other room in the house. She could sense Amanda's private thoughts as she made decisions that would affect her empire. Jess could also feel the more tender moments, with Amanda writing to her family, reaching out to those who had rejected her and caused her pain, but whom she had not forgotten.

She felt more committed than ever to the decision she had made the previous night. Oh, she had surprised them, and the memory brought a small smile. She suspected that it was one of the few times in Amanda Morgan's life when she had been speechless. But they had both recovered quickly. Amanda had been delighted, and there had been a true moment of joy in her eyes. Michael had been more reserved, but he had looked pleased, though she knew that his happiness was for her grandmother. For her there had been a momentary look of gratitude, but with it a measure of wariness and challenge. But she understood. Michael was fiercely protective of Amanda; Jess knew it and accepted it, as long as it didn't interfere with what she had to do.

She picked up the receiver and quickly dialed a number. As it rang, she braced herself.

"Good morning," a feminine voice said. "Reynolds, Armisted, Royce, may I help you?" Jess smiled; it was impossible for Sallye to keep the seductive huskiness from her voice no matter how hard she tried. She was a wonderful receptionist and totally businesslike with clients, except for that voice. Jess suspected, however, that it had brought more than one male client to the firm with his curiosity piqued. Upon arrival, the clients weren't disappointed.

"Hi, Sallye, it's Jess. How are things going up there?"

"Jess! How's the vacation? I read about you in the paper yesterday."

Jess frowned, nonplussed. "The paper?"

"Yes, in June Carter's column. She mentioned you, and that you were visiting Amanda Morgan in Pebble Beach."

"What else did she say?" Jess asked tightly. Oh great, she thought. If the item was picked up by the New York papers her father would know. The last thing she wanted right now was *that* complication.

"Not much. Just that you would probably be attending the ball to support the Monterey Jazz Festival. Will you? I hear that James Stewart and Jack Lemmon will be there."

"I have no plans to attend, Sallye," Jess said dryly. It was the first she had heard about it.

"Have you seen Clint Eastwood yet?"

Jess was mildly surprised that the columnist hadn't reported that they were having a torrid love affair. "No, Sallye, I haven't had the privilege."

"Does your grandmother know him?"

"I wouldn't be surprised." Then her voice became brusque. "Is Aaron in?"

"Yes, do you want to speak to him?"

"Please, Sallye."

Moments later Aaron Reynolds's deep resonant voice came on the line. "Jess, how are you doing down there?" he boomed.

"Apparently dancing each night away."

"So I've read," he said with humor in his voice. "You know, it wouldn't hurt you if you were."

She ignored the comment. "I have a favor to ask, Aaron."

"What's that?"

"I'm not coming back for a while."

There was a long pause; then his voice was guarded. "How long is 'a while'?"

"I don't know yet. I'm going to take Amanda's case."

"You can't be serious!" She could picture his heavy white brows dipping.

"Calm yourself, Mr. Justice. Remember your heart."

"Don't humor me, Jess. I sent for copies of the court filings after you left. There's nothing you can do there."

"Are you questioning my abilities, Aaron?" she asked calmly.

"No, I'm questioning your mental faculties. Look, Jess, I can see how you might become emotionally involved, but you can't help with this case. If I thought that you could do some good down there I would suggest it myself, but you can't."

"Yes, Aaron, I can."

There was another slight pause. "Care to tell me about it?"

Jess glanced around the room, her eyes fixing on a Grandma Moses primitive. "Nothing fits, Aaron, and there are contradictions that I can't ignore. Everything's neatly pointing to disaster, at least for Amanda. Too neatly. I can't leave until I sort this out."

"We need you here, you know." It was said with a resigned sigh, and Jess smiled.

"I know, but I think you can muddle through without me for a while. Consider it five years' worth of vacation time."

"I was afraid you'd say that. That's hitting below the belt."

"That's not all," she added. She gripped the receiver with determination. "I need Tom down here."

There was a heavy sigh at the other end of the line. "Now, why doesn't that surprise me? I suppose you expect the firm to pay for all of this."

"Whatever you think best," she said sweetly. "I had planned to assume my own costs, but if you are offering—"

"Don't push it," he said gruffly. "All right, Tom's yours. It's probably just as well; he's been trying to seduce half the girls in the office anyway. One thing I don't need with a partner gone is a randy associate running loose. You can deal with him. Anything else?"

"Not that I can think of at the moment, but I'll let you know if there is."

"I'm sure you will. Okay, then, take the time you need, and you've got Tom. I'm not happy about this, understand. We need you here, but as you said, we'll muddle through somehow. Jess, keep in touch."

"Thanks, Aaron," she said softly, hearing the concern in his voice. "Don't worry. I think I'm going to win this one."

"I hope you do, Jess. But remember something: Where emotions are involved you can't be objective. The rules change. I don't want you hurt."

She hung up, taking his last words to heart. It was a warning she had repeated to herself often since the day she had arrived. She dialed another number and waited. In spite of the fact that she had initiated the call, it jarred her when she heard his voice.

"Jess, how are you doing? Are you back?"

"No, Rick, I'm still in Monterey."

"How are things going?" There was disappointment in his voice, which surprised her.

"I'm working on a case and I need your help." She winced even as she said it. She hadn't meant for it to sound so cold.

It was a moment before he answered. "This has to do with the reason your grandmother needed you?"

"Yes," she said, wondering if he had read the column in the newspaper. She decided to hit the possibility head-on. "Don't believe everything you read, Rick. I've been working since I got here. Amanda's in trouble, and I think I can help her. At least I hope so."

He seemed to consider it for a moment, and his voice became less strained. "Okay, what can I do?"

She let her breath out with relief. "You're a good friend,

Rick. I need you to check on something for me. It involves stock in the Morgan Land and Development Company. There has been steady purchase of stock through a brokerage in Dallas. I need everything and anything you can find out about it."

"Do you suspect a takeover?"

"Possibly. But then, it might be nothing."

"How soon do you need to know?"

"Yesterday."

"I'll do my best. Give me a number where I can reach you."

She gave him the number and after a brief exchange of pleasantries, she hung up. She leaned back in the chair, staring at the phone. It was unsettling to realize that Rick was a better friend than she had realized. He had always seemed shallow, and now she wondered if she'd created his character out of her own point of view. She had expected coldness from him, even rejection. But he had offered his help without hesitation. How many other things was she wrong about? she wondered. Leaning her head back, she closed her eyes and rubbed the back of her neck against a knot of tension.

Opening her eyes, she glanced around the room, trying to decide on her next move. Instead, her attention was drawn to a low cabinet to her left, its top covered with small sculptures in porcelain, stone, marble, and silver, reflecting Amanda's fondness for tropical birds. The artworks were interspersed with photos of every size in brass frames. Rising, Jess stepped around the desk and studied them, noting pictures of her grandmother's life. There were a few photographs of Amanda with various governors, senators, and three presidents, one in the White House rose garden. The rest were of family, and those were the ones Jess paused to study. There were many pictures of Amanda and her son, captured moments of him as a baby, a toddler, and as an awkward, gangly boy. Not surprisingly, they ceased in her father's teen years. And there were pictures of Nicky Alger, some with Amanda in candid poses with forest and sea at their back, and others taken in more formal settings. Seeing their obvious happiness, Jess smiled. And then, suddenly, the hair tingled at the back of her neck and the smile disappeared. Her eyes darted back, sweeping over the collection of photographs, and her stomach tightened. There were no pictures of her grandfather. In all of

Amanda's precious collection, there was not one single picture of Jack Bellamy. Amanda's first husband was strangely and blatantly absent, as if he had never existed.

The jarring sound of the phone startled her out of her thoughts. She looked at it doubtfully, wondering if she should answer it when it suddenly stopped and she knew that Henley had answered it from somewhere in the house. Shaken, she sat down heavily on the sofa, her eyes now moving slowly over the pictures. It would have been reasonable for Amanda to remove pictures of her first husband after her marriage to Nicholas Alger, she reasoned. But Alger had been dead for fourteen years. Why hadn't Amanda brought out remembrances of her first husband since then? At the very least, pictures of Jack Bellamy with his son. Family pictures. Her thoughts turned back to the brief reference to Jack Bellamy in the newspaper announcement of Amanda's marriage to Nicky Alger. Damn, she thought, why hadn't she pursued that? It hadn't even occurred to her to search for files on her grandfather. Her head turned suddenly to the desk as the phone beeped. After a pause, it beeped again. Realizing that Henley must be paging her, she went to the desk and picked up the receiver. "Yes?"

"Miss Bellamy, there's a phone call for you on line two."

"Thank you, Henley." She pushed the lighted button on the phone. "Hello?"

"Jess, it's Michael."

She felt her breath catch at the sound of his voice, and she frowned, pushing the reaction aside. "Hello, Michael. What can I do for you?"

"Amanda just called me. We've been invited to a party at Cypress Point tonight."

We? Jess's frown deepened with puzzlement. "Where is Amanda?"

"She's still with Paul Iverson. Cocktails are at eight o'clock, I'll pick you up at seven forty-five. It's formal. Did you bring anything to wear?"

"No, nothing that dressy," she admitted. She was struck by a moment of irritation—she hadn't come here to attend formal affairs—but then she bit back her annoyance, remembering the polo match. If she had learned anything, it was that Amanda did nothing without a purpose. Aaron was right, she thought, she was becoming so emotionally involved that she was overlooking the obvious. "Can you suggest some stores? I need to do some shopping."

"Go into the village. There's Saks and I. Magnin, and a lot of boutiques. You should find something."

"The village?"

"Carmel. I'll see you at seven forty-five."

She stared at the phone after they had hung up. He hadn't been rude, exactly, just a bit abrupt. But then, why shouldn't he be? He had been ordered by his employer to take her to a party, regardless of the inconvenience in his life. She wondered, if only for a moment, why the realization brought a vague feeling of disappointment.

Jess came down the stairs at precisely seven forty. She hadn't seen Amanda since her return and she was surprised to find her in the library, dressed for the evening's event. Her grandmother looked lovely, Jess thought, entering the room. She was gowned in a soft chiffon of pale blue with diamonds glittering at her neck and ears.

"Amanda, I didn't know you were back," Jess said as she came into the room.

Amanda turned and smiled warmly, an expression that reached to her eyes. "Jessica, you look perfectly lovely."

Jess was pleased with the dress she had found at Saks, a long black silk sheath by Oscar de la Renta with long fitted sleeves. The bias-cut gown, with its heavy embroidery of silver and black bugle beads, clung to her body. Amanda's knowing eyes dropped over her and she smiled. "Jessica, there won't be a man present tonight who will be able to take his eyes off you."

"Thank you, Amanda, you flatter me."

"I'm not given to flattery, dear."

Henley entered the room just then. "Robert has brought the car around, madam."

"Thank you, Henley," Amanda said, picking up a beaded evening bag. "I'm certain that Michael will be along shortly, Jessica. I'll see you at the club."

"You're not going with us?" Jess asked.

"No, I think it best that I take my car. I doubt that I'll stay long. These events tire me, and I wouldn't want to spoil your evening."

Before Jess could protest, she was gone. Jess knew she was being manipulated again, but she didn't know why.

"Is it something I can help you with?"

She started at the sound of Michael's voice and looked up to find him standing in the doorway. As she stared at him, her emotions oscillated between confusion and a very undeniable attraction. It was the first time she had seen him in anything but jeans. Now he stood there in an exquisitely cut tuxedo, and from the fit it was obviously not something he had rented for the evening. The starched white shirt was stark against his tan, accentuating his dark eyes. He was, without question, a very handsome man.

"Help me? How?" she asked, trying to cover her surprise.

He stepped into the room, his mouth slipping into that damnable boyish grin. "You looked upset when I came in. Anything wrong?"

"No, nothing at all," she said quickly. "I just remembered something I forgot to do today. It's not important."

The look he gave her was unreadable, but she suspected he knew that she had lied. Then his eyes dropped over her and his expression warmed with appreciation. "Jess, you look absolutely beautiful." It was said simply, with genuine feeling, and it touched an unexpected soft spot inside her. She felt herself relax, pleased by the comment, but before she could respond, he held out his hand. "Shall we go?"

It was an easy gesture and she found herself placing her hand in his. This man, she realized, was supremely sure of himself and confident about who he was.

As they left the house, Jessica's eyes widened with surprise. She glanced up at Michael, but he seemed unaware of her intent regard as he led her down the steps to his car. He opened the door to the Porsche 911 Carrera and helped her in before shutting the door with a solid, reassuring sound. As he walked around to the driver's side, she watched him through the windshield. She hadn't thought about it until this moment, but she had expected to be driven to the party in his pickup. It wouldn't have mattered, but as he got into the car she wondered what other surprises were in store for her this evening.

The very private and exclusive Cypress Point Club in Del Monte Forest was the exclusive adytum of what some would consider the A-list of society. As Jess followed Michael through the room, she recognized many of those present as men and women who did business with her father, or who at one time or another had been guests of Merryhaven. Some of the guests were members of the country's oldest families, others were latter-day robber barons, and the guest list included an impressive sprinkling of Fortune 500 chairmen, presidents and CEOs.

As she and Michael circulated she greeted those she knew. They inquired politely about her father and offered their regards, and a few mentioned Justice Reynolds. It was small talk at first, but then the conversation began to shift subtly. Though it was gracefully done, a good deal of effort was made to introduce her to heads of large agribusiness companies. No one mentioned the Martinez case, but there was a good deal of discussion about shared business problems.

Jess's mind tuned out the dialogue. She knew when she was being lobbied. And now she understood Amanda's motives. If these men convinced her of the integrity and importance of large agribusiness companies, she could represent Altra Grow more successfully in court. And Amanda had chosen well; they were very likable men.

"Jessica, I see you've met everyone." Amanda appeared at her side, smiling brightly at her granddaughter. "I hope you're enjoying yourself?"

Behind the innocent smile, Amanda's eyes glittered, and Jess received the message. Returning the smile, she leveled her gaze on her grandmother. "Very much. Mr. Preston has been telling me about problems with Congress over the new tax bill. I never realized there were so many difficulties facing farmers today."

"I'm afraid we've bored you," said Mr. Preston, who owned a large agribusiness in southern California.

"Oh, not at all," Jess assured him. "I've found it quite fascinating."

"Well, the more farms that go under, the more the consumer will lose without the competition," Preston added. Then his expression changed and he turned to Amanda. "Speaking of losing, Amanda, you snatched Austin Central Bank right out from under me."

"Success is to the fleet of foot, Preston," Amanda said sweetly.

"You knew I was already bidding on it," Preston said.

"Oh, come now, don't put on that suffering act with us," said Louis Delgato, another large grower. "You lost it fair and square, and you know it. Besides, you should have moved faster when Amanda became interested. You know she's always been a maverick."

"Indeed she has." Preston grinned. "And she gets away with it. I think it's because we've always underestimated her—a product of our male chauvinism, I suppose. Never could take out the gloves with you, Amanda. But then, I've always comforted myself that I was in good company. You're the only one I ever knew who could go nose to nose with William Randolph Hearst and still be invited to San Simeon. How did you do that?"

William Randolph Hearst? Jess stared at her grandmother with interest.

"Oh, Preston, he never thought I was important enough to bother being mad at me." Amanda smiled.

"He never let go of a grudge in his life," Delgato countered, "except with you and Nicky, apparently. When Hearst dropped FDR, everyone was supposed to follow suit."

"That's the one time Hearst showed some sense," Preston interjected.

Amanda shrugged. "Perhaps he respected my loyalty."

Delgato laughed shortly. "You do realize, of course, that you're probably the only one in this room who voted for FDR."

"I'm probably the only one in this room who is old enough to have voted for FDR," she countered.

"Tell me, Amanda," Delgato said, leaning forward, "are you actually a Democrat? Was it just that damned Roosevelt you admired, or was it the fact that Nicky worked on his first presidential campaign?"

"Really, Lou, you sound more like an old woman than I do, with your propensity for gossip. And with that, now that I know my granddaughter is in good hands, there are others I should see. Have a good time, dear," she added, patting Jess on the arm. "Don't let these fools bore you to death."

Jess forced a smile, her eyes following her grandmother as

Amanda left the group. As she had listened a warm rush of heat spread over her, shock gathering into a hard knot in her stomach. Then she felt Michael's hand at her waist, his voice speaking over her turmoil. "If you will forgive us, there are some others Jess needs to meet." She let Michael lead her away, vaguely aware of the awkwardness caused by their abrupt departure. He led her to a quiet spot in a corner of the room. "Are you all right?" he asked gently.

"Of course, why wouldn't I be?" she asked, forcing a smile.

"You looked as if you'd been poleaxed. What happened?"

She looked up at him, genuinely touched by his astuteness and concern. But she had no intention of discussing her feelings with him. "Could we get out of here?" she asked suddenly.

"Of course." He didn't ask any more questions, simply responding to her need as he ushered her from the room, leaving her by the door for a moment as he collected her wrap. As soon as he dropped the shawl over her shoulders, they left the club. The cool night air helped to clear her thoughts as they walked to Michael's car and she was able to approach what she had heard less emotionally. More puzzle pieces falling willy nilly into place and beginning to form a hazy picture.

Amanda had said she had not seen Nicky again after that time in Paris. She had allowed Jess to assume that they had not met again until their later years. Was it possible that Jess had misunderstood? Yet, Amanda had been with Nicky Alger on Roosevelt's first campaign. That would have been in 1932. How involved had she been with him? There were no pictures of Jack. No pictures.

Oh, damn.

"Jess, what's the matter?"

She was unaware that they had gotten into the car or that she'd spoken out loud. He looked concerned, but what could she say to him? That Amanda could have had an affair with Nicky Alger years before her husband's death?

"Can we go somewhere?" she asked suddenly. "How about the Hog's Breath?"

"The Hog's Breath?" he repeated. Then he grinned. "Don't tell me you want to meet Clint Eastwood."

"Not really." She shrugged. "I know he owns the place, but it's the only bar I know of around here."

He started the engine; it roared to life and he backed out of the parking space. "Jess, the Hog's Breath is too crowded. Everyone's hoping to run into Eastwood."

They had pulled out on the road and she glanced at him with a frown. "I mentioned the Hog's Breath because it's the only place I know of around here. Celebrities do not impress me," she added stiffly.

"Okay, I believe you," he said. She didn't miss the amusement in his voice. They drove in silence along the winding roads toward the gate, and she glanced at him once, wondering if he knew Eastwood. "Where *are* we going?"

"To the Hog's Breath, Miss Bellamy."

They drove into Carmel and parked the car on a side street, then walked up the steep climb to the main part of the village. They turned on Fifth, and Michael led her down a long fenced walkway that opened abruptly on a small tree-filled terraced courtyard. The place was packed with people. The outdoor tables, warmed by heat lamps against the cool night air, were completely filled, as was the pub to their right and the small restaurant to their left. Through the windows she could see people elbow to elbow. The restaurant had a second story, but those windows were dark.

"What's up there?" she asked.

"Offices. And no one's home," he said. "Wait here for a moment."

He returned a few moments later. Within five minutes they were shown to a table on a small upper terrace among the trees. "Did you have someone murdered?" she asked, glancing about as the maître d' left.

"Yes, a middle-aged couple from Nebraska. What would you like to drink?" he added as the waiter appeared.

"White wine."

He gave the order and when the waiter had left she leaned toward Michael. "You know him, don't you?"

"Who?"

"Don't play games with me, Rawlings. Eastwood. You know him. That's how we got a table so fast."

"You're having delusions, Bellamy. Even if I did know him, it wouldn't help. They don't play favorites here. If they did that, the tourists would riot. We just hit it lucky."

"Bull. How well do you know him?"

"*Him*? Do you mean God or Clint Eastwood? I'm surprised at you, Jess. You grew up with the Four Hundred and spent your summers with potentates, yet you're drooling over the prospect of meeting a movie star."

"I'm not drooling."

"Yes, you are. He belches occasionally you know, just like the rest of us."

"Aha! You do know him!"

He sighed, leaning back in his chair as the waiter brought their drinks. "Enough, okay?" he said when they were alone. "If you can't love me for my mind—or better yet, my body—at least give me the courtesy of not wanting me only because you think I know Clint."

"Okay," she laughed. "I give up." She sipped her wine. The past few moments of banter had helped her relax, but she still didn't believe him. "Tell me something about yourself, Rawlings."

His gaze shifted to her with caution. "I thought we settled that."

"No, tell me something about yourself. Something personal."

"Personal? Well, I like to sail and ski, and sometimes, when Amanda absolutely insists, I've been known to play golf."

"That's not what I meant. Why aren't you married? Do you like living alone?"

"Do you?" he countered, leaning forward on the table as he turned his glass.

"You first."

"I was married once," he shrugged. "For two years. It ended badly."

"I'm sorry. That was rude of me."

"No, it's all right. It's a fact. I had known Noreen since high school. We met again the summer before I entered graduate school. She came home from USC pregnant. And I married her."

"Just like that, you married her," she said. Pregnant, with another man's child, she added silently. The realization made her somber and she studied him intently. This man was always surprising her. "You must have loved her very much."

He glanced over the boisterous, happy crowd. "No, actually I didn't. I had once, years before, but not when we were married. It was stupid, really. I guess I saw myself as some sort of knight in shining armor. But that belongs in novels. In the real world the armor rusts and gets tacky."

"What happened?"

"She saw me for what I was," he shrugged. "Blemishes, warts, and all, certainly not her hero. Noreen was—from a different world. At first the marriage seemed to work, but eventually she couldn't deal with what I planned for my future. Life at that time was boring—I was studying and working. And then she saw the life ahead of her. Noreen couldn't see herself as a farmer's wife."

Noreen sounded like a bitch. And she should know about bitchiness, Jess thought. "Where is she now?"

"In Virginia, I think. She remarried. A lawyer."

"Oh. I hope you don't hold that against me."

"No. My armor may have tarnished during those years, but Noreen had long since lost her princess status. She wasn't taken away from me; I offered her up. Gladly."

"The mistakes we commit in our youth," Jess said, smiling at the waiter as he brought another round of drinks. "They're supposed to be character-building, but they almost destroy us."

"Who was he?" Michael asked quietly.

She smiled ruefully, sipping from her glass. "Confessions, huh? Okay, I'll take my turn. Why not? At least you can claim nobility, Michael, tarnished or not. My claim was lust. Curtis Caldwell, my math professor. His politics were to the left, but his passions were centered in bed, with anything warm and willing. It's really quite trite and ugly. I gave up my virginity along with my political innocence. Maybe that's why I'm a registered Republican today. The man was pond scum, and I believed in him."

"And you're still bitter."

"Aren't you?"

"No. You have to let go, Jess."

She was feeling the effects of the white wine, but she didn't care. For the first time in years she wanted to let go. She wanted to forget the ugly thoughts she'd had about her grandmother, her grandfather, and Amanda's lover. About her father and her structured, well-organized, controlled life. "Don't patronize me, Michael. You must have felt like crud when your wife left you."

"Yes, I did. I thought I had failed. It took a long time to accept that it was just a mistake. But eventually I forgave myself."

"Noble sentiments. You are a knight, Michael. But it's different for women. It's still a man's world. There are still women who live for their men, kowtowing to their whims, suppressing their own needs no matter how painful that is. My mother was a talented artist, but she gave it all up, everything, because my father wanted a full-time hostess who would enhance his vision of himself."

His eyes narrowed as she drained the wine and ordered another. "Maybe you're being too hard on her, Jess."

"What do you know about it?"

"I don't, only what you tell me. But she was your mother, and I think I've learned a little about you. Maybe she chose her way of life willingly. Perhaps it wasn't a sacrifice."

"She was sad," Jess said, shaking her head. "Very sad."

"But you don't know why." He shrugged a shoulder at the puzzled look she gave him. "It's a mistake to think we know the deepest motives of anyone else, even someone we're close to. You can't really know what your mother thought or what she felt. You're like the squirrel that found itself in a badger's hole."

"The what?"

"A squirrel was ambling along one day, minding its own business. Suddenly it came across a hole in the ground. It was a great hole. Neat, wide, and definitely inviting. It would have taken that squirrel a lifetime to dig that hole and he couldn't resist it. He went down into the hole and explored. There were mazes of runs and deep burrows. It blew the squirrel's mind. He had found Utopia. Then he heard something from above. Quickly he found a place to hide, a small hidey-hole. And he listened as another creature drew near. It seemed to pass; then it paused, drawing back. Suddenly he was facing a large, terrifying badger. The badger glared, showing its teeth, hissing threateningly. 'How dare you invade my burrow?' it said. 'You're dead meat, squirrel.' 'I meant no harm,' the squirrel said. 'Then why are you here in my burrow?' the badger demanded. The squirrel shrugged. 'Well,' he said, 'everyone has to be somewhere.'"

She tried to focus and frowned. "I don't understand the punch line."

"It's not very deep, Jess. We're where we are because of our choices, good, bad, or indifferent. You can't live your mother's life, no matter how hard you try. And you can't see life from her point of view. You have to live for yourself." He watched her as she tried to work with that, and smiled at the confusion he saw in her expression. "Come on, Jess," he said, rising to step around the table. "Let me take you home."

"That squirrel was a fool," she said, grabbing her shawl off the back of the chair as he took her arm. "He should have stayed where he belonged."

"Really?" Michael said, dropping the shawl around her shoulders. "Jess, what ever happened, for a moment he knew Utopia."

CHAPTER 15

Amanda sat alone in the dark. Filtered moonlight from the tall windows behind her cast the room in muted grays and black shadows. She had come up to her office upon returning from Cypress Point a half-hour before. Her memories were here in the memorabilia scattered about, near but less acute than in the bedroom she had shared with Nicky. She could think here; she could face the memories in the dark, without the stark reality of the pictures of her life with him. Memories alone were softer.

Jessica knew. In those few seconds before Jessica disguised her reaction to Delgato's comments, Amanda had seen it, the unmasked shock, the beginning of the end of everything. Amanda doubted that Jess understood what she had heard, not the sum total of it. But it was only a matter of time. Michael had seen it, too. They had left immediately after, and wherever they were now—probably in a small, quiet bar somewhere—he would try to mend the damage. She knew that, just as she knew it was far, far too late.

"Oh, Nicky," she murmured. "We loved each other so much. How could such great love cause so much pain? I'm an old woman and you've left me to take care of this." I'm a selfish old woman, she added silently. I should have left well enough alone. But I just wanted to see her, to know her. She had destroyed her son's feeling for her, and now she would lose her granddaughter as well.

Her life had begun again, early in 1932 in the lobby of the Waldorf-Astoria Hotel. Nicholas Alger had stepped back into her life. He had taken her to her hotel, and he had stayed. They talked most of the night, the misunderstandings in Paris were faced, dealt with, and set aside. And she listened with rapt attention as he told her of his deep belief in Roosevelt.

He questioned her on everything that had happened in her life since she had left him in Paris. She told him about Jack, holding nothing back, not the fact of her troubled marriage or her part in it. Just before dawn he made love to her, awakening feelings in her she had never known before, and she experienced her first orgasm. She cried in his arms, overwhelmed by what he had given her. And she grieved for Jack and the unhappiness of their life.

She kept the hotel suite for the sake of appearances, but they left the hotel early the next morning and traveled to Nicky's isolated country home in upstate New York. They remained there for a glorious week, and then Nicky put her on a train to California. As she traversed the countryside, Amanda had time to consider every aspect of her life. She felt strong, filled with courage, every empty part of her filled with Nicky. They had parted with the bittersweet certainty that somehow they would be together again. But the doubts crept in as the train moved through Kansas, and acceptance as it pulled out of Colorado. She knew that she might never see Nicky again, but she didn't regret what had happened. How could a barren life reject a moment of feeling?

They had agreed not to write; that would have been impossible. But she heard from him through other sources as she began to support Roosevelt. Amanda was not a romantic fool; her commitment to FDR was not based on her affair with Nicky. She believed in FDR and his principles, and she threw herself into his campaign with a vengeance. The fact caused horror among her associates, but no one was more shocked than her husband. It became another serious wedge between them. A wedge that widened, then exploded, a few months after her return from New York.

They had just returned home from a party given for her by Samuel Morse at his large rustic lodge in Pebble Beach.

It had been a wonderful party and she had enjoyed herself more than she had in a long time. Perhaps Nicky had mellowed her, she thought with a smile. Memories of her week with him were with her constantly. It was good seeing her friends again. In fact, the evening would have been perfect except that Jack was angry. It was a frequent condition, and tonight Amanda had decided to ignore it. Normally she would have tried to appease him; it usually took little more than relaying a compliment about him from someone, or suggesting that they give a party in turn, something to fire his imagination. Jack was the consummate host, at his best when he could claim responsibility for a successful event that would have people talking for weeks.

Lulled by pleasant thoughts, as they got ready for bed in adjoining dressing rooms, Amanda was incautious. Jack's voice came through the open doorway, and she tried to ignore his enthusiasm. It was customary for them to discuss the evening's events as they prepared for bed, but tonight she wished she could simply close the door, leaving her to her own thoughts.

He was gossiping about someone and she tried to shut out what he was saying. That was her first mistake. When she failed to give the appropriate response, there was silence. Then he came to the doorway. He stood there watching her silently as she slipped into her nightgown. "What's the matter with you, Amanda?"

She should have recognized the danger in the softness of his voice.

"There's nothing the matter with me," she said irritably, wishing he'd go away. "I'm tired. I just want to go to bed."

God, she thought wearily, why didn't he just go to bed? The unpleasant thought flashed that he might follow her into her bedroom and that would mean . . . Not tonight, she thought, not ever again if she could have her way. "It was a wonderful party. I'll write a note to Sam in the morning."

"If you found it so wonderful, why did we have to leave so early?" he asked pettily.

"Jack, I told you. I'm tired. Midweek is not the best time for a party. I wish Sam had waited until the weekend. I have meetings tomorrow."

"Oh, yes, your precious meetings. Busy Amanda Bellamy. Or are they meetings for that damned Democrat? You spend too much time on that, Amanda. If you have to be a Democrat, why can't you support Garner? Hearst is backing him, after all."

Amanda paused as she hung her sable coat in the closet. She turned to stare at her husband with disgust. "And Hearst is an acceptable Democrat? Why, Jack? What makes him different?" The question was perverse. She knew perfectly well that when Jack sensed money and power he was willing to grovel for acceptance. Seeing the confusion on her husband's face, she relented, pushing aside her disgust as she tried to accept his weaknesses. "Never mind, Jack. You're right, Hearst is important. And so are Garner and his four hundred delegates to the convention. As a matter of fact, we've been invited to San Simeon next month."

Jack's eyes widened, and he stepped into the dressing room, relinquishing his grip on the door frame. His expression worked with emotion, which Amanda could read all too clearly. He was infused with excitement at the prospect of actually being invited into the inner sanctum of Hearst's famous bastion, but he was also fearful of what his wife might do. The fear won out. "Why, Amanda?" he asked. "Hearst has invited you to San Simeon several times over the years. Why have you accepted now?"

Oh, Jack, you simpleton, she thought. You know perfectly well why, though you don't want to accept it. She shrugged off the question. "I'm curious. I decided I'd like to see that ostentatious castle he's built."

But Jack wasn't as simple as she thought. Not when his senses were primed for self-preservation. "Don't humor me, Amanda. You're planning to lobby Hearst for Garner's delegates."

She sighed. "What if I am? Of what possible interest could it be to you?"

"Why, Amanda, my dear, how callous you've become." His expression took on a look of bored indifference that no longer fooled her. "You know I never interfere in your business. My interest begins only when your business affects my life."

His voice hardened on the last words, and she looked up at him with puzzlement. "How can my association with Hearst affect you, Jack?"

"Amanda, have you forgotten that part of my inheritance is stock in newspapers and radio? Hearst has been known to cause the demise of competitors who disagree with him."

"That's your problem, Jack, not mine," she said, turning toward her bedroom.

He caught her at the door, spinning her back, his face red

with anger. "It damn well is your problem! You're a fool if you think I'm going to allow you to jeopardize what's mine!"

"Jack, you're hurting me," she gasped, clawing at his hand where it gripped her arm.

"I mean it, Amanda, you're going to stay away from Hearst with your fool ideas. Do you hear me?" He released her sharply, shoving her hard against the wall. As he turned to leave, she groaned. He turned back just in time to see her rush into the bathroom with her hand clamped over her mouth.

He stood in the bathroom doorway, watching her as she bent over the toilet and retched. As she continued to be sick, he frowned, puzzled and disturbed by her violent reaction. While he regretted what he had done, abhorring physical violence, he knew he hadn't really hurt her. "Amanda, I'm sorry," he said lamely, leaning against the door frame. God, wasn't she ever going to stop? He shifted his weight uncomfortably, at a loss for what to do.

Why had she taunted him like that? Dammit, she was always poking at him, mocking him. His father had handled such situations physically, leaving Jack's mother with bruises as evidence of his control. During his college years Jack had hit a woman twice, and he had sworn to himself after the second time that he would never do it again. He had discovered that he could charm people into doing what he wanted. Unlike his father's crude methods, he found that his drew rather than repulsed people.

Now, thinking about what had just happened, Jack sensed the power his father had felt. The total control. With all of the success he had found with his own methods, Jack had to admit that he had never been able to control Amanda. He let out his breath slowly. "Do you want me to call a doctor?"

She sat back on the floor, drawing her hand over her mouth. "No, I don't need a doctor," she murmured. Color had left her face, and dark circles had appeared under her eyes.

"God, Amanda, you look ghastly."

She threw him a disparaging look and pulled herself up to the sink. Bending over, she turned on the faucet, cupping handfuls of water into her mouth and over her face. Grabbing a towel, she dried herself, then regarded him thoughtfully. "I think we better talk, Jack." She walked past him and into her bedroom.

He followed her, glancing around the room. It struck him that he hadn't been in this room for almost a year. Not that it mattered; she had never been particularly good in bed anyway. Her guilt over that left him free to his own amusements, which were far preferable to admittance to the ice lady's bed.

She sat down on the edge of the bed, clutching the towel. His eyes dropped over her, and he felt a moment's regret for their situation. She was beautiful, he thought. Small, slender, beautifully shaped, her body distinctly outlined in the mauve silk robe. Her soft honey-blond hair was tousled about her face, giving the appearance of one who had just risen from sleep—or from a night of passionate lovemaking. He felt his groin tighten unexpectedly. She could still do this to him, he thought irritably.

"Jack, are you content with our arrangement?"

The question was the last thing he had expected. By mutual, unspoken agreement, it was the one question they had studiously avoided. He detested serious confrontations, and it appeared that Amanda had exactly that in mind. "What arrangement is that?" he asked, the bored indifference entering his voice again.

"Don't do that, Jack. This is important."

He regarded her for a moment. "Amanda, we're not going to become dramatic, are we? I'm sorry I shoved you, but it is hardly worthy of a scene from *Macbeth.*"

Amanda drew a steadying breath. She knew this wouldn't be easy. "That's not what I want to talk about. I want you to answer me: Are you content with our arrangement?" She saw the stubborn expression that meant he had no intention of entering a discussion he felt was unnecessary. "All right. I'll say it. There is very little between us, Jack, except for appearances. You are devastatingly personable, an exceptional host and guest. You are a social creature, Jack, and you excel at it. We complement each other in many ways—outside this bedroom—but there is nothing personal between us anymore. Would you say that I've summed it up?"

It took him a moment, but he finally gave in to a shrug. "I think that about says it, yes."

"Is it enough for you?"

Surprisingly, her honest, blunt assessment of their relationship came as a relief to Jack. It was finally said, and she had stated it without unpleasant emotion. He actually felt himself warming to the conversation. And then it struck him why he was contented with their relationship: Amanda was like a male friend. He almost laughed out loud, realizing that he had found himself in the perfect marriage. She was a woman he could admire, even respect. They could share a friendship without the responsibilities that usually came with a woman's demands. There was only one thing he wanted from a marriage, after all, though they had never discussed it. He glanced at her, his eyes narrowing as he wondered if this could be the moment.

"Yes, I am quite content, Amanda. Since you ask, I confess that I find it wonderfully suitable." He smiled, allowing the warmth he felt to show. "In fact, now that I think about it, you are the perfect wife for me. I do have needs, of course, and some expectations from our marriage. I don't have your wealth, after all. I can't risk what I have."

Oh, she did know that, a fact that no one else suspected—that Jack Bellamy was terrified of poverty. Moreover, he was appalled by the prospect of being totally dependent on her. He enjoyed the trappings her wealth brought him, the material possessions and the powerful friends, but his ability to support himself was crucial to him.

"It's all right, Jack," she said quietly. "I won't put you at risk, I promise you."

He felt a happy rush at her calmly given statement. He knew he had been forgiven and, more importantly, that his life was secure once again. It made him bold, and he toyed with an idea. A few moments before, it would have seemed impossible, but now perhaps the moment had come. Aside from the promise she had just given to him, the most important thing in the world, a guarded dream that he had almost despaired of ever fulfilling, was the prospect of a child. A son, immortality, an heir. His head spun with the possibility that she would agree to give him this one vitally important thing.

"There is something else we must discuss," she said. Her voice caught with emotion, and her eyes strayed around the room. But he didn't notice; he was too filled with possibilities.

"Fine, there's something I would like to discuss with you." His eyes moved over her again, warming to the sight of her delicious body. He felt himself stir. This time he would arouse her, he was certain of it. "I think this is a new beginning for us, Amanda."

She frowned, wondering what he meant. Wasn't he listening? "Jack, I have something very serious to discuss with you. You must listen to me."

"I'm listening, my dear. Tell me—I am your friend, you know. Perhaps that's even more important, after all, than being merely a husband."

"I'm glad you feel that way," she said with a relieved sigh. She rose from the bed and began to pace slowly, measuring her words and what she could say to him. "When I was young, and terribly innocent, I thought marriage would be"—she turned to him with a hesitant smile—"well, like a storybook, I guess. We aren't particularly well suited, Jack, but I do think we've both tried to make the best of a bad situation."

"I agree," he said. He could be generous; she deserved that. She smiled, though it struck him that there was a certain nervousness in her expression that was quite uncharacteristic. He began to listen, wondering what she was going to say.

"I hope we can continue as well as we have in the past. We live separate lives, but the arrangement gives us both what we need. I will continue to do my part, Jack. But there is something—a situation. I'll need your support."

Her words stunned him. She was actually asking for his help? My God, what a night, he thought. He felt powerful and, with it, magnanimous. Besides, one favor deserved another. "What is it, Amanda? How can I help?"

"With understanding," she said, turning to face him. Suddenly she became terribly calm. "Jack . . . I'm going to have a baby."

He stared at her. He had heard her, but the words tumbled crazily. Then they hit him square in the gut, leaving him breathless. Rage suddenly rushed through his body, touching every nerve ending, coursing through his body with screams of betrayal, humiliation, and deceit. Then he became strangely still, a cold calm settling over him. "Who was he?" he heard himself say in a quiet voice. In his brain he screamed at her.

"I won't tell you that, Jack."

"What in the hell do you mean, you won't tell me?" he shouted. He could feel emotion closing in, taking him. She backed away from him. He saw the sudden fear in her eyes.

"You damn well *will* tell me!" He took a step toward her. "If you think I'm going to raise another man's bastard, you're crazy!"

"Jack, stop it!"

"Stop what? Who was he, Amanda? Tell me who did this? Why did you do it, Amanda? You hate sex. What did he offer you?" His voice was taunting as he walked slowly toward her. "You're the most frigid woman I know. What could he possibly offer that would make you open those legs for him?"

As he approached her, she backed away from him with horror. On his face were naked hatred and envy, sending shivers of terror through her as she silently searched her mind for a way to make him understand.

He struck her. The blow sent hot spears of pain shooting through her head and body, knocking her to the floor at his feet. The shock was so acute that it stilled the pain for a moment, and then it overwhelmed her. Her body rebelled, leaving her disoriented and dizzy. She braced herself for another blow, but when it didn't come she opened her eyes and ventured a look up at him. He was standing over her, his fists clenched as he glared down at her with fury. She fixed on that face, and suddenly anger rushed through her, outrage at what he had done. That anger saved her, though she couldn't know it then.

Her face filled with what she was feeling, rage beyond anything she had ever known. She saw him falter, the fists unclench, then clench again. But she had seen the hesitation and it gave her strength. "Get away from me," she commanded. The words came from deep within her. He took a step back, and she struggled to her feet. She fought the unsteadiness in her legs as she drew herself up to face him. "You've had your revenge. Now get out of here, Jack, and close the door behind you when you leave."

The calm assurance in her voice seemed to unsettle him. She saw the doubt that crossed his expression and she used it. "Now, Jack. *Get out!*" Suddenly he gave a strangled cry and spun around in impotent rage. He left the room, slamming the door behind him.

Slowly she moved to the bed, dropping down on it as she tried to deal with the throbbing pain in her face where he had struck her. She felt sick, and she fought to settle her stomach, willing herself to be calm. Slowly, as she sat quietly, the pain and nausea passed.

God, how she hated him. She had put up with his women, even facing some of them in unexpected moments. And always in social situations where she could do little but pretend she didn't know they were Jack's lovers. As often as not, he had stood nearby at such moments with a look of innocence, even as he dared her to react. She had dealt with those women, ignoring them until she was finally able to deal with the total failure of her marriage.

Her father had spoken against Jack only once and then had withdrawn, knowing there was nothing more he could say in face of her determination to marry Jack Bellamy. But Amanda was no martyr. She accepted that she had succumbed to Jack's charms because of her own imagined needs.

She went into the bathroom and ran the water until it was cold. After soaking a towel, she held it to her face where he had struck her. Turning to lean back against the sink, she stared at the closed door and made her decision. It came to her calmly, without passion. But then, she had always found determination and resolve to be more powerful than emotions. Except with Nicky. But she pushed those thoughts away; she needed clarity for what she had to do.

There was no possibility of divorce. The scandal would ruin her personally, and it would ruin the company as well. She wouldn't do that to her father. He had trusted her, and her marriage was her problem to solve. And then there was the child, and there was Nicky. His career was just beginning; scandal would ruin him, too. She knew that if Jack was determined it wouldn't be difficult for him to discover who was the father of her child. There was only one way to handle the situation: She would have to gain such total control over Jack that he would be forced to accept the situation in silence. And she knew a way, the only way.

It took Amanda two months to achieve her goals. There were weeks of fear as she waited for Jack to expose her secret. But she should have known that his indecisiveness was her best ally. She had no doubt that eventually he would expose the situation, while assuming the role of the injured husband. But while Jack was cunning, he wasn't particularly bright. He was shrewd enough to handle small matters, but anything serious took thought, and for Jack that meant time. The more he plotted, the more convoluted his thinking became, and that meant confusion. She saw his confusion the few times they were alone, when she would catch him looking at her, his expression clouded with doubt. In public, they continued as before. She began to realize that as long as the pregnancy didn't become obvious, there was time. He wouldn't make a declaration until he was forced to do so. And she knew that he would then make it suddenly, emotionally.

His indecision gave her the time she needed to complete her plans. The day she put the final piece into place she waited for him in the library. He had gone to a dinner party alone— something he was doing more and more frequently. She knew his behavior had begun to cause speculation and gossip, but she simply didn't care anymore. After tonight, it wouldn't matter.

It was after midnight when he came in. She had waited in the library because she knew he would come in for a nightcap before retiring. She hadn't bothered to turn on a light. She was sitting in a chair across the room, and she let him pour himself a drink before she spoke.

"Jack, we need to talk."

He spun around, almost spilling his cognac. "My God, why didn't you tell me you were here?"

She gave him a moment to collect himself. "There are some things that we have to settle."

"There's nothing I want to talk with you about, Amanda," he said, leaning back against the bar. "There's nothing you could possibly say that I am interested in hearing."

"Oh, but there is. And you are going to listen."

"Why should I?" He smirked, taking a drink.

"Because the rules change tonight, Jack." She rose from the chair and crossed the room slowly. Stepping behind the bar, she poured herself a glass of tonic water. "I'll join you in a drink," she said, glancing up at him with a smile. "We can celebrate our new understanding."

"Amanda, you've got more balls than any woman I know."

She thought about that. It was probably true, she thought. And in a moment, Jack, you will know just how much. "What I'm going to say is important, so listen to me, Jack, very carefully. Try to hold your comments until I've finished. Then, of course, you can say anything you like to me, and I'll have the courtesy to listen." When he remained silent, she fixed him with a steady regard. "First, though it will probably be meaningless to you, I want to say that I am sorry for what we've done to each other. I never wanted to hurt you, and I don't think you ever wanted to hurt me. We are just—who we are. And we were terribly mismatched."

"Are you comparing my behavior to yours?" he blurted angrily.

"This isn't a moment for accusations. Hear me out." She spoke with quiet authority, and she saw the flicker of doubt that crossed his expression. He really was such a weak man, she thought with disgust. "Jack, we are equally guilty for what happened between us. If you were a woman you would have been pregnant long ago, and certainly not by me." It pained her to compare what she felt for Nicky to Jack's endless string of meaningless affairs, but it served for the moment. He was listening. "But I never hurt you as you hurt me, Jack. I suffered your affairs, I even accepted them. But then I had no choice."

"You had a choice," he glowered, gripping the brandy snifter. "You were always so goddam cold. Maybe if I'd had a willing wife I wouldn't have had to go elsewhere."

"That's ludicrous, and you know it. We had passion in the beginning, and you would remember it if you wanted to. Your affairs began before I shut you from my bed. Oh, God, Jack, this is meaningless," she sighed, forcing away her anger. "It's the present we must deal with, not the past." Remembering the night she had told him about the baby and the humiliation and helplessness she felt when he struck her, she felt a coldness settle over her. "Tell me, Jack, have you checked your investments lately?"

It took a moment for her words to register. "Why?" As he asked the question a knot of fear formed in his gut. In spite of their differences, he had always envied Amanda's talents in business, though he found it shocking in a woman. "Why do you ask?"

"In the morning you should investigate your holdings," she said calmly. Then she looked up at him, her expression one he had seen too often to suit him. Her voice was deadly quiet. "I own you now, Jack. Lock, stock, and barrel."

"What do you mean?" He laughed nervously.

"I've bought up your stock. I now own you."

"That's impossible," he blurted. "My business manager would have called me, warned me . . ."

"How could he? You were on a cruise to Cuba. I'm certain that he did try to reach you." She smiled. "But then, your new mistress was more important, wasn't she? She's an actress, I hear. Was she worth it, Jack?"

"You're lying!" His face had grown a ghastly white.

"In the morning you can confirm what I've told you." She shrugged.

He knew it was true, every part of it. She had ruined him. The actress had been a disappointment, whining, demanding. And while he was with her, Amanda had plotted, taken him over. "How could you do this to me?"

She regarded him with a look of genuine surprise. "You really don't know, do you?" His baffled look, the panic, confirmed it. "I can't allow you to control me, Jack. I don't give a damn how many mistresses you have, but you'll never hurt me again. I will not allow you to hurt this baby or to use the fact of my pregnancy against me."

She saw him try to deal with what she had said, his face twisted with confusion. "Is this because I hit you? Is that it? I swear I'll never do that again, Amanda."

She knew he meant it. He believed, at this moment, that it would never happen again. "Yes, you would, if you had the chance, the moment you felt you had control over me and you needed an outlet for your frustration and anger. But it won't happen again, Jack. I won't allow it to happen."

He looked at her with disbelief. "You did all this just because I hit you?"

The statement angered her, and she had to force the rage back to remain calm. "Yes, Jack, just because you hit me. Can you understand what it is like to be physically at the mercy of another human being? The violation, the helplessness? No, I suppose you can't. But you will." She paused and reached over to pour him another cognac. "I considered alternatives such as divorce, but you know that is unacceptable. But I will bargain with you, Jack. I own you, but that needn't affect you. It's up to you."

He loathed asking the question, but self-preservation forced him. "What are you proposing?"

"My proposal is simple and nonnegotiable. You can live your life however you wish. I am uninterested in whom you spend your time with or how you spend it. You must learn to be discreet, of course, but I'll continue to support you, even more generously than your own investments supported you in the past. You can confer with my attorney in the morning on the details, and I don't think you'll find them ungenerous. But there are conditions: You will allow me to lead my own life without criticism or interference; you will never, ever lay a hand on me again; you will claim this baby as your own, if not by your word then by your silence. If you renege on any of these conditions I *will* divorce you, and I'll ruin you in the bargain."

He felt as if he were being strangled. He hated her as he had never known himself capable of hating another human being. She had taken everything from him, all because of a simple, warranted slap. "I have to check this out with my broker."

"Do that. You can give me your answer in the morning."

He pushed his glass aside, glaring at her with hatred, then turned and walked out of the room. At the doorway, he paused, turning back impulsively. He seemed to need to confirm that the last moments had actually happened. "This isn't the end of it, Amanda. You haven't won, not yet, in spite of what you might think. You've taken everything from me, and someday you will know how that feels. I swear it."

In the heavy silence of her small office, Amanda clutched Nicky's picture to her breast, attempting to will away the memory. Jack had done it. From his grave he had reached out and made good on his threat. Everything was gone, lost, destroyed, in one simple act of vengeance.

CHAPTER 16

It was a morning to recall the past.

Jess paused in the doorway to reflect on the absolute beauty of the day. It was the kind of morning that made one think of beginnings. The sky was a clear, bright blue with clusters of puffy white cotton clouds. The golf course beyond the terrace was lush, framed by the fringe of dense forest. The fragrance of pine and fir drifted on a gentle breeze mixed with the subtle tang of salt air from the ocean. Jess paused, drawing a deep breath. The air was sharp with the smell of fall.

Amanda was sitting on the terrace reading the papers. As Jess approached the table she noted the *Wall Street Journal*, the *San Francisco Chronicle*, the *Los Angeles Times*, and the *Monterey Herald*. "Do you read all of those every day?"

Amanda looked up and smiled. "I read all of the *Journal*, but only parts of the others. How are you today, Jessica?"

"I'm fine. Thank you, Henley, I'd love some coffee." The butler had appeared with a cup and saucer, and he poured from the Spode pot on the table. There was a plate of plain toast and crunchy English muffins—another habit Jess shared with her grandmother. Toast, no butter, and coffee for breakfast.

"Did you have a good time last night?" Amanda asked, folding the *Journal* and placing it on top of the others.

"Yes, very much so. Michael took me to the Hog's Breath."

"He didn't." Amanda laughed.

"Against his better judgment. I confess to some coercion. I wanted to see Clint Eastwood's famous establishment. But it was as crowded as Michael warned it would be, and we left after a few drinks."

"I was somewhat alarmed when you left so early," Amanda

said, sipping coffee. The point wasn't lost. Jess had thought this would be difficult, but apparently Amanda was as eager as she to discuss what was on both of their minds. How to approach it was a different matter. There was nothing to do but plunge in.

"Amanda, I'm curious about something. Will you answer a question for me?"

"I'll try."

"You told me about meeting Nicholas Alger in Paris many years ago, and about parting unhappily. I assumed that you met him again many years later, long after my grandfather's death. Last night Lou Delgato mentioned that Nicky worked on Roosevelt's first campaign for president."

"Ah, well, such is coincidence. Yes, I saw Nicky again in New York at a fund-raising event for Roosevelt. It was a brief meeting, but one in which we resolved that silly misunderstanding in Paris. He did interest me in working for Roosevelt, I don't deny it, but my dedication to FDR went beyond that meeting in New York. I saw Nicky again in 1946. Just prior to the end of the war, my father had been killed on a ship in the Pacific."

"He was in the navy?"

"No, he was an advisor to the Navy Department, on a fact-finding mission in the Pacific. The ship he was on was struck by a torpedo. Anyway, a year later, I attended the dedication of a memorial to him, a library in the old Del Monte Hotel. Our ancestor, Jeremy Morgan, built that hotel with Charles Crocker, and it is now a part of the United States Naval Postgraduate School. At the dedication, I turned around and there Nicky was, standing across the room in his naval whites. We began to correspond after that meeting. After the war he became a career officer with the State Department and eventually ambassador to Brazil."

"When did you see him again?"

"Once or twice, quite casually, when he was in California. But when your grandfather died . . . Well, I had always had deep feelings for Nicky. It wasn't long before we found each other again. The years that followed were the best part of my life."

Before Jess could pursue it further, Henley stepped out onto the terrace at that moment. "Miss Bellamy, your rental car is here."

"Finally," Jess said with a smile. "I'll see you later; I have some things to do this morning." She stood up and then paused. "I meant to ask you, what happened with Paul Iverson? Does he have more information on those stock purchases of Altra Grow?"

. "No, nothing yet, but we're working on it."

"I have a friend who is an astoundingly good broker with some very important contacts. I hope you don't mind, but I asked him to look into it."

"I don't mind at all," Amanda said, picking up another newspaper. "It was thoughtful of you, Jessica."

With an affectionate glance at her grandmother, Jess said good-bye.

Jess drove to Monterey, parked her car in a downtown lot, and set out on foot to see the sights and think things out.

What was Amanda hiding? She had appeared to be open with her answers, but Jess had sensed there was more. So why hadn't she pursued the subject instead of driving off to town? Perhaps she simply didn't want to know the truth. Or perhaps she was seeing ghosts. Pushing her unease aside, she followed the historical landmark signs through the two-hundred-year-old city.

It was late afternoon when she found herself walking along a quiet street some distance from the center of town. Jess stared at the beautiful building set amid lush, manicured grounds and rolling lawns. She felt a quiet come over her, a heavy, settled feeling along with a strange rush of joy. Jeremy Morgan had helped to build this structure. She imagined how it had looked at that time, as people came from all over the world to stay at the hotel that was once called the Queen of American Watering Places. She knew that the original building had burned down twice over the last century. But the foundation of the original Del Monte Hotel remained, as did its ghosts.

The last thought made her shiver. Everything seemed to be converging into some distorted reality, as if she had slipped through the looking glass. She had been trained to deal with complexities and angles beyond the rational. She had always trusted her instinct as a vital companion to reason. Yet now those parts of her fought, like two Titans in mortal battle. What was she trying to prove? She couldn't help Amanda unless she could remain objective and that now seemed impossible. Nothing about this case was impersonal. Each time she dealt with a fact of Rafael Martinez's death, it led her to someone she had begun to care about. And she did care about her grandmother. Amanda hadn't just touched her; Jess was beginning to care for her deeply. She let out a long, reluctant sigh, pushing away her morose feelings. Defensively, she gave in to habit and allowed her thoughts to follow their own rhythm.

Altra Grow was at jeopardy because a young man had died. His death had become important to her; Altra Grow had become important. She wanted Rafael Martinez to find justice, and she wanted to protect her grandmother's company. Were those two goals compatible? Probably not. The thought brought a brief, sad smile. It was an old legal conflict: How did one defend the guilty? Three times in her career Jess had discovered a client's guilt during the process of litigation. One principle had allowed her to do her job well: her reverence for the law and those who had created the justice system.

Jess forced herself to relax and search for the courage to face the problem. Yes, the case had become personal; she would have to defend Rafael *and* Altra Grow. Amanda might not like the outcome, but somehow the truth would benefit them all. Jess had to believe in that. If she didn't, the case would make her crazy. And though she might endure moments of tremendous confusion, she knew she wasn't crazy.

Two days later Jess was sitting in the courtyard of a small Carmel restaurant having lunch with Tom Bradin.

"Are you comfortable, Tom, is your room okay?" she asked.

"Yeah, it's great. This town is great," he said, glancing across the low stone wall to the street beyond. "If you like Fantasy Island."

She frowned with puzzlement, following his gaze. "Carmel is beautiful. It's—"

"Enchanting?" he finished, grinning at her.

"Pretty young to be a cynic, aren't you?"

"Call it culture shock."

"You're suffering from big city ass-clenching, Tom. Bus fumes have gone to your head. Take a deep breath and relax."

Jess had picked him up at the airport two hours earlier and delivered him to the Pine Inn. After dropping his luggage in his room, they had walked up Ocean Avenue, the main street of the village and searched down side streets until they selected the General Store for lunch. As they ate Cobb salads, Tom had caught her up on what was happening in the office. Then, over coffee, Jess had launched into the reasons she had sent for him.

"Give yourself a week or two," she said, putting down her coffee cup. "This place will grow on you."

"A week or two?" He stared at her bleakly.

"Trust me." She smiled to herself, understanding his reaction. She knew there was an incurable romantic beneath that thin veil of false cynicism. She wouldn't have been surprised if Tom fell in love before he left, and not just with Carmel.

"If you say so," he said with a long-suffering sigh.

"I do. Now, where were we?"

He glanced at the notes he had been taking and flipped through the pages. "I'm supposed to research the history of California from 1844 to the present and write a synopsis of it, with biographical information about anyone mentioned in the media."

"Cute."

"Why Nicholas Alger?" he asked, glancing at the last notation. "He was your grandmother's second husband, wasn't he? Can't she tell you anything you want to know?" Jess regarded the question with a level stare. "Oh," he said. I see, he added silently.

"I want a complete history of the man, beginning with his participation in Roosevelt's campaign. Look for anything that's incomplete or inconsistent."

"Pieces that don't fit."

"Exactly. You know what to do, Tom."

Yes, he did, but this was different. This was Jess's family, for God's sake. What was happening here? His eyes wandered about the patio to those eating lunch beneath brightly striped canvas umbrellas. He struggled against the urge to say what was on his mind. Her personal life had always been a forbidden subject, yet now she was asking him to treat it like part of the case. What were the rules?

"Do you have a problem?"

He regarded her for a long moment. "Yes, I have a problem. I need to know the rules, Jess. I can't work on this case if I'm under restrictions."

"I haven't put any restrictions on you."

"Haven't you? This isn't just a case," he said, tapping the notes. "It's your life. I can't do this if you're going to hold back on me."

She glanced at the passing tourists. He was right, of course, and the implications of what she was doing weighed heavily on her. "Do you remember the Simonelli case?"

Puzzled, Tom frowned, pushing his coffee cup aside as he rested his elbows on the table. "Yes, of course I do. Simonelli set out to organize a sting that would ruin his cousin's fish markets."

"Why?"

"Because thirty years before his uncle stole from his father."

"And what happened?"

"It backfired. The union got involved, and the cousin was accidentally killed by a teamster who had been laid off. Jeez, Jess, what has this to do with anything?"

"Nothing, perhaps, or everything," she sighed, pausing as the waitress appeared with the bill. "Come on, let's take a walk."

They paid the bill and left the restaurant, walking down to Ocean Avenue. Ignoring passersby, they settled on a bench in front of the library. Ever since they left the restaurant, Tom had been trying to find some parallel between what Jess had told him about Altra Grow and Rafael Martinez and the Simonelli case, but it eluded him. Glancing at her, he said just that.

"Tom, have you ever heard the expression 'what goes around comes around'?"

"Yes, I've heard it."

"Do you agree with it?"

"Yes, if you mean we get what we deserve."

"That'll do." Jessica's expression was grim as she watched the passersby. "One might say that Simonelli caused what ultimately happened. Years of hatred, a life given to revenge, finally culminated in his cousin's death."

"Are you suggesting that Altra Grow *was* responsible for the kid's death?" Tom regarded her with concern. "If that's what you think, I don't know why I'm here."

"No, that's not what I'm saying. That would be simplistic. I'm saying that my family is involved. If not directly, then possibly because of a situation they've helped to create over the decades. It's the social climate here that allowed the tragedy to happen. Look, I'm not going to say more because I need your objectivity. Take that list you made this afternoon and work with it. And don't pull back because this case involves my family. I want to see whatever you find, and I want to know your thoughts on it."

"Your grandmother ran into Nicholas Alger again in New York," Tom said, watching the tourists pass by. "He stimulated her interest in Roosevelt."

"Yes, apparently." Jess watched a couple pause at the street corner to consult their maps.

He paused, stealing a glance at her. "It became a compulsion. Roosevelt, I mean."

A family paused at the intersection. A small boy punched his brother, which caused the younger one to wail, gaining the attention of the weary parents.

"Those are the facts," Jess said, watching the family. "Bring me whatever you can find, Tom. No restrictions." Then she stood up abruptly. "Come on, we have things to do, places to go, people to meet. I want to see a labor camp, then talk with the union. For a start."

He grabbed up his notes. "A labor camp?" he asked, catching up with her.

"Yes," she said grimly. "You thought Carmel was culture shock? Brace yourself, Tom."

CHAPTER 17

Alice had fallen through the rabbit hole. After tumbling in free fall she had come to a sudden, abrupt halt and found herself in a world that seemed frighteningly familiar. A haunting melody by Tchaikovsky drifted through the seductively lighted room. Jess sat curled up on the sofa with a glass of extraordinary sherry that Michael had pressed into her hand before he left her to attend to matters in his kitchen. She could hear the occasional clattering of pots from somewhere behind her.

It had seemed simple to say yes to him, but that had been hours before when he called to invite her to dinner. Then she had walked through his door a quarter of an hour before, her thoughts on business. He had greeted her with a warm, friendly smile, and had left her moments later to see to his dinner. He left her also with the memory of how he looked in a bulky sweater and form-fitting jeans. And loafers, no socks. The hick was seductive.

Her gaze wandered over the room and she took a sip of the sherry. It didn't help that her second view of this room confirmed her earlier judgment—that he had taste. It went beyond mere appreciation for Michael's choices. If she had been asked to decorate this room for him she would have chosen the same colors and appointments, even to the piece of Steuben crystal on the coffee table. She would have, once she had seen through her original impression of him, which had been vaguely related to wagon wheels and steer horns. The fact of her prejudice was not easy to face. Nor was the realization that his tastes paralleled her own with such startling accuracy.

She forced herself to think of Rick. Urban, sophisticated, the man knew his way around Brooks Brothers, the opera, and

Renaissance art. She suspected that Michael understood those things, too. But Rick shared her pleasures, and he respected her profession. There had been no commitments.

"Dinner will be ready in about fifteen minutes," Michael said, startling her from her thoughts as he collapsed onto the sofa next to her. He planted his feet on the coffee table and tipped back a long-necked bottle of beer, taking a swallow. His choice of beverage somehow gave her comfort. She felt herself relax.

He tilted his head in concentration and frowned. "We're in for a storm."

Puzzled, she listened and turned her head to the large picture windows. They rattled then against a sudden gust of wind. Seconds later tentative drops of rain hit the window. She said nothing about the accuracy of his prediction as she sipped from her sherry, giving it her concentration.

"I'm glad you decided to stay, Jess."

She turned and looked at him. The bluntness of the statement was unsettling and walls were flung up inside her mind to block out his meaning. "If there's going to be a storm, I should go home," she said.

"I meant your decision to stay in Monterey, on the case," he said with a smile. "As for the storm, it's too late." Just then, as if to confirm his prediction, a rumble of thunder rolled from outside.

"Why did you ask me here tonight?"

He studied her for a moment, then took another swallow of beer. "Why are you always on the defensive? That burr's itching you again, Bellamy."

"So you've pointed out before. It was a simple question. And as for my burr, I thought we had a good time the other night."

"Yes, we did—after your white wine. Normally you regard me as the enemy." She opened her mouth to protest. "No, don't bother to deny it. I am on your side, you know. It would be easier for both of us if you'd believe that."

"I do believe it, Michael." She did, but she couldn't deny that she was wary of him, for reasons that had nothing to do with the case or Amanda.

"Then what's the problem?" He turned and looked at her as

his mouth slid into a grin. "Are you afraid I'm going to jump you?"

She blinked at the comment. "Should I be worried?" she asked, attempting to sound nonchalant.

"It's what you expect from a cowboy, isn't it?"

"You're never going to let me forget that, are you?" This topic of conversation was becoming irritating.

"Not as long as you still feel that way."

"I don't. I—"

He glanced at his watch and stood up abruptly. "It's time," he said. He stood above her and she stared with confusion at the hand he held out to her. Her eyes darted up to his and the grin broadened. "Dinner's ready, Ms. Bellamy."

She thought about him during dinner. The table was set in a deep bay window with a small garden beyond. The rain, pouring steadily down the panes, added to a feeling of cozy intimacy. The meal was wonderful, roasted capons stuffed with grapes attesting to another one of his many talents. Pretending to concentrate on the meal, she stole a glance at him across the small table. He wasn't Curt, and he wasn't Rick. And he certainly was not a cowboy. Or was he? It struck her suddenly that she wanted him to be. From the first moment she had met him in Amanda's library and they had glared at each other, she had sensed his strength, physically and emotionally. It hadn't been just his attire and his casual indifference to her, but his easygoing self-assurance, his lack of pretense.

She took a sip of wine, aware of the steady rhythm of the rain nearby and the sharp smell of the oak logs burning in the fireplace in the next room. Her senses seemed heightened. She set down her wineglass and picked up her fork. With uncomfortable clarity she understood why she had been so quick to apply that label to him, and why it had stuck so relentlessly. Cowboys were alien to her way of life, and she had certainly meant the comparison to be an insult—but cowboys had also been fantasy figures in her girlhood dreams. She had once been an ardent fan of Zane Grey and Louis L'Amour, though she had finally given them up in disgust when she finally realized that the hero was *never* going to kiss the girl.

"Don't you like wild rice?"

She glanced up with puzzlement, then followed his amused

gaze to her plate. She realized then that she had been busy piling the rice into a neat little tepee at one side of her plate. "I love it," she said, laying down her fork. She took a quick drink of her wine, grateful that the candlelight would not reveal the fact that she had actually blushed. "I was lost in thought. I'm sorry." Unconsciously, she bit her lower lip as she glanced at the window. "Do you think the rain's going to stop?"

"Absolutely."

She turned back to him. He was regarding her with an amused smile. "I meant soon."

"I wouldn't know. Do you want to turn on the weather report?"

"Aren't you concerned about the rain? Will it damage any crops?"

"It's not raining in the valley."

"How do you know that?"

"I know those things."

She smiled, realizing that he was teasing her.

"What were you thinking about just now?" he asked, refilling her wineglass.

"The case," she lied, pushing her plate to one side as she leaned her elbows on the table.

"Ah, yes, the case." He refilled his own glass. "Have you discovered something?"

She could hear the hope in his voice. It touched her, partly because of his unfailing concern for Amanda and partly because she had begun to like this man very much. How to explain this? "We've been discovering a lot of things, some not so pleasant. We've met with union officials, drug enforcement people, and various police departments—"

"Why?" he asked, puzzled.

"Because something smells," she said. "Look, the union has a good contract with two years left before negotiations, but radicals within the union are stirring things up. They don't like harvesting machines, and they're bitter because the machines were allowed under the current contract. They're going to try to blow up the issue when Rafael's case comes to court. You've got drugs and La Familia. They're selling cocaine and heroin off of lunch trucks in the fields. They've set up prostitutes in the labor camps, and they're trying to force some of your female workers to join their stables. Crew chiefs in many of the

companies are charging men to work or taking physical favors
from the women to guarantee their jobs. The coyotes are still
bringing up illegals, in spite of the amnesty program, and
people live on riverbanks and in caves. You exposed me to
these realities, Michael, and Tom and I have been investigating
them."

"And I'm not denying anything you've said, but I don't see
what this has to do with Rafael's death."

"Nothing, and possibly everything," she sighed, leaning
back in her chair. She struggled with her thoughts for a
moment, tempted to say what was on her mind. And then she
decided against it. She and Tom had much more work to do.

"The owners of these California agribusinesses are on a
first-name basis with governors and presidents," she said.
"These men serve on government committees and are called
upon for advice. They entertain government leaders and are
given important posts in return for their services. This is not
surprising when you consider the power the owners wield
through personal influence and strong lobbying groups, an
economic power that is equal to a world government. Yet drug
sales, prostitution, coercion, and other felonies are committed
every day of the week under their very noses. Why?"

He stared at her. His puzzled expression grew intent, then
cleared suddenly. "Jesus, is *that* going to be your defense?" He
sat up and faced her, leaning on the table as his expression
lightened with incredulity. "You're going to use the indifference of power as a defense?"

"It will be part of it. What's more important is that Amanda
has not been negligent in these aspects. I can show detailed
evidence that her company has actively fought against the more
disreputable influences. Management's efforts to keep the
company clean shows its concern for the people who work for
it."

Michael was silent, regarding Jess for a thoughtful moment.
Then he suddenly picked up their plates and disappeared into
the kitchen. She stared at the empty place he left and frowned.
She could hear the clatter of dishes in the kitchen, and after a
moment he came back. The rain had grown more insistent, and
he stared at the steady stream of water against the window
behind her. "Would you like a cognac?" he asked suddenly.
Before she could answer, he had walked into the living

room. She got up and followed him, wondering what had happened.

As Jess entered the room, he picked up two snifters of cognac he had poured from the liquor cabinet and handed her one. They stood at the windows, staring out at the rain. After a moment his voice broke the heavy silence. "I should be grateful. I've certainly put pressure on you to find a solution to this mess. At this moment, I couldn't even tell you why I feel so pissed off."

"Try." The rain pelted the patio outside the window, running in rivulets to the beds of azaleas and rhododendrons. She could feel his tension, and she truly wanted to know how he felt.

"Maybe it's that old saw about 'watch what you wish for,' " he said quietly. "I can't deny anything you said. There is criminal indifference by those who could stop it, if they cared. Maybe Amanda fought it because she was one of the first here, maybe because of her Californio blood. And I've always been ready to support her because of my own beginnings. We hoped that you would find a way to clear Altra Grow. We know we weren't negligent, but dammit, Jess, what you are proposing is just a—a ruse." He turned and regarded her solemnly. "Maybe that hydraulic hose *was* faulty and it killed Rafael. If it did, the fact that we regret his death doesn't change anything. To win the case because of our wonderful past record somehow doesn't seem honest."

This wasn't unexpected. Her voice was soft. "Michael Rawlings, you are a nice man and it's going to hurt you."

He stared at her. "Christ," he swore, then emptied his glass in a gulp. Crossing to the liquor cabinet, he refilled it.

His reaction was part of a process; she had dealt with it countless times. She waited until he had taken another drink and then she spoke, keeping emotion from her voice. "Knock it off, Michael. These are the big leagues. You wanted to play in them. You insisted on it. This is how it's done."

"No matter who gets hurt?"

"And who might that be? The owners of other large companies who might have their reputations tarnished? They can take it, and if they are guilty they need to be shaken up. They're too comfortable. We both know that, so why the anguish?"

"They're not the ones I'm worried about."

"Then who? Or is it punishment you want? You've begun to think that you're guilty, haven't you?" She saw his hesitation and played on it. "Do you suspect that Pete Maloy lied after all; that he didn't check that hose?"

"No."

"Did he doctor his log after the accident?"

"No!"

"Then it was an accident. A human error. Should an entire company be destroyed because of it? How many people would be out of work if the company folded? Do you want to see Pete in jail for criminal negligence?"

"Of course not."

"Then stifle it, Rawlings. For three weeks you've pressed me to prove that Rafael's death was the result of a regrettable accident that was not caused by criminal negligence. Now that I believe I can do that, don't confuse the issue with misplaced guilt."

He heaved a deep sigh. "You're right. I'm sorry."

"Don't be." She watched as he ran his fingers through his hair, staring out the window in silence. The gesture caused her to draw in her breath and she turned away. His vulnerability in the past quarter-hour had merely caused her feelings to sharpen. She felt a tenderness well up in her that made her want to reach out and run her own fingers through that hair, drawing his head to her breast. She hadn't known she had such motherly instincts. She collapsed into the depths of the down pillows on the sofa.

"So what now?" he said, turning.

"We keep looking." She shrugged, sipping from her cognac. "My 'ruse,' as you put it, won't be enough by itself."

"Won't it? You seemed pretty confident."

No, she wouldn't discuss her suspicions with him, not yet. But she would like him to sit next to her, she thought. "Will you answer some questions for me?" she asked.

He came to sit by her on the sofa. "If I can."

"The questions are not about the case, just some things I'm curious about." She leaned toward him slightly. "Aren't you concerned that you are poisoning America?"

"Poisoning America?"

"With pesticides and herbicides?"

"Oh. The mad farmer," he said, leaning his arm on the back

of the sofa. "Yes, we revel in killing every living thing that flies or crawls. If it moves, it dies."

"Michael, be serious," she said. She could smell his cologne, a musky scent that toppled her senses pleasantly. "People are worried about what they eat."

"I don't blame them." He leaned forward, resting his head in his hand as he bent toward her. "We love our sprays. We tank them behind tractors, and when we're really lucky we can fly them in. A crop duster at sunrise, now there's a sight—I live for it."

"Michael, stop it," she laughed. "I'm serious!"

"So am I," he said. "Look at it logically. Herbicides and pesticides are tremendously expensive. Aside from labor, they are far and away the most expensive part of farming. If consumers would put up with a few bugs in their produce, we would have eliminated the sprays long ago. Can you see it? The housewife buys a head of lettuce, takes it home, and spreads a leaf only to find a worm crawling through it. Sure, she's going to calmly flick it aside and make her salad. More likely she's going to scream bloody murder and report the offending worm to the health department and her congressman. She'll claim that the industry is trying to poison her family with worms. When she can accept that worm, the farmers will stop spraying and be glad to do so. And they'll make a hell of a lot more money."

"I see your point," she said, trying not to focus on his nearness.

"Personally, I don't use pesticides. I prefer ladybugs."

"Ladybugs? Really?"

"Yes. They're free. And they're cute. In fact, I like predators—bobcats, owls, weasels, badgers. They help to establish a natural balance. Coyotes, too. You don't want to hear what they eat, do you?"

"No."

"I didn't think so."

His cologne was assaulting her senses. "What about water pollution? I've read a lot about the water pollution from chemicals."

"Not here."

"Not here?"

He fell silent and studied her for a long moment. Suddenly

he pulled away and stood up. "Jess, I think it's time you went home."

She stared at him blankly. "Why?"

"I can take you home or call you a cab."

She glanced at her watch. "It's only ten o'clock, Michael."

He glared down at her, his expression revealing a moment of struggle. "Jess, if you don't go home right now I'm going to jump your bones."

She blinked. "How sweet."

"Sweet?"

"Sweetly put."

"Yes, well—" He had meant to put it crudely, to jar them both into reason. He liked Jess very much. Too much. He wanted her and in the last few moments it had become difficult for him to keep his hands off her. Someone like Jessica Bellamy was the last complication he wanted in his life. She was Noreen all over again. He took her coat off the hall tree and waited. She put her cognac down on the coffee table and walked over to him.

"It was a wonderful dinner, Michael," she said as he dropped the jacket over her shoulders. She was turned away from him and he couldn't see her expression, but her voice was soft and husky. He liked her perfume. And her hair was silky. His hands lingered on her shoulders as he resisted the temptation to touch it. She turned then and looked up at him with a smile. "I'm glad you asked me."

"I'm glad you came," he said, meaning it. They stood there, neither moving, as they stared at each other. His chest felt tight. Her eyes were warm and inviting and expectant. "Oh, hell," he swore. His arm went out, pulling her to him as his mouth came down on hers. The contact was stunning for them both in its intensity. Her coat fell to the floor as her arms went around his neck and he wrapped her tightly against him. He plundered her mouth as she opened to him, and his tongue launched an assault. Then he drew back, kissing the corners of her mouth, then her eyes, his sudden tenderness leaving her breathless. "Oh, Michael," she whispered, turning her head to reclaim his mouth.

He kissed her deeply again and then again as her hand moved up and she slipped her fingers into his hair. It felt just as she had thought it would, softly curling around her fingers.

His hand moved to a breast, caressing it beneath the soft wool of her sweater. She moaned against his lips, pressing against him. Bending, he swept her up into his arms and carried her to the bedroom. He had barely set her down when her arms were around his neck again and she was kissing him, fitting her mouth to his. They moved toward the bed. Feeling it against the backs of her legs, she pulled him with her and they tumbled onto the mattress. He caught himself from landing on top of her, shifting his weight as they fell.

"Jess," he murmured, pulling her to him. She was nuzzling his earlobe and her hands had slipped under his sweater. "Jess," he repeated, leaning above her on his elbows. "Slow down," he murmured. She opened her eyes and looked up at him. "We don't need to hurry this."

He felt her stiffen beneath him and saw her eyes fill with confusion, then anger. "We don't have to do it at all."

"Yes, I think we do," he said, smiling down at her. "And it's worth doing right. Unless, of course, you don't want to have to think twice about it."

Her eyes widened and she began to deny it. But he was watching her reaction and slowly she smiled. "You're right. I guess I did feel a certain amount of—urgency."

"So did I. For more than one reason." He smiled as his hand lightly stroked her body. "There's the fact of your luscious body, and I've wanted to get you in bed since the first moment I saw you in Amanda's library."

"You have?"

"Absolutely."

"But I thought you detested me."

"Part of me did. I assure you that my only motive was pure lust. As for the second reason, we've both had relationships that didn't work out. And we remind each other of them."

"You're wrong," she said, adjusting herself more comfortably under his weight. "We're both guilty on both counts." She smiled at the question that came into his eyes. "I don't want this to go to your head, Mr. Rawlings, but I think you're one of the sexiest men I've ever met."

"Really." A dark brow arched with the dryly spoken word. "Is that why you've been so frigid?"

"Cool."

"Whatever you say. Yes, it all fits now," he said, emphasizing the statement with his body as he relaxed his weight on her. "I guess we could refer to what we feel as sexual tension. So what do we do about it?"

She looked at him with disbelief. "Are you serious?"

"Yes, Jess, I'm very serious," he said gently. "I suppose we could continue with this. Maybe we both just need to go at it hot and heavy for a few moments and release the tension. But if that's all it is, I don't want it. What I'm trying to tell you, lady, is that I could get very serious about you."

She stared up at him with wonder. Something within her began to withdraw against a rush of vulnerability. And then it became still. The sudden inward calm surprised her and she studied it for a moment, marveling at the lack of resistance she felt when viewing the prospect of a relationship with him. What would it be like, she wondered, to feel alive again? To take risks?

"I think I'll take that chance," she said softly.

With a quick, gentle smile he kissed her tenderly, lingering as his hand stroked her gently. They undressed each other slowly, discovering and exploring their feelings. He slipped off her sweater and the camisole beneath. Touching her, he cupped a full, beautiful breast as his thumb made gentle circles about a nipple and as it swelled to a taut peak. He bent his head, taking the nipple between his lips, playing gently with his lips and tongue until she gasped, arching her back against him.

As he kissed her, drawing, pulling at her senses, his hand roamed. He explored and stroked her body, leaving her nerve endings tingling, her soft moans and sighs encouraging and guiding his intense pursuit.

Loving her, he murmured into her ear as he came into her, plunging into her moist softness and she folded about him. As he felt the first, tiny contractions deep inside her, she became still beneath him and he knew she was anticipating, then experiencing the tension he had been waiting for. Then she cried out softly and he plunged again, wanting to reach the moment with her. Together, they shattered apart, exploding into a mutual orgasm.

He held her against him, kissing her gently, his lips claiming the corners of her mouth and her eyes, which were moist with tears of pleasure, holding her to him until she had descended peacefully.

Later they made love again in the warmth and comfort of his bed, then got up to raid the kitchen. And then they slept, wrapped in each other's arms. Wonderfully safe, secure, and deeply sated, Jess fell asleep, feeling the warmth of Michael's arms about her. With her last thoughts her mouth curved into a sleepy smile.

Eat your heart out, Zane Grey.

CHAPTER 18

The morning sun streamed into the room and across the bed, awakening Jessica. She resisted opening her eyes, wanting more sleep; then suddenly she remembered where she was. She smiled at the deep feeling of contentment that spread through her. As she opened her eyes she reached out to touch him. The bed was empty. She sat up and glanced about the room. Then she heard a clatter coming from the kitchen. Smiling, she leaned back into the bedding. If Michael kept this up, she'd never have to learn to cook.

Moments later he came into the bedroom, bearing a tray. Her heart caught at the sight of him. His hair was tousled from sleep; it looked as if he had run his fingers through it. He was wearing a robe tied loosely about the waist, and he hadn't shaved. It was disarmingly intimate, and she felt her stomach tighten as her body flushed with memories of the past night. The cowboy was an exquisite lover.

"Good morning," he said, setting the tray beside her. He leaned over and kissed her, then took the thick Sunday paper from beneath his arm and tossed it on the bed.

"Do you have an extra robe?"

"Sure, if you really think you need one." He grinned.

He retrieved a navy silk robe from his closet, tossing it to her as he sat down on the bed. He leaned against the headboard and, grabbing a bearclaw, held it between his teeth as he unfolded the newspaper.

"I get the comics first." She slipped from the bed and into the robe, then headed toward the bathroom.

"You read the comics first?"

"Always," she returned, shutting the door. She opened it a moment later. "Do you have an extra toothbrush?"

He looked up from the paper. "I thought you were a modern woman."

"What is that supposed to mean?" she asked, leaning against the door frame.

"I would think you'd be prepared for any contingency."

"In this day and age?" she said, arching a brow. "Believe me, I don't make a habit of quick love affairs."

"Good point. There's a new toothbrush in the second drawer by the shower."

She came out ten minutes later and settled on the bed next to him and attacked the tray. There was freshly squeezed orange juice along with coffee, croissants, bearclaws, and blintzes. "My God, you did this all this morning?"

He looked up from the paper. "The food is from a bakery nearby. They even deliver on Sunday."

She chose a croissant and was delighted to discover upon breaking it open that it was filled with honey butter. She poured herself a cup of coffee and settled into the pillow with the comics. Flipping through the pages, she found "Prince Valiant."

"God, I should have known."

She looked up to find him watching her. "Known what?"

"You're an incurable romantic. I suppose you even read romance novels."

"Yep, and I love 'em." Her eyes narrowed. "And I bet you like spy thrillers."

"That's cheating. You caught me reading Ludlum the last time you were here."

"You got me."

"I sure do," he said, turning the sports page.

They spent a blissful hour reading the paper, snacking from the breakfast tray, and exchanging tidbits of information from what they were reading, including a serious discussion of events heating up in the Middle East. "Well, that guy's sure got the world by the tail," Michael said, nodding at a picture on the page Jess was reading. She studied the picture for a moment. It was of the chargé d'affaires at the Saudi Arabian embassy in Washington. "Why do you say that?"

"Well, look at him. The guy's good-looking and he gets to

run around dressed like a desert sheikh. He's got to be worth a billion dollars, his embassy post is the best in the world, and he'll probably be the next ambassador. And if that's not enough, he's got a harem."

"You don't know that," she said, her eyes shifting with interest to the black-veiled woman in the background. "I only see one wife."

"He probably rotates them. After all, he is in the States."

She laughed, but she looked at the picture again, wondering if it was true. Michael was right; the man did seem to have it all. He was handsome and very romantic-looking. Though she thought that Saudis could only have four wives. Her gaze shifted back to the veiled woman. How could Roxy have even considered a life like that? she wondered. On the other hand, at least the woman had a life. . . .

Dismissing the article along with the dreary thoughts, she traded Michael for the business section. She finished an article on a merger involving one of her clients and had just stuffed the last piece of croissant into her mouth when she looked up and caught him watching her with a strange smile.

"What?" she asked, her mouth full.

"You're beautiful," he said. There was warmth in his voice.

"You're crazy." She laughed, wiping butter off her chin. She glanced at the bed, at the crumbs left from their breakfast and the papers scattered about. The special intimacy of the moment filled her with well-being. She loved lolling in bed on Sunday morning, but she had always done it alone. Rick thought bed was for sleeping and making love, and she had never spent a whole night with Curt. The past hour with Michael somehow seemed more intimate than their lovemaking during the night. She felt light-headed, warm, and suffused with feeling. Suddenly, as impossible as it seemed, she realized that she was falling in love with Michael Rawlings.

"Jess?"

She looked at him, knowing that everything she felt was in her eyes. She saw the recognition, the flicker of surprise. She felt vulnerable, afraid of what he would say. Afraid he would simply pretend that he hadn't seen it at all. She watched as he took the tray and bent over the side of the bed, placing it on the floor. She looked away, studying her hands. Why hadn't she just left well enough alone? she thought. He'd probably turn tail and run like hell. She started as his hand covered hers. "Jess, look at me."

She looked up, afraid of what she might see. "What are we going to do about us, Jess?" he asked softly.

"What do you want to do?" Was she really ready for this?

"I think this is simpler for me than it is for you. I'm not as afraid of it as you are."

"I don't want to be hurt," she said.

"I don't want to hurt you. Neither of us can predict how this will turn out, but isn't it worth the risk?"

Her eyes moved over his face to the fullness of his lower lip, the deep brown of his eyes, and the tiny laugh lines at their corners. "I think I'm beginning to care for you, Michael, and it scares me."

"I know." His arm went around her, drawing her to him, and they sank into the blankets. "And that means trust, Jess," he said, covering her mouth with his. "Trust me."

Papers scattered to the floor. They made new discoveries, giving themselves up to their feelings. As they came together Jess said his name, offering him far more than just her body. Later, sated and breathless, they lay together, still embracing, luxuriating in the feeling until they returned to reality. Then Michael rose on his elbows and kissed the tip of her nose and smiled down at her. "I have to fly to Washington tonight for hearings before a Senate committee. Come with me."

"Washington? Now?"

"It'll only be for a couple of days at most. But I don't want to leave you, not now." He kissed her again and shifted his weight off her. She pulled herself up against the pillows, and he tucked the covers about her. "Well? Will you come?" he asked.

"No, Michael, I can't go now," she said softly. Everything was moving too fast. "There's so much to do here. Besides, a few days without you might be an advantage. I have a feeling that I won't be able to think clearly with you around."

He frowned, regarding her steadily. "On the other hand, it could be time alone together that we need. But maybe you can't handle it."

"That's not fair, Michael."

"Isn't it?" He got up and slipped into his robe. As he tied it around him, he looked down at her. "I'm falling in love with you, Jess. I don't make a habit of telling women that. I want you with me, and there's nothing here that won't wait for a few days. But do what you need to."

The bathroom door closed and she stared at it. Then she rose from the bed and dressed. Taking the tray into the kitchen, she washed the dishes, finishing just as he came into the room. She studied his face and was relieved that he no longer looked angry. "You didn't need to do that," he said.

"Of course I did," she said, drying her hands on a towel. "Don't fight it, Rawlings," she added with a smile. "I'm great at cleaning up. What you should really fear is my cooking."

"I'll remember that," he said. He covered the few steps between them and took the towel from her. Tossing it on the counter, he pulled her into his arms and kissed her. She melted against him, needing what he was giving her while wanting him to understand. "The plane is at the private terminal and it leaves at four o'clock," he murmured, kissing a point near her ear. "If you change your mind—"

"Oh, Michael—"

"Never mind. I just wanted you to know. Otherwise, I'll be back in a few days."

It was noon when Jess arrived back at her grandmother's. She was informed by Henley that Amanda was having lunch on the terrace. Jess showered and changed into a blouse and skirt, then joined her grandmother at the back of the house. "What a beautiful day," she said as she came out onto the expansive flagstone patio. Amanda looked up at her over the tops of her eyeglasses. Then she turned a page in the book she was reading. "I got your message last night that you wouldn't be home," she said. "Thank you for calling and letting me know."

Jess sat in a patio chair across the table and poured herself a glass of iced tea. "I was with Michael," she said, leaning back in her chair as she sipped the tea.

Amanda's eyes widened slightly. "Michael?" There was no mistaking the pleasure that filled them. "Jessica, I'm delighted. You spent the night with him?" Jess was taken aback by her grandmother's bluntness. Amanda laid the book in her lap and smiled at her granddaughter's flustered expression. "There are no two people in this world who are dearer to me than you and Michael. I am absolutely delighted."

"You aren't shocked?"

"Why should I be?" Amanda said, picking up her book again. "Do you think that your generation invented sex?"

"Of course not. I just didn't think that your generation was so open about it."

"You should have lived in the twenties. Didn't you ever read F. Scott Fitzgerald? Of course, things did become awfully stuffy in the fifties. But no, I'm not shocked. Besides, I know Michael; he is no playboy. He's had his share of willing partners, but I've seen the way he looks at you, Jessica. If he made love to you, he is *in* love with you. Now tell me how you feel."

Jess was speechless. The conversation was out of hand, a condition she was coming to recognize as normal with her grandmother. But she definitely was not going to discuss this. She drained her tea and set the glass on the table. "Let's talk about this later. I have some things to see to this morning. I'll see you for dinner."

As Jess disappeared into the house, Amanda's eyes followed her. She knew Michael was leaving for Washington that evening. Smiling, she turned her attention again to her book, the latest Ludlum, which Michael had loaned to her.

Jess arrived at Tom's room just before two o'clock. In spite of the hour, he looked haggard. "Haven't you slept?" she asked, passing by him into the room.

He regarded her with amazement. "You wanted this stuff quickly, as I recall." He shut the door, struggling against a yawn. "I worked most of the night."

She crossed to a table near a pair of doors that opened out onto a small garden. The table was laden with papers, and she sat down and began sorting through them as he slumped into a chair. "Here," he said, pushing a pile over to her. "The rest is unimportant." He rubbed his eyes, then ran his fingers through his hair. "There was a major court case involving La Familia last year. The transcript makes them sound like a bad facsimile of La Costra Nostra. The contract involved was bungled three times: the first time the chase car wouldn't start; the second time the gun they brought was missing a firing pin; the third time they were stopped by police for speeding. The cops got the names of everyone in the car. La Familia is a joke, Jess."

"Those men run drugs and prostitution, and they murder people," Jess said, glancing up from the papers.

"Point taken. The report on Nicholas Alger is there near the bottom of the folder. That was easy; the man was very visible. He began his political career under FDR and went on to win acclaim as a naval officer—Purple Heart and Medal of Valor. Then he went into the State Department and did twenty-five years of service. His work was exemplary, of course, and he was appointed ambassador to Brazil in 1950. He served through four administrations. There's nothing there, Jess. If you were depending on finding some dirty secrets, you're out of luck."

"Nothing?" She glanced up.

"Nothing. The man was a model of humanity."

"No one is perfect," she said, flipping through the papers.

"Give it up, Jess," he said wearily. "I'm telling you, the man was the essence of propriety. Not everyone has some dire secret, Jess."

"Perhaps," she said. Then she paused, staring at a photograph. "Where did you get this?"

He leaned forward, glancing at the picture. "There's a guy in Monterey who's got one of the best photo collections I've ever seen. That was taken in the forties, I think. Why?"

She leaned back, staring at it. Nicholas Alger was laughing. His arms were around Amanda, and they were standing in a courtyard. The edifice behind them seemed familiar to Jess. She stared at the picture, rubbing her forehead in thought. Why would the background in an old photograph of her grandmother and Nicholas Alger look familiar to her? And then she remembered. The realization came in a breathless sweep.

A weekend with Rick three—no, four years ago. They had driven down the coast. And they had stood in that courtyard along with a large group of tourists, visiting those gloriously manicured gardens, the Roman pools tiled in magnificent mosaics, and the castle itself built by William Randolph Hearst. San Simeon.

She stared at the photograph, stunned by the recognition. The massive doorway to Hearst's home was unmistakable. Within she could still see the roughly beamed great hall, the endless rooms filled with opulent possessions where Hearst gathered his guests. And in front of the castle, in the gardens, stood Amanda and Nicky, laughing. And they were not tourists. "Tom, did you notice who was in the background? That's Norma Shearer and Clark Gable. Look at the clothes; this picture *wasn't* taken in the forties."

He frowned, alert now. Grabbing the papers, he searched through his notes. "Here it is, and you're right. It was 1932."

"Nineteen-thirty-two, in Chicago, was a broker convention," she said quietly, not wanting to face what she was thinking. "Roosevelt was given his presidential nomination by Hearst. He had been supporting John Nance Garner, but at the last moment he was persuaded to throw Garner's California delegates to Roosevelt. That switch gave FDR the nomination."

Tom glanced at the photograph, his eyes widening in comprehension. "My God, Jess. Are you suggesting that Amanda Morgan and Nicholas Alger are the ones who changed Hearst's mind?"

"I don't know," she murmured. "But they were there, Tom. Hearst called Garner at the last moment and ordered him to give his delegates to Roosevelt. And Alger was part of Roosevelt's campaign. And my great-grandfather, David Morgan, was Hearst's friend."

"God, Jess," Tom breathed. "That's pretty heavy stuff."

But Jess's thoughts were taking another path. Amanda and Nicky were there together. At San Simeon. After she had left him in New York. Not years later, but in 1932. Amanda said they did not meet again for years. "Tom, what time is it?"

He glanced at his watch. "Three-thirty."

"Keep going, but now concentrate on the case," she said. She was already moving toward the door. "I want to know more about La Familia, the unions, and labor contractors. I'll get back to you in a few days."

"A few days?" he blurted, but she was gone, slamming the door behind her. He stared at the closed door, then glanced back at the papers on the table and sighed. "Shit," he said. He was all alone in Oz.

She stepped out of the cab onto the tarmac. The jet's engines were warming up, but the door was still open. Gathering up her purse and briefcase, she left the cab. As she stepped into the plane, Michael looked up. He set down the papers he had been reading. "Jess," he said, getting up as the copilot secured the door behind her.

Michael spoke briefly to the pilot, who then disappeared into the cockpit. Then he settled her into a window seat and took the one next to her as the corporate jet began to taxi for takeoff. "What changed your mind?" he asked.

"I need to see my father," she said.

He didn't question her. It was enough that she had changed her mind. He waited until the plane had cleared the runway and gained altitude. Then, as the wheels lifted, settling into the body of the plane, he leaned across the seat and kissed her, holding her in a long, lingering embrace that left them both slightly breathless. He murmured against her lips: "I'm glad you're here."

"So am I," she said, wanting him to kiss her again. She realized then how much she meant it and how bleak the next few days would have been without him. In spite of the reason she had changed her mind, she hoped that they would have some time for themselves.

Without a word, Michael flipped up the armrest between the deep, wide leather seats and unbuckled their seat belts. His arm went under her legs, and he pulled her onto his lap, enfolding her as he kissed her again. Her lips parted under his, and the kiss deepened with urgency. Finally he broke away and bent his head to nuzzle her neck and earlobe. "Have you ever made love at thirty thousand feet?"

Her voice was husky, "No, can't say that I have."

"You're about to."

She gasped softly, pulling back. "Here?" She glanced in the direction of the cockpit. "Michael, we can't."

"They won't bother us."

"How can you know that?"

"Because I told them not to when you came on board."

"You didn't!"

He smiled as his fingers began to play with the buttons on her silk blouse. "You don't have to be embarrassed—not with Dave and Frank."

"Oh?" She arched a suspicious brow at him. "And why is that? Have you done this often?"

"No, and that's not the point. Amanda may not know it—though I never know what she knows for sure—but they're the two horniest pilots in private aviation."

She blinked. "For each other?"

"No," he laughed. "Just two high-flying bachelors who appreciate their job for the fringe benefits it brings—mobility, if you will, and varied ports of call. Believe me, they appreciate our need for privacy, they don't think a thing of it, and they keep their mouths shut."

"Oh." She thought about that, and about the fact that she was sitting on Michael's lap at thirty thousand feet in a private jet with a six-hour trip ahead of them. With two pilots who would respect their privacy and were not judgmental.

"What if they want a cup of coffee or something?"

"They'll buzz first. I promise."

She glanced at the closed door to the cockpit. Then her gaze moved around the small passenger cabin, taking in the deep chairs on the other side of the aisle, and the bar and entertainment center behind them. She looked back at him, and her eyes began to dance with possibilities. "Where?"

"Right here, sweetness."

His fingers undid the buttons on her blouse and slipped beneath. He lingered pleasantly, stroking her breasts through the lace of her bra. Then he slipped his hand behind her back and undid the hooks, releasing her breasts. He pulled the bra down and bent as his mouth claimed a nipple, and his tongue began to tease. She moaned softly as he began to suck gently, and she arched her back, encouraging the blissful assault. Slowly his hand moved down her leg to her feet, where he slipped off her shoes, dropping them to the floor. Then his fingers moved up under her skirt to the tops of her pantyhose. He raised her up, slipping them over her hips, and pulled them down, one leg at a time, dropping them beside her shoes. As his mouth and tongue played at her breast, his hand slipped back under her skirt, between her thighs, parting them slightly for an invasion by his fingers, which began a gentle assault.

"Oh, God, Michael." Jess groaned with ecstasy, loving what he was doing to her, how he made her feel. The moves might be the same, but there was a tenderness in him, an attention to her feelings, that was vastly different from what she had known before and that was more than just skill.

Perhaps it was love. She swallowed, barely able to speak. "Michael, I want you," she whispered.

"You've got me, Jess." His voice was gentle and husky with his own feelings. He shifted her onto his lap, and then he pushed up her skirt and lifted her to straddle him. She looked into his eyes as he lowered her down onto him, her eyes fluttering shut as he filled her. "Oh, God," she groaned. The excitement of what they were doing made her tremble, adding to the heated tension that was starting to overtake her. She came suddenly, shuddering with an unexpected, explosive climax. Distantly surprised by her response, Michael clasped her waist and lifted her up, then plunged into her twice, bringing himself to his own release. Jess collapsed against him, burying her head in his shoulders. He wrapped his arms about her, holding her to him as he kissed her hair.

"I'm sorry." Her words were muffled against his sweater.

Michael frowned, glancing down at her bent head. "For what?"

"I couldn't wait."

He laughed softly. "I wasn't far behind, sugar. And you don't have anything to apologize for. It was great. And even if it wasn't, it wouldn't matter. We have all the time in the world to make it just the way we want it to be."

She sat up and looked at him, her arms still locked behind his neck. "It was wonderful. You know, I've never even necked in the back seat of a car."

"You're kidding."

"Nope. I went to a private girls' school. It eliminated a lot of possibilities."

"Well, that *is* interesting." He grinned. "As it turns out, I am just the man for you." He laughed at her bemused expression. "I still have my car from high school, a 1969 Camaro in mint condition. I can't wait to show it to you."

"I want to tell you about Curt and Rick."

They had dressed and were enjoying cocktails that Michael had retrieved from the galley.

"You don't have to, Jess."

"I know, but I want to. Will it bother you?"

He thought about it for a moment. It was an important question and they both knew it. He wasn't a fan of personal confessions, but he sensed that what she needed to tell him had little to do with sex. "No, it won't, not if you need to tell me."

He listened as she told him about Curt and Rick, and he began to sense that there was something she was not including, something that would explain why this talented, bright woman had chosen to involve herself with unsatisfactory partners. When she finished, the cabin was weighted by silence. He knew she was waiting for him to respond, and he measured his words, sensing that his observation was vital to her. He also knew that his thoughts would unsettle her.

"So Curt was a bastard and Rick is a friend you probably shouldn't have taken into your bed." He had settled back into his seat, swiveling it to face hers. She had chosen to sit across from him to recount her confession. "Our first love affair is experimental, Jess. We don't choose it from age, experience, or wisdom, so it's usually destined for failure. But it shouldn't be regretted. It's simply the first. And it usually hurts enough to guide us to something better. And then you found your stockbroker. And he was safe."

Her head came up. "Safe?"

"You said as much, in as many words, as you were telling me about him. He was sexually safe, a partner who was exclusive, so you didn't have to worry. That's understandable, and wise. And he was emotionally safe; you didn't make demands on each other. After all"—he paused, hoping he'd say this right—"involvement can be painful in one way or another."

He got up, taking her glass, and went into the galley to freshen their drinks, giving her a moment to let his words settle in. Returning, he handed her the drink and sat down across from her again, leaning forward. "Who aren't you telling me about, Jess?"

She regarded him with puzzlement. "No one."

"Yes, there is. I've seen the pain there; it goes beyond the death of your mother. It was there when we talked about loss that night at the Hog's Breath. And it's been there every time I've come too close. But I didn't see it when you talked about Rick or Curt. They were just the effect; they weren't the cause. Who made you so afraid of loving, Jess?"

She stared at her lap, fingering the ice in her glass. She had never talked about it with anyone. For ten years she hadn't even allowed herself to think about it, not until a month ago. She looked up, meeting his gaze unsteadily. "She wasn't just my best friend, she was my soul mate. Her name was Raokhshna Sulayman Husayn. . . ."

She talked for an hour, exposing her memories, her joys, and her pain, trusting him with them. He laughed with her when she recounted the more outrageous exploits and was supportively silent when tears came as she recalled the end. "She knew, Michael, that week in Ibiza. She knew what would happen, but she never told me."

"And you never got to say good-bye."

"No, not even in letters." She took a drink from the now warm glass.

He took it from her gently, placing it in a holder on the table across the aisle. "And the worst part is that you don't know what happened to her."

"I know what happened to her."

"You don't know the details, the where and how. And it's tearing you apart."

"The entire family was shot!"

"Jess, it's been ten years. Don't you think you should at least find out where she's buried? Then you could say a proper farewell."

"I don't want to talk about this."

"I'm sure you don't. In fact, you don't want to let anyone close to you because loving someone hurts, doesn't it, Jess?"

"You're way off, Michael," she protested.

"Am I? I'm not going to have you believing that I'm going to leave you, Jess. I'm not going to disappear."

"That hadn't occurred to me," she said defensively.

"The hell it hadn't. You're not even here now because of me, but because you needed to see your father. Amanda forced you into her life and opened a door for you. You came to Monterey because you needed to open it. But if you don't face Roxy's death—really face it—that door will slam shut again. And I'll be outside it."

"That's not true. I did love Roxy, but I've put her into the past. I've dealt with her loss."

"No, you haven't. But the saddest thing is that you put your life aside."

She stared at him, realizing that she was trembling. Impossible as it seemed, she knew he was right. And then it came with sudden, startling clarity, that her feelings for Roxy were bundled and tied up with her feelings about her family. Roxy had always seen them in a way she could not. She had encouraged Jess to seek out her grandmother; she had pressed Jess to view life in a new way. Without her, Jess had wandered through life, no longer feeling it. And though she hadn't realized it until this moment, she had been blaming Roxy for the loss.

CHAPTER 19

The plane landed in Washington around one o'clock in the morning. Jess and Michael checked into the Hay-Adams Hotel, overlooking Lafayette Square, where they managed a few hours sleep. After a quick breakfast, Jess took the plane on to Connecticut and Michael went on to his meetings, barely making the morning session in time.

The afternoon session ended about three o'clock, and Michael left the room quickly, pushing through the crowd in an attempt to catch someone he wanted to speak with. He caught up with the senator in the hallway.

"We have all the information we need, Mike," the slender, dark-haired senator said. As chairman of the committee he seemed quite satisfied with the results of the meeting. "You did a good job, thanks."

"I need a favor, Bill," Michael said.

The legislator frowned at the statement. He had worked with Michael Rawlings on three previous occasions, and the man had never approached him before for a favor. "What is it?"

"You're also on a couple of foreign relations panels, aren't you?"

"Yes," the senator said guardedly. "What do you need?"

"An introduction," Michael said. They stepped aside as a group of reporters passed, instinctively seeking shelter in an alcove. Michael proceeded to tell him what he needed, without embellishment.

"That shouldn't be too difficult," the senator said when Michael finished. "Come on back to my office with me, and I'll make a few phone calls."

• • •

Michael sat in the back of the limousine lost in thought as it moved through the Washington traffic. Fortunately his companion felt no need for small talk. The senator's aide sat facing him on the jump seat, his attention on the passing streets. Michael barely noticed their route; his thoughts were on Jess.

He thought of her the way she had been the last two days and it brought a smile to his face. He had been given a glimpse of the woman who lingered under that tough, controlled facade she showed to the world. He had glimpsed the child-woman underneath who could still feel the unrestrained joy of innocence. The fact that he had helped to bring out that side of her was astounding. It made him humble—and immensely happy, a feeling he hadn't known for a long, long time.

"We're here, Mr. Rawlings." The man across from him slipped to the edge of the seat, opened the door, and got out. Michael stepped from the car and, with some apprehension, regarded the residence set back from the quiet street. As they walked to the door, Michael glanced up at the flag fluttering from the peak of the eaves in the brisk breeze. A feeling of unreality struck him. He had come to Washington—the trip itself had been remarkable—to testify at hearings before a Senate committee on agriculture, and now he was walking boldly into the Saudi Arabian embassy. Life with Jessica Bellamy would not be boring.

They were admitted to a small, well-appointed room off of the main hallway. As they entered, two dark-complexioned men in well-fitted, expensive suits stood up. One of the men crossed the room and extended his hand to Michael. "Good afternoon, Mr. Rawlings," he said, with only the slightest hint of an accent. "Word was sent to us through your Senator Davis that you are in need of our help."

"Yes," Michael said, glancing at the other man, who was obviously measuring him. "I sincerely hope that you can help."

"We will be pleased to do whatever we can," the first man said, gesturing for Michael to sit.

"Anything you can do would be appreciated," Michael said politely. He glanced at the aide, who had taken a position by the door. He had been cautioned not to mention his knowledge of who these men were, and he almost smiled at the stiff expression of Davis's aide. Don't worry, he thought. I'm not going to screw this up.

"Of course, our host, the Saudi ambassador, is unaware of this visit," the first man said.

"Of course. And I won't remain here long enough to compromise him or his mission. Or your presence here."

"Then tell me, Mr. Rawlings," the man said, flashing a smile as he relaxed into his chair. "How might we help you?"

"Jess, I'm delighted!" John Bellamy folded his daughter into his arms, welcoming her home with a fierce hug. Then, holding her at arm's length, he gave her a hard, appraising look. "What brings you home—without any warning that you were coming? Is anything wrong?"

"Nothing's wrong." She glanced at the breakfast table. "But I could use a cup of that coffee."

"Of course. Have you had breakfast?"

"Yes," she lied. At the moment food would have stuck in her throat.

She had arrived at the private airport near Merryhaven twenty minutes before, anxious to catch her father before he left for New York. She didn't want this meeting in his office. Fortunately, he was still at breakfast when a very surprised and delighted housekeeper opened the door and ushered Jess into the dining room.

"How are you getting along?" her father asked as he turned his attention back to his breakfast. "Is Aaron still as crusty as I remember?"

"Yes. But you know that's all an act," she said, tapping her coffee cup absently.

"One that works."

She glanced at his smile, her eyes narrowing pensively. How could he pretend that nothing was wrong? But then, he had been doing it for thirty years. But no more. This morning, one way or another, the pretense was going to end. "Actually, as I'm sure you know, I haven't seen Aaron in almost a month. I've been in Monterey. With my grandmother." Amazingly, judging by his reaction she could have just imparted the next week's weather forecast.

"So I understand," he said.

If she hadn't been watching him so intently, she might have

missed the muscle that twitched in his jaw. It was a reaction she had seen often enough in the past—when he was furious. John Bellamy was a man of controlled passions. He served up his anger cold.

Now we're getting somewhere, she thought. And she plunged forward. "If you know I've been there, then you know why, so I won't bother you with the details. What is important is that I've grown quite fond of Amanda. I regret that you kept us apart all of those years."

The muscle twitched again. He picked up his coffee cup, took a sip, then set it back on the saucer carefully. He didn't look at her. Then he picked up his knife and fork to cut a piece of ham. His voice was cool. "Jessica, you know that I have reasons for what I do, and my decisions are best for all of us. I will not discuss this."

"And I've accepted your decisions all my life, even though they have cast a shadow over this family that's kept us living in dark corners. Family secrets do that, Father. We pull away from the light and tend to hide things. Most of all we hide things from ourselves, afraid to examine our emotions, or even our relationships, too closely."

When he didn't answer, she pressed on, feeling her own repressed feelings unfolding as she talked. "Perhaps the strangest thing is that Amanda reminds me so much of you. It's sad, too, to realize how much you two have in common, how much you could have shared all of these lost, wasted years. And even stranger is the fact that she reminds me so much of myself. Did you know that our handwriting is almost identical? And we like the same food. And we laugh at the same things—"

"Jessica, that is quite enough." He had finally looked up and his eyes were hard. "I do not care to discuss this further. I was quite disturbed when I discovered that you had gone to Monterey and taken on that infernal case. You know she's using you, don't you? It's inexcusable."

"Inexcusable for Amanda to want to know her granddaughter? She's waited many years for someone from this family to reach out to her."

"That's utter nonsense. She knew better than to expect anything from us. She used this case to manipulate you. I assure you, Jessica, that she has ulterior motives, and if you have an ounce of sense you'll watch your back. She's a conniving, vicious woman who will do absolutely anything to get what she wants, no matter what it costs, even if it ruins someone she professes to love."

Jess stared at him with horrified amazement. She had never heard her father speak with such bitterness and hatred. She collected herself, knowing she could use his emotion. "In just the past few days, it occurred to me why I chose the law." The apparent swift change of subject startled him, as she had meant it to do. "I know that you found my choice of careers a surprise and a puzzlement, if not an actual disappointment. You've never had any use for lawyers, after all. You voiced that opinion to me some years ago. But I understand now, and you should, too. I chose the law, with its absolutes, the comfort of structure. But with those comforts there is investigation, constant search for what lies beneath apparent motives, and a search for solutions to seemingly impossible situations. Discovery, Father, of the truth.

"All of my life I lived in those shadows you cast over us," she continued. "I lived with denials of the past, ignoring the facts of what made us what we are. The search has been everything. And I've found it." And now it comes, she thought, bracing herself. "Don't you think it's time that we dealt with that truth?"

"No. Absolutely not." His pale blue eyes glittered with anger and resolve.

"It's too late to say no." She countered his anger with calmness, but no less determination. "I came here because I want you to confirm something: Was Nicholas Alger my grandfather?"

He grew pale, staring at her for a long moment before he could speak. "Did she tell you that?"

"No. We've never discussed it. She insists that what happened is between the two of you. I began to suspect the truth about Nicky Alger quite on my own."

He leaned back in his chair, suddenly looking old and tired. "Yes. Nicholas Alger was my father."

"Did Jack Bellamy know that?"

"Yes."

"Oh, Daddy, don't you realize that it's better that we all know? I understand what a shock this must have been for you—to find out when you did. To think that Jack was your father and to discover the truth just before you were to leave for college. That was when you found out, wasn't it? That's why you never went back to California. You never forgave them." She smiled gently, understanding his pain. "But all those years of hatred, Daddy—isn't it time to forgive?"

He stared at her, his expression marked by conflicting emotions. "My God," he said, his voice weary. "I hated her for that for a long time. Try to imagine what it's like to learn that your mother has lied to you all your life and, more than that, that the man you loved and respected as your father was just a man who lived on the fringes of your mother's life. But I could have forgiven that. I'm perceptive enough to understand what might happen in a loveless marriage. If that had been all, these past years would have been much, much different."

She frowned, confused. "There was more?"

He regarded her for a serious moment. Then he took his linen napkin from his lap, laid it on the table next to his plate, and stood up. "I think we'd better go into the library where we'll have some privacy. I don't want to tell you what you're going to hear; I've tried to keep it from you. But if you're going to learn about it, and I imagine that you will"—he paused, glancing at her with deep, painful regret—"you'd best hear it from me."

When Michael returned to the hotel, he stopped at the desk to collect messages. He grinned when he learned that Jess had returned earlier and picked up her key. The knowledge that she was upstairs waiting for him was heady. He had so much to tell her, not to mention that the prospect of spending the evening together was stimulating. He got into the elevator, belatedly wishing he had made a detour by the hotel's flower shop. He should take her something—but then he realized that what he had done with his day would be a better gift than flowers.

Stepping out of the elevator he fumbled through the change in his pocket for the key, eager to see her. Had it really only been a few hours since he had left her at the airport? The thought brought a smile. God, he was acting like some lovesick teenage boy.

He opened the door and stepped into the darkened suite.

"Jess?" He glanced at the bedroom door, but there was no light coming from beneath it. He fumbled along the wall, finding the light switch. When the room was flooded with light he saw her, sitting in a chair by the balcony doors. "Jess, what were you doing sitting in the dark?" He smiled, crossing the room toward her. And then she turned to look at him. He stopped suddenly, struck with alarm. She had been crying.

"Oh, my God, Jess, what's the matter?" He knelt by the chair, taking her hand. "What happened?"

Her eyes were red, as if she had been crying for some time. "Oh, Michael." It was all she could manage before she collapsed against him, gripping his shoulders. He reached out and pulled her into his arms. He held her silently, stroking her hair as he murmured soothingly. Then, when she seemed in control, he pulled a handkerchief from his pocket and gave it to her. As she blew her nose, he pulled another chair closer and sat on its edge, leaning toward her.

"Jess, what happened today?"

How could she tell him? she wondered. He loved Amanda as much—no, even more than she did. But no more secrets, she thought, no more. They destroyed everyone. "I'm glad you're here; I wanted you to be here when I got back."

"I had something to do. I want to tell you about it, but it'll keep. Tell me what happened to you, Jess."

"Oh, God, I don't know where to begin. I saw my father. Michael"—she paused, biting her lip—"I know you love Amanda."

"Yes, of course I do." He frowned, tensing at the pain he saw in her eyes.

"You know I've come to care about her—very deeply. You believe that, don't you?"

"Yes. I believe that."

"Do you believe I don't want to hurt her?"

"Yes. Why would you hurt her, Jess?"

Oh, God, how could she go on? Odd thoughts flitted through her mind, and she remembered what the King of Hearts had said to Alice: "Begin at the beginning . . . and go on till you come to the end: then stop." She drew a deep breath. "Michael, you know that my family has been estranged from Amanda for many years. That something happened to cause my father to break with her."

He tensed, suddenly realizing what was coming. Dammit, he thought, why hadn't he expected this? Of course that's why she had come. What had she said when she got on the plane? "I have to see my father." Somewhere, through those blissful miles he had set that statement aside, not wanting to focus on it. "You know about it," he said quietly, his hands tightening over hers.

She stared at him, at his expression of understanding and regret. "You knew?" Her voice was a whisper.

"That Nicky Alger was your grandfather? Yes, Jess, I knew. Amanda had to confide in someone all of these years. She used to talk a lot about the family, about you, and she told me."

Jessica's thoughts spiraled crazily. "Why didn't you tell me?"

"It wasn't my place to tell you, Jess."

"Even in the last few days? You've listened to my confessions, you let me bare my soul, and you knew and didn't tell me?"

"Jess, that was for Amanda or your father to do." He saw the veil that dropped over her eyes and he almost groaned. She had just begun to trust him, to open herself to the vulnerability of trusting her emotions. Now to find out that he had kept something so vital from her. "Jess, please. Let's talk about this."

"There's nothing to talk about, Michael." Her voice was calm, but he heard the pain beneath it. "It's all right, Michael. I understand the loyalty you have for Amanda. I respect that. I do understand your feelings, believe that, but at the moment I need to be alone to sort this all out." She rose from the chair. He stood up and she stepped back, not wanting him to touch her right now. "I know we were planning to stay here a few days, but I'd like to go back in the morning. If that's inconvenient for you, I'll take a commercial flight."

"No, we can leave together." He wanted to hold her, but he stayed rooted to the spot and tried to keep his voice unemotional.

"Thank you. I'll be ready to leave early. Let me know what time."

She closed the bedroom door, leaving him to stare at it in impotent frustration. But there would be six hours during the flight back to Monterey, he told himself, six hours to try to resolve this before the world intruded.

The flight to California was silent. Jess sat in a window seat, staring out of the window as she dealt with her thoughts. Michael tried to talk with her, and she answered him in brief, polite statements, withdrawing without lowering the walls she had put up between them.

Jess wasn't angry with Michael; she was simply unable to deal with the conflicts that were raging within her, emotions that left her unable to respond to him. A part of her, a small part, was angry with him and the fact that he hadn't told her about Nicky Alger. She didn't want their intimacy to be compromised by Michael's ability to keep secrets from her. But she also acknowledged the newness of their relationship; after all, there had been little time to deal with anything but the fact of *them*. But she was numb and she would deal with Michael when she could. In the meantime she had to trust that he could handle whatever he was going through.

For her there was despair. There was the horror of a truth so devastating, so damning, that she couldn't come to grips with it. She could not view it from the distance of an impartial party because it wasn't impersonal, and it violated everything she believed in. She was expected to reject everything she lived by for one she had come to care for. Her passion for the law, her belief in it—she would have to suppress all of that in order to protect Amanda. If she could.

PART III

Michael

CHAPTER 20

It was with a great deal of relief that Jessica returned to Amanda's to discover that her grandmother was out for the day. She packed her things and wrote a note, telling Amanda she had decided to move into Carmel so that she could work more closely with her assistant. She paused over the note, wanting to keep it light and impersonal. A cowardly part of her was glad that Amanda was out; Jess wasn't ready to face her. Not yet.

She left the note with a rather disturbed butler after telling him where she would be staying and that she would call Amanda later. She left the house and drove to the Pine Inn, where she rented a suite near Tom Bradin's room. Then she called Tom and asked him to join her for lunch and to bring his notes.

Tom hung up the phone and stared at it for a puzzled moment. He was surprised to learn that she had moved out of her grandmother's house, but he knew better than to ask why. Perhaps it was simply a matter of convenience. Then, as he stacked his notes, shoving them into his briefcase, he thought of some of the things he had discovered in the past few days and he grew grim.

He arrived at Jess's suite a few moments later. As she opened the door for him he took a good hard look at her, cool and collected in beige wool slacks and a chocolate silk blouse. As usual, her expression was noncommittal. "Put your things over there," she said, following him into the room and gesturing to a desk near the bedroom door. "Lunch will be here in a minute. I ordered chicken salad. Is that all right?"

"Fine." He dropped his briefcase and an armful of folders on the desk. "How was your trip?"

"Informative."

"I had a couple of interesting days myself." He opened his briefcase and took out a folder. Crossing to the table and chairs by the patio window, he slumped in a chair. "Do you want to hear it now?"

"Of course."

Jess's words were clipped, and he glanced up at her with a slight frown, wondering what had happened. She was standing in profile, staring out the French doors to the patio, her arms crossed in front of her. Sighing, Tom opened the folder. "While you were gone, I met separately with two union officials, some friends and co-workers of Rafael Martinez, and the police chief in Soledad, who was particularly interesting. I don't think much goes on in the valley that he doesn't know about."

She turned her head, regarding him with a slight smile. "You've been busy."

"That's what I'm here for. What I discovered supports what you already knew, Jess. There are radical and disruptive elements in the union, and there are some heavy-hitting drug elements in the valley, including well-organized teenage gangs that work with La Familia. Some disreputable characters are operating labor camps, and—you were right—Rafael, at one time or another, had run-ins with all of them."

She turned. "All of them?"

"Apparently Rafael was a troublemaker. In the best sense. He—"

He was interrupted by the arrival of their lunch. When the waiter had left, Jess sat down at the table. "Go ahead and eat," she said, pouring iced tea.

"Thanks, I will. I didn't have any breakfast." He popped a tomato wedge into his mouth. "In the six months prior to the accident, Rafael was involved in quarrels with the union, including a steady stream of written complaints."

"He was anti-union?"

"No, he supported it. But he was vocal against the more radical elements within the union. They showed me his letters but wouldn't give me copies."

Her mouth curved into an ironic smile. "Do they think that will keep us from issuing a subpoena?"

"No, I think they expect it, but they don't want to be

personally involved. Rafael's complaints about union abuses were gaining attention, and a lot of people weren't happy about it." He took a few more bites of his salad and buttered a roll. "The police chief, Cardoza, knew Rafael pretty well. In fact, he had pulled Rafael out of some scrapes when he was younger and helped to turn him around. He was fond of the kid and is still grief-stricken over Rafael's death."

"Is his opinion prejudiced?"

"I don't think so. The guy's tough. I checked on him afterward and learned that he has a good reputation. Anyway, Cardoza painted Rafael as a kid who was fiercely protective of his brothers and sister. His dream was to finish college, then help the others through. He wanted to get them out of the fields. And beyond that, Cardoza said that in the last few years Rafael had become radical about the need for social changes in the community."

"Radical? How?"

"Two years ago he organized a secret group with his friends, and it grew as other young Hispanics joined it. They called themselves Las Voces—the Voices. They took everything on—the coyotes, the labor contractors, the companies, white prejudice. They even started a movement to put more Hispanics into city governments in the valley. They fought especially hard against the drug and prostitution rings."

"La Familia?"

"Yes, but Las Voces concentrated on drug peddling at the schools."

"How successful were they?" Chewing on a mouthful of salad Jess frowned, wondering why she hadn't heard of this before. No one had mentioned it, not even Michael.

"Marginally. As far as the public knows, they were mainly a nuisance."

"As far as the public knows?"

"Well, their membership was—is—secret, and that kind of group is always under suspicion. Letters written, notes left—you know, like the mark of Zorro. But Cardoza said Las Voces is responsible for quite a few large drug busts and for the exposure of coyotes and dishonest labor contractors. Rafael was Cardoza's main informant."

Jess's fork paused halfway to her mouth. She stared at him, and lowered it slowly. "He was what?"

"That's how it was done," Tom said, buttering another roll. "The Voices weren't vigilantes. Only Rafael knew who the other members were, and he took information to Cardoza, or they wrote directly to state and federal agencies."

Jess leaned back in her chair, fingering her iced tea glass as she stared out the window. Tom looked up in the silence, and she turned then and looked at him. He felt his stomach clench. Jesus, he thought, realizing what she was thinking. He knew that over the years Jess Bellamy's mind, like a heat-seeking missile, had developed a habit of finding the hottest, rawest, most warped of human motivations. And she was usually right.

"You're not thinking what I think you're thinking, are you?" She said quietly: "What do you think I'm thinking, Tom?"

"It was an accident, Jess," he said, denying what he saw in her eyes. "Las Voces, his involvement with Cardoza, have nothing to do with Rafael's death. They are just coincidences."

"Tom, Rafael fought against violent elements. Now he is dead."

"But, Jess, I've gone over the accident reports. It *was* an accident, you know that." He saw that she was not listening and he sighed. He saw a week in Carmel stretching into months.

"What else have you got?" Jess asked.

"Nothing much. The details are in my notes."

"I'll look at them later. You did a great job, Tom."

He smiled. "Yes, I did." He took another folder out of the briefcase and dropped it on the table next to Jess. "I found a few other things for you," he said, then poured himself another glass of iced tea.

She frowned, glancing up at him, then pushed her plate out of the way and pulled the folder over to her. Leaning back, she began to read the notes he had made. Her eyes darted up to him with surprise. "Where did you get this?"

"I went back and chatted with that photographer for a while. He gave me the name of a woman living in a retirement home near here. Her name is Alison McCrayton; her family has been here almost as long as the Morgans. In fact, her grandmother was a school chum of Elaine Morgan, your great-great aunt. She must be in her eighties, but she's as sharp as a tack. She even flirted with me."

Jess laughed, believing it. Women of all ages tended to flirt with Tom. Then she sobered, remembering what she had read. "How accurate do you think this is?"

"I checked with old newspaper files. The fire happened, but no one ever found out who started it." He studied her for a moment, aware that she was distressed by what she was reading. "What's the matter, Jess?"

She looked up and regarded him with a level stare. "Tom, Nicky Alger was my grandfather."

His eyes widened. "Jeez, are you serious?"

"Would I lie about that?"

He looked confused, then glanced at the notes she was holding and paled. Facts began to tumble in his brain and he swallowed heavily when he saw the infinitely sad look on her face. "Look, I'm sorry," he said suddenly, getting up, "but I was waiting for a phone call when you buzzed me. Let me run back to my room and see if there are any messages." He had told the switchboard to route his calls to Jess's room, but the false excuse served its purpose; Tom knew she needed to be alone.

"Yes, of course, I'd like to read this more carefully anyway."

When she was alone, Jess merely sat there, staring at the folder. She didn't need to read it again. The Jabberwock had come with eyes of flame, she thought. She closed her eyes, ridding her thoughts of the nonsense rhyme. Then a knock at the door startled her back to reality. Tom must have forgotten something, she thought. She went to the door and opened it, her eyes widening with surprise.

"Michael, what are you doing here?" He looked angry.

"Weren't you going to tell *me* where you were either?" He stepped past her and turned back as she closed the door. "What in the hell is going on, Jess?"

"I told Amanda where I was; I left her a note."

"Oh yeah, the note. That was a rotten thing to do, Jess. Couldn't you have talked with her before you moved out?"

"No." She brushed passed him and began stacking the lunch dishes on the waiter's cart.

"No? That's it, then? Amanda's upset."

"I'm sorry for that, but I can't talk to her right now. I need some time."

"Oh, great. So you're going to start another thirty-year vendetta. Problem is, Jess, she hasn't got that long."

She spun back on him. "That's a bitchy thing to say."

"It's true, isn't it? Jesus, this is unreal." He ran his fingers through his hair, trying to remain calm. Then he looked up at her and held out a hand in a gesture of reason. "Look, I know Amanda made a mistake. She was in a loveless marriage with a man who hopped in and out of every warm bed he could find. She fell in love with Nicky Alger and had a child by him. But she paid for it, Jess. I don't think you're in a position to judge her."

"Judge her? That's exactly what I'm trying not to do!"

The door opened behind Jess and she turned. "Oh, excuse me! I didn't mean to interrupt." Tom stood in the doorway, his hand still on the doorknob. He glanced at the two of them, feeling the tension in the room, and started to back out.

"Don't go, Tom," Jess said.

"But you're busy. Hello, Mike," Tom said lamely.

"No, stay," she insisted. "I want you here."

Michael glanced at her with a smirk. "You don't need protection."

"No, but you need enlightenment," she countered. "Tom has discovered some things I think you need to hear."

Tom closed the door as he looked at Jess and Michael expectantly. "Now, I think that the three of us had better sit down and talk," Jess said. She laid the folders on the table, then sat down across from Michael. "Actually, I'm glad you're here, Michael; we can save some time." She ignored the look of doubt he gave her, opened one of the folders, then leaned back and looked at him. "To begin with, Amanda's grandfather, Luke, had a sister, Elaine, and a brother, Hamilton. Hamilton was a preacher who caught syphilis and went mad. Tom, tell Michael what you found out about our mad preacher."

Tom leaned forward and pulled the folder over to him so that he could check his notes. "Well, it's actually quite a story. Hamilton Morgan used to frequent whorehouses. He enjoyed beating up prostitutes when things got too tense in the pulpit. The family began to realize that he wasn't playing with a full deck when he set fire to his father's house in order to murder his wife, who had left him for his brother, Luke Morgan. The relatives finally found Hamilton in an opium den in Salinas and locked him away in a remote house in Big Sur with a small staff to watch him. Then, in 1906, someone set fire to dozens of houses that were occupied by Chinese fishermen."

"That was China Point," Michael interrupted. "It was a small community near Pacific Grove. I remember the story. Hundreds of families lived in shanties there. It annoyed the locals because the smell of drying squid was overwhelming. But, more important, China Point had become valuable land. Everyone knew that the fire had been deliberately set, but the arsonist was never caught. One of the strangest things about the story, though, was the fact that all of the Chinese families disappeared overnight. They were simply gone in the morning, hundreds of them, to God knows where."

"Yes, so I heard," Tom said. "But it's odd that the arsonist wasn't caught because apparently it was Hamilton Morgan."

Michael stared at Tom. "Who told you that?"

"Alison McCrayton. I visited her in the retirement home."

"That old fool? Jeez, you guys are digging. When she was young she was a vicious gossip, and she's been senile for twenty years."

"Her grandmother was a friend of Elaine Morgan," Jess said.

"And did she tell you that her mother and Elaine Morgan were estranged for the last twenty years of their lives? There was no love lost there."

"Enemies are often more truthful than friends," Jess said. "The point is, Hamilton had escaped during the time of the fire and that's confirmed. When he was found, he was returned by his family to Big Sur, and he remained there until he died in 1910. And we know the man was capable of arson."

"What's the point? So the Morgans had a skeleton in their closet. I don't see what this has to do with anything."

Jess thought about it for a moment; this wasn't easy to explain. "Michael, you enjoy parables. Let me tell you one. When I was a child I had a favorite story. I read and reread it hundreds of times. I never understood it, but the fantasy appealed to a child's open mind. Once, years later, I read it as a teenager and I couldn't make sense of it. It seemed to lose its magic and its power over me. But since I've come here, for some reason, lines from that story keep floating through my head. It's crazy, but they make sense to me now. For example:

'Don't let him know she liked them best, for this must ever be a secret, kept from all the rest, between yourself and me.'"

"That's from *Alice in Wonderland*," Tom said.

"I never read it," Michael admitted. "Make your point, Jess."

"Here's my point: If Hamilton was responsible for the fire and the death of—what was it, Tom, eighty-three people?" He glanced at his notes and nodded. "If he killed eighty-three men, women, and children, and if the family knew and covered it up, then we have a conspiracy, Michael. A secret like that eats away at a family, like a cancer."

"I don't see what this has to do with our problems." Michael leaned back in his chair, tapping the table with impatience.

No, perhaps you don't, she thought, and right now I can't explain it much more than that. Tom's got the sense of it—she knew he had grasped it when she told him about Nicky Alger. Oh, he didn't know everything yet, but he was a good investigator who instinctively filled in the missing pieces. She glanced at him, then shifted her gaze to Michael, sighing at his heavy scowl, wanting him to understand. "'My notion was that you had been . . . an obstacle that came between him and ourselves and it.'"

Michael smirked. "More *Alice*?"

"More Wonderland," she said with a grim smile. "And when I'm done, you might just think you're the Mad Hatter, Michael, or wish you were. You are angry with me because I didn't stay to talk with Amanda. Perhaps I should have told you about this on the plane, but I couldn't." She got up from the chair, suddenly too restless to sit, missing the interested look that Tom gave the two of them. They had gone to Washington together? Hot damn.

"I don't want to judge Amanda, Michael, but I don't know if I can help her in this court case." She turned and looked at him. "It depends on whether or not I can live with covering up a felony."

The two men at the table stared at her. Tom blanched, glancing away, and Michael looked confused. "But the fire was over eighty years ago, and it had nothing to do with Amanda."

"I'm not talking about the fire." Her voice was soft and filled with regret.

"Then what—" He glanced at Tom, who was now staring hard at Jess.

"My father didn't leave California and put his mother out of his life because she had had a love affair with Nicky Alger, Michael. Or because she kept a secret of the fact that Nicky was his father. My father understood that, once the shock had passed, and he forgave Amanda. Keep in mind that my father grew up believing that Jack Bellamy was his father, and he loved and respected him. Jack's excesses were kept from him, by both him and Amanda. To John Bellamy, Jack was a loving and attentive father. My father's bitterness didn't stem from the fact that Amanda deceived him, but from the fact that she shot Jack Bellamy. She murdered him, Michael, and her son was witness to it."

Michael paled, regarding her with horror. "That's impossible."

"*That's* why the police and coroner's reports were so vague," Tom observed. "I checked them, Jess, and it said that Jack Bellamy died of natural causes, but he was only forty-two at the time. I thought it was strange."

"You're saying that Amanda shot Jack and then covered it up?" Michael shook his head, unable to believe what she was saying.

"That's exactly what happened," Jess said grimly. "My father heard voices arguing in the library. Just before he opened the door, he heard a shot. He entered the room to find Amanda and Nicky standing over Jack's body. Amanda was holding a gun."

"No!" Michael's voice was raspy. "I don't believe it. Amanda couldn't do that!"

"I don't want to believe it either, Michael." Jess sat down, leaning toward him. "But it happened."

"How did she cover it up?" Michael looked up at her, his expression bleak.

"She and Nicky paid off the police, I imagine. At least that's what my father thinks, and I can't discount that possibility. My father couldn't betray her; he loved her. So he went away. But he's never forgiven her."

Michael's eyes cleared slowly. "You think that she was capable of murder because of Hamilton Morgan—that she's insane, like him?"

"No. I think she was capable of it because she had been taught to protect the family. Perhaps because she had grown up with conspiracy it was easier for her than it would have been for most people, and she had learned that power could accomplish anything. I'm sure that she rationalized her actions by thinking she was protecting the company and all those who would suffer if the company collapsed. She was also protecting Nicky. Whatever her reasons, Michael, she did it."

Michael swallowed, not wanting to say the words. "What are you going to do?"

"I don't know," Jess said, slumping back in her chair. "I won't do anything until I've talked with Amanda." She looked up at him with a wan smile. "One thing we have in our favor is that I am now her attorney, as is Tom," she added, glancing at him. "She's protected by attorney-client privilege."

"And it has been forty years," Michael observed.

"There's no statute of limitations on murder, Michael. I have to confront Amanda with it; I've got to know the whole story. If I can help her, I will." She saw his disapproval and sighed. "Michael, if Tom and I discovered this, someone else could."

"But it's been forty years and no one else has discovered it." Michael forced himself to say it, even though his brain was reeling with what he had heard. He was appalled and horrified, but he couldn't turn his back on someone he had loved all of his life.

"Amanda's life has never been under this kind of scrutiny before," Jess said. "Oh, she's always been in the public eye, but not the way she is now. She's vulnerable, Michael, understand that."

"Who would attack a woman of her age?"

Tom answered, his voice grim: "Someone who wants to destroy her company."

"Can you do something about it?" Michael asked, turning to Jess.

"I'll damn well try."

"Even though you think she's a murderer?"

She saw the accusation in his eyes and she bristled. "Michael Rawlings, you still don't understand me! In spite of what I've said, I won't make any decisions until I've talked with her. If I didn't question what I heard, I would have left here weeks ago!"

Michael took a deep breath. "You're right. I'm sorry."

Mollified, Jess shrugged. "Don't apologize, not yet. I admit that I'm damned if I can see a way out of this one."

"You will." Tom was sporting a self-satisfied smile. "Something comes to mind that somehow makes me think of you, Jess: 'In my youth,'" he quoted, "'I took to the law, and argued each case with my wife; and the muscular strength which it gave to my jaw has lasted the rest of my life.'" He laughed at their amused expressions. "I read Lewis Carroll, too."

They were sprawled around the suite, pondering the problems at hand. There were two cases to consider now, though they had set Amanda's aside to deal with the more urgent one. Tom was in a deep chair in front of the fireplace with his legs thrown over an arm as he turned a glass of beer on his stomach. Odd, but he had once been curious about Amanda Morgan. Now he wished he had never heard of her. In the past few minutes he had begun to think of something he had read about the mafia. During warfare between the families they cloistered together in bleak rooms, perhaps for weeks on end. He felt something like that now. The three of them had been brainstorming for four hours; Jess only let them out of the room to go to the bathroom. Jess would have made a good mafia don.

"Okay," Jess said. She was perched cross-legged on the coffee table. "Let's go over it again."

Michael's beer stood forgotten on the coffee table. Stretched out on the couch, he groaned, opening his eyes to squint at her. Perhaps he should throw Tom out of here, he mused, trying to gather himself up to the challenge. Then he could attack Jess and make her think of something else. Wearily, he threw his arm over his eyes and tried to ignore her.

She began to recount what they knew of Rafael's case, going over it yet again. Then she halted in mid-sentence. "You're both wimps, you know that, don't you? But I understand," she said, heaving a sigh. "I apologize. I've been pushing you too hard. But you know that this proves without a doubt that women are the stronger sex."

They opened their eyes and looked at her.

"Ah, there's life there." She grinned. "That's encouraging. Okay, let's take a different tack." She had been grilling them on every detail of Rafael's background, police reports, court records, and OSHA reports, questioning them about opinions from the union, personnel records, the family, and statements of friends and opponents, including the weakest rumors. Now she sensed it was time to shift the topic, and she measured her words carefully. "Michael, what if Rafael's death wasn't an accident?"

Tom's eyes flew open and he turned his head to look at her. Michael yawned, his arm still over his eyes. His voice was bored: "Jess, we've been over that. I won't believe that Pete was negligent."

She leveled a look on him, her voice steady. "I know that, and I don't believe Pete was involved. That's not what I'm asking. What if it was murder?"

He was still for a moment; then he dropped his arm and looked at her. "What?"

"Now we're getting to it," Tom said, sitting up with new energy.

Michael sat up. "Murder? Jess, that's crazy!"

"Tell him, Tom," she said in a level voice, holding his gaze.

Tom settled next to her on the coffee table. "There are too many coincidences, Mike. Rafael was resented by some rather unsavory people. He had a lot of enemies."

"I know that," Michael said, regarding them both with disbelief. Then his eyes settled on Jess. "I told you Rafael was a radical, but that doesn't mean he was murdered! He was accidentally killed while harvesting grapes! Good God, more than anyone I want to believe the company wasn't responsible, but murder? That's insane!"

Jess slipped her legs off the table and leaned toward him. "Michael, I know this is hard to comprehend. That's why we've been going over all of this for hours. Look beyond the apparent facts and see what you come up with. Just play with this for a moment, would you? You're the only one who can."

"Me?" He looked at her as if she had lost her mind. "How can I help?"

She regarded him with a level stare. "You can tell me how a grape harvester could kill a man."

He stood up, backing away. "Oh, yeah, I suppose the machine was carrying a grudge and spent its nights plotting to kill its driver. This sounds like a Stephen King novel!"

Jess smiled. She kept her voice level, reasonable. "It's the human element I want. Michael, if you were going to kill someone with a grape harvester, how would you do it?"

He stared at her. "I couldn't. There's no way."

"Pretend, stretch your imagination. Think of the possibilities."

"No. There are too many safety factors built into those machines."

"No machine is totally safe," she said reasonably. "Think."

He gave her a doubtful glance and turned away. He began pacing, running his fingers through his hair, shaking his head. "You said to forget the facts. That would eliminate the hydraulic hose. The levelers gave out suddenly. How would I do it, if I planned it? There's the valve, but that wouldn't work, not if I didn't want the tampering to be discovered." He paused, turning to Jess. "If I did tamper with the machine, I'd make damn sure my work was undetectable, so the result would look like an accident."

"If that's possible," Jess said.

"And if we don't involve Pete, that would make the hydraulic hose a coincidence."

"Yes. Go on, you mentioned a valve," she said.

"No, that wouldn't work. The valve is encased in a housing. The accident wouldn't have concealed the fact that it had been tampered with. That would have been discovered immediately when OSHA took the harvester apart after the accident. No, the murderer would have to tamper with something else."

"Don't try to think of how someone else would do it, Michael. How would *you* do it? Plot it."

He began to pace again and came to a stop in front of the patio doors. He stood motionless staring out into the afternoon sun. Then, slowly, he turned around and stared at them. "Wires."

"What?"

"Wires. My God, it's so simple. There are positive and negative wires that go to the electronic switch that runs the automatic levelers. If the wires were switched, when Rafael hit the manual override button, it would have thrown the levelers into reverse."

"That would do it?"

"Yes, that would work. Later, when the levelers were

needed, they wouldn't work. The harvester would roll over. The wires would probably be jerked out of place during the accident, so there wouldn't be any trace of the tampering. If I had done it, though, I'd be sure I was there that night. If the wires didn't pop out by themselves, it would have been a simple thing for the murderer to pull them out during the confusion that followed the accident."

"That could narrow down our list of suspects," Tom said excitedly.

"Not much," Michael said grimly. "It took hours to get Rafael out of the wreckage. There was quite a crowd there before it was over."

Jess stood up. "Michael, that's it. That's how it was done."

He shook his head, closing his eyes against what he had been thinking. "It can't be." His eyes opened and he looked at her bleakly. "It's hard for me to believe someone would do something like that."

"Right now it's the only thing that makes sense. Unless you want to believe it was an accident—and negligence. I don't believe that anymore. Not with what I've learned."

His eyes widened suddenly. "You can't believe it was Pete!"

"No, absolutely not. That's not where I'm going, Michael, believe that."

"Then who was it?"

"That's the tough question." She exchanged a quick glance with Tom. "We're certain it's murder and you've just given us the weapon, Michael. But who did it? Our problem isn't a lack of suspects. It's that we have too many of them."

CHAPTER 21

It was early evening when Tom left Jessica's suite with a list of phone calls to make. "You work that kid too hard," Michael said as Jess came out of the bedroom. She had changed into a rose linen dress with a soft pleated skirt. His eyes warmed as he looked at her, softening the criticism in the statement.

"Tom thrives on work," she said. "And he's not a kid, though he's been known to use that boyish charm on occasion."

"With you?"

She was standing in front of a small mirror by the bedroom door. She was putting on small cluster earrings of pearls and garnets, and she glanced at him in the mirror and smiled. "Only in the strictest business sense. I'm a barracuda, didn't you know that?"

He grinned. "Is that how your co-workers see you?"

"It's what I'm called—not to my face, of course."

"Does that bother you?"

She thought about it for a moment. "Sometimes, but only when I'm feeling sensitive, which isn't too often. Besides, it isn't as derogatory as it sounds. I get along pretty well with everyone, but I am demanding."

Sensitive. He thought about her choice of words. He suspected it had more to do with vulnerability. So much about Jess made sense now. Tonight perhaps they could finish untwisting the knot and begin to put her together again. As she turned to him, he smiled. "Where do you want to eat?"

"Are you terribly hungry?"

"Not particularly."

"Good. I'd like to take a walk."

"You've got it," he said, getting up abruptly.

They walked down Ocean Avenue to the beach. It was still light and Jess became fascinated with the homes they passed. The area was a hodgepodge of architecture, each house reflecting its owner's taste, yet it was oddly congenial. There were no sidewalks; the hilly climbs and wooded landscape gave a wonderful feeling of privacy, though the lots were small and the houses tightly set.

The beach was almost deserted, and Jess and Michael walked down to the water, enjoying the solitude. Coveys of sandpipers and tiny curlews scurried out of their way as sea gulls and pelicans swooped overhead, the gulls breaking the silence with occasional cries.

They paused at the water's edge, staring out to sea. Jess had removed her shoes, and she dug her toes in, relishing the wet sand beneath her feet. "Oh, Michael, this is just what I needed," she said, glancing up at him with a warm smile.

"You'd better step back or your feet are going to get wet."

She looked down, and stepped back as the surf chased her. "Thanks," she laughed. "Wet nylons are yicky." They collapsed into the sand, which was still warm from the sun. Jess drew her legs up, wrapping her arms about her knees.

He watched her profile, encouraged by her peaceful expression as she watched the surf breaking over the beach. He understood the mesmerizing peace of the ocean; that was why he had brought her here instead of walking into town. It had been a long, unsettling day, and though he marveled at her capacity for hard work, he figured that inside she must be in a knot. "What do you do to relax in San Francisco?"

She turned her head and smiled at the question. "Have you ever lived in a city?"

"No, I haven't. Unless you count the years at Davis when I was going to school. We went into Sacramento a lot."

"A small town boy, huh? What about the traveling you do?"

"You asked me if I've ever *lived* in a city. Visits don't count, do they?"

"No, but let's start there. What do you do for fun when you're in a large city?"

"Oh, no, you don't." He laughed.

"Don't what?"

"Play lawyer with me. It was my question."

"Perhaps I was playing philosopher. Socrates answered questions with questions."

"And that served to teach his students to think for themselves. My objective is to learn more about my lover."

Her eyes softened. "We are lovers, aren't we?"

"It would seem so. But you aren't answering my question."

Her gaze drifted back to the ocean. "It's not very interesting, and painfully typical. I enjoy the theater and the symphony. I work for a few charities. For relaxation, I read. I love fiction, just about any type as long as it's well written." She glanced up at him. "Does that answer your question?"

More than she knew. She hadn't mentioned friends. He knew she attended those activities with other people, but he suspected that she kept them at arm's length. Until now. She had let Amanda into her life, and now him. He wondered what it was going to cost her.

"This has been quite a day, hasn't it?" he said.

"It has," she said, her voice weary with the memory.

"It was something, watching you today."

She turned her head to look at him. "How so?"

"You're good at what you do, and this case excites you, doesn't it?"

"Yes." She smiled. "I love the challenge." Then the smile faded. "But this case is personal, and I'm not used to that."

"How is it personal?"

"That's obvious, isn't it?"

"No, Jess, it's not. Only a couple of weeks ago we were at loggerheads over this case. Since then you've discovered some pretty unsettling facts. You can't even talk with Amanda right now because of what you've learned. And on top of that, Rafael may have been murdered, though I don't think that fact throws you much. I said that I admire the way you handle your work. What I wonder about is how you're going to handle the personal aspects of this case."

"I told you. I need to talk with Amanda before I can decide what to do."

"I'm not talking about legalities; I'm talking about you and Amanda, regardless of what she says about Jack Bellamy."

It was a moment before she could answer. "I don't know. I honestly don't know, Michael. I care about her, and nothing will change that. I'll fight for her. But what our relationship might be in the future I can't say. That's going to depend on what she has to say about everything that's happened. You might not like that answer, but it's the best I can give you."

"Love shouldn't be qualified, Jess. If you care about someone, you take the bad with the good."

"Love may not be qualified, but trust is. And I'm not sure there can be love without trust."

Not if trust is used as a test of worthiness, he thought. Fail it once, and there were no more chances. "You don't give your faith easily, do you, Jess?"

"Should anyone?" she countered. "You're right, my faith doesn't come easily. It's very hard-won. Do you know what a touchstone is, Michael? It's a rock, usually a dark quartz or jasper. When it's rubbed against gold or silver, the mark that's left determines the purity and value of the metal. Trust, for me, requires a touchstone. A test to determine genuineness."

"Proof?"

"Yes." She answered, ignoring the disapproval in his voice. "I'm not as cold-blooded as that might sound. I'll give myself to situations and people when I'm needed, but I don't expect anything in return. That's the mistake, Michael, to expect something back. If you do, you'd better test it first and be certain that what you get is genuine."

"How many people in your life have passed that test, Jess?"

"Not many."

"How many?" he pressed. "Your mother? Your father? Roxy? Who, Jess?"

"I don't want to talk about this anymore," she said. She started to get up, but he grabbed her arm, pulling her back. "Answer me, Jess. How many? Has Amanda passed it? Have I?"

She pushed his hand away, growing angry. "What do you want to hear? If I told you that I wasn't certain of you yet, would it destroy what we have? I told you that I don't give my faith easily, but you want absolutes. What about the time of discovery, of searching, the risks you said you were willing to take? Don't press this, Michael; you won't like the answers."

He let her go and she stood up, grabbing up her shoes. But as she turned away he caught her. "No, it's not that easy, Jess. There has to be some vulnerability with the discovery. You can't expect someone to chip away at those thick walls you've constructed around yourself and be content with the possibility that you might approve once they're breached. You have to take some risks, Jess, or you can't expect anyone else to."

"I'm not asking for that!" she said, trying to pull away from his grip.

"Aren't you?" he said, holding her. "You're not going to run away from this. Dammit, I love you, and I'm willing to say it. That's a risk, Jess, a big one. If you throw it back in my face right now it's going to hurt—a lot. Or do you think that I'm less vulnerable than you are? That I can't be hurt? I'll take the risk because if I don't I can only walk away. But then I would never give myself the chance to find out."

It wasn't that easy, she thought. Love took time, it came cautiously. "Oh, Michael, you ask too much," she whispered. "I don't want to hurt you, but I can't answer you. The only thing I can say to you right now is that I want your love. Selfishly, I want it. More than that, I need it. But I don't know if I can give you what you want."

He eased his grip but he didn't let her go. "That's enough, Jess, for now." He was aware of what even that guarded admission had cost her, perhaps even more than she knew herself. "At least you didn't throw it back in my face."

"I wouldn't do that!"

"Oh, yes, you would, if you didn't feel anything for me," he said softly. "Besides, I know a lot more than you think I do. Behind that protective facade you've erected around yourself, there is a warm, loving woman. You can't fake what we've shared; you just don't recognize your feelings yet. You will face them though, Jess, and I can wait."

"Then what was this all about?" She felt unsettled by the past fifteen minutes.

"It was about a beginning, Jess, a chance for you to trust yourself. You are your own touchstone, don't you know that?"

He bent and picked up her shoes, tucking them into the pockets of his jacket. Then he took her arm. "Come on. I don't know about you, but suddenly I'm hungry. There's a restaurant on Ocean Avenue that you might like."

The following morning Jess was up early, showered and dressed in anticipation of Michael's arrival. She hadn't slept very well and she kept fighting yawns and the temptation to nap. Her thoughts kept returning to the events of the previous night and the things he had said to her. The fact that he had said he loved her, the quiet, romantic dinner, and the way he had left her at her door two hours later. She had wanted him in her bed. She had needed him in her bed. As she drank her third cup of coffee the thought struck that it was exactly why he had said good night at the door. He had wanted her to think about her bed without him. She blew gently on the hot coffee as she stared around her at the flowers in the courtyard and she fought a smile. It wasn't hard to think about, damn him. She hadn't felt this much anticipation since Curt.

Memories turned back and she found that she could think about Curt with an objectivity she had never had before. There was a bird, an Australian vulture, that produced few offspring of its own; thus it made a practice of stealing chicks from the nests of other birds. It kidnapped the chicks of other vultures and even eagles and hawks until its nest contained a strange mixture of species. The image fit Curt well, a man who was incapable of committing himself to a real relationship. Instead, he surrounded himself with vulnerable young women who believed in him for a time. His ego fed off of them.

Curt wasn't to be hated; he was to be pitied. The day would come when he would no longer be able to attract young birds to his nest and would have to face the futility and emptiness of his life. So much for Curt.

Now Michael . . . She drew a steady breath against the rush of anticipation that came with thinking about him. . . .

Jess stepped out of the warm morning sun into the coolness of the room, needing to clear her thoughts. Why shouldn't she be attracted to Michael? she reasoned. She began to pace. He was handsome and unattached. He was pragmatic, a characteristic she had always admired, yet he had a wonderful sense of humor, a dry wit that delighted her. He was smart and educated—the memory of her first opinion of him brought a smile. The hick with a Ph.D. The hick who looked perfectly wonderful in a tuxedo and wore it well, who had all of the social graces but no pretensions. Michael Rawlings was exactly what he presented. Perhaps that was what drew her to him beyond anything else. He was real, and he was comfortable with his reality.

Jessica stopped, cupping the now cold coffee, and trembled

with a sudden chill. What was the old saw, that someone had walked over her grave? Why was she resisting what she was thinking? Michael had the genuineness she had been looking for all of her life. Why was she afraid to admit it? She looked up and found herself staring into the mirror by the bedroom door.

A tall, slender woman stared back at her. The face was pale, touched with artful hints of makeup that emphasized a lack of romanticism. No frivolity there. Her hair had been drawn back in a severe style, held at the nape of her neck by a clasp. She wore an exquisitely fitted suit of navy gabardine, its straight, simple lines in unquestionably good taste. And unquestionably boring. She recognized the woman; she had seen her in the mirror countless times over the years. How often had she withdrawn behind this disguise when something threatened?

She studied the woman. Boring, she thought, but effective. It was her barracuda outfit; many others like it hung in her apartment closet. "God, Roxy, look at me," she said out loud. "Madame Emilie would approve of this outfit." That did it.

She went back into the bedroom, rifling through the closet, disgusted by the things she had brought with her. Finally she found a white linen suit with a fitted jacket that buttoned down one side. She changed into it, accompanying it with a bright emerald-green silk blouse. Then she stood before the bathroom mirror, removed the clasp, and brushed out her hair. She applied a little more makeup, darkening her brows and adding a little blusher and a slightly darker shade of lipstick. Then she stood back and studied the results. The woman who stared back at her had color in her life. Her auburn hair fell in a bob around her face, accentuating her cheekbones. The cut was wonderful, she realized, sensing the frustration of her stylist in San Francisco who had so artfully styled the cut while knowing Jess would only tuck it behind her ear when she left or pull it back away from her face with a clasp.

She went back into the bedroom and found a full-length mirror that would reveal the full effect. She smiled at what she saw. Madame would tremble. And Michael? He probably wouldn't notice. In fact, he probably would have been shocked by the outfit she had chosen to start the day. And she knew now that she had chosen it to keep him at bay. He had come too close, and she had felt threatened. But not anymore.

Humming happily to herself, she went back into the living room, glancing at the clock on the writing desk by the balcony windows. Michael would be here any moment, and the prospect was wonderful. As if on cue, there was a knock on the door. She opened it and her eyes passed over him in appraisal. He was wearing beige slacks, a snowy white turtleneck sweater, and a brown tweed jacket. He looked like a tall ice cream sundae covered in caramel sauce, and she wanted to lick him.

"Good morning." He stepped past her into the room. "It's going to be quite a day, Jess. Are you ready for it?" He turned back as she closed the door.

"Oh, yes, I'm ready. But I don't know if you are."

He frowned, puzzled by the statement. The frown deepened as she stood there regarding him with a smile and a look of mischief. She looked different, somehow, besides the expression. But he liked her suit and what the blouse did to her eyes. It made them greener. Then his eyes widened as she stepped toward him, looking like a cat about to pounce on a mouse. "Jess?" She stopped in front of him and slid her hands beneath his jacket.

"Good morning, Michael." Her voice was husky, the sound startling his body to attention. "Aren't you going to kiss me?"

He looked down at the face before him, the blatant suggestion in her eyes, which were warm and languid with expectation. And her hands were under his jacket, moving over his back.

"Cashmere," she said. "I love how cashmere feels."

"Is that a fact?" he said, knowing she wasn't talking about his sweater.

"Well, are you going to kiss me or not?"

His mouth twitched suddenly in amusement. "I suppose so, if I have to."

"Force yourself."

And he did. After a few moments they were both trembling. "Jeez, Jess," he said huskily. "What's happened?" He drew back to look at her.

"I'm not sure yet. But I think maybe I'm falling in love with you."

He became very still. Apparently she'd had a revelation in the past ten hours since he had left her. He hadn't expected this to happen so soon. "That's a pretty big step for someone who needs to give people tests. Which one did I pass?"

"Don't push it, Michael. I don't want to look at this too closely. I've been running on instinct all morning."

"Now *that* is the most encouraging thing I've heard from you yet."

"You want to go to bed?"

"No. I want to savor this. I want to go crazy with it. Besides, Tom's waiting for us."

"Screw Tom."

"Jessica, really." His eyes danced with amusement.

"All right." She feigned a heavy sigh, stepping away from him. "If you need Tom to protect your virtue, so be it. But I warn you, Michael, the first moment I have you alone I plan to have my way with you."

"Oh, my God."

"Excuse me, I have to get my purse."

They met Tom in the gazebo for breakfast. He was waiting for them at a table under the open dome and was into his second cup of coffee when they arrived. He gave Jess a quizzical look as they sat down. Jessica was never, ever late. A few moments later he cleared his throat to gain their attention. Realization had dawned as he watched them. He was delighted, though he envied Rawlings's good fortune. Tom had occasionally fantasized about having Jess look at him like that. When he knew he had their attention, he grinned. "I hate to interrupt you two with anything as mundane as business, but I have some information you wanted."

"About what?" Jess asked, staring at Michael.

Tom rolled his eyes. This was more serious than he thought. "I'm working on a case you might be interested in. If you'd prefer, I'll work on it by myself."

Ignoring Michael's laughter, Jess tried to affect a serious demeanor. "I'm sorry, Tom," she said. "What is it?"

"In case you've forgotten, you asked me to set up a meeting this morning with Rafael's brothers. Mario is working on a ranch in the San Joaquin Valley. Apparently he goes with the crew at this time every year." He paused, glancing at Michael.

"If you say so." Michael shrugged. "I can't be aware of where everyone is."

"And Anselmo?" Jess asked.

"He's in jail."

"What?" Now he had Michael's attention. "What happened?"

"Apparently last Friday night he was involved in a bar fight in Salinas. There was a stabbing. Two men were seriously wounded, but they'll recover. He's been charged with assault."

"Oh, my God," Michael groaned.

"The police report?" Jess asked calmly.

"Yes, I got it," Tom said, riffling through his briefcase. He pulled out a paper and handed it to Jess.

She scanned it quickly. "There were no other witnesses?"

"No, it was around one-thirty in the morning, as it says there," Tom answered. "The bar was almost empty."

"Okay," Jess said, handing the report back to him. She looked up and smiled at the waiter who had appeared. "Coffee, please, and two eggs over easy with hash browns and whole wheat toast."

Tom gave his order; then the waiter looked at Michael. He was staring at Jess, and it took him a moment to notice that the man was waiting. "Oh—bran flakes and coffee. And toast."

When the waiter had left, Jess regarded him with an amused smile. "Bran flakes?"

"I like bran flakes," he grumbled. "They're a damn sight better for you than eggs."

"What's the matter, Michael?" she asked softly.

"Nothing's the matter." Then he relaxed a little, his glower easing into a frown. "You two might be used to this, but I'm not. You actually looked pleased to hear that Anselmo's in jail!"

"I am."

He hadn't expected that. "How can you say that?"

She exchanged a look of understanding with Tom. What she had just read was a very poorly prepared police report. "He's exactly where I want him, Michael. Trust me. I'll help him if I can." And if I can't, she added silently, he's still exactly where I want him.

But Michael seemed to accept her answer. It served to get them through breakfast, and then Michael went to get the car while Jess had a short conversation with Tom that sent him off on an errand of his own.

• • •

It took some effort to persuade Anselmo to meet with Jess. Michael was one of the few Anglos he trusted, and since Rafael's death even that relationship had become strained. He finally agreed to see her. A policeman was in attendance as they met in a small interrogation room, a small square room with a single grilled window and a table with four straight-backed chairs.

Anselmo was brought in, dressed in the orange jumpsuit of a violent prisoner, and seated at the table. Refusing to look at Jess or Michael, he stared at his hands, which were clasped before him on the table.

"You've been accused of stabbing two men, Anselmo," Jess said. She leaned back in her chair and regarded him coolly. "Did they advise you of your rights when they arrested you?" He didn't answer. "Have they been treating you well?" When he didn't answer, she looked up at Michael who was leaning against the wall at the end of the table. "I remember Anselmo speaking English quite well. Am I mistaken?"

"No, you aren't," Michael said, his eyes fixed sternly on the young Hispanic. "Anselmo's a fourth-generation American. He speaks fluent English."

"Have you spoken to anyone since your arrest, Anselmo?" she asked. He continued to stare at his hands. "I see. They said that you refused to see a public defender, and he was Hispanic, so I gather that this refusal to talk with me isn't personal. Or is it because I'm a woman? Do you feel that women are weak and ineffectual? Or is it that women should be protected, not the protectors? Your sister, for example. She needs to be protected, doesn't she, Anselmo?"

His dark eyes came up then. A sharp glimmer of alarm flickered, then disappeared, but not before Jess had seen it. "Mario is in the valley, working. And now you're in here. Who's going to protect Josefa, Anselmo? Your father? He doesn't know how much she needs protection, does he?"

"You can't help me," Anselmo said, his voice heavy with resentment and despair.

"No, you're right, I can't. Not if you won't help yourself. If you are found guilty of the charges, you could spend a few years in jail. Or, if you let me help you, you could walk out of here tomorrow."

The anger faded, to be replaced with suspicion. "How?"

"I don't want you to say anything unless you accept me as your attorney, Anselmo. Do you?"

He hesitated, glancing up at Michael. "Is she good?"

"She's a partner in one of the best law firms in the country," Michael answered.

Anselmo looked back at her and frowned. "I can't pay a high-priced lawyer."

"I won't charge you any money for this; it's on the house."

"Why?"

"Yes or no?"

"Years in jail?"

"Could be."

He hesitated another moment, his answer barely audible. "Yes."

With the answer, Jess looked up at the police officer who was standing by the door. "I want to be alone with my client." The officer glanced at Michael. "He can stay," she said. When he had left, Jess took a notepad and a copy of the police report from her briefcase. "I said that I wouldn't charge you money for my services, Anselmo, and I won't. However, there will be a fee—"

"Shit!" the young man blurted out, leaning back in his chair as he glared at her. "I knew it."

She ignored his outburst. "The fee is information, Anselmo. Information that we need to help you out of this mess and to protect your family. Nothing more. Now calm down."

He regarded her suspiciously. "What do you want to know, if I stabbed the guys or not?"

"You can tell me that if you want to; it really doesn't matter. It won't affect how I defend you. Was it your knife?"

"Yes."

"Why did the two men attack you?"

His eyes widened. "How did you know that? They said I started it, and so did the bartender."

"All right, let's look at it. There *was* one other witness. He went into the bathroom just as the fight broke out. He stated that you were at the bar and that the two men were sitting behind you at a table. It's rather difficult to attack someone at your back. More than that, the identity of the two men is your best defense. They are minor union officials, aren't they, Anselmo?"

"How did you know that?" he asked, surprised.

"I recognized their names. Your brother, Rafael, had written complaints to the union about them in the past year. Did they threaten you just prior to the fight?"

"No, they didn't say anything. But I saw them in the mirror over the bar as they came at me."

"Jess, then it was self-defense," Michael said, sitting down at the end of the table.

"It's not that easy." Jess kept her gaze fixed on Anselmo. "It was his knife. Carrying a switchblade is illegal, and it shows intent. If we have to make a deal with the DA, we'll have to show that he was carrying it for self-defense and that he had good cause to be afraid for his life." She watched for any indication that she had struck home and she got it, a subtle tensing of his jaw as he leaned back in his chair, away from her. "Why were you afraid, Anselmo?"

"I'm not afraid." His voice was defensive, and he wouldn't look at her, concentrating instead on the grilled window and the sunshine outside.

"Okay, if you say so." She shrugged. "You're not afraid. Mario's not afraid. Josefa"—she paused, seeing the jaw tense again—"Josefa, on the other hand, is she afraid, Anselmo? How will she protect herself without you?"

Michael stared at her, finally understanding Jessica's comment that she had Anselmo exactly where she wanted him. Prison wasn't the threat; the possibility of being separated from his sister was. His gaze shifted to Anselmo with curiosity. What were they hiding?

"The price is truth," Jess said sharply. "Not as my fee, but because it is the only way you'll walk out of here, the only way you'll be free to protect your sister. How many threats have been made against your family, Anselmo, and who made them? This is going to go on and on if you don't stop it, but you can't do it alone. Rafael proved that." Anselmo's head jerked back and he stared at Jessica with shock. Her voice softened: "We know he was murdered, Anselmo. If you tell us who did it, we can help you."

He looked confused and began to wring his hands on the table, glancing about with barely concealed panic. Michael leaned forward, placing his hands on the table. "Who's been threatening you, Anselmo? Someone from the union? The two men who attacked you last night? A labor contractor? Anglos?"

"I don't know," the young man groaned. "Not for sure. But a week before the accident happened, Rafael knew he was going to die. He told Mario and me. One of his jobs was to open the equipment barn each morning." He glanced at Michael. "That was before the grape harvest started. He was helping with the lettuce then. He was supposed to count out the boxes that would be used for the lettuce harvest that day. One morning he entered the barn, and when he turned on the light"—he swallowed heavily, his eyes filling with the bleak horror of what his brother had told him—"he found an owl. It was a great brown and white barn owl with a good three-foot wingspan," he said. "It was staked out."

Anselmo fell silent. Puzzled, Jess glanced at Michael. He was staring at the younger man with horror. "What does that mean?" she demanded.

It took Michael a moment before he could answer.

"An owl staked out like a cross is an ancient Aztec warning of death." He turned and looked at her. "It's a sign favored by La Familia."

CHAPTER 22

Michael shifted the car into second gear as they left the main part of Salinas and drove west along Market Street toward Altra Grow's offices. They had arranged for Anselmo's bail and ordered him to go home and remain there. Jess had made a quick phone call before they left the police station.

"I have two questions," Michael said, glancing over his shoulder as he switched lanes. "One, can you really represent Anselmo? Wouldn't that be a conflict of interest, or something? And two, how did you know that Anselmo had that kind of information?"

Jess laughed softly. "Questioning my ethics again, Michael? Nothing prohibits me from representing Anselmo; at least not for the moment. The appearance of my doing so may not be terrific, but it doesn't represent a gross violation of any kind. In fact, using it as a bargaining tool for information is a pretty standard tactic. If he becomes involved in the case *against* Altra Grow, however, I'll find other counsel for him."

"Fair enough," Michael agreed. "And how did you know?"

"It didn't take a legal genius," she answered, looking at the buildings they were passing. "If we accept the idea that Rafael was murdered, knowing what he was involved in, it was logical that his brothers and his sister were involved, too. At the very least, they would be afraid of repercussions. Besides, when I met them before I sensed they were hiding something, something that was terrifying them. But their parents were not afraid; they're innocents. Anselmo was the angry one. Instincts told me that he could provide the first clue to this mystery."

"But we still don't know who killed Rafael," Michael said grimly. "We know that La Familia threatened him, but we couldn't get the entire organization indicted even if we knew who they all were."

"That's true, but there's someone who can narrow down the list of suspects for us," she said, smiling at the puzzled glance he threw at her. "Josefa."

"Josefa?"

"She's at your office with Tom," she said. "That's the call I made, to confirm that he was there with her. It's time she confided in us as to why she needs her brothers' protection even more than they need to protect themselves."

"That's a quantum leap, I'd say."

"No, it's not. When we saw them, in an unguarded moment Josefa's expression was as militant as her brothers'. That girl's no shrinking violet. In fact, it would be my guess that she's been as deeply involved in Las Voces as her brothers. Now, if that's true—and give me that for the moment—why do they suddenly feel the need to protect her? I don't like it when something's out of sync, Michael. Trust me, Josefa's got the next clue."

When they arrived at Altra Grow, Jess asked Michael to wait outside with Tom while she went into the office alone. Josefa was standing across the room, her arms folded in front of her as she stared out the window. She turned as Jess closed the door behind her and wasted no time on pleasantries.

"Why did you bring me here?" Josefa's dark eyes glared with anger and distrust.

"I thought you would like to help your brother," Jess answered in a firm, no-nonsense voice. "Please sit down, Josefa. We need to talk."

"I don't want to talk to you," Josefa said. She turned back to the window.

Jess took one of the two upholstered armchairs facing Michael's desk. "Then why did you come? My assistant didn't twist your arm, after all."

Josefa shrugged a shoulder and answered without turning around. "I was curious."

"Nonsense," Jess said brusquely. "You are here because you don't know what else to do. You're scared to death and you have every right to be. But I can help you."

Josefa turned and regarded Jess warily. "I don't know what you're talking about."

"Josefa, I understand your reluctance. You've only met me once before; there's no reason for you to trust me. But you're going to have to if you want to help Anselmo. Have you been to see him?"

The question had the effect Jess had intended. She knew Josefa had not visited Anselmo. Josefa's eyes filled suddenly, and she turned to face the window. Jess got up and walked to the window and put an arm around the girl's trembling shoulders.

"Josefa, I can help you," Jess said softly. "Michael's outside; he wants to help you, too. Would this be easier for you if he came in?"

"No, please . . ." The girl's voice was filled with misery. "I can't see Michael. I can't talk to him."

"Then talk to me," Jess said gently. She led the girl to a chair. As Josefa sat down, Jess pulled the other chair nearer and sat on the edge of the cushion. Then she eliminated sympathy from her voice. "All right, let's talk. Let's talk about Las Voces, about the union, about La Familia."

Josefa's head came up. She looked stunned for a moment; then her eyes flashed with anger.

"Ah, that's what I wanted to see," Jess said. She was right about this girl not being a shrinking violet. And she had guessed correctly—the last thing that would reach Josefa Martinez was Anglo sympathy. "Did I strike a sensitive spot?"

Josefa's face became rigid, her mouth a compressed line that spoke volumes. She was not going to talk with Jess. "Let's not digress, Josefa," Jess said in a level voice. "You are here to find out what is happening to Anselmo. I can tell you that. You want to know what his chances are for beating the assault charges. I can tell you that, too. You want to know when he can be home with you again. I can arrange to have him out on bail in thirty minutes. . . . But all of this will cost you."

"Money?" Josefa asked, confused. "You want money?"

"No, I want the same payment that I asked from your brother—information. Truthful, detailed information."

"Anselmo talked to you?" She clearly didn't believe it.

"Yes, Josefa, he did. He told me about Rafael—about the threats. He told me about the owl."

The mention of the owl seemed to shake her. "Why? Why would he talk to you?"

"Because I can help him. And for the same reason you will talk to me—because you have nowhere else to go." Then she added a plum. "Once we have Anselmo out of jail, Michael will bring Mario home. We will relocate you and your entire family, Josefa, someplace where you will be safe. I swear it."

The room became weighted in heavy silence. Jess waited, mentally measuring the time. Pace, timing; they were everything. Know when to pull back, know when to go in for the attack.

"Rafael saw him burying bubble gum," Josefa murmured.

"Cocaine?"

"Yes. Two, maybe three kilos. Behind an equipment barn."

"*Who* was burying the cocaine, Josefa?"

The girl hesitated. "I can't . . ."

"Yes, you can. You have to give me a name. Until you do, he's in control, don't you know that? He controls what you think, how you live, what you feel. You don't want to live like that anymore, do you?"

"Herrera," she replied in a murmur.

Jess leaned forward, wondering if she had heard right. "Herrera? Dan Herrera?"

Josefa nodded.

Herrera, Jess thought. The ranch foreman—the one who sent for help the night Rafael died. Hot damn. "So Rafael saw Herrera burying drugs on the ranch. And Herrera knew he had been seen. Did he confront Rafael directly?"

Josefa shook her head. Then she seemed to steel herself against what she was going to say next. "No. But Rafael knew that Herrera knew. They looked right at each other. Herrera smiled at him," she added hotly. Then the flame of anger seemed to snuff itself out. She looked desolate. "Then—he warned our family to be silent."

"With the owl?"

"No, that was later."

"How did he warn you, if he didn't confront Rafael directly?"

Josefa looked up at Jess. Her eyes became veiled with repressed pain and her voice was emotionless. "He raped me."

Jess came out of the office, closing the door behind her. Michael was sitting behind Carolyn's desk, and Tom was perched on the edge of a desk across from him. "Tom, I'd like you to take Josefa to District Attorney Parker. Is that coffee?" she asked wearily, spying Tom's cup on the desk next to him. She picked it up and took a sip, then leaned against the desk. "I'll try to be brief. That girl needs to file charges with the D.A. and see a counselor. She was raped, Michael."

As the words sank in, both men stood up, swearing in unison. "Who raped her?" Michael demanded.

"You're not going to like this," she said to prepare him. "Dan Herrera, your Soledad foreman." She filled them in on her conversation with Josefa, finishing with: "She told her brothers but they kept the 'disgrace' from their parents."

"Herrera is La Familia?" Tom asked.

"Apparently," Jess answered. "La Familia's intention was to brutalize the family into silence."

"And Anselmo's fight with the union people?" This was from Michael.

"A coincidence, I think, one that has nothing to do with Rafael's death or Josefa's attack. But one thing is certain, that family is living in terror of retaliation."

"Dan Herrera," Michael repeated. He was filled with rage and it took him a moment to feel in control. "What do you suggest now?" He had some ideas of his own.

"Well, first I want Tom to take Josefa to Parker and have Herrera charged with rape. I made some promises to Josefa, Michael. One of them is to bring Mario home."

"You've got it," Michael said. He reached forward and picked up the phone. "And where will you be?"

Jess smiled grimly. "You and I will be in Pebble Beach. I think it's time I saw Amanda."

As they waited for Amanda in the library, Jess found herself pacing. She knew this was going to be difficult, but the past twenty-four hours had given her time to prepare herself for this moment.

She stopped before the bay windows and stared at the curving drive, the pines and oaks, the flower beds designed with artful care. Amanda wasn't just Amanda Morgan anymore; she was Jess's grandmother. And Jess loved her. No matter what she had done, she had become an important part of Jessica's life. Somehow she would see Amanda through this.

"Do you want me to leave?"

Michael's voice drew her back to the room. He was perched on the end of a sofa with a mug of coffee Henley had brought moments before. "No," she said, shaking her head. "This involves you as much as it does me. You are as much a grandson to Amanda as my brother is."

She caught the warmth of his smile, but before he could comment, Amanda came into the room. She wore a dress of lightweight blue wool; her silver hair was immaculate as was her makeup. There were sapphires at her ears, and she moved with her usual energy, her pale blue eyes darting from Michael to Jess with a quick smile. But she looked more frail to Jessica's eyes. More vulnerable. Jess wondered if she was imagining the frailty, if it was a product of her expectations, but a glance at Michael confirmed her thoughts. He set down his cup, crossing the room to Amanda as his expression creased with concern.

"Are you all right?" he asked, his voice deepened with emotion. Amanda merely gave him a quick smile as she offered her cheek for a kiss.

"I'm perfectly fine, Michael. You worry about me too much. Jessica, I'm very glad that you are here." She glanced at the coffee table. "Henley has brought you coffee, I see. It's eight o'clock in New York, and I could use a drink. Shall we have cocktails?"

Michael made them each a drink, watering them liberally, handed Amanda her usual martini, and took a vodka tonic to Jess. He poured himself a beer. Jess took the drink, grateful to have something to do with her hands. Her thoughts turned back to an event some years before when the son of an older partner was arrested for selling drugs. The man, normally a rock, had been shattered. Every normal, rational thought seemed to evaporate when he discussed his son's case with Aaron and Jess. Now, at last, Jess understood. The man was one of the best legal minds in the country and when faced with his son's arrest he had quite totally fallen apart. His opinions could have been shaken by a first-year law student. She wondered, remembering, if she could be what Amanda needed.

The room had grown awkwardly silent. It was Amanda who finally spoke. She leaned a hip on the back of the sofa and took a deep breath. "Of course, I know why you are here, Jessica, just as I knew why you left without talking with me," she said. "You've seen your father and he has told you what happened years ago. I wanted to follow you and explain, but I respect you too much for that, Jessica. The fact that you are here says that you are ready to hear my side of it."

Jess let out her breath. "Yes, that's why I am here," she said. "Do you mind if Michael stays?"

"Of course not," Amanda said, glancing at him affectionately. "It's time the truth was told and I want him to know. I'm not worried about his reaction."

The comment struck Jess to the quick, paralyzing her for a moment. "But you are worried about mine? Do you think that I'm rigid or unfair?"

"No, you will be fair, darling. But you haven't known me for very long, and your opinion of me has been colored for most of your life. I wouldn't fault you for that. Loyalty is not inherited, Jessica; it is earned. I'm afraid that I have failed you in that."

"Facts are facts," Jess said, her voice sharp with disappointment and hurt. "I'll listen to you. I want to know what you have to say about what happened that night."

"I know," Amanda said, smiling sadly. "And you will try to apply all of your considerable legalistic logic and reason to it. You will try to be objective, but can you be? Your father had thirty years with you, I've only had a month."

"Thirty years or a thousand, facts do not change; only perceptions do," Jess countered. "I know my father's memory has been colored by bitterness. I should, Grandmother; I watched it grow and fester. Tell me what happened that night."

Michael tensed on Jessica's words, his gaze shifting to Amanda. Jess had called her Grandmother, not Amanda. He saw Amanda's chin tremble as she hid it behind her drink. He was tense, hardly breathing as he watched them, knowing that at any moment all understanding could suddenly shatter, sending them both back to separate, distant lives. And they would both suffer irrevocably. Then another thought intruded, one he had tried to force aside these past few days. He had no idea how he could divide his loyalty between these two women who were so different from each other and yet so important to him.

Amanda stared into her drink for a long, thoughtful moment,

then lifted her eyes to Jess. "We haven't spoken, so I'm not certain how much you know. Forgive me if I go over ground familiar to you." She paused, forming her thoughts. "Oh, Lord, how far back do I go? You understand, of course, that no one incident, no one event happens in a vacuum. My marriage to Jack Bellamy was a total disaster from the beginning." Then, drawing a deep breath, she told them of her years with Jack Bellamy, of Nicky, and of the day she told Jack that she was carrying another man's child. . . .

Jess set her drink down on a table. Information began to drop into mental files. "Jack accepted your terms, but he must have been terribly bitter. I assume that bitterness grew, particularly after Dad was born. He must have watched and waited for something that would turn matters to his favor."

Amanda smiled appreciatively. "Exactly. And it was my fault that I didn't realize that possibility. The truth was that I didn't care. I was in love, and my arrangement with Jack had freed me to pursue my relationship with Nicky. I had Jack's silence, bought and paid for. Nicky and I continued to see each other over the years."

"Including trips, such as the one to San Simeon," Jess interjected.

"You have done your homework." Amanda smiled. "Yes, and that was a particularly bitter pill for Jack to swallow. He was a stupid man, but he was ambitious. Hearst was a hero to him. I spent a lot of time at San Simeon during the thirties, and I never took Jack with me, not once. But I did meet Nicky there. They were not merely clandestine meetings. Hearst, with his rigid morality, would have been appalled if he had known how many of us used his guest houses for *affaires de coeur*. But for Nicky and me there were political reasons as well. Hearst was a good friend of my father's, and that gave us entrée. Nicky was politically brilliant, and he used his time with Hearst to gain favor for Roosevelt, even long after Hearst was furious with FDR. I'd like to think that we did some good on those weekends, beyond what we shared personally."

Michael had listened, trying to be silent, but curiosity got the better of him. "You saw Alger all through those years?"

Amanda turned and smiled at him. "Yes, I never stopped seeing him after 1932." Then the smile faded. "It was difficult for him. Nicky was a moral, ethical man. But he knew that my marriage was a farce. What is the term the kids use? A cop-out? Perhaps it was. Lord, so many times I tried to persuade Nicky to find someone else. I wanted a normal relationship for him; I truly did want that. I caused him so much pain."

Jess remembered the night in Monterey when Amanda had told her that she understood about Curt. It was odd to think of one's grandmother as a sexual being, one who had not only felt passion but had suffered because of it. "What happened that night in 1950?" she asked. "It all came to a head then, didn't it?"

"Of course," Amanda sighed. "I should have known Jack wouldn't blithely accept what I had given to him. It was the one time in my life that I was truly naive, and the results were devastating. He threatened me once, but I didn't listen. It took him almost twenty years, but he found a way. I don't know how he found out, but it really doesn't matter now. That night . . ." Amanda paused, her hands trembling as she set her forgotten drink on the coffee table. She straightened and regarded Jess with studied control. "That night I was alone with Nicky in the library. My father's library, in the family home in which he had been born. We had moved in after my father's death.

"Nicky had just been appointed ambassador to Brazil," she continued. "He had come to tell me about his appointment. It struck me then, and again later, that he had come to me because there was no one else to go to. Nicky was an only child; his parents had died years before. He had no other family because of our relationship.

"In any case, Jack found us there and he went wild. To this day, I'm not certain if he ever would have used the information he had so painstakingly gathered. Jack was a cowardly man; otherwise I never would have had control over him in the first place. But when he found Nicky in his home, he lost whatever reason he still had. He threatened us, screaming his threats."

"Amanda," Michael said with concern when he saw how pale she had become, "are you all right?"

"Michael, I'm fine. Really. Sit down and let me finish."

Michael sank onto an arm of the sofa next to her, looking doubtful.

"He's right," Jess said, watching her grandmother with concern. "If this is too much for you we can talk about it later."

"I may be old, but I'm not dead yet," Amanda said. "Stop treating me like an invalid. These are my memories, and I'm fully capable of recounting them."

"All right," Jess said, sinking onto a window seat. "Jack was screaming threats. What threats, Amanda?"

Amanda sighed, drawing herself up to continue. "When one is bitter and filled with hatred, it's a driving force that can lead to dark discoveries. Secrets, Jess. Every family has them, though not all members may be aware of them. Some are greater than others. He discovered something that he thought could destroy the family, and the company—"

"Hamilton Morgan?" Jess interjected. "The fire at China Point?"

For a moment, Amanda looked stunned. Then she smiled. "I should have known you'd find out. Yes, the fire at China Point. The family had concealed it for over forty years. But Jack found out, and he threatened me with it."

Jess looked at her steadily. "Is that why you shot him?"

Amanda startled at the statement, paling. "My God, of course you would think that. It's what your father told you. What do you lawyers call it—the smoking gun? And I was holding it when John came into the library. And he had heard voices, angry voices. No, Jessica, I did not shoot Jack. We had been arguing, screaming at each other. He threatened to expose the truth about the China Point tragedy. I started laughing. My God, Jessica, the fire had happened half a century before. Yes, it was terrible, but I wasn't even born when it happened. Moreover, it would have caused the barest murmur of scandal. This might not be pleasant to consider now, but you must remember that minorities were considered unimportant at that time. Opinion was that *people* didn't die that day; *Chinese* did. When Jack realized that his precious information was useless, he went mad."

"Who told him?" Jess asked.

"Nicky. He never lost his composure," Amanda said. "He dealt with Jack calmly, trying to reason with him. And his reasoning was flawless, but he was trying to deal with a madman. I didn't understand that, even though I had lived with Jack for years. But he still had enough reason to understand what Nicky was saying and to understand that everything he had done was fruitless. What he knew meant nothing. I'll never forget the look on his face as he lifted the gun. He looked pleased with himself. His death, he said, would be the end of us. We could never explain it. The husband, shot in the same room as his wife and her lover. Nicky lunged for him and they struggled. Lord, I can still hear the shot. And then Jack was lying there and I reached out and took the gun. I can't explain what compelled me to take the gun from him. And I was holding it when John came into the room."

The library was deathly silent. As Amanda finished her story there seemed little else to say. Michael looked at her, glancing away at the pain in her face, and shifted his gaze to Jess. She was calm and in control. "The sheriff's report said that Jack Bellamy died of natural causes. Did you buy the sheriff off?"

Amanda didn't seem perturbed by the accusation. "Yes. It wasn't difficult. He knew, after studying the powder burns, the angle of the gunshot, and other evidence, that Jack had shot himself. Chief Martin was a friend. He knew we were vulnerable. It wouldn't have mattered that we were innocent. A newly appointed ambassador caught in a love triangle suicide? It would have destroyed Nicky. Chief Martin took charge of the whole terrible situation. He changed the report, and we went along with it. No matter what happens now, I'll always be deeply grateful to him."

"Is Martin still alive?" Jess asked.

"Yes, I believe he is living in Palm Springs."

"Oh, Grandmother, why haven't you resolved this before? Nicky has been dead for fourteen years. We merely have to get a statement from Martin that Jack's death was a suicide."

"And what about the fact that we concealed a crime?"

"A suicide," Jess amended. "I don't think it will be a problem now; it was years ago. Considering my involvement, I think it best if I give this one to Aaron. I'm certain that he can handle it—quietly."

She came to stand before Amanda, reaching out to draw her grandmother into her arms, giving her a hug. "Grandmother, I think I would have done the same thing to protect the man I loved. And after all, Nicky was my grandfather. But how could you allow my father to believe what he has all of these years?"

Amanda sank down onto the back of the sofa. "How could I convince him that what he saw with his own eyes wasn't what happened? He hated me so much. I saw it when I tried to explain, but I also had to explain who his real father was. I can't blame him for not believing me about the accident."

So much misunderstood and so many years lost, for Amanda, her father, her entire family, Jess thought. She knelt down, covering Amanda's hand with hers. "I'm so sorry, Grandmother, for both of you. And for me and Johnny, too."

Amanda eyes softened. "Does your brother hate me?"

"No, neither of us ever hated you. That's one thing you have to give Father credit for. We never understood why he felt as he did, but while he would never talk about you he never talked against you. Hate you? No, we didn't have enough facts for that. You became a mystery. But it's over now, and things are going to change, Amanda, I promise you."

Amanda smiled, patting Jessica's hand. "I know you mean that, Jessica, but don't hope for too much change in my relationship with your father. A lifetime of bitterness cannot be healed quite so easily. But if you understand—that in itself is worth something."

Michael sat on the end of the sofa with a relieved smile. "Well, if that's finally settled, there are other things to talk about. Besides, if we don't change the subject, you two are going to get sappy. And if you do, I'm leaving."

Jess and Amanda laughed, breaking the tension. "Michael's right; we do have other things to talk about," Jess said tiredly, dropping into a chair. "And I think a change of subject might be healthy at the moment."

Over the next fifteen minutes they told Amanda about the Martinez family and the events of the past few days. As she listened, Amanda seemed to recover. She was shocked by the revelation that Rafael had quite possibly been murdered, but as she listened her energy returned with renewed purpose.

"I thought I had cleaned it up," Michael said. His face looked strained, deeply weary. "Dammit, I grew up in that valley. I thought Altra Grow was clean."

"This corruption begins at the top," Amanda said grimly. "With me and all of the other owners. The kind of influence that is needed to stop the abuses begins where the money and power are." She turned, smiling at Michael. "Your grandfather used to say that a man should never leave the land; he needed to walk across it every day. The farther away he walked, the more he lost the sense of it."

"I remember." Michael smiled, then turned somber. "It's been a problem for me, one I haven't learned to deal with very well. Most of my time is spent in the office."

"Perhaps the companies are just too large," Jess said.

"Nothing else will work, not anymore." Michael shook his head. "If food production was limited to small farms, the consumer wouldn't be able to afford to eat. Lettuce would be three dollars a head."

"You're both right, but somehow we have to find a solution," Amanda interjected. "If we don't, these outrages will continue. Michael, you are too hard on yourself; you spend much more time in the field than most managers do. As I said, it will take the power of the owners to change things. Or a revolution from beneath. That's what Rafael tried to do, and we didn't help him."

"You didn't know," Jess said.

Amanda gave her a rueful smile. "That Rafael was Las Voces? No, I didn't. Why didn't he come to us? If he didn't feel he could trust Michael, the others must feel totally helpless, without any recourse."

They fell silent for a moment, and then Jess smiled, her voice bright. "Well, Amanda, you have a fresh objective, a new challenge."

Amanda tried to smile, but the effort gave in to a weary look of defeat. "Yes, I can try, but it may well be without Altra Grow."

Jess and Michael exchanged a surprised look. Michael leaned forward, worried. "What has happened?"

"A couple of things," Amanda said. "First, there's the matter of that damn stock. The purchases have continued steadily. Twenty-three percent of our stock has been bought up since it began, over three hundred thousand shares. All of the available public stock of the Morgan Land and Development Company."

"My God," Jess whispered. Michael groaned.

"Yes. Whoever they are, this will give them a seat on the board. However, even if they vote with the dissenting members of the board, with my cousin's and John's proxies, I have three more votes than I need."

"Three?" Michael asked. "Just three?"

"Yes," Amanda answered grimly. "But three is enough."

Jess listened, a knot growing in her stomach. It took an effort to ask her next question. "You mean if this new person or company voted against you with the board, your shares would be enough?"

"Yes, but just barely." Amanda sighed. "The family still holds the voting shares."

Jess had to look away, afraid that Amanda would see the concern in her expression. *If* the family held together, she said silently. She couldn't help but wonder about her father's shares.

"There is something else," Amanda said. "The second problem I mentioned. A meeting of the board has been called—Borgini hasn't been idle. I received a registered letter from a majority of the board yesterday, requesting a meeting. I had no choice but to comply."

"When is it?"

"On Thursday," she said. "The day after tomorrow. Of course, there's only one reason for this meeting," she added, glancing at the two of them. "You've worried them, Jessica. They're afraid you're going to absolve Altra Grow of its culpability in the death of Rafael Martinez. There's no doubt that the meeting is meant to finish Altra Grow before that can happen."

There was little conversation as Michael drove Jess back to the Pine Inn. As he walked her to her room, each tried to deal with the exhausting events of the day. They stood before the door, and Michael stared at the key Jess had given him. "Do you want to talk?"

"Yes."

He unlocked the door, pushed it open, and followed her into the room, closing the door behind him as she flipped on the light. "Are you tired?" she asked, dropping her purse and briefcase on the coffee table.

"Exhausted." He came into the middle of the room, fingering her key as he searched for what he could say to her.

He hadn't left, she thought. He was here, waiting for her to establish what was going to happen. "I'm torn apart, Michael. Amanda, my father, Rafael, Anselmo, the board meeting . . ." She paused, closing her eyes. "For chrissake, I'm a basket case."

"I know what you mean. Perhaps I should go." Silence fell on the room and they both felt it, the moment drawing out awkwardly. "I hate what's happening," Michael said suddenly. "I'm furious, and I'm sick about it. I don't know how much is my fault or what I could have done to prevent it. I want Rafael to be alive again, and Josefa to be as she was before. I want to protect Amanda, and I'm not sure that I can. I feel as if my life is suddenly out of control. And I don't want to leave."

"I don't want you to leave, Michael." She turned to him. "I want to fall asleep with your arms around me."

Slowly, the corners of his mouth turned up in a smile. "Well, that, at least, is something I think I can manage."

CHAPTER 23

The day of the board meeting Michael awoke early to find that Jess was already up. He showered, dressed, and followed the phone cord out onto the balcony. Jess was curled up on a patio chair, her legs tucked under her, talking on the phone. He bent down to kiss her temple, then sat across from her and helped himself to a cup of the coffee she had ordered from room service.

"Yes, I realize that, but you have to insist," she said, shoving the morning paper over to Michael as she tapped a story below the fold.

He picked it up, feeling his stomach clench as he read it. Borgini was out for blood. Apparently the reporter had cornered Sam at a large dinner party he and Helen had given the previous evening. Michael wondered why this reporter, who was a ferret for scandal, had been present instead of the society editor. Under the reporter's "insistent prodding," Borgini had "reluctantly" admitted that a board meeting had been called to determine Altra Grow's future "in light of the recent unfortunate death of one of its workers. A company must be held responsible for its actions." The article went on, in the reporter's usual yellow style, with background information on Rafael, the grieving family—interestingly, Anselmo's arrest was not mentioned—and details of District Attorney Neal Parker's charges. The story ended with items the reporter felt were examples of historical abuse of workers' rights, slanting the tone of the article. Disgusted, Michael threw the paper down and picked up his coffee. Borgini and his cronies were armed for battle.

"Try to arrange the meeting for ten o'clock. Okay. Good

work, Tom." Jess hung up and set the phone aside. Then she looked up at Michael and smiled. "Good morning."

"Good morning," he said, fixing on the warmth that leapt into her eyes. They stared at each other for a prolonged moment, remembering the pleasures of the past night, a time for them alone, to forget everything but each other. Their eyes held for another moment, sending silent promises; then reluctantly she pulled her gaze away. "Quite an article, isn't it?" She nodded at the paper.

He snorted derisively. "Borgini's publicly declared war, not that it's a surprise."

"No, but now it's all the more important that Altra Grow is exonerated. I wish I had something to take into that board meeting. Tom was with the D.A. for hours yesterday. The man's dragging his feet."

Michael was baffled. "Why? He should be jumping on it. We've solved a murder for him!"

"No, that's still only speculation, Michael. And you have to give the man some credit; we threw it on him less than twenty-four hours ago. So far his only witness is a man who's been arrested for assault."

"But he's the victim's brother! It would be different if we had made the allegations. And Josefa, what about her?"

"They've issued a warrant for Herrera's arrest, but for rape, Michael, not for murder. We're guessing that Herrera is responsible for Rafael's death. The D.A. can only deal in facts, not supposition. All we know for certain is that Rafael received a death threat, of sorts, and that Josefa was raped."

Michael thought about that for a moment. "You're right. Strange, I thought we had more."

"We'll get more," she assured him. "What are you going to do today?"

"I do have an office to go to, at least for the moment."

"And I've a meeting with the D.A. at ten," she said, getting up.

He stood up and reached for her. Pulling her into his arms, he kissed her. "I'll pick you up here at one o'clock. Is that all right?"

"I'll be here."

He began to leave, then hesitated, turning back. "Jess, try not to worry. Okay?"

"Sure, Mickey," she grinned. "And pigs can fly."

Michael spent a long morning at his office, attempting to work while his mind kept drifting to thoughts of Jess and Amanda and what they would face that afternoon. When he drove back into Carmel, he found it crowded with tourists, and Michael was forced to park two blocks from the Pine Inn. He was stopped three times and asked for directions, twice for the Hog's Breath and once by a couple who wanted to know where the best art gallery was. He sent the two families off to the Hog's Breath in their search of the elusive Clint Eastwood—he hadn't the heart to tell them that ol' Clint was on location in Europe—and directed the couple to Bill Dodge's gallery, hoping they liked American primitive as much as he did.

Fortunately Jess was ready when he arrived, and they made it back into Monterey with ten minutes to spare.

The board meeting was to be held at the Morgan Land and Development Company offices, which were housed in a small exquisitely restored Monterey Colonial. Paul Iverson, the company's CEO, greeted the arrivals, ushering them into the boardroom. His staid figure lent a needed dignity to the drama that was about to be enacted. It occurred to Jessica, however, that Iverson's world would not be affected to any great extent by the afternoon's decision. Amanda was a good judge of character and she trusted this man, but Altra Grow was only a subsidiary of the Morgan Company.

The boardroom was a large, beautiful room paneled in rich cherry and carpeted in plush emerald green. Oil portraits of family members dominated the walls; behind the chairman's chair was a painting of Jeremy Morgan. Jess found herself staring at the picture, seeing a resemblance to her father. The irony struck her deeply and she wondered what Jeremy would do now if he were here to confront what was likely to happen to his company in the next few hours.

She felt Michael touch her arm as his voice murmured in her ear: "Here comes Tweedledee. Where's Tweedledum?" She turned as Elliott Westbrook entered the room. Where was Sam Borgini?

Sam Borgini was in an office one floor above the board-room. He was standing in front of a large picture window with a panoramic view of the bay, though the spectacular sight was lost on him. The only sound in the room was the steady jangling of coins that his fingers worried in his trouser pocket. He had been waiting for almost an hour, and his nerves were worn raw. He glanced at his watch again and swore.

The door to an outside corridor opened, and Borgini spun around. "For crissake, do you know what time it is?" he barked. "The meeting is starting in ten minutes!"

John Bellamy closed the door behind him and fixed Borgini with a cold regard. "Calm yourself, Sam. It wouldn't have served our purposes for me to arrive early."

The comment seemed to appease Borgini a little, but he continued to frown. "It wouldn't have served our purpose at all if you had missed the meeting."

"You needn't worry about me," John Bellamy said with a patronizing smile. "What is of concern is whether or not you are prepared for the next hour." He joined Borgini at the window and clasped his hands behind his back as he studied the view. "Breathtaking," he said appreciatively. "Absolutely magnificent."

Borgini let his gaze sweep over the banker. He envied Bellamy the incredible way he looked in clothes. It made all the difference, to look like that, he thought. It made people trust you. Power suits didn't look the same in a size forty-eight short. And who else would have thought to wear that tie with that suit?

"Well, Sam?"

Borgini started. "What?"

Bellamy kept his gaze fixed on the bay. "What do you have to tell me? Is everything under control?"

"Of course. I told you it would be."

"So you did," Bellamy agreed in a deceptively quiet voice. "Why didn't you tell me my mother fired Julian Alcott?"

Borgini shrugged. "I didn't think it was important."

"Not important?" Bellamy glanced briefly at him.

Borgini shifted uneasily. He had heard that tone in Bellamy's voice once before—on the day that the man destroyed his company. The day that Bellamy assumed ownership of Samuel Borgini, lock, stock, and nuts and bolts. The memory pissed

Sam off, making him reckless. "Not important! If I'd thought it was, I would have called you. As for that little chit Amanda replaced him with . . ."

John Bellamy turned slightly, and his pale blue eyes turned to cold flint.

For a moment Borgini felt a stab of fear. He pushed it aside. He was sick of acting like this man's flunky. "I forgot she's your daughter. Sorry," he grumbled. "Anyway, it's almost over. Today we'll vote to close Altra Grow down. You'll have what you want and I'll have my company back—along with the bonus you guaranteed."

"You seem very certain of yourself."

"I should be," Borgini said. He assumed the same stance as the other man and pretended to appreciate the view. "I put enough into this to make it work. Besides, I didn't leave anything to chance—in spite of Julian Alcott. Never could trust goddam lawyers to do the job."

Bellamy turned and regarded Borgini with puzzled concern. "What are you talking about? What did you do?"

"Nothing you need to worry about," Borgini said smugly. "I told you that I would handle things and I did. It's going to happen because of me. Just remember that, Bellamy. I gave the lynch mob the rope to hang the company. Me, not Alcott."

"Lynch mob? What rope—" Bellamy began.

There was a soft knock at the door. It half opened, and Borgini's secretary stuck her head into the room. "The meeting is starting, Mr. Borgini."

Borgini glanced at his watch, then started for the door. "Well, it's almost time for your grand entrance. I'll go down first; then my secretary will show you the way." He paused at the door and looked back, grinning broadly. "Enjoy yourself today, Bellamy. I certainly plan to."

Borgini left the room, but John Bellamy remained there, staring at the open doorway. Lynch mob? His impassive expression slipped into a scowl as he felt a rush of apprehension. What in the hell had that cretin done?

"There he is," Jess murmured. Michael followed her gaze to the doorway. Borgini had come into the room, and he looked pleased with himself. Then Amanda entered the room, and Jess was filled with pride. Her grandmother was controlled and terribly beautiful. Jess recognized the gray suit as a Givenchy. There were diamonds at Amanda's ears and in a discreet pin on her lapel. Successful and understated. A flash of humor struck Jess when she realized that it was a power suit, definitely contrasting with Borgini's overstated look of success. Blood does tell, she thought, crossing the room to her grandmother.

"Are you certain that Michael and I won't be asked to leave?" she asked in a low voice, aware that Borgini and Westbrook were watching them.

"Nonsense," Amanda said. "You are the company's attorney and Michael is Altra Grow's general manager. I've requested that you be here." She gave her granddaughter a level look. "And that is that."

As Jess watched Amanda move away to greet the other board members, her chest tightened with pride. Then pain washed over her as she wondered how the day would end. If only she knew how he planned to sway the board, she might be able to counter Borgini's moves.

Jess stood back with Michael, watching the board members greet one another, trying to guess their thoughts. Jess had a sinking feeling when she recognized subtle gestures which suggested that they were solidly behind Borgini. The man was insufferable in his confidence. And then, a moment before the meeting was to begin, Jessica's remaining hope crumbled at her feet. She heard a gasp from someone nearby the same moment that she felt Michael grab her arm. She turned and felt as if someone had struck her. Her father had entered the room.

"Oh, my God, Father!" she whispered, leaning against Michael's solid form for support. She heard his voice in her ear, cautioning her, but she could only stare, horrified. Her eyes darted to Amanda. Her grandmother had paused in mid-sentence and turned to the new arrival. She visibly paled, but miraculously she never lost her composure as she crossed the room to her son.

"John!" Amanda exclaimed softly.

Jess pulled away from Michael's grip and crossed the room to intercept Amanda. She was acutely aware of those who were watching with morbid interest. "Why are you here?" she whispered fiercely at her father. She glared at him with all of the fury she was feeling.

In spite of John Bellamy's normal composure, he started. "Jessica, this has nothing to do with you," he murmured.

"It has *everything* to do with me!"

"Jessica." Amanda's calm voice cut through Jess's anger. Jessica's heart tightened, seeing the hunger in her grandmother's eyes as she regarded her son. "John, it is so good to see you."

"Mother." The word was uttered without feeling.

Jess swallowed, pain rushing over her. Without consciously realizing it, she moved to Amanda's side. "Why are you here?" she demanded of her father.

"I felt that I was needed," John Bellamy said smoothly, with a glimmer of disapproval of his daughter's challenge. "Altra Grow's fate is to be decided today. I know how important this is to my mother; I had to be here."

"I'm glad you are here, John," Amanda said.

Jess glanced at the two of them as voices whispered in her brain, warnings. How could Amanda be so calm? He was here to destroy her, didn't she know that? There was no longer any doubt in Jessica's mind about who had bought that large block of Altra Grow stock.

Jess felt a hand on her arm. She looked up as Michael drew her to the other side of the room. He sat her down, taking the chair next to her along the wall. "Let it be, Jess," he murmured. "We can only watch."

She didn't want to accept it, but she knew he was right. She gripped his hand.

The participants took their seats at the large mahogany conference table where a leather folder had been placed before each chair. Amanda, as chairman of the board, was at the head of the table, beneath the portrait of her great-grandfather. She called the meeting to order with aplomb, Jess thought. How could she be so in control?

"Before we begin, you will note that there is a vacant chair at our table," Amanda said. "Late last week it came to my attention that small blocks of Morgan company stock had been purchased throughout the previous month. Immediately Paul and I began to investigate the matter. We found that twenty-three percent of publicly owned stock had been purchased by one company . . ."

"What?" Elliott Westbrook interrupted. He glanced briefly

at Borgini with confusion, but Sam was looking at John Bellamy with an expression of admiration bordering on awe. Bellamy was unaware of the attention; he was scowling at his mother. Westbrook, looking confused, said, "That means that whoever it is would be entitled to sit on this board!"

"Yes, Elliott, that's what it means," Amanda agreed. "I believe that it was Julian Alcott who persuaded me to include that clause in our bylaws." She looked down the table at her son. "Isn't that correct, John?"

"I wouldn't know," John Bellamy answered. "I was not privy to your decisions regarding the formation of the Morgan Company's public offering."

"Yes, indeed. As you say," she agreed, leveling her gaze on her son.

My God, Jess thought, watching her grandmother's expression. She knows he can't be trusted.

"In any case," Amanda continued, "I was able to find out that the company that purchased the stock is American Properties—"

"Why didn't you inform us of this earlier, Amanda?" Lee Somerfield asked. A pleasant, affable man, Somerfield was a retired two-star general who had been attached to the Pentagon as his last duty. His mild demeanor hid an iron fist and a no-nonsense approach to business. He had not committed himself either to Amanda or to Borgini's camp.

"I couldn't tell you about the stock purchases until today," Amanda explained, "because I only learned the name of the company yesterday. Naturally, our Morgan Company attorneys in Los Angeles are, at this moment, developing a full report on American Properties. Had I been given more time to prepare for this meeting, you would have had the report. As it is, American Properties has been provided with its chair. They are not here, but a quorum is present; therefore we can begin the meeting. Paul, please read the minutes of the last meeting."

"I think we could dispense with the minutes," Borgini said impatiently.

"I think not, Sam," Amanda disagreed. "There was no time to prepare written copies of the minutes for you. They will have to be read. Proceed, Paul."

Jess frowned at Amanda's words. There had been ample time to prepare copies of the minutes of the last meeting. In fact, she suspected that Paul Iverson had done so some time ago. What was Amanda up to? One could almost think that she was stalling for time.

Jessica's gaze shifted to her father. John Bellamy's expression was noncommittal, though that did not come as a surprise to Jess; he loathed emotional displays. Nonetheless, she knew that behind that cold gaze was the owner of American Properties. And she was certain that when the vital vote was taken the identity of American Properties would be revealed. John Bellamy might abhor emotionalism, but he did have a flair for the dramatic.

Why should she stay to watch this? she wondered. What purpose would her presence serve? She turned to Michael. "Take me out of here," she murmured. He nodded and took her arm. Then his hand tightened perceptibly. She looked up at him. He was staring at a point beyond her. She turned, following his dumbstruck gaze.

The door to the boardroom had opened, causing a pause in the proceedings. A wave of shock rippled through the room. Three men had entered, garbed in white robes and ghotras, the black-banded Arab headdress. The tallest of the men nodded slightly to those in the room. "Please excuse my tardiness," he said in Oxford-accented English. "Our plane was delayed."

Michael stared at the man. "Jesus," he groaned, sotto voce, remembering where he had seen the man: in a newspaper photograph on a lazy Sunday morning. His eyes darted to Jess, wondering if she recognized him. She was gaping.

The man took the vacant chair as his attendants took a position behind him. Then he smiled as his dark eyes passed over the others. "I am Khaled el Ahmed. I have cause to join you in this most important meeting."

John Bellamy's expression oscillated between confusion and surprise. He had identified the newcomer immediately, though it was difficult to place el Ahmed in this setting. He addressed the others, "Prince Khaled is chargé d'affaires at the Saudi embassy in Washington." Then he turned to the Arab. "Forgive me, Prince Khaled, but I do not understand. We had no warning . . ."

"I must apologize if I have inconvenienced anyone, but I was notified only yesterday of this meeting. I am here as head of American Properties."

"*You* are American Properties?" Borgini blurted out, his eyes bugging. "But I thought—" He flushed, glancing at John Bellamy with confusion.

"*What* did you think, Sam?" Amanda asked coolly.

"Nothing," he murmured as he slumped back in his chair.

Amanda's gaze shifted to the new arrival, and she smiled warmly. "We are delighted that you could attend the meeting, Prince Khaled. And I must apologize for the late notice. I fear that we just barely complied with the forty-eight hours required to call a board meeting. Also, we didn't know how to reach you until yesterday."

Her last words stunned the other board members. John Bellamy's expression hardened. "You told us that you didn't know the identity of American Properties!"

"I didn't say that," Amanda said, giving him a soft smile. "I said that I found out the name of the company only yesterday morning and that our attorneys were preparing a report for the board. Both statements are absolutely true. I barely had time to speak with Prince Khaled about this meeting."

"Why didn't you tell me?" he insisted.

"Why, John, I was unaware that you were coming. As for the rest of the board, they're being informed now. And now that the entire board is present, let us finish reading the minutes. Paul?"

As Iverson read, Jess stared at her grandmother with astonishment. Apparently she and Iverson had been busy. But then, considering Amanda's connections, she shouldn't have been surprised. Jessica's gaze shifted to the Saudi prince. Aside from Amanda, he was the only one in the room who looked truly composed. About thirty-five, with deep olive skin and dark, almost black eyes with heavy black brows, Prince Khaled el Ahmed was an extremely handsome man. She remembered Michael's comment when they saw his picture in the newspaper, and she wondered if he really did have the world by the tail.

She definitely shouldn't have been surprised by the identity of the new stockholder, she reasoned. After all, foreign investments were surging upward every year. The Saudis were almost as active as the Japanese and the Dutch in American investments. Even the name was revealing—American Properties. And the Morgan Land and Development Company, along with its subsidiaries, was a very attractive investment.

Michael's thoughts were running along similar lines, with one difference. He suspected that he knew a little of how Judas must have felt. He didn't know how his visit to the Saudi embassy had contributed to this moment, but Prince Khaled's presence was too bizarre to be a coincidence. He stared at the Saudi, wishing he knew what was going on behind that composed demeanor. He calculated the stock votes at the table, then closed his eyes, suddenly feeling sick.

The minutes were approved, and Amanda opened the leather folder before her, the others at the table following suit. "There is only one item of business on the agenda," she said calmly. "The disposition of Altra Grow. Perhaps, for the benefit of our new board member, we should provide some background."

"Yes, I agree," Borgini interrupted, leaning across the table toward the Saudi. "But first, I want to know something about our new board member. One, how did you become aware of this company? Two, why are you interested in buying stock in a company that has an important subsidiary in serious trouble? I can't believe that you didn't know. And three, what are your intentions, Prince Khaled?"

John Bellamy winced, then spoke up before Amanda could. "Sam, your questions are inappropriate, not to mention excessively rude."

"It is quite all right," Prince Khaled said, raising his hand in a gesture of appeasement. "I am not unaware that many people in your country resent foreign investors. Is that what you are saying, Mr. Borgini?"

"It's a start." Borgini glowered.

"First, allow me to assure you that I have no desire to control the Morgan Land and Development Company. On that matter, you may rest easy. My interest, which is my country's interest, is in Altra Grow. Simply, we want your agricultural products, Mr. Borgini. Not all of them, of course, but your substantial surplus. In my part of the world, we look upon American farmers with great respect. Certainly you can understand that."

Sam's glower eased a little at the compliment, though he wondered if he was being patronized. "Yes, you're right about that—no one can outproduce the American farmer."

"It is so." Khaled smiled. "We also hope to learn from you." His gaze shifted briefly to Michael, who tensed at the attention, feeling sicker by the moment. "Surely there are enough crops to allow us to reach a trade agreement," Khaled continued. "We are aware that your Salinas Valley produces eighty percent of your country's lettuce and sixty percent of its broccoli, not to mention the over one billion dollars in total crops produced annually. Such production from such a small area astounds us." He turned his head and smiled at Amanda. "You see, I have done my homework."

"Indeed you have," Amanda returned, her lips twitching with a smile.

"But that doesn't tell us why you invested in a failing company," Borgini insisted. "If there's no Altra Grow, there's no produce."

Khaled's calm gaze turned to Borgini. "I was not aware that Altra Grow was failing."

Borgini snorted. "You Saudis may have more money than you know what to do with, but you're not fools."

"Thank you." Khaled smiled with a slight nod.

"That's not what I meant. You know there's a legal case pending against Altra Grow. I would appreciate an answer to my question."

Khaled shrugged. "I fear that at the moment I cannot give you one. Or perhaps I was misinformed. I believe that the purpose of today's meeting is to decide the fate of Altra Grow. Apparently, if I am to judge by your attitude, it has already been decided."

Sitting next to Borgini, Elliott Westbrook gave a quick snort of laughter, earning a glower of anger from Borgini. "Sorry," he said, leaning back in his chair.

"Now, if we can move on," Amanda said firmly. She leveled her look on Borgini. "I assume, Sam, that you have no further questions for Prince Khaled?" Borgini was sullen but silent. "Good. At this point, the chair will hear opinions on the matter at hand. John, I'd like to hear from you."

John Bellamy regarded his mother noncommittally. "I am here to hear what the others have to say. I have not been involved enough with the company to have an opinion."

Jess almost choked on the statement.

"Indeed," Amanda said quietly. "Well, then, who would like to speak first?"

A reply came from Charles Baird, an old friend of Amanda's and a retired CEO of one of the nation's largest computer companies. Baird, a pleasant-looking man of sixty-seven, leaned forward, clasping his hands before him on the table. "At the risk of belaboring a situation of which we are aware, I'll address Prince Khaled, if the rest of you don't mind. I, for one, appreciate your presence," he said, smiling at the Saudi. "I feel that the prospect of an additional market can only benefit us all." Over the next ten minutes Baird recounted details of Rafael Martinez's death.

"The matter at hand is the disposition of Altra Grow," he concluded. "There are those on this board who feel that the only way to protect the Morgan Land and Development Company is to close down the farming operation completely."

Jess gave in to a grudging smile of appreciation. Baird had stated the situation clearly without giving a clue to his own feelings.

"I see," Khaled said thoughtfully to the silent room. "The death of young Martinez is, of course, deeply regrettable, though in my country we would consider it the will of Allah. But to shut down the operation . . . I am confused about that. Altra Grow is one of the largest agribusinesses in your country. Considering the market portion it contributes, would this not cause hardship to many people, including the consumers who depend on its products?"

"Yes, it would," Amanda answered. "But that is not the issue here. Profits generated for the Morgan Company are the prime consideration of this board."

Khaled looked thoughtful. "Yes, I do understand the profit motive, and I do not condemn it. In fact, I look upon the situation with a certain self-interest." He paused, glancing at the others with a slight smile. "I want that broccoli."

There was a ripple of laughter around the table.

"And we want you to have it," Jess interjected. She stood up and approached the table. She was fed up with all of this pussyfooting around. "However, there are some issues of which this board should be aware."

"Jessica, this does not concern you," her father said sharply.

"Oh, yes, it most certainly does," Amanda countered

calmly. "Jessica, not everyone here has met you." Then she addressed the board. "Jessica Bellamy, my granddaughter, is with the San Francisco firm of Reynolds, Armisted, and Royce. Recently I fired Julian Alcott and hired Jessica as Altra Grow's attorney. I believe that she has information you will need to make a decision today."

Jess took a step toward the table, and her eyes swept over those present as she judged their reactions to her presence. She saw the reservations; it was a bad split. She needed to shake them up.

"This meeting comes at an inopportune moment. Rafael Martinez's death is being reinvestigated by the district attorney. We have reason to believe his death was not accidental."

"For chrissake!" Borgini exploded. "What in the hell are you talking about? That's crazy!"

Jess turned a contemptuous look on the man. "No, it is not. Other facets of this case have recently come to light—such as the fact that Rafael's sister was raped by an Altra Grow foreman. We believe that he is the one who—"

"Well, that really cooks it!" Borgini exclaimed. "If anyone has any doubt—"

"You don't understand," Jess interrupted. Her irritation with the man was reaching its limit. "We believe that La Familia is responsible for Rafael's death, and—"

"In fact, that doesn't mean a tinker's dam," Borgini countered. "The boy's death will still be associated with Altra Grow, accident or no accident, La Familia or the good fairy." Sam turned to Khaled. "You see, in this country Allah's will doesn't count; public opinion decides what is and what isn't. Normally, of course, that opinion can be controlled through creative advertising and proper promotion. But once in a while the public attaches itself to a cause. Rafael Martinez has become a cause." Borgini's voice took on an edge of contempt. "The poor farm worker who lost his life because of the negligence of the big, powerful, uncaring company. To put it bluntly, our produce won't be worth the cost to harvest it."

Seeing the effect that Borgini's diatribe had on the board members, Jess sat down. As she did, her gaze held that of Prince Khaled. He was watching her intently. She shifted uncomfortably in her chair. What did he expect from her?

There was nothing more she could do. Or was the Saudi prince merely staring at her because he thought she was a fool?

Unfortunately, Borgini wasn't finished. "This board has to look at the facts," he went on, sensing his victory. "Altra Grow is only a small part of the company's holdings. If we close it down, our losses will be manageable. We are insured against lawsuits, but not the loss of investment against growing and harvesting. Just as important is the real possibility of public *approval* if we voluntarily close down a profitable operation."

Jess felt herself begin to bleed inside. She wanted to stand up for what she knew to be the truth, but she could only sit silently, facing the inevitable. And there was no doubt in her mind where this was going.

Jess, however, was not watching her father. As Borgini had carried on, for an instant John Bellamy lost his composure. He paled, obviously staggered by something Sam Borgini was saying. A look of horror passed over his eyes; then they seemed to cool behind a veil of control. His gaze shifted to find Khaled watching him. The prince nodded slightly.

"I call for a vote," Borgini said suddenly.

"Sam, you can't call for a vote," Amanda said irritably. "There hasn't been a motion yet."

"Okay, okay," he snapped. "Then I'll do it. I move that—"

"No." The word was said quietly, but it stopped Borgini cold and drew everyone's attention. "No," John Bellamy repeated. "I'll make a motion." He leveled his stare on Borgini. Sam yielded, but he looked like someone who had been told he couldn't play.

Jess felt sick. Her father was going to destroy Altra Grow himself, she thought miserably. Did he really hate Amanda that much?

"I move that we support Altra Grow, its officers and its employees, throughout the pending legal action," John Bellamy said.

Everyone in the room was stunned by the statement—all but Borgini who obviously hadn't been listening. "I second it!" he blurted. Then it hit him what Bellamy had said. His eyes grew round, and he gasped. "You what? I—I don't second that!" he added, obviously confused.

"I second it," Lee Somerfield said.

"A motion has been made and seconded," Amanda said.

Then she repeated the motion. "Is there discussion?" she asked.

"I call for the vote," Prince Khaled said, giving in to an amused smile.

The motion passed, with only one nay. Borgini looked ready to expire.

Amanda closed the meeting, and without another word, John Bellamy got up and left the room.

As the other board members got up and began to mill around, Jess sat there, stunned. She looked at Michael, who appeared as dazed as she. "What just happened?" he asked.

"I have no idea," she answered. Then her gaze lifted to the portrait behind Amanda. "But it looks as if your company will survive after all, Jeremy Morgan. At least for now."

CHAPTER 24

"I'm ready for a party," Tom said happily. He had just joined Jess and Michael in the lobby of the Monterey Plaza Hotel on Steinbeck's Cannery Row.

Jess smiled. "It's a small celebration, Tom, not a party."

"Whatever. Where is it?"

"Amanda made reservations in the dining room for dinner," Michael answered, "but we're to join them first in Prince Khaled's suite."

"For a cocktail?" Tom asked hopefully as they walked toward the elevators.

"I hardly think so, Tom; it doesn't quite fit the Muslim profile."

"So your father showed up at the meeting," Tom said as they rode up in the elevator. "What did your grandmother do?"

"She carried it off like a pro," Michael said.

"What did she say to him after the meeting?"

"Nothing." Jess shrugged. "He left right after the adjournment."

"That's too bad. After forty years you'd think he'd stay for a few minutes."

"He didn't come to socialize," she said dryly. "I'm trying to figure out why he made that motion."

"At least it buys us time," Tom observed. "The way this case is going we need it."

"Perhaps," she mused. "But I don't trust him."

They arrived at the floor, and when the elevator door opened they were greeted by a concierge and three Saudis guarding the hall. The concierge established their identity, then escorted them to the prince's suite.

Jess had been wrong. Cocktails were being served in the prince's suite, and Amanda was having a martini. She and Khaled were sitting in large armchairs in front of a wall of plate glass doors leading out to a large deck. The sun was slipping beyond the Pacific Ocean, and the sky was slashed with streaks of bright pink and orange cirrus clouds.

"Hello, my darling." Amanda smiled as Jess approached. "Khaled and I have been having the most illuminating discussion."

Jess leaned over and kissed Amanda on the forehead. "I'm certain that you have, Grandmother," she murmured.

Amanda introduced Tom to Khaled. "He takes good care of my granddaughter," she added, smiling at the young man who was trying not to stare at the Saudi prince.

"Khaled and I have worked out some of the details of a wonderful trade agreement," Amanda added.

"A trade agreement?" Jess asked, amused. "He gets broccoli and lettuce. What do you get?"

"Money, of course. And art."

"Art?" Jess turned her question to Prince Khaled.

"We have a work of art in my country in which your grandmother is most interested. I assured her that I would loan it to her without charge, but she insists that I be recompensed."

"Is it a rug, a tapestry, a mosaic?" Jess knew it wouldn't be a sculpture, as Muslims were forbidden to create images with three dimensions.

"I have it in the other room," Khaled said. "Perhaps you should view it and give your grandmother your opinion."

"If you wish."

Khaled motioned to one of his companions, and the man went into the next room. A moment later Jess looked up and tensed. Her commitment to women's rights rushed to the surface. Across the room stood a woman draped from head to toe in a black veil.

"Ah, Jahara," Khaled said with warm affection. He stood up and held out his hand. "May I introduce you to my wife, Jahara Yamani el Khaled."

Jess tried not to stare at the woman, but she didn't know how to respond, beyond a nod. What in the world did one say to a woman so sublimated by her culture that she walked through life covered from head to toe in black cloth?

"Good evening," came a soft voice. "Has not my husband offered you refreshment? What would you like to have? A rum and coke, perhaps?"

Jess stared at the woman. Rum and coke? Lord, she hadn't had that concoction since college. But she realized that a Saudi woman would hardly be well versed in liquor. Perhaps she had heard of the drink somewhere and thought it appropriate to offer one to an American. "No, thank you," Jess said, resisting a grimace.

"Something else, perhaps?" the woman persisted. She seemed to note the drink the bartender was handing to Michael. "What are you drinking now, Jess? Don't tell me you like scotch?"

Jess stared, stunned into immobility. The voice had dropped, deepening into something vaguely recognizable. The sound of that voice pounded in her mind. The room was deathly quiet. Distantly she was aware that everyone was staring at them.

Slender hands reached up and lifted the floor-length veil. The face was there, the form, standing a few feet away in a breathtaking gown embroidered with delicate flowers on a background of ivory silk. Jess could hardly breathe. One word came out of her in a rush, a single name: "Roxy."

The beautiful, cherished face smiled. "Yes, it's me, Jess."

Jess stepped back, pushed by the force of her incredulity. "It can't be. You're dead. The mullahs killed you!"

"They tried," Roxy said. "Oh, they did try, Jess, but here I am."

Jess couldn't absorb it. Not after all these years. Suddenly she became filled with anger. "You are, you're alive. You didn't die! *Where the hell have you been?*"

"I want to tell you about it, Jess."

"Almost ten years! You let me think you were dead for ten goddam years! How could you do that to me?" Jess spun around and rushed toward the door. Michael caught her before she made it.

"Jess, for heaven's sake," he said. "You can't run out like this."

"Watch me," she hissed, reaching for the doorknob.

"Jess!" he said harshly, as he gripped her arms. "This is Roxy. Roxy, Jess. Would she have let you think she was dead all these years without a good reason?"

Jess froze. She turned back. Roxy was standing in the middle of the room, looking as bereft as Jess felt. As they continued to stare at each other the years began to tumble away. A few seconds later they were in each other's arms, laughing and crying at the same time.

A short while later they were sitting on the sofa, facing each other with red-rimmed eyes. Khaled and Amanda were sitting across from them, and Michael was perched on the edge of an ottoman to one side. Tom was standing by the fireplace, enjoying the warmth and a viewpoint that allowed him to watch everyone at once.

"I still don't believe this," Jess said, staring hard at her friend. Part of her feared that she had truly entered Wonderland and Roxy was an illusion. "Tell me everything, every detail since your last letter." She paused and glanced at Khaled. As she turned back to Roxy, her eyes widened, then began to dance with humor. "Is he the one—your prince?"

Roxy nodded and grinned. "He's the one."

"How did you escape and end up with Khaled? The last word we had"—Jess paused again, growing somber—"was that you had been shot."

"Only Fahed, my little brother, and I survived. Everyone else perished that day."

"Everyone?" Jess asked, tears filling her eyes again as she remembered holidays and the warmth and love of the Husayn family.

"Yes. Only Fahed and I are left."

"How did you manage to escape?" Michael asked, leaning forward as he rested his arms on his knees.

"A friend of my father was on the tribunal. When he heard that we had been taken, he sent a message to my father that he could save one or two of us, no more."

"No!" Amanda gasped. "Certainly your father did not have to choose."

"No." Roxy shook her head. "We had all been thrown into a cell together. A guard came. It had been arranged that he take two. Fahed and I were chosen because we were nearest the door." She paused, taking a deep breath as she dealt with her memories. "When we left the prison, I took Fahed into the underground where we joined the People's Mujahedeen. We lived that way, in hiding, for eight months. Our group was in the midst of planning a bombing to rescue two men who were being held by the Jihad. We had no way of knowing it, but the Jihad had found out about us. The next day the entire group, but for Fahed and me, were captured."

"Why weren't you?" Jess asked.

Roxy smiled sadly, remembering the loss of her friends. "Because that night Fahed and I were kidnapped." She glanced at Khaled and her smile warmed. "A group of men broke into our safe house and took us. Of course, I thought they were sent by the Jihad and that we were lost. But they moved us from place to place throughout the night. In the morning we were put on a small plane that was waiting for us in the mountains. Khaled was there when we boarded. It was he who had come for us, and he took us into safety in Saudi Arabia."

"How romantic," Jess said, her voice breathy. Then, when she realized how inane that sounded, she flushed. "I mean, of course it wasn't romantic—it must have been terrifying."

"It was both." Roxy grinned. "It seems terribly romantic— in retrospect. I had never stopped loving Khaled, though I never thought I'd see him again. I thought that all possibility of marrying him had vanished from my life. And then there he was, holding me. He had been planning the rescue for eight months."

"All right," Jess said, leveling a determined look on Roxy. "Now tell me why, in all of this time, you couldn't tell me you were alive."

"I will answer that for you," Khaled said. "Simply, Jessica, if it was known that my wife, Jahara Yamani el Khaled, was Raokhshna Sulayman Husayn, the results would be disastrous for many people. The Jihad have sworn to kill her."

"But why?"

"Because she was a very active member of the People's Mujahedeen for many years, during and long after she left Iran. Once that old fool who claimed to be the Imam was dead it became somewhat safer. But please do not ask more than that. It is best if you do not know the details."

"I was going to come to you before this," Roxy added. "But with everything that was going on here I thought I could be more useful in the background."

Jess looked puzzled. "I don't understand."

"I think I do," Michael said. "You've been watching Jess

for a long time, haven't you? You knew what was going on here, with the Morgan Company."

Roxy paused as a servant brought them small cups of thick black coffee. "Khaled, as part of his duties for the embassy, promotes trade between your country and mine. He deals with many American businessmen. And because of me, he deliberately dealt with certain men."

"Because of you? Why?"

Roxy smiled, deferring to Khaled on this one. "Some time ago the embassy began negotiations with Sam Borgini's company to purchase parts for farm equipment," he said. "The relationship was short-lived. We despised the man's business methods and had no doubt that he was dishonest. That would have been the end of it, but we soon learned that Borgini had become a member of the Morgan Company's board of directors."

"How did you discover that?" Amanda asked, clearly interested in this particular question.

As Roxy's eyes became veiled, Jess shook her head in disbelief. "No, don't tell me. You really were watching us, weren't you? Jeez, who did you have working on this—the Saudi version of the CIA?" Then her expression stiffened, a thought dawning. "Do I want to ask if you have someone working inside my father's bank?"

"No."

By the hearth, Tom let out a slow, soft whistle.

Amanda wondered about her own company.

"So it was a coincidence!" Michael blurted out.

"Yes, Michael, it was," Roxy assured him, smiling at his look of relief.

Jess frowned at Michael. What had been a coincidence? He had been acting strangely ever since Khaled walked into the boardroom. What *was* the matter with him? Later she intended to find out. But for now . . . "Okay, go on, Roxy. We're fascinated."

"There isn't much more to tell. We decided that the best defense was a good offense, so we decided to outflank your father and Borgini. Hence, American Properties."

"As it turned out, I'm not certain it was necessary," Khaled observed.

"Oh, but it was," Amanda said. "You can be sure of that. I

don't know what happened to change his mind, but John came to that meeting today to destroy Altra Grow."

"Did you find out where he went after the meeting, Amanda?" Michael asked.

"No. I have no idea," she said. Her voice was clipped and her lips compressed with hurt. "He probably went back to New York." Seeing the sympathy in the expressions of those watching her, Amanda stood up. "For heaven's sake, let's not get maudlin! Do you realize how much I have to be thankful for tonight? And I don't just mean the survival of my great-grandfather's company. I have a granddaughter whom I love dearly, and tonight she has been given a great gift." She glanced at her watch. "I've reserved a perfectly wonderful table downstairs by the window. We have some celebrating to do, so let's get on with it and leave John to stew in his own juices, since that is his choice."

For a moment Sam Borgini's face revealed all the hatred and envy he felt for this man. Beyond that, he was slightly drunk. "Get out of my house, Bellamy!" he shouted, losing a little of the effect when he slurred the words.

"Not until we have this out," John Bellamy said with icy menace. "Do you realize what you've done? Can you comprehend it, or are you totally demented?"

"Me! You're the one who screwed up! It was a done deal! Why did you make that absurd motion?"

"Because I had no choice, you idiot!" Bellamy was standing in the center of Borgini's study with his coat still on. "I knew when you were carrying on about public opinion . . . That's what you meant by a lynch mob, isn't it? I had to stop any further involvement in it right then! What in the hell have you involved me in?"

"I just did what I had to." Borgini scowled. He took a long draw on his bourbon.

"You were supposed to work with Alcott!" John Bellamy shouted. "To do whatever you had to to increase costs and create labor problems. To undermine operations! Slow up production! Not murder, for God's sake!"

Borgini took another drink. At that moment John Bellamy felt as if all the blood had drained out of his body through his feet and into the carpet. He was standing in a pool of blood and it was his. Borgini hadn't denied being involved in the murder of Rafael Martinez. Bellamy had hoped that his suspicion was wrong and that Borgini would deny it. "Jesus," he said in a strangled voice. "You did it, didn't you? You really murdered that boy."

Borgini regarded Bellamy with contempt. "Of course I didn't! I put Herrera on it. I didn't actually tell him to kill anybody, but I didn't put any restrictions on him either. What's the matter, Mr. Banker, afraid of getting your hands dirty? You want the job done and then you whine about the means used to do it."

"Whine? You son of a bitch." Bellamy lowered his voice. "You've involved me in a murder!" Staring at the other man, John felt the cold control that had ruled his life settle over him like a welcome shroud. "I'm going to give you the money, Borgini," he said levelly. "After that, you are off the Morgan Company board. I want you out of my life. I want you out of my family's life. You're to disappear. Do you understand me?"

"Sure, Bellamy." Borgini shrugged. "Whatever you say. Just be sure I get the money."

John gave Borgini a last scathing look. "If you think you can cross me, forget it, Sam. You've pushed me against the wall. I'll destroy you before I'll let you go any further—against me or my family. I *can* destroy you—and it won't be quick, like the death of that boy. You'll have to live with what I do." With that, he turned and left the house.

Borgini stared after him for a protracted moment. Then he chuckled, a deeply amused sound.

"I fail to see the humor in this situation, Samuel," Helen Borgini said, coming into the room.

"Eavesdropping again, my dear?" Borgini asked drolly. He went over to the bar and poured himself another bourbon. This time he skipped the branch water. "This is none of your business, Helen. Go to bed."

"Not this time," she said. When he looked up at her, she knew she had his attention. "We're going home to Maryland. I miss the kids."

"We're not going anywhere," he said, taking a gulp of whiskey. "We're staying right here. Don't let what Bellamy said worry you. He can't do a thing to us"—he laughed—"except support us for the rest of our lives."

"No, Sam. We're going home."

Borgini really looked at his wife then. "Shut up, Helen, and leave me alone."

She never blinked. "We're going home, Sam. You're going to take the money John Bellamy gives you and start a nice little *honest* business. And I'm going to watch my grandchildren grow up, and we're going to be the perfect grandparents."

Sam's mouth slackened; then he flushed with anger. "Who the hell do you think you're talking to?"

"To an accomplice to murder. To a bastard. But you're my husband, and I'm too old to adjust to changes if I can avoid them. I also don't want such awful publicity for our children. But don't doubt this, Sam: I can live with the publicity, and I can adjust to living by myself if I have to. I've just given you the price for my silence. Now I am going to bed. I suggest that you do the same because we start packing bright and early in the morning."

She left him in the library with his bourbon and went to bed. As she went up the stairs she was humming.

It was after midnight when Amanda returned home with Jess and Roxy. They were laughing at something Jess had said just before they got out of the car. It wasn't just that the joke had been genuinely funny; it was a night for hilarity. As they entered the silent house, Amanda waved her hand at them, though she was barely able to contain herself. "Shhhh. We mustn't wake Henley. He may be my butler, but he runs my life—the old tyrant. I can't deal with him tonight."

"Worse than that," Jess said dryly, but her mouth was working with a giggle. "We don't want to wake Conrad."

"Who's Conrad?" Roxy asked, dropping her overnight bag on the Queen Anne table.

Amanda focused on the table. "I really need to move that—"

"Conrad is the meanest, scariest—" Jess began.

"Madam."

The single word brought the three women around. Henley had come into the hall.

"For heaven's sake, Henley," Amanda exclaimed. "You needn't have waited up. But since you have: Princess—ah, Jahara will be staying with us for a few days. You may take her bag to the room next to Jess's. Oh, yes, Jessica is moving back home. Have Teresa bring her a nightgown and robe. We'll collect her things from the Pine Inn in the morning, and the princess's things from the Monterey Plaza." Amanda began to turn away, then paused. "Oh, yes, there is one other thing. There are men outside. They came with Princess Jahara. Be certain they have breakfast in the morning."

Amanda turned back to the other two women. "Now let's go into the library for a nightcap. My word, it's been a few decades since I've been to a slumber party. I am sorry, though, that Khaled has to go back to Washington in the morning. But I'm delighted that he allowed you to stay."

"Allowed?" Jess teased, flaring her eyes at Roxy. Oh, this was rich.

Roxy made a moue at Jess.

"Madam!"

It wasn't even close to a shout, but it was uttered in an octave that Henley had never used in his life. It got Amanda's attention. "Yes? What is it, Henley?"

"There is someone waiting for you in the library, madam. He has been waiting for almost three hours."

"Now? But it's past midnight!"

"Yes, madam. But you will want to see him."

Amanda frowned, moved to the double doors of the library and threw them open. Jess and Roxy could hear the sharp intake of her breath.

"John!" she exclaimed softly.

John Bellamy was sitting in a high-backed leather chair before the fire. He was still wearing his overcoat. He looked haggard. At Amanda's entrance he stood up. "Mother," he said in a quiet, pained voice.

As Amanda went into the room, Jess stepped forward and closed the doors quietly. Then she turned back to Roxy. "Well, that's a pleasant surprise. Let's hope the visit ends well," she said softly, with feeling.

"Yes, I hope so, Jess."

Jess cast a worried glance toward the closed doors, then slipped her arm through Roxy's and propelled her toward the staircase. "And now for us. Let's go upstairs, put on our jammies, and really talk."

"Isn't that what we've been doing for the last six hours?" Roxy laughed.

"Hardly," Jess said. "Let's talk about *men*. To begin with, how does it feel to be a toady?"

Soon, after changing into robes and raiding the kitchen, they were curled up on Jess's bed with potato chips, pretzels, chocolate chip cookies, and sodas.

"Amanda was right," Jess said with her mouth full. "I'm soooo glad you made the decision to stay on a few days. So answer a question for me, does Khaled have a harem?"

Roxy laughed, a throaty sound that Jess had forgotten. "No. He's allowed four wives, but fortunately I am enough for him. Besides, Jess, I'm smarter than that; I looked for a man who had been educated in the West. Khaled and I met at Oxford, and before that he went to Eton. I'm no fool." She popped the top of a can of soda. "Now it's your turn. Rick Logan is a very nice man, Jess."

Jess gasped at her. "You've met Rick?"

"No, but Khaled has talked with him on the phone. Logan found out who owned American Properties three days after you asked him to investigate it. It didn't take much to persuade him to keep silent, though. The man cares about you, Jess."

"I didn't know he cared that much."

"He assured Khaled that he was your friend; he wanted to help."

"So that's why he never called me back." Jess frowned. "I'll have to call him and thank him. People in my life have sure changed during this mess. It's brought out the best or the worst in them." Then her expression changed to one of curiosity. "Which reminds me. Ever since Khaled walked into that boardroom, Michael has been acting really weird. Would you know anything about *that*?"

"I might," Roxy said with a shrug as she munched on a pretzel. "Michael visited my country's embassy while you two were in Washington. He thought he had something to do with Khaled's interest in Altra Grow."

Jess thought her hearing had gone wacky. "He went to the embassy? Why?"

"A senator on a foreign relations subcommittee knew that some members of our staff were Mujahedeen," Roxy said as she ripped open a bag of potato chips. She glanced up and grinned. "Of course he didn't know about me. Anyway," she nibbled on a chip. "He called and said that a trusted friend wanted to meet with them. You can imagine our surprise when it turned out to be Michael Rawlings and we learned what he wanted."

"What did he want?"

"Information about me, of course. Michael asked them where I was buried. He said that someone close to me needed to say good-bye. Of course, he didn't know that the corpus delicti was two floors above him having dinner."

"I don't believe it."

Seeing her dumbstruck expression, Roxy smiled. "You don't believe that? That I was upstairs or that Michael cares that much for you?" She watched Jess's reaction. "Do you love him, Jess?"

Jess blinked. She was simply overwhelmed by what Roxy had told her. Michael had sought out the Mujahedeen to try to help her. . . . Then Roxy's question hit her. Walls of denial tried to push up. And then she looked into Roxy's open, unguarded face, a face filled with joyous expectation, after all she had been through. Roxy. Secrets, laughter, speculation, investigation—the years tumbled through her thoughts, touching her with memories. She saw the miracle of being here with Roxy, of what she was finding with Michael. She felt herself striking the stone and she saw the truth. Michael was right: Discovery was within oneself; that was where one found trust. The walls began to crumble.

"Yes," she said against the overpowering feeling of sudden freedom. "Yes, I love him."

"Good," Roxy said, emphasizing the word. "He's right for you, Jess."

Jess laughed. "And I know you're going to tell me why. You always did think you knew what was best for me."

"As you have always done for me. He's your ice cream sundae, Jess. And you need him because you tend to be anorexic."

"I do?"

"You know you do."

"You may have a point." Jess shrugged. "Anyway, I'm delighted that Michael and Khaled hit it off so well."

"Yes, they'll probably talk about farming until dawn. It's Khaled's passion. He sees the Rub' al-Khali planted and irrigated."

Jess laughed. "All two hundred fifty thousand square miles?"

"Every square inch of sand."

"Well, then, Michael—"

There was a soft knock at the door and they looked up as Amanda came into the room. "Jessica, I'm sorry to bother you and Roxy."

Both young women grew alarmed at Amanda's bleak, worried expression. "Grandmother, what is it?" Jess asked as she slipped off the bed.

"I want you to talk with your father. We need your advice, dear. I'm sorry, Roakhshna."

"It's all right, Amanda," Roxy assured her. She threw a questioning frown at Jess.

Jess shrugged slightly. "Don't eat all the chips," she said and left the room with Amanda.

Forty minutes later Jess was glaring at her father, openly angry. "How could you have done this?" she demanded. "How could you have let it go this far?"

"I didn't know until the board meeting," John Bellamy said miserably. "I never meant for any of this to happen—not like this."

Jess never realized that she could feel such disappointment in someone she cared about. "Well, Father, as they say, when you lie down with dogs you get up with fleas."

"Jessica, I understand your anger, but—" Amanda began.

"But nothing!" Jess interrupted hotly. She took a few steps away and stared into the fire, trying to find calming answers in the flames. It didn't work. She turned back to the weary form of her father. He was sitting across from Amanda in one of the two chairs in front of the library hearth. His hair was mussed; she had never in her entire life seen a hair on his head out of place. His suit was rumpled and his skin was sallow. He looked old.

Looking at him, Jess felt her anger grow. "Dad, don't pull this pathetic act with me."

"Jessica!" Amanda exclaimed.

John looked bewildered.

"Grandmother, perhaps you should leave the room," Jess suggested.

"No," Amanda answered, sitting back in her chair with a set to her chin that clearly said an army couldn't eject her. "This involves me, too."

"All right. But I want you to understand that you can't possibly be objective about any of this."

"And you can be?" John asked. His brow arched in that familiar, disapproving way of his.

Jess met his gaze levelly. "Oh, yes, Father," she said quietly. "You taught me that. No matter what the circumstances are, objectivity is vital, and it is found by cold detachment."

The glimpse of defiance disappeared and he looked sad once more. "Did I do that to you?" he murmured.

"Oh, don't apologize, Father. It made me into one hell of a lawyer. And that's what you need right now."

"Can you assess the damage?" Amanda asked.

"The damage," Jess repeated, shaking her head. This was a nightmare. "First of all, Father, stop acting like the victim. You're not, you know; Rafael was. And his family. Besides, the first rule I have for taking on clients is that they can't have given up. So cut out this suffering act or get yourself another attorney."

She began to pace. From the corner of her eye she noted that her father had sat up. "I'll go to the D.A. with this. I will look Parker in the eye"—she paused, looking heavenward for strength—"and tell him, 'Look, my father's had this vendetta against his mother for about forty years. He ruined—ah, bought out Sam Borgini's company and put Sam on the board of the Morgan Land and Development Company with the promise that if Borgini would act as his man within Amanda's organization there would be a big bonus in it for him.'" She paused, taking a breath as she glanced at her father. "Right so far?"

John nodded. He looked a little better, she thought. If he tried one more poor-little-me, she would walk out of there. She resumed pacing. "So Borgini and Alcott," she said, glancing at her father, "let's not forget Alcott—planned the demise of Altra Grow. Alcott wasn't decisive enough for Borgini, so Sam found Dan Herrera to do the dirty work for him. And he didn't care how dirty—it could even include rape and murder. And it finally did." She turned back to her father. "Is that about it?"

John looked up and met her gaze. "Yes," he said, firmly.

"Well, at this point Parker will be understandably horrified," Jess continued. "He'll be out for blood. Unfortunately"—she paused, regretting what she had to say next—"there isn't a damn thing he can do about it."

"What?" John's tired eyes widened.

Amanda sat up.

"I said that there isn't a damn thing he can do about it," Jess repeated wearily, and then she added, "Unless you testify." She sank down on the arm of Amanda's chair. "Was there anything in your dealings with Borgini—when you took over his business—that was dishonest?"

John straightened, regaining some of his old form. "I would *never* involve the bank in anything dishonest!"

She stared at him. No, she thought, I won't say it. What's the use? Then she looked down and saw Amanda's expression: It was open and raw, with the flush of forty years of guilt and pain all wrapped up in one horrified look fixed on her son. And in that moment Jess had no hope for her father. But she had to protect her grandmother.

"Well, that's something," she said. "Do you think Borgini will confess?"

John actually sputtered. "Not likely."

"Well, Herrera's not likely to confess, either; they'll be lucky to get him on the rape charge," Jess said. "You know, this case is similar to one that came up years ago." She smiled at his baffled expression. "The 'smoking gun,' Father. In spite of the fact that you have a lot to answer for, you sincerely did not mean for Rafael to die or for Josefa to be raped. But who, I wonder, would believe that? If this came out it would destroy you.

"So, my best legal advice is that if no one confesses, you don't have much to worry about," she added brusquely. "Of course, you'll have to hope that neither of your cohorts ever needs to make a deal with a D.A., or, under pressure, to confess to the murder. And you'd better hope that proof isn't found, and that I don't turn you in." She felt disgust at the look of surprise her last words brought. "Oh, I'm certain that you haven't given a lot of thought to me through all of this. But then, you never did. I'm an officer of the court, Father. If it ever comes out that I withheld this information, at the very

least my career is over." And I have to live with what I'm
doing, she added silently.

"In any case, it seems that you're safe enough," she
concluded.

"You really think so?" her father asked.

"Yes, I think so. There's just one other thing." She glanced
at Amanda quickly, then fixed him with a penetrating stare that
left no doubt as to her meaning. "You're not off the hook with
me. Ever." With that, she turned to leave the room.

"No more."

She was halfway to the door when the sound of her father's
voice stopped her. She turned back. "What did you say?"

John stood up. As he did, some of his old energy and posture
seemed to return. "I said, simply, no more. This family has
had enough secrets. You were right, Jessica, in everything you
said. I have spent enough years hiding from my past. My
bitterness has poisoned this family, providing for yet another
generation of secrets. It is time that it stopped."

Jess looked at him, then glanced at Amanda. She was
afraid to believe that he truly meant it. Amanda was regarding
her son with the same doubt, then she turned her gaze to Jess
with a tentative, hopeful smile. Jess glanced back at her
father. "How do you propose that we stop it?" she asked,
guardedly.

"For one thing, I'm going to need a good lawyer with me
when I go to the D.A. in the morning. Do you know where I
can find one?"

"Oh, John!" Amanda exclaimed softly.

As his words settled in, Jess felt almost weak with relief. At
the same time, her mind was already working with ideas of
how to defend and protect him. "I think I can manage to find
one," she said with a tired smile. Then she glanced at Amanda.
"However, I think the D.A. can wait until Monday morning.
After all these years, Grandmother deserves a few days with
her son, don't you agree?"

After a time, Jess shut the library door quietly behind her.
As she returned to her room, she thought of her father and
Amanda, and the new understandings that were beginning
there. And she thought of Roxy—who was undoubtedly
asleep by now—here, alive and well. And then she thought
about the discoveries she had made in the past weeks—about

herself and Michael. She no longer felt like she had slipped through the rabbit hole into an unreal, uncontrollable world. On the other hand, Jess thought with a smile, she hoped that, from now on, Wonderland would always remain a part of her life.

CHAPTER 25

Amanda selected a piece of melon off her plate and offered it to Conrad, who was perched on the back of her chair. The parrot took it delicately, as if aware of his mistress's slender fingers. Amanda watched him for a moment until she had determined that he was pleased with her selection; then she sighed contentedly.

Henley leaned over to refill her coffee cup. "We seem to have a full house this morning, madam," he observed.

"Yes, indeed, it appears that we do, Henley," Amanda agreed. "I hope that it is not too much for you," she added, glancing up at him with concern.

"No, not in the least, madam. Mrs. McNeely, Teresa, and I can contend with it quite handily."

"I'm certain that you can, Henley," Amanda said, fighting against a smile. She had seen him from her bedroom window that morning taking breakfast to Roxy's men who were guarding the house. He set up trays in the garden, with linen. Viewing it, Amanda had felt a rush of warm affection for her friend—and Henley was that. He always did everything with flair—and with deep, real concern.

She looked over at the far side of the room and smiled. My word, she thought, how unutterably delightful. Jessica, Roxy, and Michael were choosing breakfasts from the buffet Henley had set up. And John was upstairs sleeping. There were serious problems to be faced, but life was offering splendid new possibilities . . .

"Khaled said he'd send the plane for you at the end of the week," Michael said as they sat down at the table with Amanda.

"What time did you go home?" Jess asked as she slathered a piece of toast with strawberry jam.

"About two-thirty. Khaled's got some ideas about trying to farm in the desert—and he has an abundance of enthusiasm."

"Will his ideas work?" Roxy asked.

"No. There are some marginal things we can do, however. So, what did you and Jess talk about last night?"

Roxy exchanged a glance with Jess and smiled. "Nothing that would interest you. Just girl talk."

Just then Conrad fluttered his wings and landed on the edge of the table near Jess's plate. He turned his head and stared at her with bold yellow eyes.

"What does he want?" Jess said, drawing back warily.

"Some melon, probably," Michael answered. Then, seeing Jess's expression, he grinned. "Or maybe he wants a kiss."

"That's it," Amanda agreed.

"In a pig's eye," Jess said, exchanging stares with the bird.

Michael reached over and lifted Conrad onto the back of his chair, then offered him a strawberry. "Amanda has fruit shipped in from hothouses this time of year," he murmured to the bird. "And there's no doubt that she does it for you, Conrad, not for us. Eat hearty."

Amanda didn't argue the point.

The conversation slipped into small talk and breakfast passed pleasantly. As they finished eating, Amanda exchanged a meaningful glance with Jess. "Michael," Amanda said, gaining his attention. "There is something Jessica and I must tell you." With a steadying breath, she plunged in and told Michael what her son had told them in the small hours of the morning. Roxy listened with rapt attention.

As he listened, Michael paled. When Amanda was finished, he turned to Jess, letting her see his anger.

"I know, Michael. It's tearing me up, too."

Henley returned just then. "Miss Bellamy, your car has been delivered. There is a man waiting outside who needs your signature for delivery."

With a sigh Jess dropped her napkin on the table. "I'm glad it's come. Tom has asked to use the car for a few days."

As Jess left the breakfast room Amanda gathered up Conrad. "I shall put his nibs away, if you children will excuse me for a moment." Taking the parrot on her shoulder, she left Michael and Roxy alone.

They sat in silence for a long moment until Roxy spoke. "You must feel terrible about what they just told you."

"You could say that. The people Bellamy, Borgini, and Herrera destroyed were my friends. Now they'll need the Martinez family to testify, won't they? We planned to move them to one of the ranches in Oregon, but if Herrera has cohorts out there—and I believe he does—that won't be far enough."

Roxy didn't offer any meaningless platitudes. She knew how he felt.

"I don't think that Jess—or the D.A.—will realize how much danger this puts the Martinez family in," he added, absently. "Besides, Jess has enough to worry about. It must be hard on her, to know that her father was involved."

"She's a strong woman," Roxy said quietly. "She can handle it."

"Yes." Michael smiled for the first time. It was an expression filled with a love that showed. "She is strong. But sometimes she tries too hard to be." He fingered his coffee cup, wondering how to phrase what he wanted to say. "However, the Martinez family is not her problem. The valley is mine. Herrera worked for me. He used me to hurt people I care about. And now it's up to me to protect them. Am I wrong?" He looked up at Roxy.

She smiled ironically. "Michael, you're asking the wrong person. I come from a different world where things are handled much differently."

"Maybe you could give me some pointers." He smiled.

"I think not."

They fell silent until Roxy added, "Michael, whatever you do, don't involve Jess."

"I wouldn't."

"And, Michael, keep your hands clean."

"I never considered anything else. In fact, I won't lift a finger. If he deserves it, Herrera will hoist his own petard."

"Well," she said, with a smile, "you can't go wrong by leaving it to the will of Allah."

"Just what I was thinking."

A few moments later, Jess returned. "I sent the car on to

Tom," she said as she sat down. "Michael, Henley was going to get my things from the Pine Inn, but he doesn't have time. Will you drive me into Carmel?"

"Glad to," Michael said, "but why does Tom need your car?"

"He asked for some time off to drive down to San Simeon for a few days. He became fascinated with Hearst's castle while researching it for me." Then she became aware that Michael had developed a strange look. "What?"

He shook his head. "Probably nothing. Just a coincidence."

"What is?" she pressed.

He shrugged at the question. "Just that when I checked in at the office this morning Carolyn asked for a few days off."

They looked at each other.

"Naw," Michael said.

"Can't be," Jessica agreed. Then she smiled slowly. "On the other hand, Tom was in and out of your office a lot in the past two weeks." Good old Tom, she thought.

Roxy used the information at hand. "Well, maybe you two could take a lesson from them. Gather ye rosebuds while ye may . . ."

"All right." Jess laughed, standing up. "That's enough. We'll be back in a couple of hours."

"Don't hurry on my account." Roxy grinned, winking at Jess. As Jess and Michael left, Roxy poured herself another cup of coffee and picked up the newspaper. It would be nice to have a few hours alone with Amanda, she thought. She wanted to learn a lot more about Amanda of the Flowers.

Roxy sighed contentedly as she sipped her coffee. Jess had stopped and looked back, and there she had found her future, Roxy mused, with no little satisfaction. And now Jess was going to be all right. They all were.

EPILOGUE

The sun was setting in a red and gold blanket. As it slipped behind the craggy majesty of the Canadian Rockies it threw a few last dying rays over the lake, bathing the water's surface in rainbow hues.

It was the piper who drew them to the flagstone terrace. The sound echoed off the mountains as the mournful skirl of the bagpipe brought the sun to its repose. Jess leaned back against Michael as he wrapped his arms about her. Below them, where the sloping snow-covered grounds led away from the Chateau Lake Louise, beneath a large spreading fir tree stood a lone bagpiper in full-dress kilt. The red and black plaid of his tartan was bright against the white snow. The sound of his song drew the watchers from the hotel. And in the absolute silence, he piped down the Maple Leaf flag and the sun to their night's rest.

"What a phenomenally perfect end to the day," Jess whispered.

Michael bent and kissed her behind the ear. "Yes, it is," he murmured.

They turned their heads as they were joined on the terrace by another couple. "That was absolutely beautiful," Roxy said.

Roxy and Khaled had joined Jess and Michael for a ski week in British Columbia. Upon arrival, when first viewing the magnificent eighteenth-century hotel, Roxy had turned and murmured to Jess, "Does this compare to your last romantic ski weekend?"

Jess had shushed her with a rolling of her eyes. "No," she whispered. "This is real—and infinitely better."

It was the first time Jess had seen Khaled since the day of the

319

board meeting. Over dinner the first night at Lake Louise she'd thanked him for what he had done for her family.

"It isn't necessary," he had assured her. "What I have done has been for my wife, yet over the years I have come to think of you as family as well, Jessica Bellamy. My joy is that you are content."

"We were glad to hear that no charges were filed against your father, Jess," Roxy said.

"Fortunately, he didn't actually break any laws," Michael said. "His association with Borgini may have been for unethical reasons, but they weren't illegal."

"And now he is doing penance with Amanda," Jess added, laughing softly. "If she has her way, he'll spend the rest of his retirement years with her doing charity work." Then she sobered. "Not all endings are so neat, however. Did you hear what happened to Dan Herrera? A few days after he was released on bail he was found dead in his trailer." She shuddered. "In fact, he was found all over his trailer. I guess we shouldn't have been surprised. The D.A. hasn't been able to prove that La Familia was responsible, but there had to be a lot of worried people when Herrera was arrested for Rafael's murder.

"One good thing came from Herrera's death, however," Jess continued. "Borgini decided to plead guilty and save the state the cost of a trial. In turn he'll be given protection—for the next twenty-four years—someplace where La Familia can't get to him."

La Familia was never interested in Borgini, Michael thought. But, he imagined they were unhappy when they learned that Herrera had been cheating on them, running prostitutes, drugs, and illegal aliens without giving "The Family" their cut. Even more upsetting, he imagined, was when they learned that Herrera had set them up, pointing the finger at them for Josefa's rape and Rafael's death. Word seemed to travel quickly. They probably didn't like it much. Most importantly, however, they promised to keep the Martinez family safe. Or so Michael had heard.

"Allah's will," Roxy observed, looking at Michael.

Khaled agreed.

"Divine justice," Jess said, with feeling.

Yes, it was, Michael thought. And heaven helped those who lent a helping hand.

As the piper finished, people began to drift back into the warmth of the hotel. With a glance and a smile for her friends, Roxy tugged on Khaled's sweater and nodded toward the doors. They left Jess and Michael alone on the terrace.

"I'm so glad that we took this week for ourselves," Jess murmured, settling back against Michael. "It's the last chance we'll have until the wedding."

"You mean until the honeymoon," Michael grinned.

"Yes, until the honeymoon. You know, I've been thinking about that . . ."

"So have I."

"I think we should go to the Bahamas."

Michael frowned and glanced down at the top of her head. "I thought we agreed on Switzerland."

"The company has a resort in the Bahamas," she explained. "It would be a wonderful time to see it."

"Oh, no, you don't!" he laughed, squeezing her gently. "You can wait until Paul Iverson retires in the spring before you begin acting like Madam CEO. This is our honeymoon, and we're not going anywhere near anything that even does business with the Morgan Land and Development Company. Besides, I want to see that school where you and Roxy grew up."

"You're right," Jess smiled. "Besides, there's someone I want to see there. She's retired now but she still lives at the school. It's time to go back and see her." Her voice softened. "I've learned that it's important to tell people how much they've meant to you while you have the chance."

"We're agreed, then. Gstaad it is. Will you have time to close your practice at the firm by the end of the month?"

"Just barely." She turned her head and looked up at him with a grin. "I forgot to tell you. Aaron is making Tom an associate partner."

"That's great!"

"Yes, it is," she agreed, nestling against him again. "It's a wonderful firm. And Tom's going to be an asset."

He heard a certain wistfulness in her voice. "Are you certain about this job change, Jess? You worked hard to get to where you are. And your talent is in criminal law . . ."

"That's the odd part," she said. "I've done it because I seem to have a strange talent for it. Perhaps it was due to all the mystery in my family and a desire to discover the truth. But the fact is that I don't like it. I never admitted that to myself until Amanda offered me the CEO position when Paul retires. Being stuck in an office won't bother me. The complexities of the Morgan Company are absolutely compelling. I can't wait to get my hands on it."

"You're not worried about the responsibility?"

She thought about that. "No," she said at last. No, she repeated silently. At the moment anything seemed possible. Life seemed possible. Grab the brass ring, take a chance, drop into Wonderland. Feel it. She turned and slipped her arms under his parka and around his waist. "No, I'm not worried, not with you to help me." She looked up at his handsome face and felt a warm rush of overwhelming love. "Jessica Rawlings," she said, trying it out. "I like the sound of it."

He grinned, feigning surprise. "Jessica Rawlings? Why, Miss Liberation, are you actually thinking of taking my name? Without even a hyphen?"

"Yes, absolutely," she said. "Such is my commitment to you, Michael Rawlings. It's time for new beginnings. And speaking of new beginnings, I talked with Johnny just before we left. He's doing a bang-up job at the bank and loving every minute of it." Her expression grew soft. "Johnny's one of the good ones. I can't wait for you to meet him."

He turned, pulling her around so that he was leaning against the low terrace wall and she was now lying against him. He shifted comfortably. "Right now, Jessica Bellamy-soon-to-be-Rawlings, my mind isn't on your brother, your father, your grandmother, or anyone else. It's on a nightcap and bed. And maybe, by morning, some sleep."

"Hummm," she murmured, turning her face up to him. "Sounds heavenly. I love you, Michael Rawlings. I purely do."

"I love you, too, Jess," he said, his voice growing husky as he fixed on her waiting mouth. He lowered his head. "Jess—" He paused as he saw something over her shoulder. "For crying out loud," he murmured, "what are the odds against that . . ."

"Michael, kiss me," Jess breathed impatiently.

"There's Clint."

"Oh, Michael, really." She laughed softly. "Stop teasing and kiss me."

"But . . ."

"Michael."

He glanced down at her, amusement leaping into his eyes. "Whatever you say, Miss Bellamy." And he kissed her.